"ONCE YOU START A BRAD THOR THRILLER, THERE'S NO TURNING BACK."
—Glenn Beck

Praise for #1 *New York Times* bestselling author Brad Thor's *BLOWBACK*

"Haunting, high-voltage stuff by one of the best thriller writers in the business."

—*Ottawa Citizen*

"An incredible international thriller. . . . Riveting and superior."

—Brunei Press Syndicate

After thirteen "gripping" (*People*), "nail-biting" (*Huffington Post*) thrillers packed with "nonstop intensity" (Associated Press), Scot Harvath is still "the perfect all-American hero for the post-September 11th world" (Nelson DeMille).

Praise for the latest from Brad Thor, *HIDDEN ORDER*

"One of Brad Thor's best books to date."

—*The Washington Post*

"If *Hidden Order* does not keep you up at night . . . then you're not paying attention."

—*Bookreporter*

"[A] must-read."

—Townhall.com

"One of the best writers you are ever going to read."

—WROK

"Thor is awesome."

—*National Review*

"Brad Thor continues to write like nobody else!"

—KCBQ

"Absolutely irresistible . . . reminiscent of the best of Frederick Forsyth, Robert Ludlum, or Richard Condon."

—*Reason*

BLACK LIST

"Intense, authentic, addictive."

—Glenn Beck

"A terrific read. . . . It has you right from the very beginning."

—Lou Dobbs

"A thriller you won't be able to put down!"

—*Imus In The Morning*

"Thor and Harvath are the real deal . . . accept no substitutes."

—*Bookreporter*

FULL BLACK

"Thor has mastered thriller storytelling with fast pacing and plots that are relevant."

—*The Miami Herald*

"Enough adrenaline-charged adventure to fill several books of its length. . . . Do not miss."

—*Bookreporter*

FOREIGN INFLUENCE

"Frightening, illuminating, and entertaining."

—*Bookreporter*

"Intrigue, adventure, and adrenaline-rushing action."

—*New American Truth*

THE APOSTLE

"An out-of-the-ballpark homerun. You won't want to put it down."

—*Blackwater Tactical Weekly*

"Powerful and convincing. . . . A breathtaking, edge-of-your-seat experience."

—*The National Terror Alert Response Center*

THE LAST PATRIOT

"As close to a perfect thriller as you'll ever find. . . . Brilliantly plotted and ingeniously conceived."

—*Providence Journal*

"Wow, this guy can write."

—*The Atlanta Journal-Constitution*

"Stunning."

—*Publishers Weekly*

"The Last Patriot . . . [will] make an action addict drool."

—*San Antonio Express-News*

"[A] nonstop action machine. . . . A thoroughly researched, high-fueled thrill ride."

—*Tampa Tribune*

Books by Brad Thor

The Lions of Lucerne
Path of the Assassin
State of the Union
Blowback
Takedown
The First Commandment
The Last Patriot
The Apostle
Foreign Influence
The Athena Project
Full Black
Black List
Hidden Order

BRAD THOR

BLOWBACK

A THRILLER

Pocket Books
New York London Toronto Sydney New Delhi

Pocket Books
A Division of Simon & Schuster, Inc.
1230 Avenue of the Americas
New York, NY 10020

This Pocket Books paperback edition April 2014

POCKET and colophon are registered trademarks of Simon & Schuster, Inc.

For information about special discounts for bulk purchases, please contact Simon & Schuster Special Sales at 1-866-506-1949 or business@simonandschuster.com.

The Simon & Schuster Speakers Bureau can bring authors to your live event. For more information or to book an event, contact the Simon & Schuster Speakers Bureau at 1-866-248-3049 or visit our website at www.simonspeakers.com.

Manufactured in the United States of America

16 15 14 13 12 11 10 9 8

ISBN: 978-1-4516-0828-1
ISBN: 978-1-4165-1023-9 (ebook)

For Chase—

Welcome to the world, little one.

Hannibal ad portas

Hannibal is at the gates.

blow•back \'blō-ˌbak\ *n* **1:** process by which spent shell casings are ejected from an automatic weapon **2:** unintended consequences of a failed foreign policy or botched covert action **3:** CIA code name for an agent or operation that has turned on its creators

BLOW BACK

PROLOGUE

COL DE LA TRAVERSETTE
FRENCH–ITALIAN ALPS

Donald Ellyson tried to scream, but nothing happened. He had done a lot of reprehensible things in his fifty-five years, but this was not how he had expected to die—his throat sliced and hot blood running down the front of his parka. This was supposed to be the discovery of his life, the one that would legitimize him and land him at the top of the academic heap. But the moment of his greatest triumph had suddenly become the last moment he would ever know. And for what? Did his benefactors actually think he was going to stiff them?

Sure, he was known to gamble, and yes, he often stole artifacts from archeological digs to sell on the black market, but so did a lot of other people. It was just the way the world worked. Certainly, the punishment shouldn't be death.

It was only three years ago that Ellyson had joined a group of archeologists excavating a site southwest of Istanbul. During the dig, a hidden room with a vast trove of parchments had been discovered. Upon closer inspection, the documents appeared to be remnants of the famous Library of Alexandria, which was considered to be the greatest collection of books in the ancient world.

The library had been almost completely destroyed by the Romans who sacked and burned it in both the third and fourth centuries. It was widely assumed that the balance of the library's contents were destroyed when the Muslims, under the Caliph Umar I, laid siege in 640, but as Ellyson and his colleagues pored over the documents, they realized how wrong that supposition was. Someone at some point in history had apparently managed to preserve a large portion of what remained.

Ellyson was fascinated by what the parchments contained. One in particular was absolutely astounding. It was written in Greek and detailed a firsthand account of one of the most brilliant and most deadly undertakings in ancient history. He never catalogued that manuscript and went to great pains to make sure no one else on the dig even knew of its existence.

It was a treasure map of sorts, and though it did not have a great big X marking the spot, it promised unfathomable rewards. Once out of Istanbul, Ellyson went straight to the most likely source of funding for an expedition like this. He had been in the game long enough to know players who would jump at the chance to get their hands on what the manuscript suggested was waiting out there. And, indeed, the promise contained within the manuscript proved irresistible to his erstwhile partners.

Like Ellyson, those partners had read the classical accounts of Livy and Polybius, as well as works by renowned historians such as Gibbon, Zanelli, Vanoyeke, and a host of others too numerous to list. The more the partners read, the more they learned, and the more they learned, the more they became intrigued with the potential power of Ellyson's discovery.

Based on the archeologist's request, the partners spent millions on aerial surveys by planes, helicopters, and even satellites, combing many of the Alpine passes between southern France and Italy in hope of locating a particularly valuable item referred to in the parchment.

Ellyson had defied convention, turning his back on the more popular historical locations, as none of them fit the picture he had cobbled together from his ancient texts. Good fortune, though, did not smile upon his undertaking. Still, despite the lack of progress, the archeologist was confident he'd be successful in the end.

Though at times money was extremely difficult to come by, the men funding Ellyson's search did whatever they had to do to keep the coffers full. Their organization had been searching for decades for just this type of find and couldn't stop now. The power it promised to deliver was too important to give up on over something as trivial as money.

It wasn't until recently, aided by three summers of record-setting heat across Europe, that the snow had begun to melt, glaciers had begun to recede, and, near the Col de la Traversette, Ellyson had uncovered the first pieces of archeological evidence that proved he was on the right track—straps of leather from an ancient harness, shards of pottery, and a small collection of broken weapons. He had narrowed a staggering field of haystacks to just one, but that one was replete with fathomless gorges and crevices, any number of which might contain his needle.

The Col de la Traversette was one of the most treacherous and highest mountain passes in all of France. Over the centuries, both French and Italian authorities had attempted to sabotage parts of it in the hope of stemming smuggling between their countries, but the pass lived on. A mere ten meters wide at the summit, the remote pathway was only accessible during a short period between mid-summer and early fall—and even then conditions could still be unbearable. Locals referred to the region's weather as eight months of winter followed by four months of hell.

Despite these daunting obstacles, Ellyson had finally found his needle. He was a much better archeologist than he had ever given himself credit for. And the interesting thing about it was that the group funding his project wasn't even concerned with the entire find, only a part of it—the part he had used as bait. It was all that had been necessary to get them to finance the operation. What they wanted from the find was a mere token to him, something he could easily do without. It was, in his mind, a minor footnote that had been lost to history. If his benefactors were willing to cover the cost of his entire project, he had no intention of denying them such a small item in return.

Even now from his prone position on the floor, Ellyson could see the object they had been after—a long, intricately carved wooden chest. It was right there—theirs for the taking. He didn't need or want it. So why did they have to kill him? Nobody would have ever known that the box, or more importantly what was inside it, was missing. *Much like me,* thought Ellyson as he heard the sound of his two Sherpas approaching and watched as his killer removed a small-caliber automatic from his parka.

After calmly replacing the pistol in his pocket, the assassin stared at the wooden, coffinlike box. For over two thousand years, the ancient weapon had lain beyond the reach of man, frozen within the glacial ice of this remote Alpine chasm, but all of that was about to change. The assassin removed a satellite phone from inside his coat and dialed the ten-digit number for his employer—a man known to him only as the Scorpion.

ONE

LAHORE, PAKISTAN
ONE YEAR LATER

The narrow streets of the old city contained one of the worst slums in the world. Filth, squalor, and despair were daily accompaniments to the lives of Pakistan's lowest of citizens—the poverty-stricken Punjabi Muslims. Smaller and darker-skinned than the rest of Lahore's populace, the most fortunate among them were doomed to lives of mind-numbing menial labor, while the balance found themselves sucked up into the ranks of street urchins, beggars, and homeless. Their plight was one of subcontinental Islam's dirty little secrets, and it turned the stomach of the man sitting in the stolen Toyota Corolla outside the tomb of Muhammad Iqbal, poet and ideological godfather of modern Pakistan.

A devout Muslim, the man was humiliated to see how the promise of Muslim brotherhood had been denied the Punjabis. Pakistan was a hypocritical tangle of class divisions, and nowhere was that more evident than in the role of women. Beyond the fortunate women of the privileged classes who participated in think tanks, ran charity organizations, wrote novels and plays, and even occupied a handful of token positions in General Musharraf's cabinet, were those who suffered the daily horrors of domestic abuse, gang rape and murder at the hands of small-minded men professing their love of Allah and their devotion to the Muslim faith. Many, many times the man wished his employer's ultimate target was Pakistan, but it wasn't. As horrible as this country was, there was another that was much more evil and in much greater need of an all-powerful, cleansing blow.

His target emerged from the building across the street right on time. Every Wednesday like clockwork, the diminutive professor from Pakistan's oldest and largest university—the University of the Punjab—visited the old city for lunch. He was a man of strict routine and consistency—traits that had served him extremely well as a scientist, but which were about to lead to his undoing. As the professor unchained his small motorbike and pulled into traffic, the assassin set down the newspaper he had been pretending to read and started the car.

Two blocks before the university, the professor was still oblivious to the stolen Corolla following him. That was about to change. Approaching a busy intersection just before the campus, the professor watched in his mirror as a blue Toyota sped up as if to pass and then suddenly came swerving back hard to the right.

Bystanders screamed in horror as they watched the helmetless professor slammed to the pavement and then dragged beneath the Corolla for over half a block before the undercarriage of the speeding car spat his mangled, lifeless body into the street.

A mile and a half from the Lahore International Airport, the assassin abandoned the stolen car and covered the rest of the distance on foot. Once he was safely ensconced in the first-class cabin of his international flight, he pulled a weathered Koran from his breast pocket. After repeating several whispered supplications, the assassin turned to the back of the book and removed a coded list of names, hidden beneath the tattered cover. With the scientist from the University of the Punjab taken care of, there were only two more to go.

TWO

36° 07' N, 41° 30' E
NORTHERN IRAQ

Soldiers from the U.S. Army's 3rd "Arrowhead Brigade," 2nd Infantry Division Stryker Brigade Combat Team (SBCT) had spent enough time in Iraq to get used to the sound of enemy rounds plinking off the armor plating of their eight-wheeled infantry carrier vehicle, but ever since they had driven into the small village of Asalaam, one hundred fifty kilometers southwest of Mosul, things had been dead quiet.

The village was one of many around the Christian enclave of Mosul known for its religious and ethnic tolerance. For the most part, Muslims and Christians throughout the area lived in relative harmony. In fact, the name *Asalaam* came from the Arabic word for *peace*. It wasn't the locals, though, that the SBCT soldiers were worried about. A stone's throw from the Syrian border, foreign insurgents were one of the greatest threats they faced.

The men had seen their fair share of ambushes

in Iraq, including a devastating suicide attack within the confines of their own base, and none of them intended to return home in anything less comfortable than an airline seat. Body bags were out of the question for these soldiers.

Second Lieutenant Kurt Billings, from Kenosha, Wisconsin, was wondering why the hell they hadn't seen anything, when the vehicle commander of the lead Stryker came over his headset and said, "Lieutenant, so far we've got absolutely zero contact. Nothing, and I mean nothing, is moving out there. I don't even see any dogs."

"Must be pot luck night at one of the local madrasas," joked the radio operator.

"If so, then somebody should be manning the village barbecue pit," replied Billings. "Stay sharp and keep your eyes peeled. There's got to be somebody around here."

"I'm telling you, sir," said the vehicle commander, "there's nobody out there. The place is a ghost town."

"This village didn't just dry up overnight."

"Maybe it did. We're in the middle of nowhere. These people don't even have telephones. Besides, who'd care if they did dry up and blow away?"

"I'm sure there's an explanation for why we're not seeing anybody. Let's just take it slow," said Billings. "Do a complete sweep of the village and then we'll dismount. Got it?"

"Roger that, Lieutenant," responded the vehicle

commander as their Stryker began a circuit of the village.

For this assignment Billings had organized his men into two, eight-man fire, or assault, teams. The first team, designated Alpha, was with him in the lead armored vehicle, while Bravo team, under the command of Staff Sergeant James Russo, followed in the second Stryker. Their assignment had been to check on the status of three American Christian aid workers based in Asalaam, who hadn't been heard from in over a week.

It was scut work, and Billings didn't like taking his men out to check up on people who had no business being in Iraq in the first place—even if they were fellow citizens. Not only that, but the term *Christian aid worker* was a gross misnomer in his opinion. He'd yet to meet one whose primary reason for being here wasn't the conversion of souls for Christ. Sure, they did good work and they filled in some of the gaps that were invariably left behind by some of the larger, more established and experienced aid organizations, but at the end of the day these people were missionaries plain and simple. They also had a rather otherworldly talent for getting themselves in trouble. There were times when Billings felt more like a lifeguard at a children's pool than a soldier. While young missionaries might have the best of intentions, they more often than not lacked the skills, support, and all-around basic common sense to be living in what was still very much a war zone.

And that was another thing. The U.S. military was supposed to be in Iraq backing up the Iraqi military and Iraqi security forces, not helping lost twenty-somethings find their way. But whenever one of these situations popped up, which they did at least once or twice a month, it always fell to the American military to go out and rescue their own people. The Iraqis didn't want anything to do with them. They were too busy trying to put their country back together to be wasting their time on rescue efforts for people they had never invited into their country in the first place, and frankly Billings couldn't blame them. He had suggested to his superiors that missionaries ought to be required to post a bond before entering Iraq, or at least be required to pay the cost of their rescue the way stranded hikers and mountain climbers have to do back in the States, but his superiors just shrugged and told him it was out of their hands. If young Americans needed rescuing, even in the wilds of Iraq, then that's what the U.S. military was going to do. Never mind the fact that it might put more young American lives in jeopardy in the process.

Billings studied the faces of the men on his fire team and toggled the transmit button of his radio. "Russo. You copy?"

"Loud and clear, Lieutenant." At twenty-five years old, Russo was an old man compared to the eighteen- to nineteen-year-olds on his fire team, but not nearly as old as Billings, who was twenty-eight.

Billings heard the beep tone that indicated Russo had taken his finger off his transmit button and said, "This might not exactly be a routine check-in-on-the-children op. Let's be very careful on this one."

"We're careful on every one."

Billings smiled. Russo was right. They had one of the best platoons in Iraq. They'd been in country for three months and had chalked up some impressive wins against the bad guys and no one had suffered so much as a hangnail. "Just the same, there's something about this that doesn't feel right. Make sure your guys stay focused."

"Will do, Lieutenant. In fact, if Alpha team would rather stay nice and cozy inside their vehicle, I'm sure those of us with Bravo team would have no trouble sorting this one out." There was a chorus of chuckles from the men inside Russo's Stryker.

"Not on your life, Sergeant," replied Billings with a smile. "When we get in there, you make sure your men watch and learn from us."

"Hooah, Lieutenant."

Billings turned to the men inside his Stryker and said, "Gentlemen, Sergeant Russo seems to think we're not needed today. He says Bravo team can handle the assignment themselves."

"Fuck Bravo team," said a young private named Steve Schlesinger.

Normally, Billings wouldn't put up with language like that, but he liked his men to get pumped up before going into potentially dangerous situations. Besides, eighteen-year-old Schlesinger was their shining star. He had uncovered and helped defuse more improvised explosive devices in the last month than anyone in Iraq over the last year. The kid had a sixth sense for danger, and despite the fact that he was from Chicago and thought the Cubs were a better team than the Milwaukee Brewers, Billings liked him.

"Okay then," replied Billings. "We're all agreed?"

A chorus of "Fuck Bravo team" resounded throughout the lead Stryker. It was good-natured competition, and Billings knew his men well enough to know that when boots hit the ground, it didn't matter what team they were on, the men were all brothers united against a common enemy. He had no doubt Russo was whipping his men up as well.

As Billings felt their Stryker slowing down, he knew it was only a matter of moments before they would have to step outside and try to figure out what the hell was going on.

THREE

When the Strykers finally came to a halt in the center of the village, the soldiers jumped out and took up defensive firing positions. Though no one said anything, they were all feeling the same thing having made a complete circuit of Asalaam. There wasn't a single living soul in sight, and it had put everyone on edge.

Justin Stokes, a young, skinny private from San Diego who had a bad habit of engaging his mouth before his brain, said, "Maybe it's siesta time."

"At 10:30 in the morning?" replied six-foot-four Private Rodney Cooper from Tampa. "Stokes, my grandmother doesn't even take a nap at 10:30 in the morning."

"Whatever it is," said Stokes, "something about this place isn't right."

"It's fucked up is what it is," added Schlesinger. "Where the hell are all the people?"

"That's what we're here to find out," replied

Lieutenant Billings, cutting the crosstalk short. "We're in the game now, so let's keep communications on an as-needed basis."

"Yes sir, Lieutenant," the men responded as Billings walked over to where Russo was standing. He was using the reflex sight on his M4 to look for any movement at the far end of the road.

"What do you think, Jimmy?" asked Billings.

"I think it's too quiet," said Russo as he lowered his weapon.

"Maybe we're looking at an ambush."

"I don't think so. If somebody was going to hit us, it would have already happened."

"So what the hell's going on, then? Where are all the villagers?"

Russo double-checked his firing selector and said, "I don't know, and I've got a feeling I don't particularly want to know. This village isn't our problem. We're here to check up on three American aid workers, so let's do that and get the hell out of here."

Billings studied the cracked, sun-baked facades of the mud brick houses up and down the narrow road, some with their doors and windows standing wide open, and agreed. "All right. Here's what we're going to do. I'll take Alpha team to the building the missionaries were using as their health center. You and Bravo team do a house-to-house search, but no door kicking. If you find one that's already open and no one responds to a polite knock, you and your men can go inside and look around, but tell them not to touch anything. We'll meet back here in fifteen minutes. Got it?"

"Yes, sir. Fifteen minutes," replied Russo, who then turned to his men and said, "We're on. Let's saddle up."

One of the Strykers shadowed Bravo team along the main road, while the other followed Billings and his men as they walked a block over to a worn, low-rise building that looked like it might be a school or an administrative office.

"Provincial Ministry of Police," said Private Mike Rodriguez, from upstate New York, as he read a faded sign above the doorway. He was the only one on the team, besides Russo, with a workable grasp of Arabic.

Billings looked at the one-sheet briefing he'd been given in Mosul and cursed. "Goddamn it. They've got this piece of shit map flipped around. We're supposed to be a block over in the other direction."

"Why don't we take a look inside anyway?" said Stokes. "It's an official building. Maybe there's official information inside."

"Which we haven't been authorized to enter or look for," replied Billings. "We're here to do reconnaissance only. If we find an open door, we can go in, but if a door isn't open, we're not going to start kicking—"

Before Billings could finish his sentence, Cooper leaned into the flimsy, weather-beaten door with his massive shoulder and popped it off its hinges. As the team looked at him, he said with a smile, "Somebody must have forgotten to lock up."

"The hell they did," replied Billings. "The next person who tries anything remotely—" The lieutenant was cut short by the overwhelming stench that poured out of the building.

"Jesus," exclaimed Schlesinger. "Don't these people know they're supposed to put their garbage *outside* for pickup?"

Billings, a man all too acquainted with the smell of death, knew that they weren't smelling garbage. "Cooper, Rodriguez, Schlesinger, and Stokes, you're coming inside with me. The rest of you stand guard out here and keep your eyes peeled. The shit might hit the fan very quickly."

"It smells like it already has," said a redheaded private from Utah as he readied his weapon and took up his watch.

Tucking their noses into their tactical vests, Billings and his men stepped inside. After clearing the vestibule, Cooper kicked in the door of the pitch-black main office, and the rest of the team button-hooked inside. A chorus of "Clear—Clear—Clear" rang out from the different members of the team as they swept through the room, guided by the beams of the SureFire tactical flashlights mounted on the Picatinny Rails of their M4s.

The reason the room was so dark soon became

apparent. The windows had been completely covered with heavy wool blankets.

Rodriguez shot Schlesinger a puzzled look and whispered, "Are those supposed to be blackout curtains?"

Schlesinger traced the edge of one of the blankets with the beam of his flashlight and shrugged his shoulders in response.

"Why would these guys want to block out light here in the middle of nowhere?"

"Maybe they were trying to hide something."

"Or hide from something."

Billings didn't care what the blankets were for. "Tear them all down," he ordered, "and let's get some light in here."

Stokes and Cooper stepped over to the windows and began pulling the blankets down. Light flooded the room. As it did, Schlesinger glanced up, and his voice caught in his throat. "Holy shit."

In unison, the rest of the team looked up and saw what Schlesinger was looking at. Suspended from the ceiling were at least fifteen decomposing corpses.

Cooper, the biggest and until this point one of the bravest members of the squad, recoiled in horror. Stokes made the sign of the cross while Rodriguez and Schlesinger instinctively raised their rifles and swept them back and forth along the length of the ceiling, ready to fire. "What the fuck is going on here, Lieutenant?" implored Schlesinger, the fear evident in his voice.

Billings had no idea what the hell they were looking at. The bodies had been tied flush against the ceiling, and the heavy timber braces had completely hidden them from view when the team had first entered the room. Billings was about to say something, when a voice crackled over his radio. It was Russo.

"Alpha One. This is Bravo One. Do you copy? Over."

Billings, his eyes still fixed on the gruesome scene above him, toggled his transmit button and said, "This is Alpha One. I read you, Jimmy. What have you got?"

"We've found somebody, Lieutenant. He appears to be one of the village elders. It looks like he hasn't eaten in a week, but he's alive."

"Where'd you find him?"

"He was hiding behind one of the houses we were checking. My guys think he was foraging for food."

"Does he know what happened to the rest of the villagers?"

"He says all the survivors are hiding in the mosque. That's where we're headed now."

"Wait a second. *Survivors*?" repeated Billings. "Survivors of what? And what do you mean they're hiding in the mosque? What are they hiding from?"

"I'm still trying to figure that out. The old guy keeps repeating some word in Arabic I don't understand."

Billings motioned to Rodriguez and then said into his radio, "What's the word? I'll see if Rodriguez knows it."

There was a pause as Russo asked the old man to speak directly into his microphone. Then it came—an intense, raspy voice that sounded like a set of hinges in serious need of oiling, "*Algul! Algul! Algul!*"

"Did you get that?" asked Russo as the old man backed away from his radio.

Billings looked at Rodriguez and noticed that the soldier's already ashen face had lost what little color was left. The bodies strapped to the ceiling had gotten to all of the men, but they had to hold it together.

"You ever play Xbox, Lieutenant?" muttered Rodriguez, his eyes still glued to the grotesque forms hovering above them.

"No," said Billings, who failed to comprehend any connection between a video game and their current situation.

"*Algul* was the first Arabic word I ever learned. I learned it playing a game on Xbox called Phantom Force."

Anxious for answers, the lieutenant demanded, "What the fuck does it mean?"

"Loosely translated, it's a horseleech or a bloodsucking genie, but usually it's used to describe a female demon who lives in the cemetery and feasts on dead babies. When there are no babies left, it moves on to whoever is left in the village and keeps feeding until no one is left alive. I've also heard it's a derivative of an Arabic word which means living dead and devourer of women and children. However you slice it, *Algul* is Arabic for vampire."

Billings was about to tell Mike Rodriguez he was full of shit, when one of the bodies strapped to the ceiling above them opened its mouth and covered the soldiers with a fine mist of bloody froth.

FOUR

OUTSKIRTS OF BAGHDAD

TWO WEEKS LATER

At first, Scot Harvath couldn't tell if he had been shot or not. After the blinding white flash, his vision was blurred, and all he could hear was the thunderous pulse of blood as it rushed in and out of his eardrums. He had never expected Khalid Alomari to be carrying a *third* pistol under his robes—a knife, a razor, maybe even a grenade, but not a subcompact. It just proved yet again how desperate the man was.

From somewhere beyond the pounding in his ears, Harvath could hear the voice of his boss, Gary Lawlor, telling him to wait, telling him not to go in without backup, but Harvath had come too far to lose Alomari again.

Dubai, Amman, Damascus . . . the terrorist had always been one, if not two steps ahead. For the past two months, Harvath had been trying to close the gap and capture the man Western intelligence had dubbed the heir apparent to Osama bin Laden.

Some of the more flippant analysts and operatives at CIA headquarters in Langley, as well as some in Harvath's own Office of International Investigative Assistance (OIIA) at the Department of Homeland Security, had taken to calling Alomari "Osama Junior," or "OJ" for short.

Normally the first one to find the humor in any situation, Harvath didn't care for the nickname they'd given Alomari. It downplayed the devastation the killer had wreaked in his short but very impressive career. Not only that, but Harvath took this assignment quite personally. In Cairo, the terrorist had come within a hair's breadth of killing him. The chase had been a nonstop game of cat and mouse, and even with the resources he had at his disposal, Harvath had not actually laid eyes on his quarry until two minutes ago. If the president had simply charged him with killing Alomari instead of apprehending him for intensive interrogation, this soul-sapping assignment would have been over a long time ago, but it was precisely because Alomari was so elusive and so good at what he did that the United States government wanted him taken alive.

Hailing from Abha, the same remote mountain city in the southern Saudi Arabian province of Asir that four of the fifteen 9/11 hijackers had come from, Alomari had been born into a wealthy Saudi family, with a Saudi father, a French mother, and excellent connections to the Saudi Royal Family. Though he was highly educated, had traveled extensively abroad, and never wanted for money or creature comforts, Khalid Alomari had grown up feeling something was missing in his life. He carried a hole inside him that no amount of sailing the Greek islands, sunning himself on the French Riviera, or looking out over New York's Central Park while indulging himself in champagne and women in the Plaza Hotel's decadent Astor Suite could fill. Like another infamous Saudi trust-fund brat, Alomari eventually found what he was looking for—militant Islam.

In 1999, Khalid Alomari was only twenty-one years old when he was first introduced to Osama bin Laden. The two men hit it off instantly. Their backgrounds were very similar and they had much in common. When bin Laden mentioned that several men from Alomari's hometown of Abha were destined for greatness in the eyes of Allah, Alomari had begged to be allowed to be included, but bin Laden had other plans for the young man who had become almost like another son to him. Alomari was destined for greatness as well, but not by flying an airplane into a skyscraper. He possessed talents far and away more impressive than any of the brothers of 9/11.

Alomari had something that no other young jihadi who had come to bin Laden ever had before. The boy not only possessed exceptional taste, style, and intelligence, but thanks to his French mother, he had a wonderfully European set of facial features that allowed him to pass for almost any nationality.

No, Khalid Alomari would not be flying airplanes into buildings. He was much too precious for that. He would become bin Laden's greatest weapon—a new power that the Western world would be forced to reckon with.

Alomari trained in bin Laden's camps in Afghanistan and then was sent away for further schooling with Pakistan's infamous Directorate for Inter-Services Intelligence in Islamabad. There, the young man learned the fine arts of prisoner interrogation, blackmail, and assassination. He saw bin Laden only once more after that, just before the al-Qaeda leader had been forced to hide in one of his many mountain strongholds along the Pakistani-Afghan border. Alomari had been in the same room with bin Laden, celebrating the success of the September 11 attacks, when the famous video of his mentor was made, but unlike the other men present, Alomari had been smart enough to move behind the cameraman when the filming started. Not only did the footage prove bin Laden's complicity in the 9/11 attacks, but it was also used as a who's who of many of al-Qaeda's inner sanctum. In short, it gave the Americans more intelligence than the al-Qaeda leadership had intended. Alomari had been smart to remain behind the camera and out of sight. If there was one thing he had learned from his time in America and the West, it was that either you manipulated the media, or it manipulated you.

Now, Harvath desperately tried to wrestle the

gun out of Alomari's hand, but the man was amazingly strong. The terrorist let loose with a left hook, and Harvath lurched to the side, the blow glancing painfully off his shoulder. Harvath answered with a swift knee to Alomari's groin, which caused the man to drop the gun and also to lose his balance. Grabbing the American operative by the shoulders, Alomari took Harvath down along with him.

Before Harvath could right himself, Alomari swung an elbow and caught him right in the mouth. As he tried to recover, he could sense Alomari crawling away from him, and his only thought was that the terrorist was going for his gun.

Harvath's mind was in overdrive. He'd lost his H&K MP7 in the beginning of the scuffle and knew that it was out of his reach. He'd have to go for his sidearm, but could he pull it and fire before Alomari reached his gun and shot at him? Harvath didn't have much choice.

Reaching for his Beretta PX4 Storm pistol, Harvath drew the .40-caliber from his holster and rolled to his left. Raising the weapon, he pointed it in the direction he had last seen Alomari, but there was no one there. Quickly, Harvath spun 180 degrees. Rising to one knee, he swept the rest of the room, but Alomari was gone. There was only one way he could have escaped, and Harvath had no choice but to go after him.

The Iraqi midday sun was blinding. It took several moments for Harvath's eyes to adjust and to make out the figure of Khalid Alomari, running, almost a full block away. The terrorist's muddy-brown robes and brightly checkered kaffiyeh were unmistakable. Harvath didn't waste any more time.

Sprinting full out in combat boots and desert camo fatigues wasn't exactly an easy feat. He would have preferred the shorts, T-shirt, and Nikes he ran along the Potomac in back home. However, combat boots and desert camo were what the U.S. Special Operations Command (USSOCOM) Direct Action Team in Iraq wore, and that was what he had been issued for their coordinated takedown of Alomari. But the coordination had fallen apart.

It wasn't anyone's fault in particular. Harvath had been forced to make a command decision, and that's exactly what he had done. When the timetable had shifted and the team couldn't get in place fast enough, Harvath, right or wrong, had decided to go it alone. If he didn't catch Khalid by the time the terrorist reached the large open-air bazaar two intersections up, he knew he would end up losing him yet again. And if that happened, Harvath was going to be in even more trouble than he was now. If only he'd been authorized to kill this animal, he could probably take him out from this distance with his Beretta, but that's not what his orders were.

Harvath was very close to being SOL yet again, and he knew it. Trying to put everything out of his mind, he drew upon what little reserves he had remaining and ran even faster. Already up ahead, he could see the tented stalls of the large open-air market.

When Alomari entered the souk, Harvath was less than fifteen feet behind him. The assassin ran down one of the many narrow aisles, upending tables and pulling down anything he could behind him to slow Harvath's pursuit. No matter what he tried, none of it worked. Harvath leapt over everything and soon had the gap narrowed to within ten feet.

Harvath wanted to put a bullet in Khalid Alomari more than anything he had ever wanted before, but when he got within five feet, he opted for a brutal tackle that took the terrorist's legs out from under him and slammed his face into the pavement. The perfectly executed maneuver would certainly have earned Harvath a starting position in the defensive backfield of his alma mater, the University of Southern California.

Immediately, the terrorist began to resist, which was exactly what Harvath had hoped he'd do. He landed a quick series of rabbit punches to his kidneys, causing the man to scream in pain. When Alomari then tried to get up, Harvath mule-punched him in the back of the head and then got a good grip of his dusty kaffiyeh and bounced the man's face off the pavement three more times.

For some insane reason, the terrorist still hadn't had enough and once again reached his hand beneath his robes. Harvath didn't wait to see what sort of trick Alomari had up his sleeve this time. In one clean move, Harvath pulled the man's hand out from underneath the folds of his robes and broke his arm. Alomari began screaming even louder.

"That was for Cairo, asshole," said Harvath as he reached into the back pocket of his fatigues for three pairs of flexicuffs. "And this," he continued as he hog-tied the international assassin in the most excruciatingly painful and humiliating manner possible, "is for making me run for two months, five thousand miles, and three fucking blocks trying to catch you."

Now that it was all over, Harvath expected a string of invectives in Arabic, English, or both, but instead, Khalid Alomari—Osama bin Laden's number one hit man—began to cry.

Harvath couldn't believe his ears. Usually, these assholes were all the same—indignant, self-righteous zealots. They hurled curses at you and your country right up until the moment you put a bullet in them or slammed the cell door shut in their face, but not Alomari. Something was wrong, and it wasn't until Harvath rolled the terrorist over that he realized what it was. The man he had chased for three full blocks and beaten almost unconscious was not Khalid Alomari at all. Somehow, a switch had been pulled.

Just when Harvath thought things couldn't get any worse, he looked up into the faces of the crowd surrounding them and then locked onto something really bad—an al-Jazeera camera team who had caught the whole thing on tape.

FIVE

DHAKA, PEOPLE'S REPUBLIC OF BANGLADESH

Until today, Emir Tokay had always felt safe in Bangladesh. While most outsiders viewed it as a cyclone-prone, perpetually flooded country, he had seen it as a land rich in history and, more importantly, rich in its devotion to Islam. Dhaka, the country's capital, boasted more than seven hundred mosques within its city limits alone. Surely, it was no accident that the Islamic Institute for Science and Technology had been established here—after all, what better place to carry out some of Allah's most important work? Now, though, Emir was having second thoughts not only about that work, but whether or not he was going to make it out of the city alive.

At first, the fatal heart attack suffered by Dr. Abbas in Dubai had seemed an unfortunate but not unusual circumstance. The man was grossly overweight and had long ignored his family's and colleagues' pleas to take better care of himself. The brilliant scientist had claimed that his research took all of his time and left him little opportunity for exercise. Then there was Dr. Akbar in Amman, who was just the opposite of Abbas. Akbar broke his neck diving into the pool he swam laps in every day and drowned. After Akbar came Dr. Hafiz in Damascus. He was a relatively robust man in his fifties with no prior history of health complications who suddenly died of an acute asthma attack.

Next came the deaths of Dr. Jafar in Cairo, Dr. Qasim in Tehran, and Dr. Salim in Rabat. Then the terrible hit-and-run accident involving Dr. Ansari in Lahore. Examined individually, there was nothing unusual about these deaths other than they were unfortunate and untimely. But when Emir Tokay took them as a whole, the larger picture was terrifying. Assuming Dr. Bashir in Baghdad, whom he hadn't been able to get hold of for several days, was dead, Tokay was the last one on the research team still alive.

Tokay's first reaction was to notify his superiors, but he knew that would be a big mistake. None of the scientists were supposed to know who they were working with. The Islamic Institute for Science and Technology had cloaked the entire project in secrecy and had kept it tightly compartmentalized. The scientists were not allowed to identify themselves to each other and had only communicated via encrypted, untraceable e-mail addresses. They were allowed to share data only—nothing about their personal or professional lives. The system had seemed foolproof, but the institute had overlooked the fundamental trait that made for a good scientist—curiosity.

It was Dr. Bashir who had begun the quest to uncover not only whom he was working with, but what their research was ultimately intended to achieve. Other than that it was to be a great triumph for the Muslim people, not much had been explained to the team. It was a puzzle all of them were quietly eager to solve.

Bashir suspected that at the very least, the institute was filtering their e-mails, searching for key words that would give away any forbidden conversations, and probably was selecting random e-mails to read in their entirety. Either way, his solution required discretion.

Bashir had named one of the white lab rats in his control group Stay-Go. The name, he said in his e-mails, sprang from the way the rat bounced around its cage.

Emir Tokay, the brilliant young Turkish scientist who had been brought to the institute to help coordinate the efforts of the project members, was the first to pick up on Dr. Bashir's clever code. It was more the tone of Bashir's e-mails than anything else that made him believe the lead scientist was trying to convey a secondary message to the team. It took Tokay a while to figure what that message was, but through much trial and error he eventually discovered the key lay in what Bashir had named his lab rat. The name Stay-Go was actually a phonetic pronunciation of the word stego, short for *steganography. Steganography* was taken from Greek and literally translated to "covered writing." In cryptography it is assumed an enemy may intercept a message but will be unable to decode it, whereas the goal of steganography is to hide messages in otherwise harmless communications in such a way that even if they were intercepted by the enemy, said enemy would never even be aware a secondary message was present. In the digital world of today, practitioners of steganography could hide their messages in a wide array of data formats. Popular file attachments such as .wav, .mp3, .bmp, .doc, .txt, .gif, and .jpeg were perfect because redundant, or "noisy," data could be easily removed and replaced with a hidden message. Tokay discovered that was precisely what Dr. Bashir had done.

For three months Bashir had been embedding a simple, repetitive message inside his digital pictures of his white lab rat, Stay-Go: "Who are we and what are we doing? Be cautious with your response. Our e-mails are being watched. Dr. M. Bashir."

Once he had discovered Bashir's code, Emir worked feverishly to find a way around the institute's electronic filtering and monitoring of the team's communications. Like many organizations, the institute was far more concerned with attacks originating from outside their computer system than from within. Soon, Tokay was confident that he had devised a way for the team to send and receive e-mails without the institute's knowledge. In time, the scientists began trading clandestine messages on the average of once a week. From what they could tell, the project they were working on was more a game than anything else. No one could understand what practical application their research could possibly have.

It wasn't until the final stages of the project that Dr. Bashir floated a terrifying supposition about what they might be working on. Before they could fully discuss the possibility, thc team was officially disbanded. Only Emir was kept on at the institute to assemble the team's research. Immediately thereafter, team members began dying. *But why?*

Alone in his lab in Baghdad, Dr. Bashir had come up with the correct answer. Each of the team members had been recruited to help give birth to an abomination. It was the only thing that made sense, but Emir Tokay had no intention of continuing to be a party to it. The type of Islam he believed in would never allow what the institute planned to unleash on the world. It was pure evil, and Islam was a religion of peace. He wouldn't allow any more fanatics to hijack his faith for their own vile ends.

The one problem he had was that he couldn't prove anything if he was dead. He needed to get back to Turkey and the safety of his family. The airport was out of the question, as was the train station. They were too dangerous, too obvious. If he could catch a bus south to the port city of Narayanganj, he could board a ship and everything would be okay. But, before he did that, there was one last thing he needed to do at the institute.

After sending off a final e-mail and gathering his files from his office, Emir wound his way through the bustling old town and emerged on one of the crowded streets parallel to the Dhaleswari River. When he saw his bus coming, he allowed himself to believe that he just might make it.

His thoughts were soon interrupted by a speeding black Mercedes that screamed to a halt alongside him, filling the air with the smell of burnt rubber and tire smoke. When three masked men armed with AK-74s leapt from the car and surrounded him, he knew he had been a fool to think he could ever make it out of Bangladesh alive.

SIX

WASHINGTON, DC

Pennsylvania Democratic senator Helen Remington Carmichael watched the footage for the thousandth time, and it still gave her the chills. It wasn't that she abhorred violence. On the contrary, she saw the calculated application of force for exactly what it was—a necessary means to preserve liberty. In this case, though, what the images on her television screen represented, what the footage millions of Americans were seeing repeatedly on Fox and CNN and Muslims around the world were watching on their respective channels, was the beginning of the undoing of American President Jack Rutledge.

She had known it was only a matter of time. The man's approval ratings had been ridiculously high. It started with sympathy over the loss of his wife to breast cancer during the first campaign, then it followed him through his first term as president with his kidnapping, his dismantling of several high-profile terrorist organizations, and most recently a successful showdown against the Russians. It had seemed as if the man could do no wrong. And then this. The heavens had opened, and God had handed Helen Remington Carmichael the one thing she had been praying for since considering a run for the vice-presidential slot on the Democratic ticket.

One step at a time, she had told herself. She knew how the press perceived her. She was the power-hungry bitch who had used her successful husband to catapult her into a Senate seat. She didn't even like Pennsylvania, but when it became obvious that aging senator Timothy Murphy wasn't going to run again, she had grabbed her husband by the balls and had moved the entire family out east to establish residency and make a run for the Senate.

The people of the state liked her fire, and Murphy had thrown not only his endorsement but all of his political weight behind her. The young Republican the GOP put up against her never had a chance.

Ever the savvy politico, Carmichael had been working hard to soften her image, but no matter what she did, everything about her still screamed *bitch.* While some of her aides privately debated whether or not she should ditch the pantsuits and grow her hair out, there were others who said none of it would matter. No matter how you dressed or coiffed her, the woman not only acted like a bitch, she just plain looked like one.

The word among her staff was that maybe all she needed to soften her up was a little sex, but her husband was too busy chasing other women.

The fact of the matter was that the only way Carmichael was going to get elected to the presidency of the United States was to serve as one hell of a vice president first.

But to even get that far, there was something very serious standing in her way—Jack Rutledge. The Democrats didn't have a single candidate they could stand up against him and hope to win with. The only way they were going to win was to politically batter the incumbent president until his numbers were so low they could walk in and take the office right away from him.

SEVEN

THE WHITE HOUSE

President Jack Rutledge waved his chief of staff, Charles Anderson, into the Oval Office and signaled that his phone conversation was almost complete.

"Yes, Your Majesty, I realize that, and we appreciate the lengths you have gone to to keep militants in your own country in check. Your help in the war on terror has been invaluable. Let me assure you that this is one of my top priorities and we are going to get to the bottom of it," the president said. He paused and then said, "I've heard that rumor, too, and I can understand why your people would be upset, but let me again state that there are always two sides to every story. We're going to get to the bottom of this, and as soon as we do, we'll brief you on our findings. I guarantee you that we are taking this very seriously."

The president paused again and then answered, "And I thank you for your time as well. Goodbye, Your Majesty."

As the president hung up, he turned to Anderson and said, "This is an absolute nightmare. That's the sixth call I've had today from an Arab head of state. You know what they're calling it over there? The showdown at the al-Karim corral."

"Yeah. I've heard that one," replied Anderson. "Not very original, if you ask me."

"Original or not, this is a big black eye for us. The Muslims take an extremely long view of history, Chuck. Much longer than we do. To many of them, the crusades are as fresh in their minds as if they happened last week. All of this on the heels of the whole Abu Ghraib prison fiasco. That might as well have happened ten minutes ago as far as they're concerned."

"Abu Ghraib was bad. No question about it. And this al-Jazeera thing has got the potential to be much worse—"

"*The potential?* Chuck, I have no idea how the view is from where you're sitting, but this has gone way beyond the *potential* for being worse. It is worse. Monumentally."

"I'll admit it doesn't look good, but I want to remind you, as you yourself just said, we don't have all the facts yet."

"That soldier is an American. That's all that matters," said the president. "We're not fighting this war on terror in a vacuum. Every single move we make is watched around the world. Every single thing we do has countless repercussions. It takes us years to gain a mere foot of credible ground in that region and only seconds to lose it."

"Agreed," said Anderson, "but the Muslims' long view of history notwithstanding, I don't think the United States should have to wear the weight of the crusades around its neck. America didn't even exist in the eleventh century. Europe launched the crusades."

The president leaned back in his chair and looked at the ceiling. "It doesn't matter. In their minds we're an extension of Europe. Everything the West does, whether it's Europe or America, is connected. Seven minutes or seven centuries ago, it's all the same to them. They paint us with the same brush. It's frustrating as hell, but these people just don't think the way we do."

"Nobody thinks the way we do. We have a unique spirit, and that spirit is what defines America. Freedom, democracy, liberty, and the willingness to use force when necessary to help preserve those ideals—that's what we're all about. You pick any man or woman on the street in the Middle East and give him or her the option of staying put or coming to America to start their lives over again with the rights and freedoms we identify ourselves by, and they'll choose the good ol' USA every time. They might burn our flag for the cameras, but throw a handful of green cards in the air and they'd cut each other's throats to get their hands on them."

"I wonder what al-Jazeera would do with that

footage," said the president as he shifted his gaze and focused on his chief of staff.

"Don't get me started on al-Jazeera. We could be passing out blankets, medicine, and gold-plated copies of the Koran over there, and they'd still find a way to make us look like the bad guys."

"Too true," replied Rutledge, "but lack of journalistic integrity at al-Jazeera is a conversation I'm tired of having. What did you want to see me about?"

"I take it that was King Abdullah you were speaking with?" asked Anderson.

The president nodded his head.

"And the rumor you were referring to was that the man seen being beaten by our soldier was just a nobody, a fruit stall vendor, right?"

Again the president nodded.

"Well, that's not a rumor any longer. He *is* a fruit stall vendor."

"That's fantastic," said the president, as he threw up his hands and stood up from behind his desk. "It couldn't have been a terrorist off our most wanted list, could it? That would have been too easy. Heaven forbid we get an opportunity to bolster our credibility in the region by taking a known killer out of circulation."

"Even if the guy was a known terrorist, from a PR standpoint I still don't think this is how we would have wanted it to go down for the cameras," replied Anderson as he watched the president pace.

"You know what I'm trying to say. Our credibility is so thin over there, all you have to do is hold it up to a light bulb and you can see through it. We talk about being a just nation—a nation that observes the rule of law, a place where people are innocent until proven guilty—but those are only words, aren't they? And what speaks a thousand words? Pictures. And what pictures are being watched the world over by anyone who has turned on a television set in the last eight hours? A faceless American soldier beating the pulp out of an Iraqi fruit stall vendor. What a picture that made, straight out of Central Casting. A uniformed American GI and a typical local citizen complete with turban."

"It was actually a kaffiyeh, sir, not a turban. There's a difference."

"I know there's a difference, and you don't have to tell me," barked Rutledge. "I saw the footage."

"Of course. I'm sorry, sir."

"My point is that we can't just talk the talk. We have to walk the walk—all of us. From the lowliest buck private all the way to the people working in this building. Damn it. Just when it seemed we were getting some PR traction in that part of the world, this happens."

Anderson waited a moment for the president to cool down and said, "There may be a piece of information that could work to our favor in all of this."

Rutledge stopped pacing for a moment and raised his eyebrows. "Really? Like what? Are you going to tell me that the attack was self-defense somehow? Maybe the fruit vendor was selling bad dates, because if he was, then this whole thing is okay, isn't it? I mean, if this guy had the balls to sell bad dates, then the gloves understandably come off. God knows we're not a nation that stands for bad dates, and heaven help any fruit vendor who tries to sell them to us."

The chief of staff knew that the president was only one step away from blowing his stack and decided to tread very lightly. "The fruit vendor's stall was nowhere near where this incident took place. In fact, it's completely on the other side of Baghdad. He should have been manning his stall when this all went down, but it turns out he paid one of his cousins, and not a small amount of money, to man it for him."

"Why would he do that?"

"Because somebody paid him even more money to take the day off and hang out a couple of blocks from the al-Karim bazaar."

"Who? And why?"

"The Iraqi Security Forces have been trying to get that out of him, but the man claims he doesn't know," said Anderson. "And before you make any remarks about the effectiveness of the Iraqi Security Forces, keep in mind that they were almost immediately on the scene at al-Karim and shut the al-Jazeera crew down before they could get our soldier's face on tape. We're lucky that it was all shot from behind."

"Who cares if they got his face? They got that little two-by-three-inch patch with the stars and stripes on his upper arm," said the president, not at all convinced there was anything positive about this catastrophe. "That's all they needed to get."

"True," said Anderson, "but the fact that his face wasn't shown will definitely help buy us a little more time."

"Time? Time for what? Time to hope this story will just fade away, because that's not going to happen. This isn't something we can claim ignorance of and quietly sweep under the rug. People are incensed, Chuck. The entire Muslim world is up in arms. They see this as a direct attack on Islam and are *literally* out for blood. I've been asked by no less than four governments in the region to hand the soldier over once he's been ID'd so he can stand trial under Islamic law. Not only has every two-bit imam across the region issued a fatwa against him, the U.S. military, and the United States in general, but some of these people are calling for a war crimes tribunal in The Hague."

"Well, if the Muslims want to try our soldier, they'll have to take a number, because the Democrats on the Hill are already calling for their own hearings."

The president sat back down in his chair and massaged his temples with the heels of his hands. "Why doesn't that surprise me?"

"We *are* in an election year."

"Even if it weren't an election year, it wouldn't matter. Our side would be all over this as well if the situation was reversed. This is just too juicy to pass up." Looking up, he asked, "Who's leading the charge?"

"Helen Carmichael," replied Anderson. "And here's the kicker—she wants the hearings televised."

"Why doesn't that surprise me either?"

"It shouldn't. She's looking to score major points with her party before Governor Farnsworth's campaign team and the DNC nail down who the number two person on their ticket is going to be. What's surprising, though, is that she's launching the hearings from her own seat on the Senate Select Committee on Intelligence."

That *did* surprise Rutledge. "*The Intelligence Committee?* What the hell for? This doesn't have anything to do with them. Why isn't she giving it to Armed Services?"

"We think it's because she smells blood in the water."

"Of course she smells blood in the water. We're hemorrhaging. Islamic fundamentalists are going to use that al-Jazeera footage as a perpetual recruiting tool, and it's going to work. Thousands of Muslim youth who might not otherwise have signed up are going to be asking themselves, *What if that was someone I loved or cared about being beaten by an American soldier?* We handed them this one on a silver platter. It's going to take us decades to recover. But that still doesn't explain what possible interest the Intelligence Committee could have in holding hearings on this."

"You might change your mind about the committee's interest once you know who the American in the al-Jazeera footage is," said Anderson.

The president leaned forward in his chair. "Who's got him? The Army? Do they know who he is?"

"The Army doesn't have him, and they don't know who he is."

Rutledge waited for the other shoe to drop, but when Anderson didn't say anything, his mind started turning. "I don't suppose this guy is a private contractor we can plausibly disavow?"

"We're not going to be that lucky on this one. If it was a contractor, this entire thing would be over already."

"He's an operator then, isn't he?" said the president.

Anderson nodded his head. "Part of one of the direct action teams authorized by the DOD and this office."

"Is he CIA?"

"I don't think you should know any more at this point. There's a good chance Carmichael is going to be issuing subpoenas, and I don't doubt there'll be one with your name on it."

"My name? What the hell for?"

"We've got him on a C130 en route to Andrews Air Force Base right now. He won't be on the ground until much later tonight. In the morning, there'll be a thorough debriefing, and afterwards I'll come to you and we can talk. In the meantime, I'd rather you stay outside the loop on this."

Rutledge had known his chief of staff long enough to trust his judgment. Shielding the president from political fallout was part of Anderson's job. "Until the morning, but that's it," said Rutledge. "Now, what about Carmichael? Does she know we've got him?"

"I don't think so. Not yet," replied Anderson.

"Does she know who he is?"

"She's got her teeth into something, and she's working around the clock turning over every rock in town."

"Well, if we've got him, then we have to get out in front of this story and control how it unfolds. I don't care about the elections. They don't supersede the sanctity of this office. We're going to do the right thing on this, and if it means this operative has to take one for the team, then he's going to have to take one for the team," said the president.

Anderson shook his head and reached for the BlackBerry device vibrating on his hip. "You might not feel that way once you know who we're talking about."

"Are you saying I'm familiar with this person?" asked the president.

Anderson didn't respond. He was too busy reading the message he had just been sent.

"Chuck, I'm asking you a question," repeated the president. "Is this person someone I know?"

The chief of staff looked up and said, "I'm sorry, Mr. President. We'll have to take this up later. You're needed in the situation room immediately."

EIGHT

WHITE HOUSE SITUATION ROOM

Within twenty minutes, the situation room was packed with bodies and the air was thick with tension. Based on an emerging terrorist threat, the White House had gone into full crash mode.

"Ladies and gentlemen," called the president. "It appears we've got a lot to cover, and I'd like to get started, so if you'd all take your seats please."

The attendees did as they were instructed, and as a subdued hush fell over the room, the president nodded at the chairman of the Joint Chiefs of Staff, General Hank Currutt.

"Thank you, Mr. President," replied Currutt, who stood to address the room. "Two days ago, soldiers from the U.S. Army's Third Arrowhead Brigade, Second Infantry Division Stryker Brigade Combat Team out of Fort Lewis, Washington—now based in Mosul, Iraq—responded to a call that three Christian aid workers had failed to check in with their organization and had gone missing. Traveling to the remote village near the Syrian border where the workers had been based, the soldiers uncovered something the likes of which we have never seen before.

"To brief you on what exactly it is that they found, I'm going to turn the floor over to Colonel Michael Tranberg. For those of you not familiar with Colonel Tranberg, he is the commander of the U.S. Army Medical Research Institute of Infectious Diseases at Fort Detrick, Maryland. I have asked him here because USAMRIID is the Department of Defense's lead laboratory for developing medical countermeasures, vaccines, drugs, and diagnostic tools to protect U.S. troops from biological warfare agents and naturally occurring infectious diseases. After the CDC in Atlanta, USAMRIID houses the only other Biosafety Level Four laboratory in the entire country, which allows Colonel Tranberg's team to study highly hazardous viruses in maximum biological containment. I think that's about it introduction-wise. Colonel Tranberg?"

"Thank you, General Currutt," said Tranberg, a tall, gray-haired man in his sixties. He picked up a digital remote from the conference table, pressed a button, and the two plasma monitors at the front of the room came to life with the revolving USAMRIID logo. "The footage you are about to view was shot a little over a week ago in northern Iraq by the aforementioned Christian humanitarian aid workers from a group called Mercy

International out of Fresno, California. Three of Mercy International's workers had been based in the remote village of Asalaam, about one hundred fifty kilometers southwest of Mosul. When they failed to check in with Mercy's main Baghdad office, calls were made, and eventually soldiers from one of the U.S. Army's Stryker Brigade Combat Teams were sent to check up on them. It was these same soldiers who uncovered this footage. We've edited it down to the most important parts, but I have to warn you, it's not easy to watch."

Tranberg pressed another button on the remote and sat down.

Everyone in the room watched with rapt attention as a young female aid worker, who couldn't have been more than twenty-two years old, chronicled a strange flulike illness, which was sweeping through the village. By the second day, though, the woman, as well as her two colleagues, fell ill and quickly grew too sick to continue filming. "From this point on," narrated Tranberg, "we believe it's one of the villagers, maybe a local person who had been working with the aid workers, who continues the filming."

The group watched as the video further chronicled the sickness spreading throughout the village. Those who were infected needed to be physically restrained. All of the patients eventually exhibited extremely aggressive behavior, with many trying to bite their caregivers, or anyone who came across their path. In many of the afflicted, a bizarre state of heightened sexuality was also observable. Many of them complained of severe insomnia and headaches. They were hypersensitive to odors, particularly garlic, and couldn't stand to see their reflection in anything from a mirror to a bedpan. In addition, they seemed to suffer from hydrophobia and had to be completely nourished intravenously, and even then, the few IV bags the village had available had to be hidden beneath towels, as patients who saw anything even remotely resembling water would fly into a rage and their throats would swell up, making it impossible for them to breathe. They were hypersensitive to light, and their skin had taken on a very strange pallor. The presentation cut to the final footage of the aid workers in the end stages of the illness.

Everyone around the table watched in silence as the aid workers began convulsing. Soon a strange, dark fluid began to pour from their nostrils, and moments later they were dead.

In the background of the video, villagers who had not yet become infected recoiled in horror.

When the clip was over, the video footage was replaced once again by the spinning USAMRIID logos. For a moment, no one spoke. It was obvious from the faces around the table that the footage had scared the hell out of everyone, including the president.

Dr. Donna Vennett, the surgeon general and a

family medicine physician by trade, was the first to speak. "What is it? Some sort of Ebola strain? Hemorrhagic fever?"

"No on both counts," responded Tranberg. "This is not like anything we've seen before."

"What was that substance running out of the nasal passages before the victims died?"

"That's a mystery as well."

"Well, what do we know?" said Steve Plaisier, secretary of Health and Human Services. "We've obviously been called here for a reason. Is there a chance we might see an outbreak of this thing in the U.S.?"

"There's more than just a chance," responded General Currutt. "We're counting on it."

Homeland Security Secretary Alan Driehaus cleared his throat and said, "Why?"

"Because the village of Asalaam wasn't infected by chance. It was specifically targeted."

"Intentional infection?" said Plaisier.

Currutt nodded his head.

"What makes you so sure?"

The general activated his own laptop and projected a series of photos via the monitors at the front of the room. "Not only were all communication lines into Asalaam taken out, but the handful of vehicles the villagers collectively owned had been sabotaged—tires slashed, things of that nature. No one was going anywhere. Someone wanted that village completely isolated."

"Who?"

Now it was Director of the Central Intelligence Agency James Vaile's turn to speak. "We have some parallel intelligence we think might answer part of that question. Over the last two months, a high-ranking al-Qaeda operative named Khalid Sheik Alomari has been sighted in Dubai, Amman, Damascus, Cairo, Tehran, Rabat, Lahore, and Baghdad. And while he was in each of those cities, a highly respected Muslim scientist died. On the surface, all of the deaths appeared to be accidents or the result of natural causes. Originally, we thought that Alomari was doing the Middle East circuit to either fund-raise or coordinate a multicity attack. We had no idea until one of our analysts started connecting the dots that the man was there committing assassinations."

"You said this Alomari was high-ranking," stated Paul Jackson, the president's National Security Advisor. "How high-ranking are we talking about?"

"Alomari is bin Laden's protégé—handpicked to handle only the most sensitive assignments. It's exceptionally concerning that we've attached him to what happened in Asalaam because Alomari's main responsibility for al-Qaeda is to help conceptualize and orchestrate the most devastating attacks he can think of against the United States. He's the only person in al-Qaeda said to hate America even more than bin Laden himself."

"But how do we know Alomari and those dead

scientists are connected to what happened in this village?" asked Secretary Driehaus.

"Because, besides probably being killed by Alomari, the scientists were all working on a highly secretive project for something called the Islamic Institute for Science and Technology in Bangladesh. Its mission statement is to improve the lives of Muslims worldwide through advancements in science and technology, but we've suspected for some time those aren't their true marching orders."

"Why is that?"

"They get paid lots of visits by scientists from Islamic countries we believe are involved with covert chemical, biological, or nuclear weapons programs. One of the institute's directors, in fact, is especially fond of quoting Dr. Shiro Ishii, the head of Japan's bioweapons program during World War II. Ishii was the one who said that if a weapon is important enough to be prohibited, it must be worth having in one's arsenal."

The secretary of state, Jennifer Staley, replied, "Director Vaile, do we have any hard evidence connecting this institute with any covert weapons programs?"

"Yes, we do."

"What's the connection?"

"Jamal Mehmood."

"Who is Jamal Mehmood?" asked Driehaus.

Vaile looked to the president, and when Rutledge nodded his head, Vaile explained, "He's a Pakistani nuclear scientist. A couple of years ago, we found the schematics he designed for an anthrax-spreading device in an al-Qaeda training camp. The CIA was part of the team that helped track him down and detain him outside of Karachi. We were never able to substantiate his claims that the designs had been stolen."

"I still don't see the connection."

"Both Mehmood and A.Q. Khan—the father of the Islamic bomb, who sold nuclear secrets to Iran and Libya—have not only been visiting professors but major fundraisers for the Islamic Institute for Science and Technology."

The secretary of state held out her hands in front of her, as if balancing what she'd been listening to, and said, "So we have a serious mystery ill ness seen only in some remote Iraqi village on one hand and a high-ranking al-Qaeda operative who killed a bunch of scientists tied to some Islamic research group on the other. I'm still not seeing any connection here."

General Currutt advanced to the next slide on his laptop and responded, "A few days before the people in Asalaam started becoming sick, Khalid Sheik Alomari was spotted crossing the Iraqi-Syrian border less than forty-five kilometers from the village. We believe Asalaam was a live test site for the virus."

That was all it took. There wasn't a single person in the situation room who could ignore the al-Qaeda link.

"So that's it then," said Jackson. "Al-Qaeda is now actively in the biowarfare game."

Currutt brought up an organizational chart for al-Qaeda. Those who had been killed or captured had either a slash or a red X through their photo. "Unfortunately, it would seem so. We've inflicted such significant damage on them that they're growing desperate. In a sense, we've forced them to branch out in drastic new directions, one of which happens to be in the realm of chemical and biological weapons. They're using Iraq and Afghanistan as justification for employing whatever weapons they can get their hands on to drive us from all Muslim lands."

"Jesus," responded Driehaus. "Talk about blowback. Every single move we make, whether successful or not, seems to come back to bite us in the ass twice as hard."

It was exactly what everyone around the table was thinking.

"The good we're doing over there far outweighs the bad," said the secretary of state.

"I hope so," responded Driehaus, "but I have to be honest. I'm worried our losses may soon overshadow whatever gains we might make."

"What's that supposed to mean?"

"It means that for better or worse, I'm more concerned with the welfare of the American people than I am with the Iraqis or anyone else over in that part of the world."

"So what? We're supposed to just bury our heads in the sand and hope that the terrorism problem will just go away? Because we all know that's not going to happen."

"All right," interjected the president. "I respect that we've got a wide range of opinions in the room, but let's all try to settle down and focus on the matter at hand."

After several moments of awkward silence, the surgeon general said, "I suppose that if we don't know what we're dealing with, it's pointless to ask if there's a cure."

"Pretty much," said Colonel Tranberg, relieved to get back on track.

"How about the fatality rate? What can you tell us about that?"

"Well, that all depends upon how you interpret the data. If you look at the village of Asalaam, one out of every two people died, which gives us a fifty percent fatality rate, which is extremely serious."

"If the village is our only benchmark," asked Plaisier, "then how else could you be looking at this?"

"We're looking at the village, of course, but more importantly, we're looking at the one out of every two villagers who died. You see, the area around Mosul is one of the largest Christian enclaves in the entire country. It isn't unusual for

Christians and Muslims to live side by side there. Asalaam was a perfect example of this. So perfect, in fact, that it was about fifty-two percent Muslim and forty-eight percent Christian."

"And when you look at the deaths by religious affiliations?" asked the surgeon general.

Tranberg shook his head slowly. "Only the Muslims survived. If you weren't Muslim, the illness was one hundred percent lethal."

NINE

Alban Towers Apartments
Georgetown

Helen Carmichael didn't have to sleep with the young CIA analyst—the promise of a position in her cabinet would have been enough in itself, but the sex was a nice bonus. It wasn't only powerful male politicians who attracted good-looking, hard-bodied young things. Powerful female politicians did as well, although they tended to be a lot more discreet about it.

Carmichael reached for the half-empty bottle of Montrachet in the ice bucket next to the bed and filled their two glasses. As she handed the sandy-haired twenty-five-year-old his wine, she said, "Tell me about work."

Brian Turner knew it was part of the deal, but just once he wished they could talk about something else. "I have a friend who keeps a sailboat on the eastern shore of the Chesapeake who said I could use it any time I wanted," he said, changing the subject. "How about this weekend?"

"Brian, you know I'm not a big fan of boats," replied the senator.

"That doesn't matter. It's supposed to rain anyway. We'll just keep it in the slip and stay below deck. There's a DVD player on board. We can rent a bunch of movies and stock up at Dean & DeLuca on the way. We'll get those lobster rolls you like so much. I'll bring along a case of wine. It'll be perfect."

For a moment, Carmichael was tempted. She couldn't remember the last time she had dropped everything to run off on a carefree, romantic weekend. There might have been one or two in the beginning of her marriage, but that was so long ago she couldn't really be sure if they'd happened or if she was just inventing them in her mind to make herself feel better.

She stared at Brian Turner's tan, firm body lying on top of the crisp Frette linens and tried to figure out a way to clear her schedule, but it was impossible. There were too many important things going on. She needed to see and be seen around town, especially as she moved to get her committee's investigation of the al-Jazeera incident off the ground. "I can't, Brian," she said. "I've got way too much on my plate right now."

"I understand," replied Turner, and he did. In fact, he was glad she had turned him down. He had already extended the same invitation to a much younger and more attractive congressional staff assistant, also known in DC parlance as a "staff ass," rumored to have an insatiable appetite for wild, marathon sex. Turner was just playing Carmichael. The senator never accepted any of his "romantic" getaway overtures anyway. The thought of spending an entire weekend having to play warm and cuddly was not really his idea of a good time. Not that he found her unattractive. She was okay, but he wasn't with her for the sex, he was with her for what she could do for his career.

Carmichael was Turner's ticket to the big time, his ticket out of the monotonous, post-9/11 slog at the CIA. Short of spending the weekend nailing the pretty little blond staff ass from South Dakota, there was nothing Brian Turner wanted more than to go to work for Senator, and hopefully soon to be Vice President, Helen Carmichael.

He was ruminating on the perversions the staffer was said to be fond of when Carmichael began nudging him about work again. "What's going on at Langley?" she asked. "What are you hearing about the al-Jazeera footage?"

"*Seeing* is more like it," said Turner, who, somewhat relieved that the intimacy portion of the evening had come to a close, slid his feet over the side of the bed and walked to his desk.

The senator watched him walk. His body was a testimony to youthful strength and vigor. She looked down at her own body and was proud of what she saw. She worked out regularly and had the body of a woman at least fifteen years younger. She especially liked the piercing Brian had talked her into getting. They both wore matching, stainless steel studs—the senator in her navel and Brian Turner through the head of his penis in what was known as a Prince Albert. It was a reminder to Carmichael of her secret indulgences, and she liked to discreetly finger the stud while surrounded by other important DC figures—people who would never even guess at the double life she led.

In a moment of concern, Turner had asked the senator what her husband might say if he ever saw her piercing, but Carmichael had set his mind right at ease by telling him that her husband hadn't seen her naked in years.

Turner returned to bed carrying a file folder. He tucked a pencil behind his ear and brushed the hair away from his forehead. "I asked one of the DOD liaisons at the agency to review the footage."

"And?" asked Carmichael.

"And same as you, the first thing he noticed was that the uniform the American soldier was wearing—"

"Didn't have any insignias other than the U.S. flag," said Carmichael, finishing the young man's sentence for him.

"Exactly."

"Which means the soldier was probably operating in some semi-covert capacity, maybe on one of the Special Operations Command's direct action teams."

"Right again," said Turner.

"Do you know who he is?"

Turner smiled. "Nobody, it seems, wants to help hang this guy. I had to be very careful who I talked to and what information I pulled. He's very highly thought of—kind of a hero in intelligence circles."

"Quit dragging this out," purred Carmichael as she grabbed the file folder away from him.

The young man watched as the senator pored over the pages, a smile curling the edges of her mouth.

"This is incredible," she whispered as she continued to read. Toward the end of the dossier, she concluded, "This is beyond good, Brian. This guy is the president's goddamn golden boy."

Turner smiled again. "I thought you'd appreciate it."

"I more than appreciate it. This is the find of the decade."

"His résumé is pretty lengthy. For some reason, he doesn't seem to stay in one place too long. He served on both Navy SEAL Teams Two and Six, before the Secret Service hired him to come work at the White House. While he was there, he knocked one out of the park by rescuing the president during that whole kidnapping thing in Park City, Utah. That's the move that earned him all his cachet around town. Shortly after that, he linked up with the CIA and started doing occasional assignments with members of the Special Operations Group. One involved a hijacking and the dismantling of the Abu Nidal terrorist organization, and another involved the Russians and the suitcase nukes they were threatening to detonate here."

"He seems to be behind a lot of the president's successes."

"He does," agreed Turner, "but then all of a sudden he got dumped over at the Department of Homeland Security. He's now working in some innocuous police and intelligence liaison unit called the Office of International Investigative Assistance."

Carmichael closed the folder and tapped it against her chin for several moments. "Something tells me we're going to find that the Office of International Investigative Assistance is anything but innocuous and that our new friend is up to a lot more than just liaising with police and intelligence people."

"Where are you going?" asked Turner, as the senator slid out of bed and began getting dressed. "I thought we were going to spend the evening together."

"I can't. Not now. There's much too much to be done. But I want you," said Carmichael as she bent down and gave Brian a deep kiss, "to sleep like an angel tonight. You deserve it. I also want you well rested, because I'll probably need you in the morning. Keep an eye on your hotmail account. If we need to talk, I'll send you a message, and then we'll use the Breast Cancer Forum chat room like before."

Before Brian Turner could respond, the senator was out the apartment door and on her way down to the lobby.

The moment she stepped outside, Carmichael pulled out her cell phone and speed-dialed her assistant's home number.

"Hello?" said an obviously tired voice on the other end of the line.

"Neal, it's Helen. I want you in the office in twenty minutes. As soon as you get there, start pulling everything you can on an ex–Navy SEAL who used to work Secret Service at the White House and is now over at DHS named Scot Harvath. I want you to dig as deep as you can. Get my black Rolodex out of the safe and start calling in favors. We need to know everything about this guy, especially what he's been involved with since he began working at the White House a couple years ago. Am I clear? Do you have all that?"

"Yes, Senator," said the assistant, who was now wide awake.

"Good," replied Carmichael. "You've now got eighteen minutes to get yourself into the office. Get moving. I want to make the morning news cycle."

TEN

MANDARIN ORIENTAL HOTEL
WASHINGTON, DC

Chief of Staff Charles Anderson found the Swiss ambassador at a quiet table in the Mandarin's lobby bar.

"Can I buy you a drink, Chuck?" asked Hans Friederich as a waitress set down his martini.

"I'll have a light beer," said Anderson. "I don't care what kind."

"Light beer?" said the ambassador as the waitress smiled and walked away. "Since when does Charles Anderson drink light beer?"

"Since my trousers started getting a little too snug around the waist."

The ambassador laughed good-naturedly.

"I'm also going back to the office tonight," added the chief of staff. "We've got a bit of a situation brewing."

"I've been watching your situation brewing all day on TV," said Friederich.

Anderson grimaced. "Yeah. The al-Jazeera

thing. Believe it or not, that's shaping up to be the least of my worries at this point."

"Then I'm sorry that I might soon be adding to them."

"Why?" asked Anderson. "Are Mitzi and the kids okay?"

"They're fine."

"How about you? You look like maybe you should start thinking about switching over to light beer too."

The ambassador smiled and shook his head. "I'll take it under advisement."

Friederich tilted his head in the direction of the approaching waitress and fell silent. Once the young woman had poured Anderson's beer and left the table, the ambassador continued. "I have some information for you, but before I give it to you, I want you to know that we're only an intermediary. My government has no way of corroborating what I am about to share."

"Understood. What do you have?"

"The sword of Allah."

"The sword of Allah?" repeated Anderson. "I've never heard of it."

"If what I hear is true, you are about to become extremely familiar with it. It's a weapon with which Islamic fundamentalists intend to purge the world of all but the most devoted Muslims."

"And exactly what kind of a weapon is this?"

"It's a sickness that infects all but the most devout followers of Islam."

Anderson almost spit his beer back in his glass.

How the hell did the Swiss ambassador know about this? He took a moment to glance around the bar to make sure nobody was listening to them. "Where'd you get this information?"

"I'm here on behalf of a man who does a tremendous amount of business with my country."

"Who?"

"He's not a Swiss citizen, but he has been extremely—"

"Damn it, Hans. I don't have time to fool around. Who the hell did you get this information from?" demanded Anderson.

"Ozan Kalachka."

"Kalachka the Turk? The terrorist?"

"The terrorist characterization is malicious and unfounded," replied Friederich.

"*Unfounded,* my ass. Western intelligence, in particular the CIA, knows—"

"Western intelligence knows precious little. In fact, Western intelligence, your CIA in particular, has been *trying* to compile a detailed dossier on him for years without any luck."

"We know enough about him," said Anderson.

"I don't think so. In fact—"

"Hans, let me save you some time. If you're here trying to promote Ozan Kalachka for U.S. citizenship in exchange for whatever dubious information he may or may not have, forget it. We don't want anything to do with him. And frankly, I can't understand why Switzerland bothers with him either."

"Mr. Kalachka is a businessman. He has many legitimate international contacts that have proven very profitable for Switzerland."

"And lots of not-so-legitimate contacts that have proven very profitable for Switzerland's private banking industry."

"True," said Friederich as he took another sip of his martini. "But in all fairness, the United States had their Adnan Khashoggi to help cement its relationship with the Saudis and their mountains of money. One trillion they have in your economy now, if I recall correctly. It's no wonder you remain so loyal to them. If they pulled their money out of America, your economy would collapse."

"What's your point?"

"My point is that Ozan Kalachka serves much the same function for us as Khashoggi has for you—he drums up capital for our ventures in other parts of the world."

"*Capital*. It sounds so clean when you put it that way."

"Come on, Chuck. We both know how the game is played. The difference with the Swiss, though, is that we recognized the value of doing business with Kalachka straightaway. I believe Khashoggi didn't get his job with the White House until he accidentally 'forgot' a briefcase with a million dollars in it at the home of your President Nixon. After that, as I understand it, Mr. Khashoggi became quite popular over here. Your country even thought enough of him to allow him to act as the middleman during the whole Iran-Contra affair, didn't it?"

"Those were different administrations," replied Anderson, exasperated. "Can we please get to the point here?"

"The point is that you shouldn't allow your preconceptions to cause you to dismiss the information Ozan Kalachka has—"

"*Allegedly* has, and I'm not dismissing it. I just don't like the taste I get in my mouth when I say the guy's name."

"Does that mean you're interested?"

"I still don't completely know what we're talking about. You're going to have to give me more than just this cloak and sword of Allah routine."

"Fair enough," said the ambassador as he removed a small digital video player from his suitcoat pocket. "Mr. Kalachka thought you might need some additional convincing."

Anderson watched in disbelief as he was shown virtually the same footage he had seen in the situation room that morning from Asalaam. "Where did you get this?"

"I told you," said Friederich. "I'm just the messenger. You'll have to ask Mr. Kalachka."

"No doubt he wants something in return."

"Yes. Mr. Kalachka apparently needs a favor."

Anderson was understandably wary. "What kind of favor?"

"Mr. Kalachka is prepared to tell the United

States what he knows about the weapon and will even provide access to one of the scientists who worked on it—"

"One of the scientists is still alive?"

"According to Mr. Kalachka, yes. But there is only one person he will give this information to, and he wants to arrange a meeting with him in private, at which point he will ask favor face-to-face."

The chief of staff had known the Swiss ambassador for many years and could read him like a book. "Absolutely not. I won't allow it."

"Allow what?" asked Friederich. "I haven't even told you who he wants to meet with yet."

"I know you, Hans, and I can't believe you thought for a second I'd allow the president of the United States to meet with a man like Ozan Kalachka."

The ambassador couldn't help laughing. "That would indeed be a historic meeting, but thankfully, President Rutledge is not the person Mr. Kalachka wishes to meet with. He has someone else in mind."

Anderson was trying to guess who in the U.S. government Kalachka might want a favor from and why he would need the Swiss ambassador and the president's chief of staff to put it together for him. "As long as this person is not the president or a cabinet member, I'm willing to consider arranging a meeting. Who are we talking about?"

The ambassador leaned forward and said, "Agent Scot Harvath."

ELEVEN

THE WHITE HOUSE
NEXT MORNING

"What the hell do you mean, I'm *fired*?" said Harvath.

"I mean, *you're fired,*" replied Charles Anderson, "and I don't care how upset you are; this is the White House, and I will not tolerate that kind of language in this building."

Harvath was never at a loss for words, but this time he honestly didn't know what to say. He was absolutely stunned, and on top of that, he was completely exhausted. The debriefing had started the moment he touched down at Andrews Air Force Base, and the questions hadn't stopped until a team of Secret Service agents came and whisked him away to the White House at nine o'clock this morning.

Before leaving Andrews, he had been given a few minutes to clean up. For the first time in his life, as he looked in the mirror of the men's latrine, Harvath not only felt older than his thirty-five years, but thought he was starting to look it too. His constant workload had caught up with him. His bright blue eyes were bloodshot and rimmed with fatigue, and while the hair on his head was still light brown, traces of gray were starting to sneak into the stubble that covered his chin.

While in the SEALs, he had earned the code name Norseman, not for his rugged good looks, which were more Germanic than Norse, or because he fought like a fearsome Viking warrior, but rather because of the long string of Scandinavian flight attendants he had dated. As he splashed some cold water on his face and examined his haggard appearance, he wondered what he would look like in two or three more years if he kept going at this pace.

The one thing that didn't seem to belie his age was his body, a testament to how hard he worked to keep himself in top physical condition. At five foot ten, and a solid one hundred seventy-five pounds, Harvath was in better shape and carried more muscle mass now than he had at twenty-five. The only effect that aging seemed to have on his body was that the pain that came with the invariable bumps and bruises of his job seemed to linger a lot longer than it used to. While an unfortunate byproduct of the way he lived his life, pain was one of the few things he felt he could exercise some semblance of control over. He had been taught time and again in the SEALs that pain was largely psychological.

What the mind can perceive, the body can achieve—and with that mantra playing on an endless loop in his mind, Harvath had forgone everything else in pursuit of his career, which now seemed to be coming to a screeching halt.

"I'm going to ask a stupid question," said Harvath. "Does the president know I'm being dropped?"

Anderson reached into his drawer, removed a blue folder, and slid it across the desk to Harvath. "What he knows is that you're resigning this morning."

"So now I'm *resigning*?" replied Harvath as he slid the resignation letter out and read it over.

"You really screwed up in Baghdad," continued the chief of staff. "The president didn't like seeing you on TV."

"Neither did I, but there was nothing I could do about it. It was a set-up."

"I got that much from your debriefing report."

"So what's the problem?"

"The problem," replied Anderson, "is that you've created a firestorm with that takedown. A million and one fatwas have been issued against you, and every Muslim country on the planet wants to see you stand trial under Islamic law."

"So?"

"So they're not the only ones who want your head on a stake."

"Who else does?"

"Senator Carmichael."

"Carmichael?" scoffed Harvath. "I'm not going to have anything to do with that woman."

"You don't get a say in the matter."

"The hell I don't."

"Scot, I warned you about your language—"

"Chuck, give me a fucking break here, would you? We're talking about my career. If you release my name and face to the public, not only will I never work again, I'll be looking over my shoulder for the rest of my life. You said it yourself—a million and one fatwas have been issued against me. Every radical Muslim on the planet will be looking to book the perfect corner table in Paradise by taking me out."

Anderson leaned forward over his desk and looked at Harvath. "You see, that's where you're wrong. This isn't about you or your career. This is about the president, and I'm not about to see him go down in flames trying to cover for you—not with the election around the corner."

"So you're just giving me up?" replied Harvath in disbelief.

"We're not giving you up."

"What the hell would you call it then? Carmichael has nothing at this point. From what I've heard, the Iraqis rolled up that al-Jazeera crew before they could get a shot of my face. All they've got is the back of my head. Seems to me that'd be pretty hard for the senator to build a case on."

"Do you think we'd be having this conversation if all Carmichael had was the back of your head? She's got you dead to rights as the person doing the takedown."

"How? How could she possibly have me?"

"She's been talking to a lot of people."

Harvath's temper was starting to get the better of him. "People like who?"

"Like everybody. She's on the Intelligence Committee, for Christ's sake. She has contacts all over the community."

"Just because she's connected doesn't mean she's figured out I'm the guy in that footage."

"She has."

"*How* do you know?"

Anderson took a deep breath and tried to calm everything down. "I got a call this morning."

"Carmichael called *you*?"

"No, someone else did. It was an old contact of mine—someone who's in a position to hear things. He told me Carmichael has been asking a lot of questions about you."

"What kind of questions?"

"She wanted to know about your time at the White House, why you left the Secret Service, and what you've been doing over at DHS. She even asked what the Apex Project was."

This last revelation was too stunning for Harvath to even believe. The Apex Project was the code name for everything he did at the Department of

Homeland Security. Only a handful of people even knew of its existence. Its secret budget was buried so deep and drawn from so many places it was supposed to be untraceable. *How the hell had Senator Carmichael gotten her hands on it, or on any of this information?* Harvath wondered. Somewhere they had a leak—a human leak who needed to be plugged, literally.

"Don't you see what she's trying to do?" continued Anderson. "She wants to burn the president, and she's going to start the fire by torching you with the biggest flamethrower she can get her hands on."

"Maybe she's just trying to see what she can smoke out."

"Come on, Scot. Face facts here. Out of all the people in this town she could possibly name, she names you? You've been made."

Harvath wasn't ready to give in so easily. "Chuck, until we're absolutely certain, I don't think we should—"

"We *are* absolutely certain," responded the chief of staff, cutting Harvath short. "Your subpoena is going to be ready by three o'clock. She's already made some vague statements to the press this morning that something big is coming down from the Hill. We need to put as much distance between you and the president as possible. Your desk at DHS has already been cleared out."

"You don't waste any time, do you?"

"We've got to focus on the big picture."

"So what exactly am I supposed to do?"

"First, I'd like you to sign this letter of resignation."

"And second?" asked Harvath, mad as hell that no one seemed to be considering what he had done for this administration.

Anderson looked at him and replied, "You might want to start thinking about a new career."

TWELVE

GREENBELT PARK

LATER THAT AFTERNOON

"Do you want to explain to me why we had to meet all the way out here?" demanded Harvath, whose temper had only gotten worse since his meeting with the chief of staff.

"Because right now," replied Gary Lawlor, as he walked past his thirty-five-year-old protégé and headed for one of the park's paved jogging trails, "you have the unfortunate distinction of being politically toxic."

"Politically toxic," mused Harvath as he fell in step with the man who was not only his boss, but also a long-standing friend of his family and someone who had become like a second father to him. "This isn't exactly how I had imagined my career coming to an end," he continued. "It's not only a bit undistinguished, but the timing's off by about a good twenty years. Jesus Christ, Gary, how the hell did I become the bad guy in all of this? If Carmichael goes public with my identity, that's it. I've

screwed the pooch. It's all over. What the hell am I supposed to do?"

"For starters, stop feeling sorry for yourself," suggested Lawlor.

"I don't feel sorry for myself. I feel sorry for my country. You know I wasn't exactly in this for the paycheck. I was in it because I believed in defending what America stands for."

"And what? You've stopped believing? You don't want to defend those things anymore?"

"Were you not listening when I told you Charles Anderson had me sign a letter of resignation?" asked Harvath.

Lawlor stopped and turned to face him. "What did you expect? He's the president's chief of staff. His job is to protect Jack Rutledge, not Scot Harvath."

"In pursuit of which it's okay to throw me to the wolves on the Hill?"

"If necessary, you bet," replied Lawlor.

"But why me? Why make me the sacrificial lamb?"

"Why not you?"

"Because I do a very dangerous job for my country and I've never asked for anything in return."

"Now you've hit upon the right word," said Lawlor. "*Dangerous.* Your job is *extremely* dangerous. Not only for you, but for this administration as well."

"You still don't get it, do you?" Harvath asked.

"I didn't do anything wrong. I don't care if that guy in Baghdad was some jackass fruit vendor. He got paid to be a decoy. He knew he was doing something he shouldn't, and as a result, he got the beating I was intending on handing Khalid Alomari. Maybe he'll stick to selling fruit from now on."

"I think you've guaranteed that the man's decoy days are well behind him, but that's not what we're talking about."

"Really?" inquired Harvath. "Then what is?"

"Senator Carmichael. She isn't after you for what you got caught doing by al-Jazeera."

"The hell she isn't."

"Scot, I know you're angry, but shut up a second and listen to me. The whole al-Jazeera thing is only a pretense. Does it make us look bad in the Muslim world? Yes, it does. Can we repair that damage? Of course we can. It might take some time and a lot of PR, but we can definitely do it.

"You need to remember that Senator Carmichael didn't get to be where she is by being stupid. She's a savvy woman and an extremely adept politician. Would I have liked it if you had never popped up on her radar screen? Of course, but now that you're there, she's using lots of little crumbs of information to bake a very big cake—one which she hopes to cover with candles and use to celebrate the Democrats taking back the White House."

"But how do we know she can even prove anything?"

"She doesn't have to prove anything. This is Washington. All she has to do is have enough to suggest that the president may have been sanctioning off-the-books black ops, and it'll hurt him in the election. It doesn't matter that Jack Rutledge has been proactive as hell and has had the balls to do whatever is necessary to keep this country safe, there's a good percentage of the voting public out there who don't like the idea of their president operating outside the scope of his power and not having to answer to anyone."

"But that's not how he works, and you know it," replied Harvath.

"Of course I know, but what I say isn't going to make a bit of difference. Carmichael is going to make him look like an egomaniacal despot waging his own war via his own private assassin. It'll decimate the public's trust in him."

Harvath was silent. How could he argue? Lawlor was right.

"I don't need to tell you what a battlefield DC is," said the older and often wiser man, "and I also don't need to tell you that on the battlefield, you never underestimate your opponent. The president and his chief of staff are certainly not underestimating Helen Carmichael right now."

"You can say that again," replied Harvath. "According to Anderson, they expect her to have a subpoena ready for me by three o'clock this afternoon."

"That's one of the reasons I wanted us to meet

here. Carmichael means to drag you out in front of the media, and the sooner the better, as far as she's concerned. But if she can't find you, she can't serve you. And if she can't serve you, then she can't expect you to appear before her committee and the media."

Harvath was quiet for a moment while he tried to divine his boss's meaning. "Are you telling me you want me to duck a congressional subpoena?"

"Right now? Yes. I want you to duck it as hard as you can."

"You know what that means," replied Scot. "It means not going to the office, not going home—not going anywhere I normally go. What do you suggest I do?"

"Disappear."

"For how long?" he asked.

"For as long as it takes for us to fix this thing," said Lawlor. "The last thing the president wants is for you to appear before Senator Carmichael's committee."

"But why did he have me sign a letter of resignation then?"

"He didn't have you sign it, Anderson did, and it's just a fail-safe. The president has no intention of accepting it," he replied as he handed Harvath an envelope. "In fact, he has something else in mind for you."

THIRTEEN

BRITISH AIRWAYS FLIGHT 216
SOMEWHERE OVER THE ATLANTIC
LATER THAT EVENING

As Harvath's flight sped across the Atlantic, his mind was reeling. He doubted if anything could have prepared him for the contents of the envelope Gary Lawlor had handed him only hours earlier. The photos and description of what had happened in the village of Asalaam were horrific. In addition to the non-Muslim population, the illness had claimed five U.S. soldiers, all members of the Stryker Brigade Combat Team sent to look for missing American aid workers.

Harvath ran through the images again in his mind's eye, reliving every horrible stage of infection as it unfolded. A crack containment team from USAMRIID had been dispatched to Iraq as soon as it was discovered that the SBCT soldiers had become infected. It was no use. Hours after the body strapped to the ceiling of the Provincial Ministry of Police had covered them in a fine bloody mist, they began to show symptoms of contamination. Immediately, the soldiers were placed in quarantine, which helped to prevent the illness from spreading, but despite being pumped full of antibiotics, there was nothing that could be done to save them.

The illness worked faster than anything anyone had ever seen. The only thing the USAMRIID team was able to learn was that the black sludge that exited the nasal passages right before death was actually the remains of the victim's liquefied brain matter.

Despite their express desire to get their hands on weapons of mass destruction to use against the West, no one could understand how al-Qaeda had been able to come up with something this sophisticated. The idea that they could have bioengineered a substance to attack all but the followers of Islam was beyond comprehension. Harvath was beating himself up for not having apprehended Khalid Alomari sooner. Somehow he was involved in all of this, and Harvath couldn't help but feel that if al-Qaeda succeeded in carrying out whatever they had planned, he would be largely at fault.

Based on everything he had learned from Lawlor, it was painfully clear that Khalid Alomari hadn't been on a fund-raising or planning tour of the Middle East, but had been ticking names off a very special hit list. Whoever those scientists were, they had obviously been involved in engineering this mystery illness and had been taken out one by one in an effort to tie up loose ends.

While that much made sense, it still didn't explain Ozan Kalachka's connection to everything.

As the flight attendant removed his dinner tray, untouched, Harvath reflected on the somewhat unusual friendship he had developed with one of the East's most elusive and fabled underworld figures.

The two had first crossed paths when Harvath had been tasked to SEAL Team Six. He had been part of a joint DEA task force charged with taking down a notorious Mediterranean drug trafficker who had branched out into the black-market arms trade. The problem, though, was that the team had been operating on faulty intelligence. After a very thorough investigation, the DEA, along with local authorities, had been able to apprehend a significant mid-level player out of Morocco. That player in turn agreed to roll over and finger his superiors in exchange for being cut loose. No one had any idea that the man's superiors had set him up in order to have the DEA do their dirty work for them.

The mid-level Moroccan provided excellent intel, but it didn't lead to his superiors; instead it led to Ozan Kalachka—a man whose arms-trade turf the Moroccans were trying to cut in on. Despite all the Monday morning quarterbacking, no one disputed that the agents working the case had done everything exactly as they were supposed to. It was the first and *last* time anyone ever got the better of the DEA in a case of that magnitude, but it could not be denied that during its execution Scot Harvath had almost made one of the biggest mistakes of his career, if not his life.

At six feet tall and well over three hundred pounds, the sixty-two-year-old Ozan Kalachka nearly measured the same side-to-side as he did up-and-down. With his impeccable taste in clothing and neatly groomed silver hair, he bore an uncanny resemblance to the actor known as the Fat Man—Sydney Greenstreet. Many mistook Kalachka's excessive weight as a sign of lethargy and weakness—an indication that he was soft and slow. That was the mistake Harvath had made when the joint task force attempted to arrest the reputed Turkish mobster, and it nearly cost Harvath one of his eyes. Though one would have to look very closely to see it, he still bore the scar from the encounter above his left cheekbone. And in what was more of a testament to his hot temper than his training as a SEAL, Harvath had bestowed upon the Turk the limp with which he still walked to this day.

Both men, each in his own way, had misjudged the other and had lived to regret it—Kalachka for his limp, and Harvath, not so much for his scar, but rather for the shame of underestimating an opponent and letting him get the better of him. When the physical and legal dust had settled, the encounter had resulted in lessons neither of them would ever forget. The DEA, having been duped by the Moroccans, had nothing substantial they could charge Kalachka with, and were forced to stand down. Kalachka, though, had been wronged and intended to inflict maximum damage on the Moroccans who had set him up. Two months after checking out of the hospital, Kalachka sent the lead DEA agent a file three inches thick, which led to the absolute ruin of the Moroccans' organization.

The entire experience was unusual at best, but even more unusual was the friendship it spawned—a friendship between the man with the limp and the man with the scar. The relationship had actually served Harvath well on more than one occasion. Not that Ozan Kalachka was generous with information. Kalachka was the epitome of the word *profiteer*. The man never made a single move that didn't somehow benefit him first and foremost. That said, Kalachka exhibited something that could only be loosely described as a sort of paternal fondness for Harvath. When all was said and done, the man liked him, and to a certain degree, Harvath felt the same way in return.

"Fixer" was the best way to describe Kalachka and what he did for a living. He brokered everything from arms and real estate deals to crooked foreign elections, banana republic revolutions, and assassinations many felt were too difficult or too politically sensitive to attempt. Even the Israelis had employed Kalachka at one time.

Though Israeli Kidon agents had carried out the hits, Kalachka was the person who had blueprinted the assassinations of all the members of Black September—the Palestinian terrorists responsible for the killing of Israeli athletes at the 1972 Munich Olympics. The Israelis hired him again in a consulting capacity in 1976 and were rewarded with the successful recovery of Israeli hostages from Entebbe, Uganda.

In an attempt to broaden his revenue base, Kalachka, it was said, had offered his services to the United States on two separate occasions and both Presidents Kennedy and Carter had turned him down. Kennedy had said no to Kalachka's suggestions for taking out Castro in lieu of what would become known as the Bay of Pigs fiasco, and Carter had passed on Kalachka's ideas for how to successfully recover the American hostages from Tehran. Despite the affinity of several other countries for Kalachka's talents and abilities, the United States had never warmed to him.

As far as Harvath was concerned, though, as long as Kalachka was helping to organize the assassinations of known terrorists and overthrow corrupt regimes, he was okay. His dealings in the black-market arms trade were among the gray areas that were easier to look at in light of the good he'd done elsewhere.

Kalachka was one of the few people he had ever met who not only knew who he was, but made no apologies for it. No matter how charming and cordial on the outside, the real Ozan Kalachka was a ruthless creature who worked the very outermost fringes of what was legal and would stop at nothing to get what he wanted. The hundred-thousand-dollar question at the moment, though, was what did Kalachka want from him?

Closing his eyes, Harvath tried to put the question out of his mind and was immediately burdened by something else. If Carmichael was successful in dragging him into the media spotlight and destroying his career, what was he going to do with the rest of his life? Depending on how bad a number the senator did on him, he might or might not be able to go into the private sector as a consultant.

Regardless, if Carmichael forced him into the spotlight, there would always be a bull's-eye painted on his back, and no career other than what he was doing right at this very moment would ever be satisfying for him. Harvath had spent most of his adult life in service to his country and had no desire to see that change.

For the time being, though, he had very little control over his situation. He had to trust that people like Gary Lawlor, the president, and even Chuck Anderson were not going to let him burn for simply doing his job. In a matter of hours his plane would be landing and he would discover what Ozan Kalachka wanted from him.

FOURTEEN

Büyük Hamam
Nicosia, Cyprus
Next day

Harvath leaned back against the octagonal tiles and breathed deeply. The searing heat of the saunalike chamber known as a *göbek tasi* felt like bags of broken glass being poured into his lungs. He fought back a coughing fit and willed himself to relax. Taking another deep breath, Harvath realized that he'd become so wrapped up in his job that he'd actually forgotten how to relax. He knew it was an integral component of rejuvenation, and as he felt his lungs loosen up and the dry heat overtake him, he tried to remember the last time he had allowed himself any legitimate downtime. *As long as there are terrorists,* he began to say to himself, but pushed the thought from his mind. Whether he chose to take a vacation or not had nothing to do with terrorism. It had everything to do with him. It was easy to make the excuse that he had no time for anything else but work.

In the post-9/11 world in which Harvath lived,

relentless dedication to one's work had stopped being admirable a while ago and was now simply de rigueur. While no one would say his priorities were out of whack, they definitely came at the price of his social life. Even his on-again, off-again girlfriend, Meg Cassidy, was reaching the end of her rope with him. How could you have a relationship with someone who was never home? Harvath didn't blame her. He had watched his mother go through the same thing with his father. It wasn't until Michael Harvath had transferred out of active Navy SEAL duty to become an instructor at the Navy's Special Warfare School near their home in Coronado that his mother had been truly happy. Harvath had no intention of becoming an instructor of anything at this point in his career and had told Meg that he would understand if she chose to move on with her life. She was a great lady and he had no desire to hold her back. Besides, getting married and starting a family were not what he wanted to do right now.

When Meg asked him what he *did* want to do, he was brutally honest with her. "This. I want to keep sticking it to the bad guys before they stick it to us."

It was at that moment that Meg knew she not only didn't have him, she never would. However Scot Harvath wanted to paint it, he was married to his career and there wasn't much room for anything or anyone else in his life.

They had kissed in the driveway of her cottage

in Lake Geneva, Wisconsin, over two months ago, and that was the last time they had seen or spoken to each other. Harvath still had no idea when he would be back home for any real stretch of time, nor did he have any illusions that she'd be waiting for him. In fact, she had all but said that she was going to move on with her life. As difficult as all of that was to deal with, right now he was grateful for the few precious moments he'd been granted to rest his tired mind and somewhat battered body in this sauna halfway around the world. The reprieve, though, was short-lived.

A cold rush of air signaled the arrival of a newcomer. "Interesting choice for a rendezvous, Ozan," said Harvath.

Kalachka joined Harvath on the long, porcelain-tiled bench and responded, "I'm a Turk, and like all good Turks, I cling to my heritage. The Hamam has been an integral part of our lives for centuries."

"Let's cut to the chase, Ozan."

Kalachka wiped the sweat from his heavily perspiring face and said, "As you know, I've proposed a trade."

"Yeah, my government's very aware of that. I want to know everything you know about this illness, why Muslims seem to be immune to it, and how al-Qaeda has been able to pull this off. And finally one very big item: my government wants to know how the hell you got your hands on classified video footage."

"All in good time."

"Bullshit, let's start with the footage," said Harvath. "I knew you were well connected, but this is unbelievable. Who the hell do you have on your payroll? Or are you blackmailing someone in the Department of Defense?"

"Scot, you should know me better than that. I am no blackmailer."

Harvath laughed. "I don't even know the first thing about you, and you know what? I don't want to know. Tell me about the illness."

Kalachka shook his head. "First, I need something from you."

"Of course, right to the price tag. I forget that everything costs with you, doesn't it, Ozan? Even friendship."

For a moment, Kalachka didn't look at Harvath. Finally, he turned to him and said, "It's about my nephew."

"You've got a nephew?" replied Scot.

"He's my sister's only son, and even though he's always been a little *too* Muslim for my taste, he's still family and I promised to—"

"Ozan, I have no time and even less patience. Regardless of how you see yourself, you've blackmailed my government into a corner, and I've been instructed to work with you and do anything within my power to facilitate this exchange, so enough beating around the bush. What kind of trouble are we talking about here? Spit it out already."

As Kalachka looked at Harvath, it was difficult to tell whether it was sweat or tears rimming the older man's eyes. "My nephew has been kidnapped."

"By whom?"

Kalachka hesitated. "I have my suspicions, but I can't be positive about anything."

"You'd be surprised how accurate suspicions can be in these situations. Let's back up a second, though. How do you know he's been kidnapped? Has there been a ransom demand?"

"No, but there were witnesses. Dozens of them," said the Turk. "He was grabbed off a street in Bangladesh in broad daylight. Three men, wearing ski masks and carrying automatic weapons, plucked him off the sidewalk near his office in Dhaka and then drove him away."

"What about the car?" asked Harvath, still skeptical.

"Stolen. The police found it abandoned the next day."

"Any idea why somebody would want to take him?"

Kalachka wiped his face yet again and replied, "I think it has something to do with what he was working on."

"Which was what?"

"He's a scientist, neuromolecular biology something or other. I have never pretended to understand it. Suffice it to say that he's a very intelligent young man."

"Ozan, what was he working on?" repeated Harvath, who was starting to get a very bad feeling.

Kalachka couldn't stall any longer. He threw up his hands and answered, "He was one of the scientists working on the sword of Allah project."

Harvath was beyond shocked. "Your nephew is responsible for all of this?"

"Trust me," said Kalachka, "when he accepted the position with the Islamic Institute for Science and Technology, he did so intending to do great things for the Muslim world. The scientists there had no idea what they were working on. Everyone on the project was kept separate from one another. It wasn't until they were nearing the end that Emir was able to fit the pieces together. But by then, someone had begun silencing all of the people involved. It had to be someone from the institute."

Harvath took a towel and wiped the back of his neck. "I think you're wrong."

"What do you mean, *wrong*?" replied Kalachka. "It makes perfect sense. He put the pieces together, they found out that he was going to expose them, and so they kidnapped him."

"To do what? Scare him to death? Put him in a room with nothing to do and bore him to death? Think about it, Ozan. All the other scientists were *killed*. Not kidnapped. The only reason that would have happened was if he was of value to someone. Did anyone else know what your nephew was working on?"

Kalachka was silent for several moments. "I asked him the same thing right before he disappeared."

"And?"

"He was e-mailing someone."

"Who?"

"Another scientist. Someone he went to university in England with. She's a specialist who Emir thought might be able to help him better understand what he was dealing with."

"So why are you talking to me? Why not this woman?" asked Harvath.

"Because she's not an operator. She's not in the business of recovering hostages."

"But she's your only lead."

"There's something else," said Kalachka, as he reached next to him and lifted several photos that had been encased in clear plastic sleeves.

"Pictures of your nephew," said Harvath, resigning himself to what he was going to have to do. "I suppose they would be helpful."

"They might be more helpful than you think," stated Kalachka. "Look at them carefully."

Harvath studied the first two photographs. They showed the actual kidnapping in perfect detail. "Where'd you get these?"

"There was a newly installed security camera on the exterior of the bank across the street. What do you see?"

"I see what looks like the kidnapping of your nephew," replied Harvath.

"Look at the last picture in the series, as Emir is being shoved into the car. The Mercedes's windows are blacked out, but in the frame when the door opens, you can see that there's a man inside."

As Harvath looked closer at the photo, he saw that Kalachka was right. There definitely was a man sitting inside the Mercedes, and he wasn't wearing anything to disguise his appearance. It wasn't a tight enough shot, though, to make a positive identification. Harvath was just about to mention that, when Kalachka handed him the final photograph and said, "I had it digitally enhanced. Tell me what you see now."

Harvath looked at the photo and saw a face he had hoped never to see again. It was now apparent why Kalachka had asked for him. "You know goddamn well who that is," he said.

Kalachka's eyes sparkled as he replied, "And so do you, don't you?"

Harvath's head was awash with images. Timothy Rayburn was ex–Secret Service. He had been one of the agency's best and also one of its most dangerous. He had been Harvath's earliest mentor, and Harvath had personally seen to it that the man's employment was terminated and that he could never work for another federal, state, or local law enforcement agency ever again.

"Find Rayburn," said Kalachka, pulling Harvath's mind from the past, "and you'll find the information you need to stop the illness."

FIFTEEN

As his dented taxicab crawled through the crowded streets of Nicosia, Harvath's mind spun. After the Secret Service had effectively barred Rayburn from ever working in law enforcement again, it shouldn't have come as a surprise that the man had found a way to ply his trade overseas. Harvath reminded himself that there were people out there who would pay big money for what Rayburn could do for them, regardless of his ethics. Based on what Harvath had seen, the man would sell his services to the highest bidder and relegate any pangs of conscience to a remote and dark corner of his psyche. If nothing else, at least Rayburn remained consistent. He had always been about the money, and that was what had gotten him cut from the Secret Service.

Harvath remembered the affair, and more importantly the betrayal, in vivid detail. Ex-military himself, Rayburn had taken a shine to Harvath the moment the new recruit had transferred from the SEALs to the Secret Service. Like many federal law enforcement agencies, the Secret Service often rotated highly skilled field agents through the classrooms at their training facility in Beltsville, Maryland. That was where Harvath and Rayburn had met. Not only did the two become close friends, but Rayburn became somewhat of an older brother figure to Harvath, riding him harder than the other students and saying he owed it to Harvath to be tough on him. Insiders like Rayburn knew why Harvath had been recruited to the Secret Service. They were all very well aware that it was because of his vast counterterrorism background and that he was headed for a special post at the White House.

A self-confessed "old dog in need of some new tricks," Rayburn took a keen interest in Harvath's SEAL career and the current way things were being done in the world of counterterrorism. The two spent many late nights bonding over pitchers of beer in several Beltsville taverns. Though Harvath hadn't noticed it at the time, Rayburn was slowly and methodically picking his brain. And it didn't end in Beltsville. When Harvath graduated, Rayburn had himself assigned to spend time with the freshly minted field agent.

The pair worked several grueling cases before the White House finally decided Harvath was ready for the big leagues of presidential protection.

Harvath's new position kept him very busy, and gradually, the two friends fell out of touch. Harvath had felt guilty about it. Had he known that Rayburn had purposely let the friendship lapse because he had no further use for the former SEAL, he probably would have felt a lot different. It wasn't until Rayburn was forced back onto Harvath's radar screen that the young Secret Service agent realized he'd been taken.

Rayburn headed a team of Secret Service agents that had been assigned to complement a State Department security detail protecting a high-level foreign dignitary visiting the United States. Two days into the visit, the dignitary was assassinated.

Because of his expertise in counterterrorism, Harvath was asked to consult in the investigation. The deeper he dug, the more his gut told him the killer, or killers, had somehow received help from the inside. As much as he hated to go in that direction, he had no choice but to conduct a thorough examination of the security detail.

As Harvath connected the dots, a picture began to emerge—and it wasn't flattering. His hunch had been right. Someone had been bought. The trail eventually led to the door of one of Rayburn's men, but there had still been something about all of it that didn't feel right, so Harvath kept digging, quietly.

Harvath's involvement in the investigation was something Rayburn had never planned on. The older agent had picked a fall guy and had planted the evidence implicating him so deep that by the time the investigators found it they would be not only exhausted but completely convinced they had their man. Harvath, though, was no stranger to being wrongfully accused of a crime he didn't commit, and had worked overtime to help clear the agent he sensed wasn't guilty. Nailing Rayburn as the real bad guy was another story entirely.

When it came down to it, most of the evidence against Rayburn, as well as how Harvath had uncovered it, wasn't admissible in court. There was, though, enough to get him booted from the Secret Service and to make sure that he never worked in law enforcement again. Fueled by the anger he felt over Rayburn's betrayal, Harvath continued to work outside official channels and eventually tracked down a numbered account in the Caymans that Rayburn had used for his blood money. Working through an "unofficial" contact, Harvath had the funds discreetly transferred to a compensation fund established for the deceased dignitary's family.

Draining the account provided only a small measure of satisfaction. As far as Harvath was concerned, the man should have stood trial for murder. After the investigation had been officially closed, Rayburn disappeared. But Harvath had never forgotten him. He figured the U.S. government hadn't either. Somewhere within the intelligence community, somebody might still be keeping an eye on him, but as long as Senator Carmichael was looking to put Harvath's head on a stake, Gary Lawlor had made it clear that he didn't want him reaching out to any of his contacts within the community, including Lawlor himself. Gary had established a roundabout way for Harvath to get in touch with him, but only if he absolutely had to. For the time being, Harvath was operating without a net, and given the current situation back in Washington, if he fell, no one was going to step forward and identify his remains.

That left Harvath with only one option—he would have to get creative, and the first thing he would have to get creative with was a way to get his hands on the specific intelligence he needed.

With a ban in effect on reaching out to any of his official intelligence contacts, he realized he would have to go outside his normal circle. It took him a moment, but he soon came up with somebody who could help him. The only question was, would Nick Kampos be in the mood to do him such a major favor?

SIXTEEN

After parting with Kalachka, Harvath had needed only one phone call to the Cyprus office of DEA agent Nick Kampos to get his answer. When his cab dropped him later that night at an outdoor taverna near the port of Kyrenia, Kampos was already sitting at a table by the water.

"Classy," said Harvath as he pulled out the plastic chair opposite the man and sat down. The squat wooden table was covered with a red-and-white-checkered tablecloth, complete with paper napkins, dirty flatware, and a chipped hurricane lamp. "If I didn't know you better, Nick, I'd swear you were just trying to impress me."

"Are you kidding me?" said the DEA agent as he swept his arm toward the harbor and its brightly colored fishing boats. "Look at this view."

"It's terrific," replied Harvath as he leaned over and shoved a stack of napkins under one of his chair legs to even it out.

"If I really cared about impressing you, we would have eaten at one of the fancy joints up the road. It would have cost twice as much, but the food wouldn't have been half as good."

"I guess I'll have to take your word for it," said Harvath as a waiter arrived with an ice bucket and a bottle of white wine.

"I took the liberty of ordering us something to drink."

"I can see that."

"You're not going to give me any macho bullshit about only being a beer drinker, are you?" asked Kampos.

Harvath laughed and shook his head. It was funny to hear Nick pimping him about being macho. The man was a six-foot-four solid wall of muscle with gray hair, a thick mustache, and a craggy face weathered with a permanent tan from a lifetime spent out-of-doors. Divorced, with two daughters in college back in the States, Kampos liked to joke that it was the women in his life who had grayed his hair, but Harvath knew better. Nick and his ex were still on good terms, and he adored his daughters more than anything else in the world. He put up a pretty tough front, but underneath it all, the guy was a complete teddy bear.

"Good," replied the DEA agent as he politely waved the waiter away and poured full glasses for both of them. "Local stuff. A little rough at first, but you get used to it. Cheers."

Harvath regretted not chickening out and ordering a beer the minute the wine hit his taste buds. "Smooth," he said between coughing fits.

"You're getting weak, sister. Too much time in DC and not enough in the field."

"I'm never out of the field, it seems," replied Harvath as he took another swig and this time managed to get it down without registering how bad it tasted.

"There you go. That's the Scot Harvath I know and love," said Kampos with a wide grin. "After this, we'll move you onto the hard stuff."

"Bring it on," Harvath stated with a smile.

Kampos discreetly belted out the army yell, "Hooah!" and took another long swallow of local vintage.

Scot couldn't help liking the guy. In fact, when he thought about it, the DEA was one of the only agencies he'd ever worked with where he'd actually liked every single person he'd come in contact with. Though they shared many of the same facilities as the FBI training academy at Quantico, the two cultures couldn't have been more different. While the FBI focused on hiring lawyers and accountants, most DEA agents were ex-cops, or ex-military like Kampos. What's more, they were the best close-range shooters in the business. In fact, the DEA was so good at close-quarters battle, or CQB as it was more commonly known, that they trained all of the president's Marine One helicopter flight crews.

When Harvath transferred from the SEALs to White House Secret Service operations, he'd been so impressed with the HMX-1 Nighthawks' level of CQB proficiency that he had asked if he could train with them in his off time. Shooting, after all, was a perishable skill, and any law enforcement officer who carried a gun was always encouraged to log as much range time as he could—especially in his off time. The bottom line was that the more you fired your weapon, the better shooter you became, and that was certainly true in Harvath's case, especially while Nick Kampos was his instructor.

Harvath had learned a lot about the DEA, both on and off the range. What struck him the most was their dedication not just to their jobs but to each other. One of the guys told him a story about how they had turned a founder member of one of Colombia's largest drug cartels and while they had him in a hotel awaiting a trial he was set to testify at, he regaled his two DEA protective agents with stories of what his immense wealth had been able to buy—local cops, state cops, judges, politicians, but never a single DEA agent.

Though they had boots on the ground in fifty-eight countries around the world, including those of Kampos, who had put in for the Cyprus position just before Harvath left the White House, for some reason, the powers that be in Washington had never invited the Drug Enforcement Administration to sit at the big kids' table when it came to sharing intelligence. This oddity had its pros and its cons, but for the most part, the DEA agents Harvath knew were okay with it. It meant they weren't bound by a lot of the same rules, requirements, and restrictions as other federal agencies. It also meant, at least for right now, that Harvath had someone he could reach out to for help and be one hundred percent certain that it wouldn't get back to Senator Helen Remington Carmichael.

"If you don't mind my saying so," said Kampos as he put a little float atop each of their glasses, "you look like shit."

"Thanks a lot," replied Harvath.

"If the job's gotten too much for you, maybe you ought to think about getting out."

"What are you, a career counselor now?"

"Nope. I'm just a Wal-Mart greeter currently employed by the DEA."

"Get serious," said Harvath.

"I am being serious. If things ever get to the point where I don't want to do the job anymore, I'm going to be the best damn greeter Wal-Mart has ever seen. But you didn't come all this way to talk about my employment prospects. Why don't we talk about why you're really here."

"I'm visiting an old friend."

"Let me guess," said Kampos. "A big fat guy who walks with a very pronounced limp."

"Hey, go easy on the limp," responded Harvath. "That's some of my best work."

"What could you possibly want with him?"

Harvath tore off a piece of bread and dragged it through one of the dips the waiter had brought out. "He's got some info related to a case I'm working on."

"The case you can't talk to me about."

"Right."

"The one where you have to ask me to do your scut work for you because apparently you can't go to anyone in DC."

"Right again."

Kampos looked at his old friend and said, "Scot, what are you into?"

"Nothing illegal, I can promise you that."

"Can you? I haven't talked to you in at least a year, and all of a sudden you pop up out of nowhere, balls-to-the-wall cloak and dagger, and ask me to run names for you on the QT because you're *persona non grata* back home? What would you think if you were in my shoes?"

"I'd think I must be pretty special for Scot Harvath to come to me for help."

"Bullshit. You'd have just as many questions, if not more than I do," replied Kampos. "What the hell is going on? And don't give me any *I could tell you, but then I'd have to kill you* secret agent crap either. The reason the DEA is able to work in so many countries around the world is because we don't do any spy shit. We only work in the drug world."

"I know, and I'm not asking you to do any spy stuff."

"You asked me to compile two dossiers for you. That's a pretty big favor. Granted it wasn't like sneaking microfilm across the border, but we're getting into semantics here. Why did you come to me instead of going to somebody at your own agency?"

Harvath had a tough decision to make. Sure, Kampos liked him, but the man probably liked his career and his pension a hell of a lot more. Kampos wasn't about to stick his neck out for Harvath without having a good reason. If Harvath was asking the man to trust him, he was going to have to do the same thing in return. His gut told him the DEA agent could keep his secret, and Harvath always went with his gut. "Have you seen the al-Jazeera footage they've been running from Baghdad?"

"Where that GI is beating the camel humps off that poor fruit stall vendor?"

"There was nothing poor about him, but yeah, that's the footage I'm talking about," said Harvath.

"What a fucking mess. You know they're going to fry that GI once they figure out who he is."

"Right after they use a very big axe to chop off his wee-wee."

"Hold on a sec," said Kampos. "Are you telling me that—"

Harvath put on the best grin he could muster considering the subject matter and said, "Yup. Yours truly."

"Turn around."

"What do you mean, *turn around*?"

"I've seen that video about a thousand times already. That GI had one badly shaped head. I want to see the back of your head to see if it matches up."

"Fuck you," replied Harvath.

Kampos checked him out from across the table. "I can tell from here. It's you. Jesus, what a head. How many times did your momma drop you on it?"

"Fuck you," repeated Harvath.

"What'd she do? Use Crisco instead of baby lotion?" said Kampos as he pretended to have a baby that kept shooting out of his arms. "Whoops, there he goes again."

Harvath held up his middle finger and went back to his food.

"Only you couldn't have waited until the camera was off."

"Yeah, I couldn't help myself. Very funny, Nick."

Kampos tried to put on a straight face. "No, you're right. This is serious. Just let me ask you one thing."

"What?"

"You were cussing that guy out pretty good while you were zip-tying him, right?"

"So?"

"So, technically I think that counts as a speaking role. You've arrived, son. You must be eligible for a Screen Actors Guild card now."

"And *I'm* the wiseass. Listen, I told you this because I thought I could trust you to keep quiet about it. It's for your ears only."

"And I promise you it will go no further," replied Kampos, who took a moment before continuing. "I'm not the only one who knows you're the guy in that footage, am I?"

"No, you're not, and that's why I'm having trouble at the office."

"Is it the president?"

"No. It's somebody who's trying to get to him by burning me."

"And they're going to do it by going public with your identity?"

"I sure as hell hope not, but don't be surprised if I end up joining you as a Wal-Mart greeter."

"Junior greeter," said Kampos. "I don't share top billing with anybody, not even big TV stars like you."

"Fine, *junior* greeter," replied Harvath. "Now, are you going to help me out or not?"

Kampos reached down into the briefcase next to his chair, removed a thin manila envelope, and slid it across the table to his colleague. "That's the best I could do on such short notice."

Harvath removed the documents from the envelope as Kampos continued to speak. "After that Rayburn character got the boot from the Secret Service, the trail on him goes so cold it's sub-Arctic. It's like he just vanished. No tax returns, no passport renewal, no credit card activity, no hits on his social security number—nothing."

"What about the other name I gave you? The one for the woman."

"That one I had a little more luck with. Jillian Alcott. Age twenty-seven. Born in Cornwall, England. Attended Cambridge University and graduated with her undergraduate degree in biology and organic chemistry. Went on to attend the University of Durham, where she secured a graduate degree in molecular biology, followed by a PhD in paleopathology."

"What the hell is paleopathology?" asked Harvath.

"Beats me," replied Kampos, "but whatever it is, it apparently qualifies her for her current position, which is teaching chemistry at a very exclusive private high school in London called Abbey College. I never did understand the Brits. They call high-school college and college university. Anyway, it's all there in the file. In the meantime, I'll see if I can dig up anything else on Rayburn for you."

"Thanks, Nick. I appreciate it."

"Don't appreciate it. Just get whatever's screwed up straight and come out on the right side of it."

Harvath's attention drifted toward the water, and Kampos seemed to be able to read his mind. "You're going to London, aren't you?"

"Yes," replied Harvath.

"Well, if you need anything else, let me know."

"Actually, there is," said Harvath as he opened his wallet and counted several bills onto the table to pay for their dinner. "I need a ride to the airport and a gun."

SEVENTEEN

NIKOS TAVERNA
PLAKA DISTRICT
ATHENS

Khalid Alomari tried to keep his anger under control as he flipped his cell phone closed and tossed it onto the wooden table in front of him. As the noise of motorbikes whizzing past mingled with the sounds of shopkeepers hawking their wares to the tourists who crowded the dusty sidewalks, Alomari wondered once again why none of his contacts was producing. Secrets didn't keep long in a country like Bangladesh, but for some reason this one was eluding him. As he tried to piece together what had happened, he thought seriously about having one or two of his lowlife associates there killed to help motivate the others.

None of it made any sense. Men like Emir Tokay didn't simply vanish. They didn't have the aptitude. Tokay was a scientist, after all, not a trained intelligence operative. *There had to be a way to find him,* thought Alomari. The assassin had gotten to all the other scientists on the list and didn't like coming up one short. His situation was made even more difficult by the fact that there was very little time left.

The last time he had spoken with his employer, who was known to him only as Akrep, or the Scorpion, the man had been enraged. He had chastised the assassin for moving too slowly with the kills and somehow knew, as he always seemed to know everything, that the last scientist had disappeared. Once more, Alomari questioned the benefit of ever having gotten involved with such a man.

True, Alomari specialized in killing for hire, but his targets had always been the obvious enemies of Islam. The only comfort he took in this assignment was that the Scorpion himself was a true believer and had pledged his life in service of the faith.

His faith notwithstanding, the Scorpion was known for being absolutely ruthless. Even bin Laden, a man not frightened by anyone, was said to conduct himself toward the Scorpion with an amazing degree of respect and admiration. It was even hinted that al-Qaeda had been the Scorpion's idea, hatched in the mountains of Afghanistan with bin Laden during the great holy war against the Soviets.

In the end, Alomari held no illusions about why he had taken the assignment—he needed the money; or more importantly, al-Qaeda needed the money. With bin Laden cut off from a significant portion of his funds and forced into hiding along the Pakistan-

Afghan border, the al-Qaeda organization was starved for cash. While the cell in Madrid might have sold drugs to keep themselves afloat and finance their spectacular train bombings, there were plenty of other good Muslim members of the organization who would not stoop to such a thing, and Alomari was one of them. He had had no choice but to take the Scorpion's assignment.

It had been months since he had last been able to make contact with his mentor. Bin Laden was constantly on the move, and he expected his followers to be able to think on their own and make their own decisions. He couldn't be expected to hold their hands like children. Throughout the grueling assignment, Alomari had tried to remind himself to be thankful. The Scorpion could have selected any number of other assassins to do this job. Alomari knew that bin Laden had played some part in recommending him, and that only made him feel doubly guilty for having failed. At first, it had seemed as if Allah himself was smiling down upon him by handing him this assignment. But he had no idea why Allah would want to halt his progress when he was so close to closing out his list and collecting his much-needed money.

The Scorpion was someone Alomari had never met face-to-face. They had only spoken by telephone. Any actual face-to-face contact was always through his second, a man named Gökhan Celik. As Alomari watched Celik enter the taverna and make his way toward the table, he slid his hand along the outside of his sport coat, just to reassure himself that the ultra-compact Taurus PT-111 pistol was still there. He cared little for whatever relationship existed between bin Laden and the Scorpion; he was taking no chances, not even with this wiry shadow of a man who was the Scorpion's second.

Gökhan Celik was seventy-five years old if he was a day, with a pair of narrow, dark eyes and a long pointed nose that floated above a set of terrible teeth. The man was devoid of any chin, and as a result, his face seemed to be only an extension of an otherwise twig-thin neck.

Despite his appearance, Alomari knew the man was brilliant. It was said that Celik had been the Scorpion's counselor since he was a teen, and almost everything the Scorpion had learned, he had learned from Gökhan Celik. In other words, Celik was not a man to be underestimated either.

Dressed in a chic linen suit, Celik could have been any aging Greek businessman out for an early, run-of-the-mill business lunch with a colleague, except that Celik was no Greek and this was no run-of-the-mill luncheon. Celik had come to pink-slip one of the world's deadliest assassins.

Ever affected by his mother's cultured influence on his upbringing, Alomari asked his guest if he cared for something to eat or drink before they began.

Celik looked at him and replied, "Let's not waste any more time, Khalid. You know why I'm here."

"To discuss the remaining scientist."

"No. That subject is no longer open for discussion. I'm here to dismiss you. You're fired."

"Fired?"

"Of course you can keep the two-hundred-and-fifty-thousand-dollar deposit you were paid, but that's all you are going to receive."

"But that doesn't begin to even cover my expenses."

"Too bad. You knew the deal when you took it—all the items on the list were to be taken care of. You failed."

Alomari had suspected that this was the reason Celik had demanded the meeting, but true to his Arab heritage, he haggled desperately for a few moments in an attempt to keep the assignment alive.

"The contract is canceled, and that's final," said Celik as he placed his gnarled hands on the table and rose from his chair. "I thought we owed it to you to tell you in person."

That was the least they owed him, and if nothing else, it should have been the Scorpion himself sitting across from him, but Alomari let it slide. "I can still finish the assignment," he said. "There's still time."

"No, there isn't, and this has gone far beyond your capabilities."

"What do you mean?"

"*What do I mean?* I mean that if you had acted faster, maybe you would have gotten to Tokay before he talked."

"He talked? To whom?"

"That's what we're going to have to find out. Now, we not only need to locate and silence Tokay, but we also need to silence anyone else he may have talked to. But we're going to do that without you. Consider yourself lucky that your ineptitude isn't getting you silenced as well."

Alomari was seething, and subconsciously his hand began to move for his pistol. When he realized what he was doing, he tried to calm himself. *Not here. Not now. It must be someplace else, away from witnesses.*

As Gökhan Celik left the taverna, the assassin came to the conclusion that the Scorpion had made a very grave error in underestimating him. For that, Gökhan Celik was going to lose his life. The key would be in making it look like an accident, but accidents were the al-Qaeda operative's specialty.

An hour later, his anger only partially cooled, Khalid Alomari crossed the lobby of the most elegant hotel in Athens, the Grande Bretagne. He was disgusted not only with how the Scorpion conducted business but also with how he protected, or more appropriately didn't protect, his people. Gökhan Celik was supposed to be the man's most important lieutenant, but the Scorpion allowed him to stay, unguarded, in the same suite of the same hotel every time he came to Athens. The Scorpion's reputation might frighten most of the people who knew him, but it didn't frighten Khalid Alomari, especially when so much money was on the line.

"How dare you?" demanded Celik as Alomari forced his way into the suite and knocked the old man to the floor.

"I want to know everything you know about Emir Tokay and who he was talking to before he disappeared."

"You've already been told that's no longer any of your concern."

"You should have paid me what you owe me, Gökhan."

"What do we owe you? You failed. We owe you nothing."

"It was a small price compared to what it's going to cost you now."

"What do you mean, *what it's going to cost us now*?"

"We both know that Emir Tokay has knowledge you don't want anyone else to have. I'm going to find him, and when I do, I'm going to sell him back to the Scorpion at ten times what you should have paid me," replied the assassin as he slammed his foot down into the old man's hip and heard the bone snap like dry kindling.

"You are a dead man!" howled Celik.

"Everyone must die," replied Alomari, "but not

all of us get to choose when. Answer my question and I will let you live. Who was Emir talking to before he disappeared?"

Celik spat at the pants leg of his attacker. "I will see you dead. Do you understand me? Do you know what Akrep will do to you?"

Alomari shook the spit from his trouser leg and said, "You have cheated me out of what is rightfully mine. Do you just expect me to slink away? I will give you one last chance to answer my question. What do you know about Tokay?"

Celik glared at the man in defiance.

"You should have known I wouldn't give up, Gökhan. Things will only get worse from here. If you do not answer me, I will track down your daughter and your grandchildren, and they will be next. I am a man of my word. You know I will do it. Even if it takes me the next five years of my life, I will not stop until I have visited upon them deaths more horrible than any you can possibly imagine."

Celik's body was trembling.

"What will it be, Gökhan?"

"Akrep will know you did this."

"I don't think so," said Alomari as he withdrew an empty hypodermic syringe from his sport coat pocket. "Embolisms are quite regrettable, but not uncommon in men of your age. Our friend the Scorpion may have his suspicions, but with the fall you took that broke your hip, I don't think they will trouble him for too long."

"You will be punished for this," moaned Celik.

"As you will have Allah's ear in Paradise before I do, I am certain you will do all you can to make that so. In the meantime, it is not too late for you to save your family."

Celik didn't need any further convincing to know the man was telling the truth. The assassin's reputation was assurance enough.

EIGHTEEN

The White House
Washington, DC
Next day

The president stood staring through the glass doors of the Oval Office onto the Rose Garden and said, "I couldn't be more serious. I want this entire thing to go away, Chuck. Do you understand me?"

"Yes, Mr. President. I understand. Believe me, we all want it to go away, but just wishing isn't going to make it happen. We can't put the genie back in the bottle. Not now."

"I don't care about putting it back in the goddamn bottle," snapped Rutledge as he turned to face his chief of staff. "I just don't want some self-aggrandizing senator forwarding her career by pulling the mask off of one of the good guys. After everything he's given to his country, forcing Scot Harvath to wear a scarlet letter is not only unfair, it's just plain wrong."

"With all due respect, sir," replied Charles Anderson, "it's not Harvath she wants wearing that scarlet letter. It's you."

The president turned away from the doors and walked back over behind his desk. "Then why doesn't she come after me?"

"She is coming after you, Jack. This is how it's done. You know that."

"Well, the way it's done stinks."

"I'll second that," agreed Anderson.

"You don't ruin good people who this country depends on. If she wants me, she should come get me."

"I'll be sure to tell her that when she gets here. If you have any compromising photographs of yourself that you'd like to hand over to me now, maybe I could get her to agree to a trade."

The president appeared to smile, but it could have very well been only a grimace as he mentally moved on to his next topic. "What do we have from the Joint Chiefs and USAMRIID?"

Anderson removed a briefing report from the folder in front of him and said, "It's not good. USAMRIID has cultured the illness, but it seems resistant to everything they're throwing at it. They've got representatives from the CDC and the Mayo Clinic's exotic disease department working with them now, but they've yet to make any progress. At least it's still contained to that one incident in Asalaam."

"For now," replied the president, "and that's only because for the moment it suits the purposes of whoever's behind this thing. What's our state of readiness if it makes an appearance here?"

Anderson referred back to his briefing report and replied, "First responders are going to be primary care physicians and hospital emergency rooms. We've put out a bulletin via the Healthwatch system to report any cases involving the symptoms we're aware of to their local public health department. Those departments will report back to a crisis center at the Department of Homeland Security. The key is being able to contain any outbreak as quickly as possible."

"What do we do if we can't contain it?"

Anderson tried to calm the president. "Let's worry about that if and when it happens."

"Chuck, you know as well as I do that it's only a matter of time. They may have finally been able to come up with the biggest stick on the playground. A stick that spares only the most faithful to their beliefs."

"Which makes us confident there has got to be a way around it—a way to be immunized against it."

Rutledge wanted to share his chief of staff's optimism, but he'd always been one to prepare for the worst and then, and only then, hope for the best. "If we can't contain it and we can't immunize against it, what then?"

"USAMRIID is still developing scenarios."

"Let's cut to the chase. What are we talking about worst case?"

The president's chief of staff was reluctant to answer, but he had little choice. "Worst case, we initiate the Campfire protocol to guarantee we stop this thing dead in its tracks."

The color drained from Rutledge's face. "Making me the first U.S. president to ever authorize a thermonuclear strike on his own soil and against his own people."

NINETEEN

LONDON

Jillian Alcott, chemistry teacher at London's prestigious Abbey College, carefully picked her way through the swollen puddles along Notting Hill's Pembridge Road. Arriving at the Notting Hill Gate Tube station, the five-foot-eight redhead with deep green eyes and high cheekbones politely but firmly shouldered her way through the crowd that had gathered at the entrance to take shelter from the storm. After collapsing her distinctive Burberry umbrella and giving it her customary three firm snaps to rid it of any residual rainwater, she tucked it beneath her left arm and removed her Tube pass from her wallet.

Though Jillian was in fine physical condition and could have easily walked the distance, saving time by cutting through Kensington Gardens, the weather was just too disagreeable for her. Ever since she was a small child, she had never liked thunderstorms.

Jillian was seven years old when her parents left her alone with her grandmother to drive inland to sell some of their livestock. It was a late Friday afternoon, and the weather began to kick up half an hour after her parents had left. She stared out the front windows of their little stone house at the enormous white caps forming on the ever-darkening Celtic Sea. Her grandmother pulled out all of her board games and they played every one of them in an effort to take Jillian's mind off the storm raging outside. Jillian tried her absolute hardest to be brave, but with each booming knell of thunder the house shook, and she was certain the next would send the tiny structure toppling over the nearby cliffs and into the sea.

Jillian's grandmother tried everything to calm the little girl, but nothing seemed to work. Finally, she decided to draw Jillian a hot bath and infuse it with lavender.

With the bath drawn, Jillian's grandmother was just about to put her in when another flash of lightning blazed and all of the power in the house went out. A roaring clap of thunder followed that shook the small dwelling and rattled the windows so hard the glass seemed poised to fall out of its panes.

Jillian's grandmother left her in the bathroom for just a moment while she went to search for candles, but she never came back.

The little girl used her hand to feel along the wall and guide her toward the kitchen. Floorboards creaked beneath her feet, and every cold brass doorknob she touched along the way sent chills racing up her spine. When she finally made it into the kitchen, she immediately sensed that something was wrong.

She called out softly to her grandmother but received no response. The candles were in a drawer on the far side of the room, but Jillian was afraid to cross the kitchen in the dark. Something inside her told her not to move. She waited and waited until another flash of lightning came, and when it did, she had the shock of her seven-year-old life. Lying on the floor was her gran. Apparently, she had tripped in the dark and in her fall had hit her head on the kitchen table. Upon seeing the pool of blood that was quickly covering the floor, Jillian screamed and ran.

She dashed into the front hall and picked up the telephone to call the police. *If there is an emergency, always call the police first,* her parents had told her. Jillian picked up the phone, ready to dial the number she had learned by heart, but the phone was dead.

Still in her pajamas, Jillian thought only of her gran. Grabbing her mac from the front closet, she quickly pulled it on, followed by her bright red Wellington-style boots. When she opened the front door, she was greeted by an enormous burst of wind that almost pushed her back inside. The little girl had no choice; she had to get help.

Through the storm, Jillian ran the mile and a

half down their muddy road to the junction only to find that it had been washed out. She was trapped. There was no way she could cross the torrent of floodwater. There was no way she could get to the neighbors, or anyone else for that matter. There was no way she could get help. There was nothing she could do but return to the house.

When she did, she realized she would have to tend to her grandmother. Mustering her courage, she reentered the kitchen and found a towel, intending to begin by cleaning the blood from her gran's head wound. As she approached, though, she realized her grandmother wasn't moving. There wasn't even the rhythmic heave and fall of her chest as she took in air. Jillian crept closer and, placing her hand alongside her grandmother's cold flesh, realized that she was gone.

The storm raged for two more days. Seven-year-old Jillian couldn't bring herself to remain inside with the body of her dead grandmother lying in the kitchen, so she stayed in the barn, keeping warm beneath a pile of horse blankets. When the police finally did arrive, she wondered how they had even known she needed help.

The police came with Jillian's aunt. When they found her in the barn, her aunt suddenly began to cry. She blamed the weather, the terrible weather. She was crying so hard that one of the policemen had to tell Jillian himself that her mother and father wouldn't be coming home. They had died in a car accident on the way back from selling their sheep. They had fetched a good price early and were trying to beat the storm back to the farm, but they had seriously misjudged it.

One horrible storm had managed to take away the three most important people in Jillian's life. It was no wonder that rough weather still made her feel so uncomfortable. In fact, storms had grown to become a metaphor for Jillian, representing the uncertainty and cruelty that could be disproportionately visited on one person's life no matter how little that person had done to deserve it. It was, in part, why she had surrendered herself to a life of science. Science was a world of constants—rules and processes, which could always be counted on. The part she cared not to think about was that science was also a world that was to a significant degree cold, unfeeling, and exceedingly inhuman.

Of course there were people passionate about their pursuits, but very rarely were they passionate about other human beings. In the academic world of "publish or perish," very few put anything above their love of science. It was indeed a cold place, incredibly enriching for the mind but not so enriching for the soul.

As a remarkably attractive woman, Jillian Alcott was a rarity in the academic world and constantly found herself treated as an object to be possessed rather than as a woman deserving of love. Throughout her education, both her fellow students and many of her professors had desired her simply for her stunning outward appearance. None of them had the courage to look beyond her all too often cold demeanor to see the person she really was. Had anyone taken the time to really study her, to study her with even half the vigor with which they pursued their vaunted scientific investigations, they might have seen a woman who had not yet been able to make it past those two horrific storm-plagued days in Cornwall when she was seven years old, a woman who, though braver than most on the outside, was still, on the inside, incredibly frightened. Life, her career, and even the prospect of learning to love someone again only to have them ripped from her, all terrified Jillian Alcott.

The worse the storm, the worse her feelings of impending doom, and today was no different. On days like this, her only comfort came from indulging herself. And though it sounded terribly clichéd, even to her, the one thing that made her feel better was shopping. And her favorite place to shop was the Harvey Nichols department store in Knightsbridge.

As she exited the Tube station and raced through the rain across Sloane Street, Alcott decided that with nothing but the day's mail awaiting her at home, she'd make an evening of it at her beloved Harvey Nics. It was either that or the television at home, and as much of a social cripple as she was,

Alcott knew it was better for her to be out among the living and breathing.

Alcott decided to head up to the store's Fifth Floor Café for something to eat before she began her shopping. Finding a small table for two, she placed her belongings on the opposite chair and sat down. The rain pounded against the glass roof and ran down the windows at the front of the café in white foamy sheets that made it appear as if she was sitting behind a waterfall. As a streak of lightning ripped through the sky, followed by a booming peal of thunder, Alcott decided she wanted a glass of wine.

Forty-five minutes later, the storm was still raging as Jillian paid for her meal. Despite the two glasses of Pinot Gris she had consumed, she couldn't shake the feeling that there was something bad out there with her name on it. Blaming her unease on the storm, she got up from her table and decided that it was time to do a little shopping.

Taking the escalators to the third floor to browse through the lingerie section, she felt a chill along the back of her long, slender neck. She was even more frightened than before and didn't know why.

As she moved through the lingerie department, her feelings of impending doom came to a crescendo and finally made sense as a powerfully built man grabbed her urgently by the arm and said, "Come with me if you want to live."

TWENTY

"What are you doing?" demanded Alcott as she was muscled toward the back of the department.

"Saving your life," replied Scot Harvath as he kept her moving toward one of the green emergency exit signs.

Alcott tried to twist out of his grasp. "You're hurting me. Let me go."

"Someone has been following you since you left the Abbey College."

She had wanted to blame her unease on the storm, but on a more primal level Jillian had sensed all afternoon that something wasn't right. It was as if she had felt someone's eyes on her. But the only way this man could have known she was being followed was if he had been following her as well. "Who are you?"

"That's not important right now," said Harvath as he increased their pace.

"If you don't stop this, I'm going to scream. Do you hear me?"

"You scream and we're both dead."

Alcott was about to show him she was serious when she felt something hard pressed into her back. Without even seeing it, she instinctively knew what it was—a gun. "Why are you doing this?"

"Over your shoulder, by the elevator."

Alcott looked. "What about it?"

"The tall man standing next to it. Do you see him? Dark hair. Dark skin."

"Yes, why?"

"He's been sent here to kill you," responded Harvath as he turned Jillian back around and continued to maneuver her toward the door marked *Emergency Exit.*

Alcott was just about to tell this man one last time that he was insane and to unhand her when she heard gunshots and all of the mannequins around them began exploding. "Get down," yelled her captor, knocking her to the ground as they were showered with pieces of flesh-colored fiberglass.

As Alcott started to scream, Harvath counted to three and rolled off her, coming up on one knee with the compact eleven-shot, .40-caliber Beretta Mini Cougar Type D pistol that had been waiting for him when he arrived in London. As good an agent, and a friend, as Nick Kampos was, arranging weapons for Harvath in foreign countries was something even he couldn't do. For that, Harvath reluctantly had to call on Ozan Kalachka and ask him for a favor. A favor the man was only too happy and able to arrange.

Catching sight of their assailant, Harvath began firing.

The unsilenced weapon bucked in his hand as Harvath let loose with a deafening three-round volley. The store was in complete pandemonium, with shoppers screaming and running for their lives. Keeping low while he expertly weaved his way through the racks of clothing and display stands, the attacker was less than twenty yards away and closing fast. Harvath desperately wanted to get off another round of shots, but there were too many people in his way.

"We've got to get out of here now," he said as he maneuvered back over to Alcott.

Jillian wanted to respond; she wanted to say something, but the words caught in her throat. Her heart was thudding against her chest so hard she thought for certain it would burst.

"Do you see that exit sign back there?" asked Harvath as he helped her up into a crouch.

Alcott had trouble responding, and Harvath realized that she must be in shock. Grabbing her chin, he turned her head in the right direction and asked her again if she saw the sign.

This time, Jillian nodded.

"Good. When I say go, I want you to run as fast as you can to that door. I'm going to be right behind you and—"

"Who are you?" she managed.

"That's not important," replied Harvath. "We've got to get out of here. Now, when I say *go*, we're going to make a run for that emergency exit door. Do you understand?"

Jillian nodded her head.

"Okay, get ready. One, two, three, *go*!" yelled Harvath as he pushed Alcott forward and laid down a wide swath of cover fire behind them, careful to avoid hitting any of the fleeing shoppers. When they arrived at the emergency exit door, Harvath kicked it open and pulled Jillian in behind him. They ran down a narrow service corridor until they found the emergency stairwell and then began bounding down the stairs two at a time. Alcott's legs seemed to be moving entirely of their own accord, her will tied to the sheer force of the man in front of her.

Instead of descending all the way to the ground floor and out some side door, as she assumed they would, they instead exited the fire stairs on the first floor and cut across the length of the store to the other side. Finding another staircase, Harvath led the way down to the ground floor, where he spirited Alcott through the perfume section and straight out the front door with the rest of the panicked shoppers.

Harvath quickly scanned the street through the torrential downpour and saw that not only were all of the buses packed, but so were the taxis. The

Tube was an option, but they couldn't get on it here. Not at Knightsbridge. It was only a matter of time before Khalid Alomari realized he'd been tricked and doubled back to look for them. They had to get out of the area as quickly as possible.

Tightening his grip around Alcott's arm, Harvath steered her away from the department store and down the sidewalk. Without her trusty Burberry umbrella, which she had lost somewhere in the lingerie department along with her briefcase, Alcott had nothing to keep her dry. Growing colder, wetter, and more scared by the moment, she tried to think of something to say—something that would cut through all of this insanity. "Please, let me go."

Harvath wasn't listening. He was only concerned with putting as much distance between them and Alomari as possible, and right now that meant they had to keep moving forward—together.

Harvath was in no condition to tackle the highly skilled assassin. He was running on empty, summoning up reserves of energy and recycled adrenaline he knew he was going to pay dearly for in the very near future. All he wanted to do was lie down and sleep for a week, but right now, sleep was not an option. Knowing that a very deadly disease could be unleashed upon America at any time was all the inspiration Harvath needed to increase his pace.

As they got closer to the South Kensington Tube station, Harvath realized he still had no idea where they were going. He hadn't thought that far ahead. They couldn't aimlessly wander London all night. They needed an end point, a destination. "We need to find a place where we can get out of the rain," he said more for his own benefit than hers. "A place where we can talk. Quietly."

"How about a police station?" replied Alcott. "They're quiet enough, and we'll both be safe there."

"We can't go to the police."

"We can't?" she mustered up the courage to say. "Or *you* can't?"

"It's the same thing now," stated Harvath. "We're in this together." Through the rain, he could make out a pub sign about half a block down. After glancing over his shoulder he said, "There's a pub up ahead. We can talk there. Let's go."

"I don't want to go anywhere with you," said Alcott. "I don't even know who you are. The only place I want to go is to the police."

Harvath was anxious to get off the street and out of the rain. Any minute now, the area would be crawling with police. He could already hear the Klaxons, and even though he'd been careful to avoid showing his face to the department store's security cameras, there was no telling if any eyewitnesses had gotten a good look at him.

Harvath needed time to think, and like it or not, for at least the near future, he and Alcott were going to be joined at the hip.

He thought about using the gun and telling her she had no choice, but playing hardball was only going to make traveling with her more difficult. He needed her to trust him. "If you don't come inside with me, not only will you be putting your life in further jeopardy, but Emir Tokay's as well."

The look on the woman's face told him that he'd struck the right chord. The resistance drained from her body, and Harvath was able to quickly steer her off the street and into the dimly lit pub.

TWENTY-ONE

It was called The Bunch of Grapes and turned out to be one of London's oldest pubs. As Harvath led Alcott to a quiet table in the back, he noticed a sign that said it had been in existence since 1777. The rich, wood-paneled interior was steeped in London history and was exactly what one would expect to find in a traditional English public house, especially one that had been around for more than two hundred years.

After hanging their soaking wet coats near the door, Harvath ordered two Irish coffees from the bar and brought them back over to their table.

Jillian reached for her drink and in the most confident voice she could summon said, "I'm giving you five minutes to tell me who you are and what this is all about. Why would somebody want to kill me?"

Harvath was famished. He opened the package of salt and vinegar chips he had bought at the bar, took a couple of bites, and then washed them down with a mouthful of hot Irish coffee before responding. "My name is Scot Harvath, and I work for the American government. The man from the department store who tried to kill you is named Khalid Sheik Alomari. He's an al-Qaeda assassin."

"An al-Qaeda assassin is after me?"

"Yes."

"And you just let him follow me all the way to Harvey Nichols?"

"I wasn't able to get a good look at him until just before everything happened."

"This is preposterous. Why would an al-Qaeda assassin be after me?"

"Because of your relationship with Emir Tokay."

"My *relationship*? But Emir and I are just friends," responded Jillian. "We went to university together. Why would someone, much less al-Qaeda, want to kill me over that?"

Most people would have missed it, but Harvath noticed a subtle shift in her facial muscles that signaled she was not being completely truthful. It was called a microexpression, and through their extensive training, U.S. Secret Service agents were the only human beings consistently capable of detecting them. It was a skill Harvath had worked tirelessly to keep sharp, and it was precisely at moments like this that he was glad he had. "There's more to this than that," replied Harvath, "and you know it.

Emir was working on a very serious project that he contacted you about for help."

"I don't know anything about any project Emir was working on."

There it was again, the tell. "Dr. Alcott, everybody on that project is dead now. Everybody except for Emir, and if you don't want the same thing to happen to him, I suggest you cooperate."

Jillian was silent as she decided what, if anything, she should divulge. This man knew that she had been followed since leaving Abbey College because he had been following her too. In her opinion, that made him just as suspect. Just because he managed to get to her first didn't automatically make him one of the good guys. What proof did she have that he was telling her the truth? Emir had warned her to be extremely careful about whom she spoke to about anything regarding his work.

Jillian quickly made up her mind that before she would answer any of Harvath's questions, she had a few more of her own she wanted answered. "If you work for the American government, why can't we go to the police?"

"It's tricky," he replied.

"I can only imagine," said Jillian, her courage bolstered by the Irish coffee and the presence of other people at the front of the somewhat crowded pub. "You are quickly running out of time to explain it to me."

Harvath took a moment to compose himself as

he chose his next words very carefully. "The man who shot at you at the department store—"

"Allegedly," replied Jillian.

"What do you mean, *allegedly*?" said Harvath. "What do you think those mannequins were doing? Bursting with pride because they found work in the lingerie department?"

Jillian looked Harvath square in the face and said, "How do I know he wasn't shooting at you and I was just in the wrong place at the wrong time?"

Harvath couldn't believe what a state of denial this woman was in. "Trust me. Khalid Alomari came to London to kill you."

"Really?" she replied. "Then what was he waiting for?"

"What do you mean?"

"You said he'd been following me since I left the school. Why? Why follow me all the way to Harvey Nichols, then wait around while I was in the café? Why not kill me outside the school or even on the Tube? Why draw it out?"

"I don't know," replied Harvath. "The only thing I can think of is that he must have wanted something from you."

"Like what?"

"Information, probably. Like how much you knew about Emir's work and who else he might have been talking to."

"Which are exactly the same things I assume

you want," she said as she looked at Harvath. "But that still doesn't explain why he waited."

"Maybe he planned on following you home. Do you live alone?"

"I'm not going to answer that."

Harvath read her face and said, "You live alone, I can tell, but that doesn't matter. Alomari is ruthless. He would have killed anyone who stood in his way of getting the information he wanted."

"But I don't have any information."

Harvath could tell she was lying again, but he let it go. "When he saw me at the department store, he probably realized he wasn't going to be able to get to you, and so he figured if he couldn't, then no one would."

"How romantic," replied Jillian. "How do you know so much about this Alomari person?"

"Until recently, it was my job to hunt him down and bring him in."

"So how come he's still on the loose?"

"He's very good at what he does and extremely adept at not getting caught. For over two months he's been my number one priority, but all that's changed now."

"Why?" said Jillian. "What's happened?"

"Emir Tokay is what happened. He and his colleagues have engineered an illness, which poses a serious threat to the West."

Jillian's mouth was agape. *They had done it.* "How come word of this hasn't made it into the press?"

she asked as she stared at the man sitting across the table from her. There was something about him, something she couldn't put her finger on. She was torn between wanting to trust him and wanting to get up and run like hell. He could very well be one of the bravest, most confident men she had ever met, or the most insane and dangerous. There was a chance that he was just the wrong mix of all of the above. Until she uncovered why he refused to go to the police, though, there was no way she could even begin to consider answering his questions. Taking another sip of her drink, she said, "I'm sorry, Mr. Harvath, but I find it extremely disconcerting that you still haven't explained why we, or more particularly *you*, can't go to the police."

Harvath looked past her to the small television in the bar area that had just been switched to the evening news. Already the press was reporting breaking news of a shootout at the upscale Knightsbridge department store. In some small way it was a relief to see something other than his al-Jazeera footage leading the news. His relief was short-lived, as the footage from the al-Karim bazaar was the next story the anchor cut to. There was no getting away from it. Harvath had a decision to make.

He had taken a chance with Nick Kampos, and now he was going to have to take a chance with Jillian Alcott. If he didn't trust her, there was no way he could expect her to trust him. "Turn around," he said.

Jillian half expected to see either the police or the assassin from Harvey Nichols standing in the front of the pub, and it took her a moment to figure out what Harvath was looking at—the television. The footage was all too familiar to her by now, but she watched again as the American soldier mercilessly beat the unarmed Iraqi. Each time she saw it, it was more distressing than the last. When it was over, she turned back and looked at Harvath. "Not a good day for America's public image."

"Nor mine," replied Harvath.

"Why?" said Jillian. "Wait a second. Are you telling me that was you? You're the man beating that innocent Iraqi?"

"He was far from innocent, believe me. That man was paid a lot of money to act as somebody's decoy."

"Whose decoy?"

"Khalid Alomari. The man who tried to kill you less than a half hour ago."

"That's why you can't go to the police?"

Harvath nodded his head. "That's part of it. It's important I keep as low a profile as possible right now."

Jillian looked at him and replied, "You might want to start by not shooting up department stores."

"Thanks. I'll make sure I remember that the next time I see someone getting ready to use the back of an innocent high-school teacher's head for target practice."

Jillian ignored his remark. "What about going to the American embassy?"

"I definitely can't go to the embassy."

"Why not?"

"Because a subpoena has been issued for me back in the States. The president's political opponents want to run him out of office on a rail. They think the way to do it is to have me testify in open court about what happened in that market in Baghdad."

"So why not do it? If you didn't do anything wrong, why not go and clear your name?"

"Because the whole Baghdad thing is just the tip of the iceberg. That's only where it starts. Regardless of how it's handled, it could be extremely embarrassing for the president."

"Is there anything he's done that should make him embarrassed?" she asked.

Harvath didn't like talking about sensitive political matters with an otherwise perfect stranger, so he once again chose his words very carefully. "Absolutely not."

"Then what's the problem?"

"The *problem* is how his opponents could make it all look. Often the mere suggestion of impropriety is enough to ruin someone."

Jillian respected Harvath's apparent loyalty to his president.

"The other thing I'm not too crazy about," continued Harvath, "is that they want to televise the hearings. Even if I'm cleared, my career will be over, but that's not the worst of it. There have been more fatwas issued against me than you can shake a falafel at, and once my face is made public, I'll have to look over my shoulder for the rest of my life. I don't want to do that."

"It sounds like you are in a very difficult situation, and I would like to say that I sympathize," said Jillian, "but none of this makes me any more inclined to believe you. I don't even know if that's really you in that al-Jazeera footage. All I can see is the back of that soldier's head."

She didn't trust him, and Harvath couldn't blame her, but by the same token, he could still sense that part of her wanted to believe that he was here to help her. "Listen, when this thing is all said and done, I don't really care about my career, or the president's for that matter. I care about the threat to my country. Foreign policy isn't my department, but I can tell you one thing: I have seen how this illness kills, and no one deserves to die like that. No one."

Jillian tried not to appear too interested, but her scientific curiosity was on fire. Emir's accounts had been somewhat vague, and she was very keen to know what Harvath had seen. "You've actually seen the illness at work in human beings?"

Harvath nodded his head.

"How does it manifest itself? What's the progression like?"

Though he hated to even relive it in his mind, Harvath explained in detail what the disease was like from the moment it first made itself known to the last horrifying minutes of a victim's life.

Jillian was quiet for a moment as she thought about everything she'd been told. If it weren't for the fact that Emir Tokay had completely fallen off the face of the earth and had stopped returning her e-mails, she would have already left the pub. Draining the last draught of warm liquid from her glass, she asked, "What's happened to Emir?"

Finally, progress, thought Harvath as he replied, "He was kidnapped a couple of days ago not far from his office in Dhaka. Do you have any idea who might have wanted to kidnap him?"

"God, that's awful. No. I have no idea at all."

Harvath studied her face. She appeared to be telling the truth. "What did Emir want your help with?"

"How much do you know about what he was working on?"

"I know that his team had engineered something called the sword of Allah," said Harvath, "and that it's a weapon of some sort intended to cleanse the world of all but the most faithful Muslims."

"You obviously don't know much then," replied Alcott, "because you're wrong on both counts."

TWENTY-TWO

"How am I wrong?" asked Harvath.

"First of all, Emir had no idea what he was working on. That's why he contacted me," said Jillian. "And second, his team didn't engineer anything. What they were dealing with was a *discovery.*"

Harvath leaned forward over the table. "What kind of discovery?"

"It's a paleopathologist's dream come true, but it's also something that probably should have stayed buried and never been found."

"Why do you say that?"

"The project Emir was working on bore striking similarities to accounts of a very old and virulent bioweapon."

"How old?"

"Over two thousand years."

Harvath thought she was pulling his leg. "They had bioweapons over two thousand years ago?"

"And chemical as well."

"That's impossible. You need established, modern science to effectively wage chemical and biological warfare."

"Tell that to the enemies of the Hittites over three thousand years ago who found themselves beset with human plague bombs. Or how about the soldiers on the receiving end of barbed, poisoned arrows shot by Scythian archers more than five hundred years before Christ?"

"Pretty nasty stuff," replied Harvath, "but not very scientific."

Jillian expected as much. Most people had a tremendously naïve view of ancient warfare. It was one of the things that made her field so interesting and yet so very frustrating. She often felt as if she had to be equal parts salesman and scientist. "Were you aware that these same Scythians had perfected a composite reflex bow which allowed them to outshoot any archer of their day by double the distance?"

"No, I wasn't."

"I'd say being able to project a payload twice as far as your enemies constitutes a pretty technologically advanced delivery system, regardless of its day, wouldn't you?" Before Harvath could respond, Jillian pressed on. "How about the fact that the Scythians had learned how to agitate human blood to separate out the plasma, which they then used to make their poison arrows even more lethal?"

"But how could a bioweapon over two thousand years old still be viable after all this time?"

"You'd be surprised how long ancient poisons remain lethal. The Victoria and Albert Museum just discovered that the heads of several arrows from India in their collection were coated with deadly substances that are still lethal today, over a thousand years later. If the substance in question here was even somewhat volatile, as long as it was preserved in an anaerobic substance like honey, which was well known to the ancients, or sealed within a container crafted from a nonporous material like faience, gold, or glass, it could remain quite deadly and still be quite dangerous today."

If what Emir was dealing with was some ancient bioweapon, it was becoming painfully clear why he had reached out to Jillian Alcott for help.

"How these poisons survived is really not what's important," she continued. "The point is that for some reason historians all too often choose to overlook the ancients' skillful manipulation of nature. They'd rather believe that soldiers of old adhered to the highest moral codes in battle, but this just isn't the case. The ancient world was filled with terrifying precursors to today's sophisticated chem-bio weapons: from flamethrowers and incendiary devices, all the way to poison gases and dirty bombs. And they did it all without the help of modern science."

"I'm willing to concede," replied Harvath, "they

had a handle on chemical and biological warfare, but what does this have to do with what Emir was working on?"

"How familiar are you with *Islamic science*?" asked Jillian.

"If you mean the state of science in the Islamic world, I know a little."

"That's not what I'm talking about. In the context of what Emir Tokay was doing, the term *Islamic science* refers to a rather bizarre hybrid of modern science and Islamic mysticism practiced by Muslim fundamentalists."

At the mention of Muslim fundamentalists, Harvath leaned forward even further and began listening even more intently. She was speaking his language now, and a connection was finally starting to form.

"Many of the people involved with Emir at the institute are Islamic scientists," continued Alcott. "They believe that things like Ebola, smallpox, and atomic energy all contain powerful, unseen spirits called *djinns*—from which we take the English word *genie*. The scientists think that these *djinns* can be commanded via secret knowledge contained within the Koran. They're fascinated with things such as Pandora's box and the plague demons King Solomon supposedly harnessed to build the great temple at Jerusalem and then sealed up within its foundations."

"This all sounds pretty strange," said Harvath.

"It is," replied Alcott, "especially to the Western mind, but it bears scrutiny. There are many fundamentalists, particularly in the Arab world, who are absolutely obsessed with harnessing the power of ancient biological weapons. The older the weapon is, the more powerful they believe the *djinn* inside it to be. The scary fact is that they are fixated on possessing these ancient weapons and have been on a mad, Indiana Jones–style quest to do so for decades."

"The David effect," said Harvath.

"Exactly," replied Alcott. "A scenario by which a significantly smaller player, with access to the right technology, is able to severely damage a much larger foe, which in this case appears to be the enemies of radical Islam."

"If this isn't something that Emir and his group bioengineered themselves, how is it possible that it only targets non-Muslims? Muslims weren't even around over two thousand years ago."

"I don't know," said Jillian. "Unfortunately, I never got far enough with Emir to figure it out."

"You said that over two thousand years ago there were accounts of a bioweapon similar to the one we're seeing today. Where were those accounts from?"

"In a book called the *Arthashastra*. It was written in India in the fourth century B.C. It urged kings to set aside their conscience and liberally employ diabolical methods to ensure victory against their enemies. It also contained hundreds of recipes for toxic weapons, as well as countless instructions for waging ruthless, unconventional warfare."

"And this is how you were helping Emir?"

"Yes, I was using my background in paleopathology, the study of disease in antiquity, to help him ascertain what it was he was working with."

"That's what Emir thought he was working on? A disease from antiquity?"

"He had his suspicions. He'd heard enough rumors that certain people affiliated with the institute had been searching for ancient diseases and ancient bioweapons to know it was a possibility."

"What about you?" asked Harvath. "What did you think?"

"Did I think it was possible? I thought it was very possible. In fact, I think that in this case, where the brain of the victim liquefied to a black sludge and ran out the nasal passages, we have a spot-on match for accounts within the *Arthashastra*."

Harvath was fascinated, yet underneath it all he sensed a *but*. "But?"

"But the rest of the symptoms seen in Asalaam—the aversion to light, water, and strong odors, as well as the patient's aversion to his own reflection and so on—don't fit."

"Could Emir's group have orchestrated that—added it in somehow?"

Jillian shook her head. "From what I gathered,

this mystery weapon had been discovered, and Emir's team was responsible for putting it back into circulation, not improving or modifying it."

This time it was Harvath who shook his head.

"What?" asked Jillian.

"It's hard for me to believe that Emir didn't know what he was working on."

"According to him, they were duped. They'd been given samples of the weapon, told it was something that had been engineered by the West and that there was a good chance it was going to be used against Muslims somewhere in the world. They had no idea that the reverse was true. Emir Tokay is a good man."

"As far as I'm concerned, that has yet to be proven," replied Harvath. "In the meantime, what were they hoping to gain by working with the weapon?"

"Apparently, there was some sort of way to inoculate or build up resistance against it. Emir's group was supposed to find out how Muslims could be protected from it."

Immediately, a bell went off in Harvath's head. "Then this weapon wasn't bioengineered to decimate non-Muslims, it was engineered to kill anyone who wasn't vaccinated against it."

"*Vaccination* in the strict sense of the word might not be exactly how it works," said Jillian, "but you're in the right vicinity."

"What else can you tell me?" he asked. "I need to

know more, especially about the *Arthashastra*. Maybe there's an answer in there—a formula or an antidote we can use."

"It's a very complicated book."

Harvath was about to assert that it couldn't be that complicated if a group of nutcase fundamentalist scientists had figured out how to crack it, when the TV at the front of the pub caught his attention again. Several of the patrons had gathered around to watch some sort of update on the Harvey Nichols shooting. "Stay here," he said. "I'll be right back."

He quietly walked up behind the group of customers at the front of the pub and watched as a reporter explained that three people had been shot to death at the upscale Knightsbridge department store—one of them an off-duty London police officer. The reporter then cut to video from the store's security cameras showing the shooter in action. It was like the al-Karim bazaar all over again. All of the attention was focused on Harvath, and Khalid Alomari was nowhere to be seen. The only thing Harvath had going for him was that none of the footage showed a full shot of his face. Not that it mattered. According to the reporter, eyewitnesses were already working with police sketch artists, and they were confident they would have a composite soon. What they did have now, though, were several shots of a woman police were saying might have been kidnapped by one of the gunmen. Harvath watched as they ran several pieces of video that clearly showed Jillian's face.

Hurrying back to the table and positioning his body so that Alcott would be less visible from the front of the pub, Harvath asked, "How'd you pay for your meal in the café? Cash? Check? Credit card? What was it?"

"I paid cash," responded Jillian. "What's this all about?"

"Good. That means they won't have your name, at least not right away."

"Who won't have my name?"

"The police. They've just released images from the store's security cameras. Apparently, they can't decide whether I kidnapped you or if you were my willing accomplice."

"Accomplice to what?"

"To the shooting. Three people back at the store are dead. One of them was an off-duty policeman."

Jillian didn't know what to say. "Did you shoot him?"

"Of course not."

"How can you be sure?"

"Because," replied Harvath, "I know who I was aiming at."

"Khalid Alomari."

"Exactly."

"This is too much," replied Jillian. "We have to go to the police. Now."

"I already told you. I can't go to the police, and neither can you. There's no time."

"If Alomari was in that store, then they'll have footage of him too."

"He's a professional. If they do, they won't have much."

"But it's something, a start. They could help us look for him."

"At this point, Khalid Alomari is one of the last things I'm concerned about. I need to get to the bottom of how this illness works and how and where al-Qaeda intends to use it. I can't do that, though, without your help. I need to know more about what Emir was involved with."

Jillian knew she had to do something. She might be Emir's only hope. Finally, she said, "I'm not the one you need to talk to."

"Of course you are. You're the person Emir was speaking with outside the institute."

"I'm not exactly the only one."

Harvath looked at her. "If there's anyone else you think he might have spoken to, you need to tell me. They could be in a lot of danger right now as well."

"I doubt it," said Jillian. "There's no trail connecting them. Emir didn't even know I was talking to anyone else about his work."

"*You*? Who were you talking with?"

Jillian paused for a moment. "Two people who know a lot more about this stuff than I do."

"Other paleopathologists?"

"They were professors of mine at university," she replied. "Vanessa and Alan Whitcomb."

"Where can I find them?" asked Harvath.

"About five hours north of here in Durham. Do you have a car?"

Harvath shook his head.

"Then it looks like we may be sticking together for a little while longer."

TWENTY-THREE

THE WHITE HOUSE
WASHINGTON, DC
SAME DAY

"You want me to *what*?" said Senator Carmichael as she accepted the crystal highball glass from Charles Anderson and set it on the table in front of her.

"Come on, Helen," replied the president's chief of staff. "You didn't think I asked you over here so we could have a nice bipartisan bourbon and chat about the future of American democracy."

"No, but I was expecting a little cordiality."

"Well, you picked a bad week," said Anderson as he sat down on the couch across from her. "We're all out of cordiality."

"You know what, Chuck? You've changed."

"No, Helen, you have. You're so obsessed with clinching the vice presidency that you'll do anything to make it happen."

"As any member of my party would," countered Carmichael.

Anderson took a sip of his bourbon and said,

"No. We're not talking about party politics here, Helen, and you know it. We're talking about you and your rabid desire to ultimately become president."

"Me? What about you? Are you going to sit there and tell me that your boy's desire is any less than mine?"

"First of all, we refer to him as the president of the United States in this office—"

"Don't scold me, Chuck—"

"And secondly," replied the chief of staff, plowing right ahead, "you damn well know the arm-twisting we've had to do to get him to run again."

"If he doesn't want to run," said the senator as she lifted her drink, "then why is he?"

"Because the country needs him, and more importantly, it *wants* him."

"This country doesn't know what it wants."

"Really? Look at any poll out there, Helen, and you'll see it's clear. America wants Jack Rutledge to stay for another term, and that's what it's going to get—four more years."

"Not if the Democratic Party has got anything to say about it."

Anderson leaned forward. "The Democratic Party already knows they're beat. I had the chairman of the DNC in this office this morning, sitting right where you are, and he told me the very same thing."

Carmichael was flabbergasted. "Russell Mercer never would have admitted that."

"I'll tell you, Helen, Russ is a smart guy. There are a lot of times I wish he were on our side. But with the president's numbers the way they are, nothing short of a full-blown scandal in this administration is going to close the gap enough to give your party a shot at the Oval Office."

"Well," said the senator, a smug look on her face as she sat back and raised her bourbon to her lips, "you'd better mind the gap."

"We're minding it all right, but I want to tell you what else Russ Mercer said while he was here."

"More nonsense, I'm sure, but go ahead. I'm all ears."

"It's no secret that the Democratic presidential nomination is going to go to Governor Bob Farnsworth of Minnesota. All things considered, I think it's a pretty good choice. He's got a good voting record, he's a veteran, and to tell you the truth, in a nose-to-nose election race with him, I'd probably lose more than a little sleep at night, but this isn't a nose-to-nose race."

"What's this have to do with what other drivel Mercer had to say?"

"They're not going to put you on the ticket, Helen. Not this time."

"What do you mean, they're not going to put me on the ticket? How the hell would you know?"

"I know, because Russ told me so. You may be one of the party's rising stars, but you don't have the juice to make an election like this happen."

"Well, I'm just going to have to—"

Anderson cut her off. "Russ also told me that you are on very shaky ground as far as the DNC is concerned. If you don't watch your step, you might turn around and find that the party isn't there for you anymore."

He was playing her. He had to be. The self-righteous son of a bitch was trying to fluster her. Well, he had another think coming. She was a United States senator, and she did not fluster, not that easily. "I'm apparently going to have to have a chat with our beloved DNC chairman and get a few things straightened out with him," said Carmichael.

"Helen, let's cut the crap. You saw an opening, probably smelled what you thought was a little blood in the water, and took it upon yourself to get these hearings launched."

"So what if I did?"

"If you did, and the hearings blow up in your face, nobody from your party is going to be there to help you pick your teeth up off the ground."

"Chuck, let's be clear here. Are you threatening me?"

"No. No threats, Senator. Just friendly advice."

"From the incumbent *Republican* president's chief of staff. You'll pardon me if I take your advice with more than a grain of salt."

"Take it with two grains if you like, but these hearings could end up ruining your political career."

"Or yours," replied Carmichael with a grin.

Anderson ignored her and pressed forward. "Have you even polled this, Helen?"

"What? The hearings? I don't have to. People are outraged. The *American* people are deeply disturbed by what they have seen, and they want justice to be done."

"No they don't, and they're not outraged. This is exactly why you should have run this by your party leadership before you kicked this whole thing off. The Abu Ghraib prison photos outraged people. One of our servicemen kicking the crap out of a suspected terrorist is something entirely different."

"Did *you* poll it?" asked Carmichael.

Anderson was silent.

"Jesus, you did. Didn't you? What kind of numbers did you get?"

"I'm not going to do your homework for you, Helen. If you want to float a poll, you go right ahead and see what you get back. But I will tell you this. Unless you're polling in Ramallah, Tehran, or downtown Baghdad, you're not going to find an overwhelming amount of support for your hearings. Nobody wants this soldier dragged out in front of the media and nailed to a cross, and they'll want it even less when we release our side of the story."

"And what exactly is *your* side of the story?"

"Press with the hearings and you'll find out."

"Now that sounds like a threat."

"You know what, Helen? I'm tired of this," said the chief of staff as he stood from the couch and walked back over behind his desk. "You take it however you want to, but I'm warning you—you're biting off more than you can chew."

"Why? Because Scot Harvath, the man seen beating that defenseless Iraqi, is some kind of American hero for all of the things he's done? Do you think you'll be able to wrap him in the flag and the public will just give him a pass? How about the president? Do you think he can parade out that same trite line that he's got a tough job to do and sometimes that job involves doing things others might not have the stomach for in order to keep this country safe? If you think that crap is going to work, you are sorely mistaken."

"What I think is that you've got no idea what it takes to run this country, Senator."

"I know it doesn't take things like the Apex Project," replied Carmichael, pausing for Anderson's reaction to her bombshell.

The chief of staff was ready for her, though. "I've got no idea what you're talking about."

"I'm talking about the president's own special black ops team that funds its budget with monies approved by Congress for a wide variety of fiscal and social programs. Since you're such an expert, Chuck, how do you think Americans would feel if they knew what the president was really up to? Running his own private assassination teams out of the White House? How do you think that would poll?"

"I've got no idea what you're talking about, and I'd tell your committee the exact same thing under oath."

"Good," replied Carmichael as she threw two subpoenas down on his desk—one bearing his name and another with the president's. "I'll look forward to it. Consider yourselves served."

TWENTY-FOUR

DURHAM, ENGLAND

The Whitcombs lived in a small Victorian cottage just off the University of Durham's main campus. The drive had taken more than six hours, and though Harvath was tempted to try to steal a little sleep along the way, he couldn't risk it. They both needed to keep their eyes out for the police.

As Jillian pulled the tiny MG into the Whitcombs' gravel drive and killed the engine, Harvath glanced at her in the pale light spilling from the cottage. It was the first time he had really taken the opportunity to consider how attractive she was. Because the police would be looking for a woman with a tight bun, Harvath had suggested she let her hair down. It was a tremendous improvement. Her thick auburn tresses hung in loose curls around her shoulders, dramatically softening her features and causing her deep green eyes to stand out against her almost translucent white skin. Jillian Alcott now looked much less like the prim schoolmarm Harvath had pegged her for when he had first seen her leaving Abbey College.

When they reached the porch, Harvath peered through the curtains and noticed that despite the late hour, both of the Whitcombs were awake and waiting for them inside. Alcott didn't wait for a response. She simply knocked and let herself in.

Vanessa Whitcomb, a stylish woman in her mid-sixties with platinum chin-length hair and designer glasses, met them in the entryway. "Thank heavens you made it. Are you okay, my dear?" she asked as she threw her arms around Jillian and gave her a big hug. "Your message had us so worried. Then we saw the news. Do you know that there was a shooting in London? They're looking for a woman who could be your twin sister. The resemblance is uncanny."

"It's not uncanny," replied Alan Whitcomb, a taller, heavyset man with gray hair who appeared several years older than his wife. He looked Harvath up and down and with his eyes still locked on him said to Jillian, "It's you in that footage, isn't it? And this is the man who was there with you, the man with the gun. He's the one the police are looking for, isn't he?"

"Alan," Jillian implored, having come to a decision during their time together in the car that she might actually be able to trust Harvath. "It's not like that. Scot saved my life."

Whitcomb didn't know if he should believe her, and it was written all over his face.

"I mean it. If it wasn't for him, I wouldn't be standing here right now. I wouldn't be standing anywhere for that matter. You have to believe me."

Harvath stuck out his hand toward Whitcomb.

Alan looked at the hand warily, as if deciding how much bad luck might rub off on him from shaking it, and then gave in. "You two are in a lot of trouble."

Harvath smiled and said, "I've seen worse."

"Why do I get the feeling you're not exaggerating?"

"He's not," replied Jillian, who turned to Vanessa and said, "It's been a very long day. Do you mind if we come in?"

"Of course, dear. Of course," said Vanessa as she ushered them into the house, every square inch of which was covered with books. Even the dining room where they ended up was lined from floor to ceiling.

Satisfied, for the time being, that Harvath had not brought Jillian to their home against her will, Alan disappeared into the kitchen and returned several minutes later carrying a large plate of antipasto, along with a bottle of wine and four glasses. "It's not much, but I thought you might be hungry after your long drive."

"Starving, actually," replied Harvath. "Thank you."

As they ate, Jillian filled the Whitcombs in on what had happened at Harvey Nichols, who Scot Harvath was, and why he wanted to meet them.

The Whitcombs were deeply disturbed to hear about the disappearance of Emir Tokay, who had also been one of their students. Even so, Emir's situation didn't take them entirely by surprise. They had harbored reservations about many of the people associated with the Islamic Institute for Science and Technology for some time.

When their meal was finished, Harvath tactfully moved the conversation back to the reason he and Jillian had come. As it was a chilly evening, Vanessa suggested they move into the living room, where Alan built a small fire in the fireplace. Once they were all installed, Mrs. Whitcomb cut right to the heart of the matter. "Based on the materials we've seen that Jillian got from Emir, it would appear that what we are dealing with is most definitely a *pestilentiae manu factae*."

"I'm sorry," said Harvath, his mind not as sharp as he would have liked it to be. "A what?"

"It's Latin for man-made pestilence. That's where our initial investigation is pointing. In fact, this is one of the first times Alan and I have both agreed on something like this right off the bat."

"You don't normally agree?"

"We practice two different brands of science, so we often have different ways of interpreting things."

"I'm confused," replied Harvath as Alan poured a little more wine into his glass. "I thought both of you were Jillian's paleopathology professors."

"Not exactly," said Jillian. "I studied molecular

biology under Alan in the graduate program here, and then he recommended me for Vanessa's PhD program in paleopathology."

"The brightest and most apt pupil either of us ever had," replied Mr. Whitcomb.

"And I dare say we grew much closer to Jillian than any of our other students," added Vanessa. "Even if we'd had children of our own, she still would be very special to us."

"I don't doubt it," said Harvath as he began to better understand their relationship, especially Jillian's role as a surrogate daughter. "So what about Jillian's hypothesis?"

"I only know enough about Islamic science to know that I don't like it. Though I can't speak extensively to what relevance it may have to this case, I can speak to *pestilentiae manu factae* and say that they themselves have been used to affect society, political society in particular, for a long, long time."

Harvath's interest was definitely piqued. Taking a sip of wine, he asked, "How?"

"The term *pestilentiae manu factae* was coined by Seneca, the Roman philosopher and advisor to Emperor Nero, in the first century. It was meant to describe the deliberate transmission by mankind of plagues or pestilences. The ancients were very adept at manipulating their environment, and the history of the ancient world, particularly Roman civilization, is rife with stories of people who intentionally spread disease. In Rome, it often happened by pricking unsuspecting citizens with infected needles in order to undermine confidence in the empire's leadership and topple unpopular governments."

"Jillian said this mystery illness we're dealing with resembles an entry in some kind of ancient Machiavellian cookbook called the *Arthashastra*?"

"Yes, it does."

"I find it hard to believe that anybody in the modern world would be interested in something like that. Outside of academics, of course."

"You'd be surprised," responded Mrs. Whitcomb. "For some people, the *Arthashastra* still holds a lot of relevance, even to this day."

Harvath looked at her. "Like whom?"

"I can give you a perfect example. As recently as two years ago, the Indian Defense Ministry began funding a study of the *Arthashastra*, hoping to uncover what they referred to as 'secrets of effective stealth warfare,' including chem-bio weapons, which could be used in the present day against India's enemies."

"Such as Pakistan," said Harvath.

Vanessa nodded her head and continued on. "Military experts and scientists from Pune University looked into things like a recipe of wild boar's eyes and fireflies, which was supposed to give soldiers enhanced night vision capabilities. There was another recipe that called for shoes to be smeared with the fat of roasted pregnant camels or bird sperm along with the ashes of cremated children which would then give wearers the ability to march for hundreds of miles without getting tired."

"No offense, but that's ridiculous," replied Harvath, at the same time wondering if the United States should be looking at a possible connection between the illness and India.

"Is it that ridiculous?" asked Mrs. Whitcomb. "It wasn't so long ago that the American government was experimenting with mice and fruit fly genes in the hopes of developing some kind of magic potion that would allow its troops to go for weeks, even months, without sleeping."

"If they ever find a way to bottle that, I'm going to be the first one in line, but in all honesty this just seems too far-fetched."

"You are certainly entitled to your opinion, but it shows the lengths, even in this day and age, to which countries are willing to go to get the edge," replied Vanessa.

"True," said Harvath, "but how could a mere book have had so much power, even back then?"

Vanessa waited until Alan had topped off their glasses once more and then responded, "The *Arthashastra* was a very diabolical and much-feared corpus. It was infamous throughout half the world, just as its author had intended. Mere mention that a king was in possession of it was enough to make invading armies turn and flee. The knowledge contained within the *Arthashastra* represented enormous power, and we're all familiar with the saying 'Power corrupts, and absolute power corrupts absolutely'?"

Harvath nodded.

"Well, there were many kings and military leaders who couldn't help themselves. Once they got a taste of the power that lay inside the book, they were hungry for more. It spawned a bloodlust. Many kings who had access to the book quickly lost all respect for human life—regardless of whether those lives belonged to their enemies, or even members of their own family whom they suspected of plotting against them. They killed indiscriminately. But even the most bloodthirsty among them were still terrified by some recipes in the *Arthashastra*—recipes they dare not toy with. One such recipe, I believe, is playing a part in what we're talking about right now."

"What is it? What is the recipe?"

"It's for a very deadly poison, one of the only Western accounts of which comes from Alexander the Great during his campaign through Pakistan into Southeast Asia in the fourth century B.C. The campaign encountered something they had never seen before—a purple snake with a very short body and a head described as being as white as milk or snow. They observed the snake and didn't find it to be particularly aggressive, but when it did attack, it did so not with its fangs but rather by vomiting on its victim."

"*Vomiting?*" repeated Harvath.

Vanessa tilted her head as if to say, *Wait, there's more,* and kept speaking. "Once, let's say, one of your limbs was vomited upon, it would putrefy and you would die very quickly, although there was a small percentage of victims who were known to have died a slow and lingering death over several years, helplessly watching as their bodies wasted away with necrosis."

Harvath, who had just lost his taste for anything, set his wine glass down and said, "I don't see the connection."

"You will," replied Vanessa. "The breed of snake that Alexander described was completely unknown to science until the end of the nineteenth century. Paleopathologists and herpetologists alike believe that it is the *Azemiops feae*, a viper indigenous to China, Tibet, Myanmar, and Vietnam. There is still very little modern science actually knows about this animal.

"The author of the *Arthashastra*, on the other hand, knew quite a bit. The book cited the use of the snake's venom for several deadly weapons." Vanessa took a sip of her wine and said, "Now, here's where I think things will start getting interesting for you. Extracting the venom from this snake was a very complicated process. While still alive, it had to be suspended upside down over a big pot to catch all of the poison as it dripped out."

"Jesus," replied Harvath.

Alcott saw the look on his face and asked, "What is it?"

"The village in northern Iraq, Asalaam—where we believed the terrorists tested the virus."

"What about it?"

"In one building, people who had been infected with the illness were hung from the ceiling, apparently while still alive."

"It would appear that you've just learned something else," said Vanessa. "Anecdotal, of course, but potentially useful."

"Which is?"

"We may be looking at an illness that needs to grow *in vivo,* rather than *in vitro.*"

"You mean it has to be grown inside of people?"

"Maybe not every batch, but if this illness had been lying around for over two thousand years, whoever is behind it might have wanted to increase its potency by exposing it to the human immune system and letting it figure out how to beat it before setting it loose."

"Are you saying this thing can learn?" asked Harvath.

"All living things learn. Their survival depends on it. They must adapt and overcome. What doesn't kill us makes us stronger."

Harvath contemplated that possibility as Mrs. Whitcomb continued. "After dripping down, the snake's venom would then collect in the bottom of the pot and congeal into a yellowish gumlike substance. When the viper eventually died, another pot was placed beneath it to catch the watery serum as it drained from the carcass. It took about three days for those secretions to jell into a deep black substance. At this point, you had two completely different poisons that killed in two completely different ways. Neither of which was very pretty."

"How did they kill?"

"Well, the black substance was said to cause the lingering-style death over several years, while the yellowish poison derived from the pure venom—are you ready for this?"

Harvath nodded his head and leaned toward her.

"The pure venom concoction caused violent convulsions followed by the victim's brain turning to a black liquid that ran out his nasal passages," said Vanessa as she sat back in her chair and folded her arms across her chest as if to say *beat that*.

Harvath looked at Jillian, who simply nodded her head. "And there's nothing else that causes the brain to liquefy and run out the nose like that?" he asked.

"Not one single thing on this earth," replied Vanessa.

TWENTY-FIVE

As the facts tumbled around the fertile soil of Harvath's brain looking for places in which they could take root, he asked, "If this is about snake venom, why can't we use some sort of antivenin?"

"Because," said Alan Whitcomb, "we don't exactly know for sure what we're dealing with here. Improper use of antivenin can not only delay a patient's recovery, but more often than not, it can actually speed up the mortality process. Unfortunately, because of the rarity of this snake, there are no test kits or special instruments available for the conclusive identification of the presence of *Azemiops feae* venom. There is also no known antivenin."

Harvath was frustrated. What good was discussing what kind of venom they might be dealing with if there was no sure way to detect it and no sure way to treat it? "I don't understand," he replied as he looked at Alan. "Jillian said that she had come to *both* of you for help because she believes the illness is derived from something in antiquity. If you're not a paleopathologist, how do you fit into all of this?"

"Well, as Jillian said, my field is molecular biology—which encompasses both biophysics and biochemistry. In short, I study the building blocks of life, specifically something called aDNA. In case you're wondering, the *a* stands for *ancient*. Many people in my field like to refer to it as molecular archeology. You see, for a very long time the scientific powers that be didn't see a need for our expertise in helping examine human remains. The commonly held belief was that degradation of DNA occurred within hours or days after an individual's dcath.

"The tide turned in our favor, though, in the early eighties when a group of scientists reported finding a significant amount of viable genetic information in a four-thousand-year-old Egyptian mummy. A few years later the PCR, or polymerase chain reaction, technique was invented and voilà, molecular archeology was born. Ever since, it has been possible to extrapolate a lot of data from minimal traces of DNA."

"How minimal?"

"Theoretically, one needs only a single molecule for a positive result."

"Like *Jurassic Park*?" asked Harvath, slightly embarrassed that his contribution to the conversation was nothing more than a pop culture reference.

Not that anybody could fault him for reaching. The concepts they were discussing were very difficult to comprehend.

"*Jurassic Park* was a good story, but it seriously stretched the bounds of credibility. As far as we can tell, DNA probably can't last much more than ten thousand years and definitely not beyond one hundred thousand years, so the concept of finding viable DNA in a mosquito from over sixty-five million years ago gets a bit of a laugh from those of us in the scientific community."

"So *Jurassic Park*–style cloning couldn't be done then."

"We don't know that for sure. If we could isolate DNA that's on the order of ten to fifteen thousand years old, science might, and I stress *might*, be able to bring back Pleistocene era species, but it wouldn't be easy. A perfect example of the best-preserved Pleistocene species we've found to date would be woolly mammoths. In their case, though, we've only recovered short strands of mitochondrial DNA, not the nuclear DNA necessary for cloning. It's a very tricky business, all this cloning stuff, and one I'm glad I'm not involved in."

Vanessa could tell Harvath hadn't fully grasped what Mr. Whitcomb's specialty was, and so she tried to elucidate. "For lack of a better term, what Alan does is listen carefully to very old DNA. It talks to him."

"Kind of like *The Horse Whisperer*," joked Jillian.

Vanessa nodded her head and smiled. "Ancient DNA can tell us lots of things about how people lived, such as what their diets were comprised of and what their lives were like, but more importantly ancient DNA can often tell us more about how people died. This is Alan's primary area of expertise—the makeup, if you will, of ancient disease on a molecular level. By studying how the organic structure of diseases has changed over time, we can hopefully develop a better understanding of how to combat and maybe even overcome the diseases we face today."

"For instance," said Alan, "we're now learning that the smallpox pandemics of the Middle Ages, not the plague, mind you, but smallpox, left generations of people with a rare genetic defect that protects them against infection by HIV, the virus that causes AIDS. We estimate that approximately one percent of people descended from northern Europeans are virtually immune to HIV infection. And of that one percent, Swedes are the most likely to be protected. The Middle Ages may not exactly be *ancient* history, but this is the type of science that falls within my bailiwick."

"You see," added Jillian, "if we were able to locate the original illness, or organic matter from someone who was exposed to the original strain of this mystery illness and had survived, Alan might be able to tell us a lot about the disease itself."

"Could we cure it?"

"That's a pretty difficult question, but if we had either the original form of the disease itself or organic material from someone who had been exposed to it and survived, we'd have a fighting chance," said Alan.

For all intents and purposes, the Whitcombs were investigators, and while Harvath couldn't begin to fathom how they did what they did, he could relate to how they went about their search for answers. "So, let's assume for a moment that what killed the people in Asalaam is based on this purple viper venom. Where are the other symptoms coming from? I mean, when you see the people in the advanced stages of this illness, they look like attendees at a Count Dracula convention." Yet another pop culture reference, but it was the most apt description Harvath could think of.

"You raise an excellent point and one that has been bothering us since Jillian first presented this case to us," responded Mrs. Whitcomb. "We can only assume that this is either a derivation of *Azemiops feae* venom that we are not yet familiar with, or that it is being used in conjunction with something else. I have searched the *Arthashastra* from cover to cover, but can't find anything that would cause the full range of symptoms that we're seeing."

"What also doesn't make sense is why the illness only seems to affect non-Muslims. How could this thing have been specifically bioengineered to attack specific religions?" asked Harvath.

"I don't think that's what we're looking at," said Alan. "In my opinion, it must be something else, like contamination of food or water supplies—which has been a popular method of subduing an enemy since the dawn of time."

"As for the symptoms beyond the known effects of *Azemiops feae* venom," added Jillian, "what we may be seeing here is something the scientific community occasionally refers to as duplexing."

"What is duplexing?" replied Harvath.

"Duplexing is the combining of two illnesses to make them more lethal than they would be on their own. Australian researchers recently proved this theory quite inadvertently when they incorporated an immunoregulator gene into the mousepox virus. The result was a seriously enhanced, monster mousepox virus that was more virulent than anything they had ever seen before.

"The concern, especially among bioterrorism experts, is that this technique could be applied to other naturally occurring pathogens like smallpox or anthrax, which would dramatically increase their lethality."

"Let's just suppose for a second that what we're seeing here *is* a case of duplexing and that the snake venom is being added to something else in order to create a more potent bioweapon. I still don't understand how only non-Muslims were infected while none of the other indigenous people in that village seem to have been," said Harvath.

"The duplexing itself can be a one-two punch," replied Alan. "It could be that only people infected with substance A get sickened when exposed to substance B, and the resultant AB combination ends up being more lethal than A or B on their own."

"Or, as we discussed," said Jillian, "there could be some sort of immunization we're not aware of."

"What about the *Arthashastra*?" asked Harvath. "Does it talk about how the viper poison might be distributed?"

Vanessa nodded her head. "There are many suggested means of delivery—swabbing arrowheads, coating the edges of swords and spears—but one of the most interesting items I came across was a means by which it could be transformed into a rocklike substance, much like crack cocaine, and then ground into a fine powder. The toxic powder could then be left in fields for troops to walk through and pick up on their clothes, infection occurring through both skin contact and inhalation. The ancients were also very adept at employing toxic smoke to carry their chemical or biological agents across the battlefield. The key lay in the winds not turning and blowing the substance back on you.

"Modern-day troops certainly don't do much

hand-to-hand with enemies using edged weapons; I'm prone to lean toward the powder or smoke angle. But I could be wrong. We need more time to study this.

"Speaking of which," Vanessa continued as she looked at her watch, "it's getting late. I have a lot of e-mails yet to return, and I want to get an early start tomorrow. Why don't we call it a night? Both of the spare rooms are made up, so you two can stay here. We'll meet at my office in the morning, say, eight o'clock?"

"Eight o'clock sounds great," said Jillian, answering for both of them. "We'll be there."

When Harvath went to bed, he began to question what the hell he was doing. With all the scientific jargon still spinning in his head, he realized he was way out of his league and seriously doubted whether he was going to be able to pull this assignment off. An unfamiliar feeling gnawed at the edge of his thoughts, an insecurity that questioned what his life would be like if he was forced to resign and live out his days as an international pariah—the overaggressive American agent who beat the defenseless Iraqi in the al-Karim bazaar.

Harvath found it difficult to breathe and wondered if this was what a panic attack was like. Regardless of what it was, he didn't like it. It made him feel weak.

He forced his mind to turn to something else—something he could focus his energies on. As he did so, the face of Timothy Rayburn floated to the surface of his consciousness, and he struggled to understand what his involvement in all of this might be. Soon, Khalid Alomari's face took Rayburn's place, and as Harvath began to slip into the fathomless darkness of an exhausted sleep, he visualized killing both of them—as slowly and painfully as possible.

TWENTY-SIX

UNIVERSITY OF DURHAM
NEXT DAY

Vanessa Whitcomb's tiny third-floor office was much like the woman herself—compact, neat, and perfectly organized. A large mullioned window behind the desk, which normally would have fed bright sunlight into the room, instead framed thick black clouds outside which were threatening another downpour. Bookshelves took up every inch of wall space. A short Formica table, usually reserved for holding even more books, had been cleared off and set in the center of the office with two chairs taken from a nearby classroom. On top of the table were two neatly stacked piles of documents, each with a Post-it note designating which batch was for Harvath and which was for Jillian. In addition, Vanessa had laid out legal pads, ballpoint pens, and two green highlighters.

The trio wasted little time chatting. Vanessa was busy on her computer as Harvath jumped into the first article in his stack. It was a passage from the

Arthashastra, which talked about specific ways to injure an enemy. In particular, it focused on a host of recipes for powders and ointments made from things like animals, minerals, plants, and insects that could cause blindness, insanity, disease, and immediate or lingering death. It described a magical smoke that could kill all life forms as far as the wind would carry it, but what was most interesting to Harvath was the concept that the deadly poisons could be used in such as way as to contaminate "merchandise" like spices or clothing and then be surreptitiously sent to the enemy. He knew that the British had done the same thing when they gave blankets and handkerchiefs infected with smallpox to American Indians and made a note on his legal pad.

There was an examination of Sophocles' play *Philoctetes*, in which Hercules died in a Hydra-poisoned cloak, suffering many of the same symptoms as those associated with smallpox. Not only were the Greeks evidently aware that clothing and personal items could spread disease, but so were civilizations as far back as ancient Sumer in 1770 B.C.

Harvath then became acquainted with the word *fomites*, a term used by modern epidemiologists to describe items such as garments, bedclothes, cups, and toothbrushes, which were known to possess the capability to harbor infectious pathogens. Regulations prohibiting citizens from coming into contact with known fomites went back almost four thousand years. Harvath was beginning to wonder if some sort of fomite was responsible for infecting the non-Muslim population of Asalaam.

The articles Vanessa had printed out for him went on to describe other ingenious attempts at infecting an enemy, such as forcing him to camp or march through disease-infested swamps, as well as the use of "poison maidens"—seductresses with highly communicable infections, who were sent to do away with military leaders like Alexander the Great.

Just as Alan had mentioned, there were also discussions about the poisoning of an enemy's food and water supplies. Short of discovering how the victims had been infected, and by what, Harvath knew the only way to get to the bottom of the illness was for him and Jillian to discover who had kidnapped Emir Tokay. At this point, Tokay seemed to be the only one who could unravel the mystery.

Harvath read through more articles, one of which detailed how, just as today, surgeons and scientists in the ancient world rushed to keep up with advancements in biowarfare. They were constantly trying to discover and develop new antidotes, treatments, and inoculations against the wide range of poisons and toxins that were being used against their soldiers and fellow citizens.

The Roman writer, encyclopedist, and foremost authority on science in ancient Europe, Pliny the Elder, claimed that resin from giant fennel and a type of laurel known as purple spurge were effective at curing wounds caused by envenomed arrows. In fact, Pliny went so far as to claim that there was an antidote for every kind of snake venom except the asp—a highly venomous snake of the cobra family. Harvath wondered what category the modern world might eventually be forced to put *Azemiops feae* in.

The article went on to list the efforts of citizens of the ancient world to develop resistance to snake venoms. It was widely understood that people who lived in lands home to venomous creatures such as snakes and scorpions often possessed some degree of immunity against their poisons. Bites or stings from these creatures were often nothing more than mildly uncomfortable for their victims. In some cases, local inhabitants' resistance was thought to be so significant that their breath or saliva could cure venomous bites in anyone. According to Pliny, the *Psylli* tribesmen of North Africa were so resistant to snake bites and scorpion stings that their saliva was considered a highly effective antivenin, and they were drafted for every campaign the Romans ever conducted on the African continent.

Harvath was familiar with how antivenin was derived from antibodies to live snake venom, but he was amazed at how far people had gone over the centuries, often unsuccessfully, to immunize themselves against all sorts of toxins. Throughout the ancient world, people believed in ingesting small amounts of poison along with the appropriate antidotes to help develop full-scale immunity against whatever it was they wanted to avoid contracting.

Harvath wasn't surprised by the practice. Even today, many Southeast Asian nations still made their soldiers drink snake blood as part of their jungle training in the belief that they could become immune to snake venom.

The one thing the ancients did that seemed to make the most sense, and which was still relevant in today's world, was questioning captives about what kind of bioweapons their militaries were using and how to defend against them. That was the kind of scientific method Harvath could relate to—pure interrogation.

"I think you two should have a look at this," said Vanessa, interrupting Harvath's thoughts.

"What is it?" asked Jillian as she came around the desk.

Vanessa leaned back so they could see her computer screen. "It's a reply from someone on my paleopathology listserve. I put a question to the group asking if they'd noticed anyone taking any interest recently in our little purple viper and its connection to ancient biowarfare."

"And?"

"Someone sent me this," said Vanessa as she scrolled down to show the photo that had been included with the e-mail.

Harvath watched as an ancient piece of armor, a breastplate to be exact, came into view. The leather straps were surprisingly well preserved, as were the only somewhat rusted clasps, but that wasn't the piece's most remarkable feature. Right in the center of the breastplate was one of the most interesting crests he had ever seen. Carved in relief was the head of a snarling wolf with two snakes wrapped around its neck—and not just any kind of snakes. Their bodies were made up of brilliant purple stones, while their heads were fashioned from oblong pieces of what looked like creamy white marble.

"Who did the photo come from?"

"It was taken by the wife of one of the paleopathologists on my server list. Her name is Molly Davidson. She works with Sotheby's arms, armour, and militaria division in London."

"Sotheby's? As in the auction house?" asked Harvath.

"One and the same," replied Vanessa. "A new client wanted the value of this piece appraised for auction. Apparently, Molly has had a devil of a time placing it in any sort of historical context, and when her husband received my e-mail regarding *Azemiops feae,* he had Molly e-mail me the photo. They thought there might be a connection and maybe we could help each other out."

Harvath studied the image more closely. There was definitely a connection here. "Does she have any idea where the piece came from?"

"Originally? She thinks it might be from Carthage, probably around the third century B.C."

"But the Carthaginians were from North Africa in the area that's now Tunisia. How would they have known about *Azemiops feae*? You said it was indigenous only to China, Tibet, Myanmar, and Vietnam."

"I did say that and it's true," replied Vanessa. "*Azemiops feae* is not a reptile that ever would have been seen anywhere near Carthage."

"So what's the connection?"

"Let me answer your first question. Carthage was originally a colony founded by the Phoenicians, who were great seafarers. Tyre and Sidon, Carthage's two most renowned ports, are even mentioned in the Bible. In fact, the word *Bible* comes from the word *Byblos,* another Carthaginian port from which the majority of Egyptian papyrus was exported. Most early books were made from papyrus, and the word *Byblos* or *Biblos* became the ancient Greek word for 'book.'

"Just like their ancestors, the Carthaginians were incredibly adept merchants, skilled at buying and selling just about anything. Even more important, they were also extremely accomplished mariners and traded throughout the Mediterranean. Most scholars don't believe they traded any farther east than Greece, but it's possible. There are stories of Carthage foraying into Asia Minor and beyond via the monsoon trade route. If this is true, it's conceivable that they could have come across the *Arthashastra*, as well as *Azemiops feae* and the knowledge of how to extract its venom. This, of course, is all dependent upon whether or not they did in fact establish some sort of trade relations with ancient India."

"Even if they did. What does that have to do with this breastplate?"

"What do you know about the Carthaginian general Hannibal?"

An adept student of history, Harvath replied, "He was one of the most brilliant military strategists of the ancient world."

"Correct," said Vanessa, "and Hannibal was probably best known for his daring sneak attack on the burgeoning Roman Empire."

Harvath knew the story well. Hannibal had set out from Spain with approximately forty war elephants and, according to some reports, upwards of more than a hundred thousand soldiers to launch his attack. All that stood between him and his enemy were the towering peaks of the French-Italian Alps. But, by the time he made it over the top and descended into Italy's Po Valley, near present-day Turin, Hannibal had lost many of the elephants and more than half his men. While ambushes and skirmishes with marauding Gaulish tribes in present-day France and Spain accounted for a good amount of his losses, many more soldiers were lost to precipitous mountain paths, as well as numerous Alpine landslides and avalanches.

"Not so well known," continued Vanessa, "is a rumor that at the forefront of his forces, Hannibal posted members of his most elite guard. They were said to be transporting a weapon of unimaginable destruction—a weapon which would all but assure their victory over the Romans."

Despite his knowledge of the Carthaginian general, this was something Harvath had never heard before. "Let me guess, you think this weapon was biological or chemical in nature?"

"Since we're talking about Hannibal," interjected Jillian, "most definitely biological."

"Why?"

"Hannibal was one of history's earliest and biggest proponents of biological warfare."

Harvath was stunned. "He was? What kind of weapons are we talking about?"

"The best example I can think of, especially because it demonstrates his penchant for venomous snakes, happened sometime around 190 B.C. Severely outnumbered by the Pergamum navy, Hannibal sent men ashore to gather as many poisonous snakes as they could. They sealed them in clay jars, and when the Pergamum ships were within range, Hannibal's men catapulted the jars onto the enemy's decks. The jars shattered and sent the snakes in every direction, forcing the Pergamum sailors to abandon ship and giving Hannibal a decisive victory over a much larger foe.

"If Carthage had developed contact with India,

and from what we know of Hannibal's aggressive pursuit of biological weapons, this all might fit together quite logically," said Vanessa.

"Well, I see a very obvious connection here," replied Jillian. "Whoever wore this breastplate had to be wielding a weapon of some sort that used *Azemiops feae* venom."

"I agree with you about there being a connection," said Harvath, "but how can you tell that whoever was wearing the breastplate was using a weapon that incorporated our venom?"

Vanessa could see what Jillian was driving at. "Both the depiction of the wolf and the *Azemiops feae* vipers on the breastplate were meant as scare tactics. The ancients believed very strongly in the power of psychological warfare. Some were even known to carry banners into battle advertising the types of poison they would be using against their enemies."

"So you think the breastplates were an advertisement?"

"Most definitely," replied Vanessa, "and let me tell you why. Are you familiar with the Scythians and their archers?"

"Jillian mentioned them."

Vanessa drew a quick picture on her pad and turned it around so Harvath could see it. "The shafts of the Scythians' arrows were painstakingly painted to look like the snake from which the venom was taken. Even if one of these arrows simply landed next to you, the psychological effect would be enormous. It's hard to believe, from a modern perspective, but these techniques absolutely terrorized opposing armies.

"Tactics like these were in widespread use hundreds of years before Hannibal. It's reasonable to assume he would have employed them as well. He was an extremely cunning warrior. We have to imagine he would have used every advantage to overwhelm his enemies."

"I agree," replied Harvath. "Everything you're suggesting is completely in keeping with Hannibal's character. But where I'm getting lost is with this *weapon of unimaginable destruction.* I've read a lot about Carthage, but I've never seen anything like that before."

"Not many people have. That's probably because everything we know about Hannibal comes from his enemies, the Romans. Once the Romans conquered Carthage, they carried out something they called the Carthage solution. They absolutely decimated the country, sold most of its people into slavery, burned all of Carthage's libraries, and then, as a final assurance that the Carthaginians would never return to threaten Rome again, sowed every inch of soil with salt.

"When it comes to accounts of Hannibal and Carthage, Polybius was regarded as the most reliable of Roman historians, followed by Livy, who was born one hundred fifty years after Hannibal's march across the Alps. But what a lot of people don't know is that there were actually two Greeks, war correspondents if you will, who were embedded with Hannibal during his march on Rome. One was named Sosilos, who wrote Hannibal's biography, and another was named Silenus. Sosilos stuck to Hannibal like glue, studying the general's every move, while Silenus, who was proficient in several languages, spent a lot of time among Hannibal's various troops."

"And one of these Greek war correspondents made mention of this weapon of unimaginable destruction?"

"Yes, Silenus did, as well as the crest on the breastplates worn by Hannibal's elite guard."

"So where is this Silenus reference? Maybe we can learn something more from it?"

"That's the problem," said Vanessa. "No one in modern civilization has ever seen it. The original was said to have been lost when the Library of Alexandria was sacked in 640 A.D. by Muslims under the Caliph Umar I."

"Any idea how long the breastplate has been in Dr. Davidson's possession?"

"Her e-mail doesn't say, but the fact that she referred to it as coming from a *new* client makes me think it can't have been that long."

Harvath was quiet for several moments as he pondered what their next move should be.

"What are you thinking?" asked Jillian.

"I think we need to get a look at that breastplate."

"And what exactly do you expect to glean from it that a foremost expert in the field hasn't been able to already?"

Harvath went back to the small Formica table and began gathering up his notes. "May I take these with me?" he asked Vanessa, as he motioned to a reference book and the stack of documents she had printed out for him.

"Of course you may," she replied.

"Scot," interrupted Jillian. "You haven't answered my question."

Harvath accepted a rubber band from Vanessa to put around his stack of pages and said, "I don't believe in coincidences. There's some sort of connection here, and I want to find out who this new client of Sotheby's is."

"Dr. Davidson won't tell you that," responded Jillian. "When it comes to the anonymity of their clients, Sotheby's makes the Swiss banking establishment look loose-lipped."

"Well, we're going to have to figure out some way around that," stated Harvath.

"I'm sure if you had an official from Washington contact Sotheby's on your behalf they would—" began Vanessa, but she was interrupted by Harvath.

"I can't deal directly with Washington right now."

"Why not?"

"Trust me, it's a long story," answered Jillian.

Assembling his papers, Harvath looked at Vanessa and asked, "I'll want to contact Mrs. Davidson myself and set up a meeting. Do you have a phone number for her in London?"

Vanessa looked back at the e-mail on her computer screen and replied, "She's not in London. According to this, she's in France working out of Sotheby's Paris office."

On the street below, that was all Khalid Alomari needed to hear. Harvath should never have allowed the Alcott woman to abandon her briefcase at the London department store. Just as her e-mail correspondence with Emir Tokay had led him to London, so had the hard copies of her correspondence with the Whitcombs led him here to Durham. As he packed up his parabolic listening device and climbed back into his rental car, Alomari decided he could come back for the old couple later. Right now, though, he needed to get to Paris. Somehow, a knot from his past had come untied. Both the archeologist and the two Sherpas from the Alps were dead. He was sure of it. He had killed them himself, but the artifacts they had uncovered were now making their way onto the market. If he had any hope of collecting his money from the Scorpion and maintaining favor in his mentor's eyes, Alomari needed to tie up his loose ends.

As he drove away from the university campus, he wondered what it was going to be like to watch Scot Harvath die.

TWENTY-SEVEN

PARIS

It was easily the worst flight Scot Harvath had ever taken in his life. A severe storm had buffeted the plane all the way across the Channel to France. Even the most stoic of passengers had death grips on their armrests, and from where Harvath sat, he could see Jillian Alcott was on the edge of absolutely falling apart. For security, they had traveled separately on a budget carrier out of Newcastle International Airport. The British police would have been looking for a man and a woman traveling together.

Once they were on the ground in Paris and had cleared both passport control and customs, Harvath finally breathed a silent sigh of relief. While he was traveling under an assumed name and a false passport, Alcott had only her authentic passport. The fact that she had been able to make it through without being stopped meant that the police must have still only had shots of her face to go on and hadn't yet put a name to them. They had been lucky, but they couldn't hope for that luck to hold out forever. They needed to make some headway, fast.

Harvath normally liked Paris—the fashionable bistros of the Marais, the intimate cafés of St. Germain-des-Prés, the smoke-filled bars of the Latin Quarter. There was no city in the world like it, but as their taxi splashed through overflowing puddles on the way to Sotheby's, the city seemed alien to him. There was something different about it—something just didn't feel right. Maybe it was the lightning. Harvath had experienced all kinds of Parisian weather before, but never this.

The afternoon sky was as black as he'd ever seen it, punctuated only by the erratic stabs of lightning. By the time their cab pulled up in front of a rather derelict-looking façade in the Les Halles neighborhood, a light rain was already beginning to fall.

"Are we in the right place?" asked Jillian as she looked at the building.

Harvath double-checked the address on the piece of paper Vanessa Whitcomb had given them. "This is it," he said as he paid the driver and then held the door for Jillian as she got out of the cab.

The edifice they were standing in front of was supposedly a storage and restoration annex. Whatever it was, it was a far cry from the resplendent auction house Sotheby's had on the rue du Faubourg Saint Honoré—a stone's throw from the Paris Ritz. This shabby, rundown building, which leaned precariously to the left (like many in France), was easily three hundred years old. It looked as if it wouldn't take more than a seismic hiccup to bring it crashing to the ground.

As they ran up to the door, Harvath heard a loud roar and felt the sidewalk shake beneath their feet. It took a moment for him to realize that they were standing above one of the many Métro lines that crisscrossed at the nearby Châtelet Les Halles Métro station.

Émile Zola had called Les Halles the belly of Paris—a fitting sobriquet as it had long been the city's main food market, where citizens, restaurateurs, and merchants alike traveled on a daily basis to purchase the wide variety of staples that made up the Parisian diet. Les Halles was also practically the geographical hub of Paris as it lay just north of the Louvre—the point from which all of Paris's arrondissements, or administrative districts, spiraled out in clockwise fashion, much like the continuous ring of a conch shell.

Sotheby's three-story annex was bordered by some sort of warehouse to its left and a butcher shop to its right. Beneath the eaves of the butcher shop was a mural that Harvath thought he recognized. Before he could give it further thought, he heard a buzz as the lock on the annex door was released and he realized that Jillian was already on her way inside.

The interior of the annex was incredibly modern and bore little resemblance to the building's dilapidated exterior. The only hints of its age were the timeworn wooden floors, which had been polished until they shone like honey-colored mirrors. Rows of halogen lighting illuminated a variety of paintings and sculptures displayed against the stark white walls. A sleek, brushed aluminum reception desk sat in front of a frosted pane of glass complete with an etched Sotheby's crest. Behind the desk was an impeccably dressed young woman, flanked by two armed security guards in crisp black uniforms. The guards were not your everyday rent-a-cops either. Their eyes had an unmistakable *Don't fuck with me* look. Judging by the Heckler & Koch MP5s slung over their shoulders, the body armor strapped to their chests, and the .40-caliber Berettas at their sides, their employers took security of this annex very seriously. Harvath knew the price tag for all of the art stored in this facility had to have been astronomical.

Jillian announced herself to the secretary, while Harvath nodded pleasantly at the two powerful-looking security guards. Neither of them returned Harvath's greeting. They just stared, sizing him up.

"Oui, d'accord," said the attractive receptionist as she hung up the phone and turned to Jillian. "Dr. Davidson is officing on the top floor at the end of the corridor. I will need to see your identification, please."

Jillian and Harvath both proffered their passports. The receptionist copied down their information and then took digital photos of each of the visitors. Moments later a machine beneath her desk spat out two laminated badges. "If you would please be kind enough to pin these visitor passes to your clothing," said the woman to Jillian, "you may proceed upstairs."

They walked up a narrow, winding staircase together in silence. When they emerged onto the third floor, it looked as if they were stepping onto the set of a Three Musketeers movie.

The rough-hewn plank flooring was complemented by a series of wooden beams that lined the low ceiling. Eighteenth-century oil paintings of life at court, pastoral scenes, and a variety of still-life subjects hung in gilded frames and lined both sides of the hallway. Beneath the paintings was the occasional antique chair or collection of leather-bound books piled artistically on sturdy, farmhouse-style tables. If not for the modern halogen lighting, Harvath would have sworn they had traveled back in time.

Davidson's office was at the end of the hall on the right. When they arrived at the heavy wooden door, Harvath knocked, and a voice from inside instructed them to enter. Rising from behind her desk to greet her two guests, Dr. Molly Davidson was not at all what Harvath had expected.

She stood at least two inches taller than him, and with her long blond hair and deeply tanned skin looked more like a beach volleyball player than one of the world's foremost experts on ancient arms and armor.

"Dr. Davidson," said Jillian, offering her hand as they met her halfway across the room. "I'm Dr. Alcott, and this is Sam Guerin," she continued, using the alias Harvath was traveling under.

Except for its extraordinary length, the office, with its petite sink, sloping roof, and small windows set into the eaves, resembled a typical Parisian-style garret apartment, or *chambre de bonne* used for housing domestics. The long room looked as if it was predominantly used by Sotheby's for storage, but someone had shoved most of the office furniture and cardboard boxes toward a back corner to clear space for the arms and armor expert from London.

Workbenches with microscopes, illuminated magnifying glasses, and a host of other research tools lined the interior wall. A short row of bookcases ran along the opposite wall beneath the windows, while down the center of the room was an enormous worktable that had to be at least seven feet wide and twice as long. Half of the table was covered with a series of white sheets on top of which were the artifacts Dr. Davidson was currently investigating, including the breastplates.

Davidson shook both of their hands and then shut the door behind them. "I have to apologize for the modest quarters. This was the best they could do for me on such short notice."

Through the room's closed windows, Harvath could still hear the rush of whining Vespas and noisy diesel delivery trucks from the busy street below. He also could hear the muted melody of a song he thought he recognized. It seemed to be coming from inside the room itself. It took him a couple seconds of intent listening before he could place it. It was the seventies funk classic "Love Rollercoaster" by the Ohio Players. If Dr. Davidson had a stereo hidden somewhere, Harvath had to hand it to her, she had good taste.

"I also have to apologize for that noise," added Davidson. "The shop next door rented out their upstairs apartment to a young DJ who's home all day and gone all night. Half the time, I end up having to take my work home with me just to get away from it." Davidson walked down the length of the room, pounded on the far wall, and yelled in French for the music to be turned down. The command seemed to work, for seconds later it was barely audible.

Harvath, though, didn't much care for Dr. Davidson referring to music of the Ohio Players as noise.

"I'm sorry I couldn't tell you much more over the phone," continued Davidson as she crossed to a computer workstation and reached for a box that was inside one of the drawers. "But as I indicated, I was still waiting for a couple of key test results to come in this afternoon. We've only had the artifacts for a little over a week now."

"That's okay," replied Jillian. "Have the test results come back then?"

"Yes. I just got them."

"What can you tell us?" asked Harvath as he lifted an enormous battle hammer from the table and shifted it from hand to hand, gauging its weight.

"I can tell you," snapped Davidson as she brought a box of white cotton gloves from her drawer over to the table and handed a pair to Harvath, "that I would rather you not handle any of the artifacts without my permission, and even then, only whilst wearing proper gloves. These items are quite old and need to be treated with extreme care."

"Of course," said Harvath, setting the battle hammer down and pulling on the gloves. "I'm sorry."

Davidson looked slightly mollified. "I suppose there's no harm done. Out of everything you could have picked up, you selected the sturdiest item. It's quite an amazing piece. According to our testing, the hammer's head was forged from metals mined in North Africa, and the handle itself, interestingly enough, is made from Indian teak—the hardest wood known to mankind."

"Why is that interesting?" asked Harvath.

"It's interesting because we've dated the piece to the third century B.C., and it was believed that

Greece was the only common point of contact for those two cultures. India and North Africa were not known to be direct trading partners."

"Could the Greeks have traded in North African metals or Indian teak?" asked Jillian.

"I don't profess to be an expert on either culture," replied Davidson. "This is a bit out of my league. My expertise runs more along the lines of arms and armor of the Middle Ages and that sort of thing, but I suppose anything is possible. There's just as much about the ancient world that has been lost to us as has survived."

Jillian nodded her head in agreement as Harvath walked along the table and asked, "Are all of these items part of your investigation?"

"Yes. According to our client, all of the items were discovered together."

"And where was that?"

"We don't know," replied Davidson.

"You don't?" said Harvath, somewhat skeptical. "Why not?"

"Our client wouldn't say."

"That certainly can't make your job very easy," offered Jillian.

"No," answered Davidson. "In fact, it makes it a lot more difficult for us. But for some of our clients, items have been in their families for generations and there's the possibility that they are simply unaware of the actual origins."

And there's also the very likely possibility, thought

Harvath, *that more than a few of the artifacts that come your way are criminally tainted and their owners say as little as possible to help them remain under the radar.* Harvath had done his homework on the prestigious British auction house at a public internet terminal at Newcastle Airport before arriving in Paris. Sotheby's had been involved in numerous scandals over the years dealing with the sale of stolen artifacts, and they were anything but naïve when it came to the ways of the world. That said, they had built a reputation on protecting their clients' anonymity at all costs. He didn't relish the prospect of having to sweat Molly Davidson, but if it came down to it, he'd do it. For the time being, though, he wanted to know more about her research and what she'd been able to uncover. "You mentioned in your e-mail to Dr. Whitcomb that you thought the breastplates came from Carthage, around the third century B.C. Why is that?"

"I can trace the materials used in the breastplates to the region during that time," replied Davidson, "but it's the other artifacts discovered along with them that really push me in that direction."

"How so?"

"Well, we have coins from the Iberian Peninsula, spearheads from ancient Egypt, arrowheads from Gaul, even the stirrup of a Numidian cavalry soldier. It's a real hodgepodge. Based upon the weapons and armor, my hypothesis is that this collection belonged to either a military unit that was widely traveled throughout the ancient world, in and around the Mediterranean in particular, or—"

"It came from an army made up largely of mercenaries from in and around the Mediterranean," said Harvath. "Just like Hannibal's."

TWENTY-EIGHT

"I didn't know Hannibal's soldiers were mercenaries," said Jillian.

"According to one of the articles Vanessa had in her office," explained Harvath, "the Carthaginians were predominantly merchants. There was no need to maintain a large standing army when they could just hire out the best one money could buy whenever they needed it."

"Which would explain the presence of a Numidian cavalry soldier," said Davidson. "They were considered some of the best horsemen of their day."

"Normally each family in Carthage," continued Harvath, "committed at least one son to a life of military service, and like Hannibal, those men were extremely well trained. They were the ones who led Carthage's mercenary army."

Dr. Davidson watched Harvath as he walked over to the breastplates. "What can you tell us about these?" he asked.

"Not as much as I would like," responded Davidson. "That's what I was hoping you could help me with. Based on what my husband told me, your colleague at the University of Durham seems to believe that the snakes represent the *Azemiops feae* viper?"

"They do bear a great resemblance," replied Harvath, "but like you, we're feeling our way around this to a certain degree as well. What else can you tell us?"

Davidson pulled a pair of white cotton gloves from her pocket and put them on before handling the armor. "Each one of the plates shows exceptional workmanship, especially for the third century B.C. The Greeks were some of the best armorers of the period, but these surpass any of their work. Based on our metallurgical testing, we know the metal came from somewhere in North Africa."

"Just like the war hammer," said Harvath.

Davidson nodded her head.

"How about the purple stones used for the bodies of the snakes," he said. "What are they?"

"Amethysts," replied Davidson.

"Interesting," said Jillian. "Any special reason amethysts might have been chosen?"

"I wondered about that too and did a little research. Like most stones, amethysts have a long mythological history. Da Vinci believed they possessed incredible powers, not the least of which was the stone's ability to dissipate evil thoughts and quicken the intelligence."

"But we're talking about a time period way before da Vinci," interjected Harvath.

"Right," agreed Davidson. "That's why I went as far back as I could, to locate the first reference to amethysts having any sort of special power. After all, it wasn't unusual for ancient armies to employ specific talismans to give them particular advantages over their enemies in battle."

Jillian couldn't help but anxiously coax the woman forward. "And you found a connection of some sort?"

"Sort of. Ancient Greek mythology claims that Dionysus, the god of wine, had been insulted by a passing mortal and swore that he would take revenge on the next one that came his way. He conjured up a team of ferocious tigers just as a beautiful young maiden was approaching. The maiden's name was Amethyst, and she was on her way to pay tribute to the goddess Artemis. As Dionysus released the tigers, Artemis turned Amethyst into a statue of pure crystalline to protect her from the tigers' claws. Upon seeing the beautiful statue, Dionysus wept wine-filled tears of regret, which stained the statue a deep shade of purple.

"From that moment on, the amethyst stone was known to hold significant protective properties. Apparently, as the myth recounts, amethysts could even protect you from the wrath of the gods themselves."

"So knowing that the Carthaginians had extensive contact with the Greeks, it's possible they might have been familiar with this myth?" asked Harvath.

"Most likely," replied Davidson. "We know that a tremendous amount of religious practices in the ancient world were actually borrowed from the Greeks."

"Do you have any idea where these particular amethysts came from?" Scot asked as he took a closer look at one of the breastplates.

"Most of us in the modern world automatically think of South America when we think of amethysts. Places like Brazil, Uruguay, Bolivia, and Argentina come to mind, but most of the amethysts in the ancient world actually came from Africa."

Yet another African connection, Harvath thought to himself, though at this point he needed no further convincing that the artifacts were connected to Hannibal. "What about the stones used for each of the snakes' heads?"

"Rather unimpressive milk opals. They can be found all over the world."

"Any significance there?"

"I don't know, though they certainly aren't being used as talismans in this instance."

Harvath tilted the breastplate he was holding in the light. "Why not?"

"Amethysts," said Davidson, "are revered for offering protection. But opals, on the other hand, are traditionally known to bring bad luck. The combination of the two stones seems to send a mixed message. *Protect me, yet bring me bad luck.*"

"Or from a soldier's perspective," offered Jillian, "they could mean *Protect me from the bad luck I am bringing upon my enemy*."

Davidson set her breastplate down thoughtfully. "That's also a possibility, but if these are *Azemiops feae* vipers, why would the Carthaginians depict them on their breastplates at all? What's the purpose? From what my husband tells me, *Azemiops feae* is an East Asian viper. Armies in the Mediterranean never would have seen one, much less have known how deadly they were. If these breastplates were intended to inflict some sort of psychological damage, why not depict cobras, which were much feared and much better known? Or better yet, since we're very likely talking about the Carthaginians here, why not use obviously ferocious creatures from their part of the world like crocodiles, rhinos, or even lions?"

"If these are in fact representations of *Azemiops feae* vipers," replied Jillian, "then they must have been very significant to the men who were wearing the breastplates."

"I'd have to concur," replied Davidson. "But significant how? And why?"

Jillian looked up from the table and caught the

look in Harvath's eye. They were both thinking the same thing. It was time to get to the bottom of things. "Dr. Davidson, we need to know who sent you these artifacts," said Jillian.

"Why?" she asked incredulously.

"Because people's lives may depend on it," stated Harvath.

"People's lives may depend on a table full of military relics over two thousand years old?"

"This goes much deeper than military relics," said Jillian.

"How?"

"We're not at liberty to share that with you."

"Mr. Guerin," said Davidson as she used Harvath's alias, "don't insult my intelligence. Any lives concerned with what I am doing here have long since passed. If you'd like to tell me the real reason we're talking, maybe then we can help each other out. Are you suggesting that these relics are connected to some sort of crime? If so, I'd like to know how a respected paleopathologist like Vanessa Whitcomb fits into all of this."

"We can appreciate that you have questions of your own," said Jillian as she tried to take control of the conversation and prevent things from turning too adversarial. She was a scientist herself and understood the way Davidson's mind worked. She wouldn't respond well to intimidation, and Harvath looked all too ready to jump into his "bad cop" uniform. It was obvious what her role was going to have to be. "We, on the other hand, need you to appreciate that we're limited in what we can tell you."

Davidson walked over to her desk, folded her arms across her chest, and sat down on its edge. She said, "Why don't you start with what you *can* tell me. Because until you do, I'm not sharing anything else."

"Dr. Davidson, you're obviously an intelligent woman—" began Harvath.

"Don't try to flatter me, Mr. Guerin," she shot back.

"Believe me, flattery is the least of my intentions," he responded. "I'm trying to be nice, so why don't you cooperate and listen to what I have to say? Your employer, Sotheby's, has been involved in multiple cases of fraud and trafficking in stolen and otherwise illegally tainted merchandise over the years."

"How dare you?" snapped Davidson. "Sotheby's has never knowingly participated in any illegal activity whatsoever."

"Dr. Davidson, not only do I not care, but the general public at large is not going to care either when this story breaks. I guarantee you it will be the end of Sotheby's. A stolen painting, a forged diary, they're nothing in this day and age compared with colluding and providing material aid to terrorists."

It was preposterous. Davidson couldn't believe her ears. "Terrorists? That's how they're making their money now, by trafficking in relics over two thousand years old? Are you serious?" she laughed.

"Deadly serious," replied Harvath.

"I don't think you are. If you were, you wouldn't be speaking to me. You'd be speaking to someone else here with a lot more power than I have."

"You're the one studying these for the client," said Harvath.

"Mr. Guerin, you're not only wasting your time, you're wasting mine, and I want you to leave."

Harvath was about to give it to Davidson with both barrels when Jillian motioned for him to back off. Shaking his head in exasperation, Harvath walked toward the other end of the room and the faint music bleeding through the wall.

"Dr. Davidson," said Jillian, "I can assure you this is a very serious matter. We need to know where these artifacts were discovered and who found them. In answer to your previous question, yes, we believe they are connected to a major international crime."

"So you lied then. You're not a paleopathologist at all," said Davidson, breaking her silence. "What are you? Interpol?"

"Dr. Davidson, I didn't lie to you. I *am* a paleopathologist, but this case is very complicated. Please. We need your help. You have to tell us who sent these artifacts to you."

"Let me disabuse you of that notion right now," snapped Davidson as she rose from her stool. "Unless you want to make all of this very official, I don't have to tell you anything. It is strict Sotheby's policy not to divulge the names or any other personal information about our clients. If you have reason to believe that these artifacts or the person or persons who supplied them to us are tied to some sort of criminal activity, then I suggest you speak with a local magistrate. Unless this company is properly served with the appropriate legal paperwork, we will give you nothing."

"You're asking us to start legal proceedings? Through the French legal system no less? Do you know how long that will take?" beseeched Jillian.

"That's not my problem."

"Dr. Davidson, I am imploring you—"

"What the hell is he doing?" demanded Davidson, standing up.

"Cutting through the red tape," stated Harvath, who had walked back to the head of the table and was now rifling through a stack of file folders. "We don't have time to wait for French or any other jurisprudence. We need this information now."

"I'm calling security," said Davidson as she reached for her phone.

"Stop her," Harvath ordered Jillian.

Alcott couldn't believe how rapidly things were deteriorating. "Let's just all calm down here."

Harvath had no intention of calming down. In the world Davidson and Alcott lived in, people might patiently sit back and move at a snail's pace dictated by science, but that wasn't his world. In Harvath's world, either you set the pace or somebody else set it for you. Too many people were depending on him to get to the bottom of things as quickly as possible. Jillian had had her chance and failed. Now they were going to do things his way.

Harvath dropped the files he was looking at, came around the table, and got to Davidson just as she began speaking. He yanked the phone's cord from the wall and said to her, "I always try my best to be nice until it's time not to be nice, and guess what time it is now?"

Davidson fixed him with an icy stare. "What is it you want?"

"You know what I want," said Harvath as he moved into her personal space, hoping to increase the intimidation factor. He didn't like having to play hardball with a woman, but she wasn't leaving him much choice. "I want all of the information you have on whoever sent you these artifacts, and I want it now."

Davidson pointed to the pile of folders spilled on the floor and replied, "It's down there in one of those."

She was lying, and the lie was accompanied by a not so subtle shift of Davidson's weight from one foot to the other. She wasn't trying to get away—she was trying to obscure something from Harvath's vision. *What was it?* Then Harvath figured it out. *Her computer.*

"I don't suppose you want to make this easy for me?" he asked.

Davidson just glared at him.

"Okay, have it your way," said Harvath as he pulled her chair out for her. "Take a seat." The woman refused, and Harvath had no choice but to physically encourage her. The move scared her more than anything else, and she immediately dropped down in front of her computer. Harvath kept one hand clamped around her upper arm just in case there was any resistance. Little did he know that the resistance was going to come flying through the door at him like a Mack truck.

Before he could get Davidson to open any of her computer files, the office door exploded inward, and a powerful, black-clad, uniformed body came sailing across the desk toward him. Harvath let go of Davidson's forearm just in time to raise his hands to protect his face. The security guard crashed into him and sent him tumbling over backward. His head smacked against the hardwood floor, and before he could clear the stars from his eyes, the security guard began pounding on him. Despite the stars, Harvath's instincts immediately kicked in.

In two quick moves, he had gotten the better of his attacker and was on top of him, holding the man's head and neck in a hammerlock. There was only one problem—Harvath had forgotten that the man had a partner.

Before he could free one of his arms to parry the

blow away, the second security guard had landed a searing kick to his ribs. Harvath thought for a fraction of a second that he might be able to hold it in, but inevitably the air rushed from his lungs. His hammerlock collapsed, and his body crumpled to the floor as it heaved for oxygen. Somewhere off in the distance, he thought he heard Jillian scream as a round was chambered into an MP5 and its muzzle was pressed against the side of his head.

TWENTY-NINE

CAPITOL GRILLE
WASHINGTON, DC

Helen Remington Carmichael weaved her way through the crowded steak house and found DNC chairman Russell Mercer at his usual table behind a large porterhouse and an even larger glass of Archery Summit Pinot Noir. "Helen," said the portly man as he rose to meet his unexpected guest. "How nice to see you."

"Cut the crap, Russ. I've been trying to get hold of you for two goddamn days."

"I've been a bit busy."

"I can see that," said Carmichael as she looked at the three attractive young women seated with him. "Let me guess. *Polling*?"

Mercer could smell a showdown coming, and the last thing he wanted was witnesses. "My tab should still be open at the bar," he said as he stood and politely shooed the women from his booth. "I'll let you know as soon as we're done here."

Once they had filed past, Carmichael sat down

and snapped her fingers at the nearest waiter. "Ketel One martini up, very dirty with lots of olives." When the waiter had disappeared, Carmichael focused her ire back on Mercer. "Judging by the looks of your companions, they charge by the hour, so I'll make this short."

"I'm not going to even dignify that remark with a response," replied the DNC chairman.

"Well, let's see what you will dignify. I heard you had a very candid meeting at the White House with Chuck Anderson."

"Yes, I did."

"And you told him I wouldn't be on the Democratic ticket?"

"That's what I told him."

"How dare you?" she hissed.

Mercer leaned forward over the table, and his eyes bored right into hers. "Listen to me, Helen, and listen good. Your ball-busting routine might have charmed the voters of Pennsylvania, but you're in the big leagues now, and we play by a different set of rules here. If you want the party's nomination, you've gotta damn well earn it. You don't just sashay up to my table, insult my guests, and demand I hand it to you on a silver platter."

Carmichael was indignant. "And you don't control the party, Russ. The ticket needs a strong vice-presidential candidate, and there isn't anyone else out there as strong as I am."

"You think so?" replied Mercer. "I happen to

think Senator Koda of Maine could do a lot to help the ticket."

"And if assholes had wings, this whole fucking town would be an airport," she replied, rolling her eyes. "Listen, Koda may be good, but I'm better, and you damn well know it."

"So what? You haven't earned it."

"*Earned it?* How dare you say I haven't earned it? I've busted my ass for the party."

"And it hasn't gone unnoticed."

"Then how can you say I haven't earned a spot on the ticket?"

"You haven't earned your stripes," replied Mercer as he held out his sleeve and patted his forearm. "Nobody gives a shit what you've done for the state of Pennsylvania. If it weren't for your husband, you wouldn't have that job in the first place. What's more, you've got a shitty public image. Half of voting Americans, hell, half of your own constituents think you're a raging bull dyke, and the other half think the only reason you're in office is to help facilitate your husband's business deals. It won't sell. Not where we need it the most."

Carmichael waited for the waiter to set down her martini and back away from the table before responding. "My own people have been encouraging me to work on my public image, and I'll admit I've been slow to respond, but I can change that. I'll even bring in outside consultants if I have to. Whatever it takes, I'll do it. You want me to soften things up? Consider it done. Just don't scratch me off the list of possible contenders for the ticket."

The woman was amazing. She was an absolute chameleon. One minute she could be the Beltway's biggest brass-balled bitch, and the next she was turning in a "Please, sir, may I have some more?" performance worthy of the best Dickens novel. Mercer, though, had seen it all before. Political ambition came in a million shapes and styles. If Helen Carmichael wanted the Democratic nomination so bad, she was going to have to work for it, and Mercer knew just how to make her do it. Regardless of whether they put her on the ticket or not, if the DNC kept her focused, Senator Carmichael could broadside the Republicans so bad there was no way President Rutledge's campaign would be able to bail water fast enough.

Mercer settled back into the booth, reached for his wineglass, and said, "Maybe we can work something out. Tell me, how are your hearings progressing?"

THIRTY

Hotel Gare du Nord
Paris

Tell me some more about Hannibal and his love of biological weapons," said Harvath, unbuttoning his shirt as Jillian emptied the ice bucket on top of the mini bar into a plastic bag and handed it to him.

"First things first," she replied. "Let me take a look at your ribs."

Harvath pulled back his shirt so Jillian could see the softball-sized bruise that was setting up shop along his left side.

"Does anything feel broken?" she asked as she reached her hand out toward his side.

"Hold on a second," said Harvath as he caught her hand. "You're a doctor of paleopathology, not medicine."

"For your information, I rode ambulances to help pay for school and doubled as a nurse's assistant on several archeological digs during my summers off from Durham."

"Imagine my luck," said Harvath as Jillian's fingers slid across his flesh. "Any of your patients actually live?"

"Very funny," she said, applying pressure to an obviously sensitive part of the bruise. "This looks tender."

Harvath sucked in a painful breath as Jillian continued, "You know, this all could have been avoided if you hadn't lost your head."

"I lost my head?" said Harvath. "Is that what you think happened?"

"I've seen it before," she said as she continued probing for broken bones. "It's a typical male reaction. You're the hammer, and any problems you encounter in life are nothing more than nails."

"Hammer this, lady," said Harvath as he stood up from the bed and put his shirt back on. Even if he had managed to crack a rib or two, Jillian Alcott wouldn't be able to tell just by touching him. And broken or not, there was nothing she could do for him. His ribs would just have to heal on their own.

"Sit back down," ordered Jillian. "I'm not done examining you yet."

"If you want to see any more," he replied, walking over to the mini bar to retrieve a small bottle of Moskovskaya vodka, "you're going to have to buy me dinner and tell me you love me first."

Jillian smiled. "That's not what I meant."

"I know what you meant," he said as he poured

the vodka into a glass and looked around for some ice. "Let's get back to Hannibal."

Jillian picked the ice pack up off the bed and threw it to him. Harvath untied the bag, removed a couple of cubes, and dropped them into his glass. "I'm all ears."

"There isn't much else to add. Like Vanessa said, what we know about Hannibal comes to us mostly from Roman accounts, and there aren't many. We do know that he was extremely brilliant and would go to any lengths to get the ultimate edge. There was no one else like him."

"I'll drink to that," said Harvath as he took a sip of Moskovskaya to kill the pain in his side. As he set his drink on the nightstand he asked, "What about the India connection? Is it possible Hannibal had contact with them?"

"There's no arguing with those breastplates. Those are *Azemiops feae* vipers, no doubt about it."

"How does the wolf image fit in?"

"Wolves were considered very fierce, very ferocious animals. They were also a symbol of Rome. Hannibal might have been attempting to steal some of the Romans' thunder by using their symbol in that way."

"Possibly," said Harvath, though he had a feeling that theory was off the mark.

"What we do know," said Alcott, "is that the weapon itself had to have been the most frightening thing he had in his arsenal. That's why the *Azemiops feae* were depicted on the breastplates. He would have wanted everyone, especially his soldiers, to be constantly aware of the weapon they were carrying."

"Are you saying that replicating poisonous snakes on arrow shafts and depicting *Azemiops feae* vipers on breastplates could be used to scare the enemy *and* embolden your own troops at the same time?"

"Exactly," replied Alcott. "Once the snake plan had been announced, Hannibal's navy felt confident they couldn't lose, even in the face of a much mightier opponent."

Harvath sorted through the logic, trying to tie everything together. "So let's assume that Hannibal got his hands on a copy of the *Arthashastra*."

"Which would have been no small feat at the time. It was a pretty powerful book, and I doubt they were just giving it away on street corners, especially to nations that could wind up as potential enemies at some point down the road."

"I'll put my faith in Hannibal. He was a pretty crafty guy, but whether he bought the *Arthashastra*, stole it, or it was given to him doesn't matter. Let's just say he got a copy of it."

"Okay."

"Then he got hold of someone to translate it for him. Maybe he even brought some enterprising Indian scientist or soldier to the Mediterranean to help out with it. He could have even sent teams back and forth to India to get the snakes they needed, since *Azemiops feae* wasn't native to the Greco-Roman world, and then used members of the Psylli tribe to handle them and extract the venom."

"All possible," replied Jillian, "but Vanessa said she'd been through the entire *Arthashastra* and couldn't find a recipe that matches up with all the symptoms seen in Asalaam."

"I know," said Harvath, "but what if the Carthaginians only used the *Arthashastra* as a base or a jumping-off point of some sort? What if they came up with an *Azemiops feae* hybrid? What if they duplexed it and came up with an illness nobody had ever seen before?"

"Also possible," said Jillian as she paused to think about it, "but where does that leave us? We have no idea where all of those artifacts came from, much less who gave them to Sotheby's in the first place, and nothing short of a court order or official government request is going to get that auction house to open their doors again for us."

"Suppose we didn't need them to actually *open* their doors for us?" suggested Harvath as he reapplied the ice pack to the bruise on his side.

It didn't take a genius to intuit what Harvath was contemplating. Jillian sensed he wasn't the type to give up easily. "We were lucky enough to get out of there once without being arrested," she said. "I don't think the odds will be very heavily in our favor for a second go-around. Especially if you're contemplating breaking in."

Harvath smiled.

She had pegged him correctly. He was definitely a hammer.

"I think you're wrong about today," continued Harvath. "There was no way they were going to arrest us. Davidson can't be sure the artifacts didn't come from an illegitimate source, and she's wary of bad press."

"Even so, how do you propose we get back inside? From the security I saw, it has to be next to impossible."

"Magic," replied Harvath with a smile.

"What kind of magic?"

"We're going to walk through walls."

THIRTY-ONE

When Jillian came down to the Hotel Gare du Nord's lobby, she was dressed in the secondhand clothes Harvath had sent up to her room earlier in the evening. She couldn't figure out if he'd incorrectly guessed her sizes or if he had purchased the black turtleneck and black jeans slightly snug on purpose. Regardless of what his intentions had been, with the battered, secondhand leather jacket she felt that she looked perfectly Parisian. She was also glad to have the warm clothes, as a second storm front had moved in and the rainy night air was bitterly cold.

At exactly midnight, Harvath appeared in the lobby and motioned for her to follow him. Outside on the street, he hurried her through the rain to a tiny, windowless van. He had left it running, and though the wheezing heater was cranked all the way up, its effect was barely noticeable.

"How do the clothes fit?" he asked as they pulled away from the curb.

"Strangely enough," replied Jillian, "the boots are a perfect fit, but everything else is a little tight."

Harvath glanced over at her before turning right onto the boulevard de Magenta and said, "No they're not. They're just right."

Jillian should have known better. Anyone who could nail her shoe size after having only spent two days with her certainly knew what he was doing with everything else. "Where'd they come from?"

The tires of the tiny van wobbled as they splashed through puddles making their way south. "I got them at a flea market."

"And the van?"

"I know a guy who knows a guy."

Jillian looked into the cargo area behind their seats. "And I assume everything in back is from—"

"The same guy," said Harvath, hanging a right onto the boulevard de Strasbourg and speeding up in order to make the light at the next corner.

"So what is all that stuff?"

"Skeleton keys."

"Skeleton keys?" repeated Jillian, looking behind her at the duffel bag and two plastic Storm-brand cases. "You've got to be kidding me."

"I couldn't be more serious. Trust me. You'll see."

Ten minutes later, they had threaded their way through the bustling Les Halles neighborhood and had managed to find a parking space around the corner from the Sotheby's annex. Walking around to the back of the van, Harvath opened the double doors and leaned inside to get his head out of the rain. He slid the two Storm cases and heavy black duffel toward him, opened them, and checked their contents one last time.

"I thought you said you had a set of skeleton keys in there," said Jillian, who had darted behind the van and was now leaning inside next to him.

"I do," replied Harvath as he withdrew a small sledgehammer about a foot long from the duffel. "This one unlocks the downstairs door."

Jillian looked at him as if he was nuts. "You realize that when I said you were like a hammer and that you approached all your problems like nails, I was speaking metaphorically, right?"

Harvath ignored her and tucked the sledgehammer beneath his coat.

"I'm serious," said Jillian.

"I know."

"So tell me what your real plan is."

"I told you. I'm going to use my skeleton key to open the downstairs door."

"What about the security guards?"

Harvath zipped up the duffel and then slung it over his shoulder. He grabbed the larger of the two Storm cases and indicated that Jillian should take the other. As he closed the rear doors of the van, he said, "If we do this right, they won't have any idea what we're up to."

"And if we don't do this right?"

"Then I hope your tight jeans don't prevent you from running."

"That's a good one," said Jillian. "You sure know how to kid a girl."

"Who's kidding?" replied Harvath as he set off down the block.

Jillian peppered him with questions the entire way, but Harvath didn't feel like talking. Despite his leather jacket, the nylon straps of the overweight duffel were cutting into his shoulder. He couldn't wait to finally set it down. Thankfully, the heavy Storm case had built-in casters that allowed it to be dragged behind him.

For her part, as much as Jillian wanted to trust Harvath, she couldn't help feeling he was acting out of desperation. Smashing through the glass front doors of the Sotheby's annex with a sledgehammer was the most insane plan she could ever imagine. They wouldn't make it more than five feet before the armed guards would be on them. She was just about to say as much when Harvath pulled up three doors short of the annex. Ducking into a small alcove, he set his heavy duffel down, leaned his Storm case against the wall, and produced a pack of cigarettes and a lighter. "Here," he said as he offered them to her.

"I don't smoke."

"Neither do I, but that's not the point."

"Then what is?"

"Everybody in Paris smokes."

"So?"

Harvath turned the pack over, tapped out a cigarette, and handed it to her. "So, standing around with nothing to do looks suspicious."

Jillian didn't see the sense in his logic. "But it's okay to stand around with nothing to do as long as you have a cigarette in your mouth?"

"In Paris it is," replied Harvath as he raised the lighter for her.

"You know, I quit smoking these things about three years ago," said Jillian as she bent over the flame. When she had it lit, she leaned back and took a deep, long drag. She felt that old familiar feeling as the smoke filled her lungs and the nicotine began to race through her bloodstream. Though she knew it was terrible, the cigarette tasted fabulous. It was like coming home. "What I do for queen and country," she sighed.

Harvath hated cigarettes. "I didn't say you actually had to smoke it, you know."

"What am I supposed to do with it?"

"Fake it. Don't inhale."

"Too late now," she replied as she took another hit. The damage was already done. "While I'm standing here throwing away three years of willpower and hard work, what are you supposed to be doing?" she asked.

Harvath tucked his hands in his coat pockets, rocked back and forth on his heels, and nonchalantly said, "Me? I'm just waiting for the Métro."

"Waiting for the bloody Métro? You're aware that it runs below ground in these parts?"

"Quite aware," replied Harvath as he continued rocking.

Jillian had no idea what to make of him. "If you see the bus for Piccadilly coming, you'll be a dear and let me know, won't you?"

"No problem."

Jillian stepped to the edge of the alcove and watched as the heavy rain pounded the roofs of cars parked up and down the street. There were flashes of lightning accompanied by peals of thunder somewhere off in the distance. Jillian counted the seconds between them. The storm was getting closer, and as it did, her unease grew. As she stared out into the rainy street, her mind was taken back to the night she had lost both her parents and her grandmother.

"The French call it the *danse macabre*," said Harvath, figuring she was staring at the disturbing mural under the eaves of the building across the street. "It means—"

"Dance of death," she replied as Harvath stepped out of the shadows of the alcove to join her for a moment.

"Do you know it?" he asked.

"Of course. It's probably one of the single most popular allegorical art themes in the paleopathology field. People in the fourteenth and fifteenth centuries believed that skeletons rose from their graves to seduce the living to join them in a mysterious dance that ended in death. From the pope on down, no one was immune. The murals served as a *memento mori*."

"What's a *memento mori*?"

"Simply put, it's a reminder that no matter what we do in life, we're all going to die. It supposedly comes from Imperial Rome when victorious generals had their triumphal processions. A slave was said to have accompanied each general as he passed through the streets repeating the chant, 'Remember thou art mortal.' Kind of a reality check, I guess."

"Interesting. Do you know where the first mural was painted?"

Jillian looked at him and said, "Germany. They refer to it as the *Totentanz*. It depicted a festival of the living and the dead."

"Actually," replied Harvath, "the first depiction of the *danse macabre* was painted three blocks from here in 1424, in the Church of the Holy Innocents."

"How do you know that?"

"I've been to Paris a couple of times. I like to learn about the history of the places I visit."

"You're sure that the first *danse macabre* was painted here?"

"I double-checked it this afternoon," replied Harvath, a flash of lightning illuminating his face.

Jillian counted the seconds in her head until the thunder. "I suppose then that it must have something to do with what we're doing here?"

"In a way."

"How so?"

The ground beneath them began to rumble with the sound of an approaching Métro. "I'll tell you in a minute," replied Harvath as he removed the sledgehammer from beneath his jacket. "Right now, we've got a train to catch."

THIRTY-TWO

While Jillian kept an eye on the street, Harvath used the noise of the Métro to cover the three full swings of the hammer it took for the heavy wooden door, with its thick metal lock, to splinter and give way. The door to the apartment upstairs proved much easier to get through.

As Harvath set up his gear, he explained to Jillian that on their first trip to Sotheby's today, he noticed that this building had the same *danse macabre* under the eaves as the one across the street. It reminded him of a story he had once read about what the French did with the bodies from the Holy Innocents cemetery when it got too full and they needed to make room for new arrivals.

Originally, they placed them in charnel houses adjacent to the church, but they didn't have enough space to keep up with demand. So they started quietly buying up buildings in the neighborhood to use as undisclosed charnel houses.

Sometimes they'd wall the bodies up and rent out the apartments to help recoup some of their costs. Sometimes they'd place the bodies on the top two floors and rent the floors beneath. Everything was going just fine until the walls and floors began rotting away and dead bodies started falling into people's living rooms.

Even building to building, corpses were falling through the walls. At this point, Paris caught a break. They had pretty much stopped mining stone under the Right Bank because they were afraid that all of the tunnels had weakened it close to the point of collapse. It was the perfect place to transfer the contents of the charnel houses. They hauled the dead out in the dark of night by the wagonload, stacked their skulls and bones throughout the tunnels, and voilà, the Paris catacombs were born.

Seeing the murals earlier that day had gotten him thinking. He tracked down the club where the DJ who lived in the apartment worked and learned that the man would be working a rave in Calais for the next two days. After that, he did a little research at the Bibliothèque Nationale and learned that all of the buildings on this block were at least several centuries old. The wall that separated the apartment from what they wanted in Molly Davidson's office next door was constructed in exactly the same way as buildings over five hundred years ago—stone and mortar.

"I hope you've got a bigger sledgehammer if you're planning what I think you're planning," said

Jillian as Harvath unlocked the lid of the larger Storm case and flipped it open.

Along with another weapon, Ozan Kalachka had come through for him yet again. Inside the case was a device called a Rapid Cutter of Concrete, or RAPTOR for short. It looked like a large fire extinguisher with a long muzzle attached to it. It was a helium-driven gas gun that could fire steel nails at 5000 feet per second, five times the speed of sound, cracking concrete over six inches thick.

"What the hell is that?" she asked.

"Our ticket in," replied Harvath as he removed a long black silencer tube from the Storm case and screwed it onto the end of the RAPTOR. "There's one other thing we need."

Harvath walked over to a stack of milk crates stuffed with record albums. As he began sorting through them he said, "First, we have to remove the coating of plaster on this side of the wall with the sledgehammers and then we'll use the RAPTOR to help us get through the wall itself. But even with the silencer, we're still going to make a good amount of noise. I don't want to have to depend on intermittent Métro trains coming and going all night to help cover us. Besides, I like to whistle to something while I work. Don't you?"

"That depends what we're whistling to," she replied.

Harvath held up *George Clinton's Greatest Funkin' Hits* and said, "How about the Master?"

THIRTY-THREE

Harvath turned the stereo speakers around so they faced the wall and then let the music rip.

Not only was George Clinton great to swing a hammer to, but a song like "Atomic Dog" had enough bass in it to disguise any sounds that might be heard on the third floor of Sotheby's. As crude as his plan was, Harvath felt fairly confident they were going to be able to get in and out without anyone knowing, until tomorrow morning, that they had been there. By then, it wouldn't matter. They'd have what they needed and be on the trail of whoever sent the artifacts to Sotheby's.

Once the plaster was successfully chipped away, Harvath got to work with the RAPTOR. After loosening several large blocks of stone, he removed a set of telescoping titanium poles from the duffel bag along with a block and tackle set. Jillian and Harvath both used small pry bars to edge the stones out to a point where a web harness could be slipped around each one of them and then they could be lowered to the floor on their side. It was two and a half hours before they had finally cleared a space big enough to crawl through. After packing the equipment, Harvath punched through the plaster on the Sotheby's side as quietly as he could and crawled inside.

Using the filtered blue beam of his SureFire to light his way, Scot stepped into Molly Davidson's office with Jillian right behind him. Rain lashed the windows and very little light from the street below found its way inside. The room was a disjointed jumble of shadows, and it smelled different for some reason. There was a mix of odors he couldn't exactly place. It was a combination of melted plastic and something else—something not as strong, but definitely distinct. Though he didn't know why, Harvath had a very bad feeling in the pit of his stomach. That little voice in the back of his head that never steered him wrong was trying to tell him something. As they moved farther into the room, the hair on the back of his neck began to stand up.

Harvath swept the beam of his flashlight over the long table and noticed all of the artifacts seemed to be there. That was strange. *Why wouldn't Davidson have locked them up?*

As they crept closer to her desk area, Harvath saw something that stopped him dead in his tracks. Not only did the blue filter on his SureFire reduce the intensity of the light, making the beam harder to see, it also caused certain substances to stand out under dark conditions.

Harvath noticed the splatters on the wall first. It looked like someone had flicked a heavily soaked paintbrush at it. As he angled the beam toward the floor, he moved it forward and saw a large, dark pool spreading out from the direction of Davidson's desk. Suddenly, there was a flash of lightning and the room was illuminated for just a fraction of a second. It was enough for Harvath to see a bludgeoned body and, lying next to it, the ancient war hammer.

Harvath risked flipping the hinged filter up from his SureFire to get a better look at the body as he ran over to it. The war hammer was covered with blood and little pink morsels of tissue, which could only be pieces from Molly Davidson's scalp. The scene was horrific. Jillian choked back a scream.

Harvath took one look at the intense damage to her skull and knew there was no way she could be alive, but he reached down and checked for a pulse anyway. The body was still warm—too warm, especially considering the massive loss of blood. Whoever had killed her had done so very recently, maybe even as Harvath was in the final stages of breaking in. He didn't like the thought that they might have been able to do something to save her, but there was no way they could have known what was going on while they were busy punching through the wall.

The other thing Harvath didn't like was that they might have interrupted the killer midway through his work. He swept the flashlight in a slow arc around the room. There were very few places a person could hide, but he wanted to make sure they were absolutely alone.

Understandably, Jillian was extremely frightened and stayed as close to Harvath as possible. "What is it?" she asked as he lit up the different corners of the room.

"Nothing. I just wanted to make sure we were alone."

"Who do you think did this to her?"

"I have no idea," replied Harvath, "but—" Harvath stopped mid-sentence as he focused the beam of his flashlight on Davidson's desktop computer and then responded, "Goddamn it!"

"What is it?" she asked, carefully stepping around the body to see what Harvath was so angry about.

"Whoever killed her was concerned enough about what was on her computer to crack the tower and burn everything inside before leaving." Now he knew where the burned plastic smell had come from. Davidson's blood had turned out to be the other odor.

Jillian looked at the computer's blackened and melted circuitry. "How do you create a fire that burns something that bad without setting off the smoke alarms?"

"You need a type of fire that burns with very little smoke—a real hot one. Whoever did this must have had some sort of a handheld blow torch or soldering iron with him."

"So much for this being a spur-of-the-moment crime of passion," said Jillian.

Harvath couldn't argue with her. Whoever did this had come prepared. And, as he had just pointed out, there must have been something on Molly Davidson's computer that they were desperate to erase.

"What do we do now?" asked Jillian.

"I don't know," he responded as he looked at his watch and realized it was nearing four o'clock in the morning. There had to be something. They were already in the building. Sotheby's had to have another copy of the information somewhere, but where? *Think,* he told himself. *The hard part is over—we're already inside. Where would Davidson have kept backups of her files? Was there a central server in the building? Did they have hard copies in a file room somewhere?* Harvath laughed at that idea. If Sotheby's did have a file storage area, there was no telling how big it would be. With all of the transactions they did in Paris each year, the room would be enormous. It could take up an entire floor. It could even comprise a completely different building. Not only were they searching for a needle, they had no idea where the haystack was.

Then, something hit him. "Didn't Davidson say

she worked from home sometimes when she needed peace and quiet?"

"Yes. She most likely had copies there of everything she was working on. I often do the same thing."

"So do I," replied Harvath as he opened one of Davidson's desk drawers. "She must have carried a purse, or a wallet or something that might have her address in it."

After several moments of looking, it was Jillian who found the purse inside a tiny cabinet beneath the small sink in the corner. "Got it," she said, pulling it out so Harvath could see it.

"Good job."

Jillian cleared a spot on the nearest workbench, and while Harvath held the flashlight for her, she turned the purse upside down and emptied its contents. Among an assortment of useless items were a wallet, cell phone, and set of keys. Immediately, her attention was drawn to a Swiss Army knife, just three inches long, hanging from the key ring.

"What is that?" asked Harvath as Jillian extended a rectangular piece of metal-tipped plastic from beneath one of the blades.

"It's a compact flash memory stick," she replied. "It's like a portable hard drive or storage device. I use the same thing to transport files between my computer at work and the one I have at home. Dr. Davidson must have been doing the same thing."

"That might be exactly what we're looking for," said Harvath as another flash of lightning exploded.

Jillian, who was standing near the windows, suddenly saw a figure dressed completely in black, perched on the sloped roof and staring through the glass at them. But before she could scream, Khalid Alomari raised his pistol and fired.

THIRTY-FOUR

When the window exploded in a hail of razor-sharp glass, Harvath was already in motion. Leaping across the large table covered with artifacts, he knocked Jillian to the ground and drew the .40-caliber H&K USP Compact he was carrying at the small of his back. Raising himself up onto one knee, Harvath prepared to fire, but was forced to hit the deck when Khalid Alomari raked the room with another fusillade. A screeching, high-pitched siren soon joined the sound of gunfire. The shattered window had triggered the alarm system. Harvath could almost hear the heavy boots of Sotheby's well-armed guards pounding their way up the stairs at that very moment. That was all he needed. He had no desire to dance with those guys again. They had to get out of there—now.

Rolling to his right, Harvath pounded the area around the window frame with six rounds from his H&K. Turning back to where Jillian lay, he said,

"When I count to three, I want you to take off running for the hole in the wall. Stay low and don't stop for anything."

"I don't think I can move," she wheezed as her breath came in short gasps. Her hands were trembling and her eyes were wide with fear. Seeing Molly Davidson's body and now this, it was all too much and had resulted in classic adrenaline dump. Her fight-or-flight mechanisms were overloaded and she was completely paralyzed. Harvath needed to get her focused on moving.

Handing her the keys to the van, he said, "I'm going to hold him off while you run. I want you to take the van and go back to the hotel and wait for me. Got it?"

Alcott nodded her head.

"Good. I'm going to count to three. Are you ready?"

"Wait," she said, scared and trying to stall. "What about you?"

"Don't worry about me. I'll meet you there. Here we go. One. Two. Three!"

Harvath let loose with another volley of six shots while Jillian ran for the far end of the office. When Harvath had fired his final shot, he ejected the spent magazine and inserted a fresh one. He put seven additional rounds through the eaves above, hoping to get lucky and nail Alomari outside on the sloped roof, but there was no way to be sure. All he knew was that he was no longer returning fire. Either Harvath *had* gotten lucky or Alomari was on the run. Like it or not, Harvath knew he had to go after him.

Grabbing a stool from one of the workbenches, he knocked the remaining pieces of glass from the windowpane as the sound of Sotheby's security guards racing down the hallway could be heard. Reaching for the best handhold he could, Harvath pulled himself up and out of the window.

The fierce rain was being driven horizontally by the wind, and it tore at him like sheets of nails. It was all Harvath could do to hang on. The sloped roof was slick with rain and an accumulation of Paris grime. Realizing he was going to need both hands, Harvath reluctantly tucked the H&K back into the holster at the small of his back, sucked up the pain from his ribs, and scrambled upward.

As he reached the top of the roof, the parapet exploded in a hail of gunfire and Harvath lost his grip. He came sliding downward on the slimy tiles, grabbing frantically for any sort of handhold he could find. Clawing at the sloped surface, he was finally able to stop his precipitous slide.

Harvath struggled his way back up the roof. When he arrived beneath the parapet, he steadied himself and drew his pistol. He grabbed hold of the ledge and swung himself up and over the top. Rolling along the flat surface, he took cover behind a large stone chimney. He listened for any sign of Alomari, but all he could hear was the raging of the storm. Taking a deep breath, he tightened his grip around the pistol and sprang from his hiding place.

All of the roofs of the block's buildings were connected, and through the driving rain, Harvath could make out the silhouette of Alomari no more than fifty yards away. With no civilians this time blocking his line of fire, Harvath didn't hesitate. He pulled the trigger five times in quick succession and on the last round saw Alomari spin, as if he'd been hit in the back, and go down.

Harvath began to advance, ready to finish the job, when he heard voices behind him. The Sotheby's security guards were scaling the roof, and there were the sounds of police Klaxons closing in on the street below. He had no choice. Though he didn't like it, he had to get out of there. Spotting what looked like an access door two rooftops over, he took off at a sprint.

THIRTY-FIVE

WASHINGTON, DC

Growing up in South Philly, one thing Neal Monroe was not was a punk. He had learned early on to mind his own business and never anyone else's. At the same time, his grandmother had brought him up as a good Christian and someone who knew the difference between right and wrong. And what his boss, Senator Carmichael, was doing was wrong. There were no two ways about it. That was why he had put the call in to Charles Anderson, tipping him off that Carmichael was on Scot Harvath's trail. While Monroe didn't know Harvath personally, he had learned enough about him over the past three days to know he didn't deserve what the senator was preparing to do to him, all in her pursuit of the White House.

Contacting the president's chief of staff, especially when he was of the opposing party, was tantamount to committing political suicide, but Neal

Monroe didn't care. He had come to Washington for one thing—to make his country a better place—and promised himself that no matter what, he would always do the right thing. If Carmichael knew what he was doing, there was no question she'd fire him. There was also no question that he probably would never find another job in DC either, but at least his conscience would be clear.

As an African American, Monroe liked to joke with the other two minority staffers in the senator's office—a young Asian woman named Tanya, and George, a Hispanic guy who grew up in Neal's neighborhood—that they formed the perfect little Rainbow Coalition right there in Carmichael's office, demonstrating how worldly and open-minded she thought she was. Though the senator didn't intentionally mean to be patronizing, she always was whenever she asked them how "their people" might feel about a specific issue or piece of legislation she was working on. Tanya was so removed from her Asian heritage that she was the first one to ask for a fork every time they ordered Chinese, and though George put on a good show of being of Mexican descent, he couldn't speak a word of Spanish.

The bottom line was that Carmichael only saw what she wanted to see, and in slow-roasting Scot Harvath over an open flame, she saw her ticket to the White House. Maybe it was that his distaste for his boss had been simmering for so long that it was bound to bubble over onto the stove at some point;

maybe it was because he had put himself through college on the GI bill and saw Harvath as a fellow soldier; or maybe it was just the Christian thing to do, but however you cut it, Neal Monroe didn't care if he lost his job or not. At the end of the day, he wanted no regrets.

Once he had called Rutledge's chief of staff, Neal felt totally absolved of any further responsibility. But all of that changed when he discovered how the senator was getting her information.

Now, as he walked through the Discovery Creek Children's Museum, he thought about what he was going to say to the man Charles Anderson had sent to talk with him. Standing near a small placard that illustrated how trees grow, Monroe spotted his contact. "They didn't have any of this in the neighborhood I grew up in," said Monroe as the man joined him.

"In my neighborhood, we didn't even have trees," replied Gary Lawlor.

Monroe offered the man his hand, and Gary shook it. "You're a brave guy, Neal. You know that?"

"Why? Because I'm airing the senator's dirty laundry?"

"If what you told Chuck is true, her laundry is well beyond dirty."

"Suffice it to say that I don't like the way she's conducting the people's business."

A group of children was approaching, and so Lawlor suggested they take a walk. As they did, he looked around and said, "I've had clandestine meetings in a lot of interesting places over the years, but this is certainly one of the most unique. Why'd you pick it?"

"I knew it was the one spot where we'd never bump into Helen. The senator hates kids."

"But I thought she had a daughter," replied Lawlor.

"That's a neighbor's kid. They just rent her for photo ops."

Gary laughed. "So what have you got? Chuck mentioned you're pretty confident you know where Senator Carmichael is getting her information."

Neal nodded his head. "I knew it was coming from one of the intelligence agencies. I just didn't know which one. Until this morning that is."

Lawlor couldn't believe it. "You know who's feeding her the information?"

"No. I only know where it's coming from, not who's behind it."

"That's still a start," said Gary. "What's the source?"

"Langley, Virginia. The Central Intelligence Agency."

THIRTY-SIX

PARIS

Harvath and Alcott found a small, twenty-four-hour Internet café a few blocks away and ordered two mugs of coffee. Except for a couple of backpackers waiting for an early morning train, the place was deserted. Harvath chose a computer in the back, sat down, and got on line. The first thing he did was log on to the public bulletin board site he used to covertly communicate with Gary Lawlor. He left a brief, coded summary of what had happened so far and then plugged in Davidson's flash drive and began scrolling through her files. It took over twenty minutes of searching, but when he finally found the record of Sotheby's mysterious client, he knew it couldn't be a coincidence. There were two names, one of which he recognized and another which he didn't. The name he did recognize, Elliot Burnham, was one of the aliases Harvath had uncovered during his investigation of none other than ex–Secret Service agent Timothy Rayburn.

His address was listed as being in care of a hotel called the Queyr' de l'Ours, or the Skin of the Bear, somewhere in southeastern France. Harvath had never heard of the village before and had to look it up online. Once he found it, he also pulled up the SNCF web site and began scanning timetables for the next high-speed TGV train to Nice. He knew driving the distance would take way too long, and the last thing he wanted to do was hassle with airport security. At least traveling by train, he'd be able to quietly carry his gun along with him. In Nice, they could rent a car and drive north into the Alps for the rest of the trip to the village of Ristolas.

After they gathered their belongings and checked out of the hotel, they took a cab across town to the Gare de Lyon. Once their train was safely outside of Paris and well on its way to the south of France, Harvath finally felt comfortable enough to close his eyes and get a few hours' sleep.

In Nice, they used Harvath's Sam Guerin credentials to rent the last car the agency had available, a midnight blue Mercedes. It was well into the evening by the time they pulled across the old wooden bridge and into the tiny village of Ristolas. The three-story, barnlike Alpine hotel known as the Skin of the Bear was located just off the main street. A series of low stone walls surrounded the building and looked as if they might have once been used for grazing livestock. They parked their rental in the driveway and climbed the wooden steps to the hotel's ornately carved front doors.

A large stone fireplace with books covering its mantelpiece anchored the deserted reception area inside. One book in particular caught Harvath's attention, and he walked immediately over to it and took it down. It was an autographed first edition of John Prevas's *Hannibal Crosses the Alps*. Harvath held it up for Jillian to see. She looked at it for a moment and then went back to studying the many photographs that covered the reception area's walls. They appeared to be of different climbers who must have used the hotel as a base camp over the years. In each one, there was a big bear of a man whom Jillian assumed was the hotel's owner as well as a mountain guide.

Harvath had come over to join her and was hoping to spot Rayburn in one of the photos, when a petite, gray-haired woman of about sixty, her face as craggy as the mountains in the photos, emerged from the kitchen and said, *"Bon soir. Puis-je vous aider?"*

"Bon soir," replied Harvath. *"Avez-vous une chambre?"*

Wearing a white, lace-trimmed apron over a loose-fitting peasant's smock, the experienced hotelier recognized Harvath's accent and replied in perfect English, "You're American."

"Yes."

"And British," added Jillian.

"You're on your honeymoon," said the woman, raising her eyebrows conspiratorially. "I can always tell."

For some reason, people often came to that conclusion when they saw Harvath with an attractive woman. He had no idea why. He figured he must have had a look about him that suggested he was perfect marriage material. He had learned the hard way, though, that at this point in his life, marriage or any kind of reasonable relationship was not in the cards for him. "No, we're not here on our honeymoon. We came to climb. We've heard very good things about your hotel."

"Really?" said the woman as she looked at the ground and smoothed the creases of her apron. "We don't get many guests here anymore. Not since Bernard has gone."

"Was Bernard your husband?" asked Jillian as she turned toward the photographs. "Is he the one I see in all of these?"

"Yes," she said, managing a small smile. "Guests used to say they came for three things—Bernard, the climbing, and my cooking, in that order."

"He sounds like he was very special."

"He was. Everyone loved him."

"What happened?" replied Harvath. "If you don't mind my asking."

"Bernard went climbing about a year ago and never came back."

Tears began to form at the corners of the woman's eyes, but she removed a tissue from her sleeve and quickly dabbed them away.

"I'm sorry for your loss," said Jillian.

"It's how he would have wanted to go," responded the woman, "but you didn't come to listen to the sad stories of an old woman. You came for a room. I have one available for fifty euros a night. I hope you don't think it is too expensive, it's just that—"

"No," said Harvath, interrupting her with a smile. "Fifty euros is fine."

"But we'll need two rooms if possible, please," Jillian added.

Definitely not on a honeymoon, Harvath thought to himself.

After unpacking his few belongings, Harvath walked downstairs for dinner. A small table had been set in the kitchen, and Marie, not expecting guests, apologized that all she had available was pottage. That didn't bother Harvath. The temperature had dipped below freezing outside, and the weather was forecasted to get worse. It was a perfect night for soup. Actually, it was a perfect night for the fireplace, a good book, and a large glass of bourbon, but Harvath knew there was no way in hell that was going to happen.

As they ate their pottage, Marie explained that her husband, Bernard, had named the hotel the Queyr' de l'Ours after an old French saying, *Don't try to sell the skin of the bear until you have already gone out and killed it.* She spoke fondly of him and of how Bernard had been born in Ristolas and had started hiking and climbing as soon as he could walk. Mount Viso and its surrounding mountains, valleys, and gorges had been his métier. The people of the village joked that his body had been formed from the mountain's granite and that glacier water ran through his veins.

They still had a hard time believing that he had just gone off on a climb one day and never returned. Marie Lavoine had a hard time believing it too.

Without Bernard, the hotel had suffered. He had been the draw—the larger-than-life personality who organized and led top-of-the-line climbing and hiking trips throughout the area. Without him there anymore, even the most loyal clients began finding other guides and inns to stay at. When Bernard disappeared, it heralded the end of an era. It was obvious that Marie Lavoine had been struggling since his disappearance both emotionally and financially. As hard as it was going to be, Harvath decided it was time to address why they had come. "Marie, we need to ask you a question about one of your guests."

"One of *my* guests? Who?"

"Elliot Burnham. An American."

Lavoine looked up at the ceiling for a moment as if trying to recall the name and then back at Harvath. "I'm sorry, we usually received more Europeans than Americans, so you would think it would be easy for me to remember, but I'm sorry, I don't."

Harvath could see Marie Lavoine was lying to him. "Marie, this man is very dangerous. People have died because of him."

At the mention that people had died because of Burnham, a sudden change came over her. Marie grew tense, and even Jillian could read it in the strained creases of her face. Lavoine's small hands nervously twisted the napkin in her lap. "Who are you? Why are you asking me these questions?"

Jillian placed her hands atop the widow's and tried to calm her. "Marie, your name, along with Elliot Burnham's, was listed as the owner of a group of artifacts being authenticated for sale by Sotheby's. Why is that?"

"I have no idea."

It was there again, the tell. This time it was even more pronounced. Marie Lavoine was not a good liar. Harvath could see that she was on the edge of coming unraveled. "Marie, I can tell just by looking at you that you know who we're talking about."

Lavoine's eyes started to tear again. "Why would you want to torment a lonely old woman?"

"Why would you want to protect a killer?"

"I am protecting no one."

"You're protecting the man who calls himself Elliot Burnham," said Harvath as he raised his voice and tried to apply just a little more pressure. He could see she was almost there. She wanted to come clean about something. The guilt was eating away at her. She had a confession and it was right on the tip of her tongue. "If you don't talk to us, we have no choice but to go to the police with this. I don't want to do that. You seem like a very nice woman to me. Whatever your connection to this man is, I'm sure you had no idea what a bad individual he was; but if you don't cooperate, we're not going to be able to help you."

"I needed his help," said Lavoine, breaking down into tears.

"Help with what?" asked Jillian as she tried to comfort the woman.

"Selling some of the treasure."

"Treasure?"

"Yes, the artifacts. I have no pension—nothing. Bernard left me only with the hotel and my memories. And only the memories are completely mine. The bank still expects its payments on the hotel. The artifacts are all I have. Please do not take them from me. Please," the woman begged. "Monsieur Burnham and I were going to split the money. That is why he wanted to use the hotel for his address."

After taking a moment to collect her thoughts, Lavoine told them that two years ago Elliot Burnham arrived at the hotel and asked for Bernard by name. Not only had Burnham been looking for the most knowledgeable guide in the region, he also wanted the most discreet. Bernard fit the bill on both counts. Over the years, many celebrities had called the Queyr' de l'Ours home while they tackled Mount Viso, and despite the pressure from lifelong friends in the village, Bernard had refused to divulge even the smallest bit of gossip about his guests. He had a sterling reputation and it paid off in spades with the arrival of Elliot Burnham.

Burnham presented himself as the director of a large archeological foundation in America. After leaving a sizable deposit, in cash, along with a list of equipment and supplies that would be needed, he returned a week later with the "chief archeologist from his foundation," Dr. Donald Ellyson.

In Lavoine's opinion Ellyson seemed to her a man who had been broken by the world, but at the same time, there was a confidence about him that suggested a hopefulness about the future. He was a confusing man of terrible habits—a hard drinker, a gambler, and a tomcat who liked to womanize in the surrounding villages, but someone who always had a kind word for her, especially when it came to her cooking. Ellyson's death, as well as that of Maurice Vevé, whom Bernard often hired on as a Sherpa on his more involved expeditions, only made the death of her husband more painful. For just one of them to have been lost due to a misstep or maybe the poor placement of a crampon or ice axe would have been difficult to bear, but for all three men to lose their lives on the same day was an absolute tragedy.

"So he came to mount an expedition then?" queried Jillian, coaxing Marie Lavoine forward.

"Did Burnham share with you what they hoped to find?"

"No," she said, shaking her head. "Bernard and Maurice had been sworn to secrecy. They were instructed not to discuss their work with anyone. Not even me. Monsieur Burnham booked out the entire hotel. He paid for all the rooms and did not care that they went empty."

Jillian shrugged her shoulders in agreement and waited for Marie to continue.

"At first, Dr. Ellyson was extremely secretive. Even Bernard had no idea what the man was looking for. They made many trips to the Col de la Traversette—"

"What's the Col de la Traversette?" asked Harvath.

"It's a pass located just to the north of Mount Viso."

"Did you know why Ellyson was so interested in it?" asked Jillian.

"Not at first," said Lavoine. "But I had my suspicions. He was occupying two rooms. One he used for sleeping and the other became an office. I was never allowed in the room he used as an office. He kept it locked, and Bernard had turned over all of the keys to it. The room he used for his living quarters was something different. We had a young girl from the Czech Republic who did our cleaning, but Dr. Ellyson didn't trust her. I was the only one he would allow to clean his room."

Alcott nodded encouragingly.

"I did my best to respect Dr. Ellyson's privacy. But one day, I noticed something unusual on his bedside table. There were three books I had not seen before. I assumed that he had brought them from his office across the hall so that he could read them in the evening before he went to sleep. What was interesting, though, was that there were three copies of the exact same book. Each had been highlighted with a specific color, but all in different places."

"That's odd," replied Jillian.

"That's exactly what I thought, especially as we knew the author of the book quite well. He had spent many summers here doing research and climbing with Bernard."

"Who was it?"

"His name is John Prevas."

"Hannibal Crosses the Alps," replied Harvath. "I saw it in your reception area."

"Yes, Monsieur Prevas was kind enough to send us a signed copy when it was published," said Marie.

"Why was Ellyson so interested in this particular book? What's so special about it?"

"It is different from other books about Hannibal and the route he took over the Alps. The Col de la Traversette has always been very dangerous, not only because of the steep terrain, but because until the 1970s smugglers controlled it as a way to get from France into Italy. Scholars had avoided investigating the Traversette as a possible route for

Hannibal's army because of, as a man named deBeer put it, 'the ease with which triggers were pulled in the area.' I was never very much interested in the subject until Monsieur Prevas became our guest, but then I began reading. I am certainly no expert, but his book is the most convincing I have ever encountered regarding the true route Hannibal and his army used when crossing the Alps."

"So Ellyson was interested in retracing Hannibal's path?" asked Harvath.

"That was the way it seemed, and the more time Bernard spent with him, the more Dr. Ellyson began to trust him," said Marie. "He was a lonely man. He had no wife, no family. Many evenings, he kept Bernard up all night so he wouldn't have to drink alone. The doctor would tell Bernard stories about how Hannibal had almost succeeded in changing the face of history."

"What did he mean by that?" Jillian eagerly asked.

"He believed Hannibal's army was bringing with them a magic weapon that could completely decimate the Romans—men, women, children, even their animals. This idea is completely crazy. A magic weapon which kills people and also their animals?"

"How did Ellyson know this? Where did he get his information? Was it from Burnham?"

"Bernard wondered the same thing. Like me, he was also beginning to think Ellyson was crazy. Of course, we were being paid good money, but at some point the money was not so important. Ellyson was, how do you say? Obsessed.

"One night, after they had been drinking, Bernard forgot himself and told the archeologist that he thought he was crazy. They had been searching for some time and had found nothing. Ellyson was furious that Bernard did not believe in him. He made Bernard go upstairs with him to the room he used as his office so he could show him his proof."

"Proof?" repeated Harvath. "What kind of proof?"

"In the office, Bernard watched Dr. Ellyson take the key he kept on a chain around his neck and open a metal attaché case. Inside was a book made from pages of very old papyrus. According to the archeologist, the pages were written in ancient Greek and were a firsthand account of Hannibal's journey over the Alps."

Jillian turned to Harvath and said, "The Silenus manuscript. Silenus was the Greek war correspondent who spent all his time amongst Hannibal's different soldiers. That must be what it was."

"Not only were there Greeks with Hannibal, but Roman spies as well. From what Dr. Ellyson learned, word of Hannibal's attack had been circulating for some time. It wasn't the attack itself that the Romans were most concerned with, but rather the magic weapon the Carthaginians were said to be bringing with them; and the Romans found a way to stop this magic weapon from ever reaching Rome."

"How?"

"The Roman spies paid some of the Carthaginian soldiers to betray Hannibal. The men responsible for guarding the magic weapon were killed as they slept, and their bodies and beasts swept off the face of the mountain by a terrible avalanche."

"Did Ellyson ever say how the book came into his possession?" asked Harvath.

"Mais oui," replied Marie. "Of this, the man was very proud. He told Bernard he had discovered it himself."

"Where?" said Jillian.

"At first, he would not say. It was as if maybe he was embarrassed or something. But you have to know Bernard. There was something very special about him. He was a very powerful man, and other men were drawn to him. He was like a rock. He never judged them, and for that, they felt that they could unburden their souls to him."

"And Dr. Ellyson?" asked Harvath. "He unburdened himself to Bernard?"

"With the help of two bottles of Chateau Margaux," said Marie. "One night the doctor must have had a vision of Christ because he unburdened himself of all his sins. He admitted to Bernard many things we already knew about him. He admitted the drinking, the gambling, and of course the women, but it was the thing he saved for last which was the most interesting."

"Which was?"

"Dr. Donald Ellyson was a thief."

"A thief?" echoed Harvath.

Marie smiled and said, "He had assembled quite a personal collection of antiquities over the years. The only ones that were of any value were the ones that were stolen."

Harvath shook his head knowingly. It didn't surprise him that in the frothy pool of international malfeasance, two floaters like Rayburn and Ellyson had managed to bump up against each other and had found a way to improve their shitty lot in life by throwing in together. "What did your husband think of all this?"

Marie Lavoine laughed. "Bernard found it quite amusing. The funny thing about Dr. Ellyson was that he had basically stolen from everyone else's archeological discoveries his entire life, but the minute he made his very own find, he unequivocally forbade my husband and Maurice to steal from him."

"Wait a second," said Jillian. "*His find*? What did he find?"

"Dr. Ellyson was a better archeologist than he thought. With the help of the book in that attaché case, he found part of Hannibal's army."

"Which part? Which part of the army did he find?"

"The part the Romans paid a fortune to make sure never made it to Rome."

THIRTY-SEVEN

Neither Harvath nor Alcott could believe it. Ellyson's find was absolutely amazing. "He found it here? In the Alps?" asked Jillian.

"Yes, somewhere near the Traversette."

"Where exactly?"

"I don't know. Bernard never told me. He only told me about the discovery itself."

"How soon was this before they disappeared?" asked Harvath.

"Two weeks, maybe more. They had only just begun to excavate the site. It was located in a very deep ice chasm that was extremely difficult to get their equipment into."

"I'm confused. You said Ellyson forbade Bernard and the other man working with him—"

"Maurice."

"Right. Ellyson forbade your husband and Maurice from stealing objects from the site, but they did, didn't they?" said Harvath. "That's how the artifacts came into your possession."

"No," replied Lavoine. "They did not steal anything. Dr. Ellyson was extremely concerned with what he called the structural integrity of the site. An avalanche, a shift in the ice—it wouldn't have taken much for everything to be lost."

Jillian looked at the woman and asked, "So what did they do?"

"Dr. Ellyson catalogued everything. Very carefully, he recorded where each piece had been found, and then Bernard and Maurice helped carry them back here. The smaller artifacts were easy enough to transport; it was the bigger ones they were just starting to decide how to handle when they disappeared."

"So Ellyson reported his find to Burnham, and that's how he knew you had them."

"The artifacts? No, Dr. Ellyson said the artifacts were none of Burnham's business."

"But Burnham was funding the expedition."

"Ellyson didn't care. He said Monsieur Burnham was only interested in one thing from the dig, and since that was all their agreement called for, that was all he was going to get. Anything above and beyond that, Dr. Ellyson said Monsieur Burnham had no right to."

"And what was the one thing Burnham was interested in?" asked Jillian.

Lavoine had no idea. She just turned up her palms and shrugged her shoulders.

"How did the man claiming to be Burnham even figure out then that you had the artifacts?" asked Harvath.

"Because I told him. As I said, we haven't had many customers since Bernard disappeared. The bank still must be paid, and I have very little money left. So, I offered Monsieur Burnham a chance to buy the artifacts from me."

"But technically he had funded the expedition. Those would have rightfully belonged to him and his institute. What if he had gone to the police?"

"I didn't care. I lost my husband. My life was ruined. Besides, I knew Monsieur Burnham wouldn't want anything to do with the police. As I told you, Dr. Ellyson was very secretive and always kept the door to the room he used as an office locked. He had every copy of the key, and even I wasn't allowed in there to clean. When he, Bernard, and Maurice failed to return, I had my neighbor help me take the door off the hinges. On the other side, there was absolutely nothing. No sign of the boxes of books and papers he had brought to the hotel with him. No computer. No attaché case, nothing. Someone had been in the hotel and had taken every single thing out of that room. Who else would have done that but Monsieur Burnham?"

"So a year passed and you decided to do what?"

"I decided to sell Monsieur Burnham the artifacts. We would fix a price and he could have them all."

"But that's not what happened."

"No. He told me he didn't have any money. Not right now, at least. He offered to give me a small deposit and pay me later, but I wouldn't agree."

"Smart lady," said Harvath.

"I told him I needed all of the money right away. He became very angry, telling me they belonged to the foundation. When I told him I knew there was no foundation, he tried to make excuses. Finally, I threatened to go to the police and tell them everything I knew if he didn't cooperate."

"I bet he didn't like that," replied Harvath as he remembered what a temper Rayburn had.

"Not at all, but he was in a similar position as me. He had no choice. He could not afford to pay me, and he definitely did not want me taking the artifacts or my story to the police, so we settled on the compromise of selling everything through Sotheby's."

"So what's at Sotheby's represents everything Ellyson uncovered?"

Lavoine looked away for a moment before responding. "No. Not everything."

"There's more?" asked Jillian.

Lavoine tried to explain. "Even though we were dealing with Sotheby's, I still didn't trust Monsieur Burnham. I thought he might find a way to cheat me. I couldn't risk everything on the first venture. Besides, Ellyson had never even told Monsieur Burnham exactly where the site was, much less what he had recovered from it. Monsieur Burnham had no idea what I had in my possession. By doing it my way, if the first sale went well, I could wait a while and then quietly go back to Sotheby's with more."

"And without having to split the money with anyone."

Marie nodded her head.

Harvath stood from the table and said, "We need to see those remaining artifacts."

"Why?"

"Because even though your husband never made it back from that chasm, the weapon the Romans paid so dearly to prevent getting to Rome actually did."

Lavoine was shocked. "What do you mean?"

"I mean, the man you call Elliot Burnham has been working with Muslim terrorists, and they plan on using Hannibal's weapon against the Western world."

"The weapon actually exists? What is it?"

"An illness of some sort," replied Jillian. "Please, Marie, whatever artifacts you have still, we need to take a look at them. We promise you, that is all we want to do. We have no intention of taking them from you. Millions of lives may be at stake here. We know Bernard had no idea as to whom he was helping, but you can help us to fix this. Please, we need your cooperation."

Lavoine thought about it for several moments and then said, "Okay," as she stood. "Get your coats. You're going to need them. It's very cold outside."

THIRTY-EIGHT

WHITE HOUSE SITUATION ROOM
WASHINGTON, DC

Once the secure videoconference link with CIA headquarters in Langley had been established, the president began speaking. "I assume I wasn't called out of my meetings upstairs because you have good news."

"Unfortunately no, Mr. President," responded the director of Central Intelligence, James Vaile. "Two days ago we made a very important electronic intercept related to the village of Asalaam."

"If you made it two days ago, why am I just hearing about it now?"

"With all due respect, sir, our Arabic translators are seriously overworked and dangerously backlogged."

"I know. I know," said Rutledge, "and I'm doing everything I can to get you additional funding to hire more of them, but now's not the time for this discussion. Why don't you tell me what you've got."

"We intercepted a posting in an Islamic chat room that commented on the hand of Allah successfully striking down all but his most faithful followers in a remote location referred to as the *place of peace*."

"Asalaam?"

"That's what we think," replied Vaile. "The fundamentalists like to describe Iraq as the crusaders' burial ground. The people talking in that chat room signaled that the place of peace was within the land known as the burial ground of the foreign crusaders."

The president was silent as the DCI continued. "One of Osama bin Laden's most beloved was also said to have been present to witness the power of Allah firsthand."

"Khalid Alomari."

"We think so. There were enough allusions to his past accomplishments for us to be fairly certain it's him. We've been monitoring the room, but the poster hasn't returned, or at least not under the same handle as before. We're not holding out much hope of tracking him down. Just like cell phones, these guys will use a chat room once and then never come back to it again. They know it makes it impossible for us to trace them that way."

Though none of this was exactly good news, Rutledge knew his DCI well enough to know that he was saving the very worst for last. "What else did you find out?"

"One of the people in the chat room claimed that what happened at the place of peace was only a small example of what Allah and his most holy warriors had planned for the enemies of Islam, in particular the United States."

The president was again silent for several moments as the confirmation of their worst fears began to sink in. Finally, he asked, "Is that it?"

"No sir," replied Vaile. "There was one other thing."

"What is it?"

"According to the transcript, the means by which Allah intends to decimate all but the most faithful followers of Islam has already arrived in America. It says that it's only a matter of days before the bodies of our citizens begin piling up—overflowing our hospitals, morgues, and cemeteries."

THIRTY-NINE

FRANCE

Carrying flashlights, Harvath and Alcott followed Marie out into the bitterly cold night and were led behind the hotel to a small barn at the far end of the property.

"You keep the artifacts in here and don't even keep it locked?" Harvath asked as Marie pushed the door open.

"No one locks their doors here. If you do, you send a message that you have something worth stealing. Besides, how long do you think it would take if someone really wanted to get in here?"

The woman had a point.

Marie closed the door behind them and then used her flashlight to point to a stall in the middle of the structure. "In there."

After moving several bales of hay and kicking away the loose pieces of straw, Harvath found the trapdoor. Drawing it back, he played his flashlight down a series of stone steps, which led into a large cellar.

Jillian joined him, and with Marie bringing up the rear, they descended the steps. The cellar was enormous. Marie found a box of matches and lit several of the lanterns hanging from the low ceiling. As the lanterns illuminated the room, Harvath heard Alcott draw a sharp intake of breath.

Perfectly arranged on clean sheets across the cellar floor were hundreds of artifacts contained in clear plastic bags. Jillian couldn't help herself and she rushed over to get a closer look. "How were they able to transport all of this?"

"Strong backs, big packs, and many, many trips," replied Marie.

Joining Jillian, Harvath carefully picked up one of the sealed bags and examined its contents. Inside was a weapon he recognized from his study of military history—a Celtic *falcata*. With its inward curving blade, legend had it that the powerful short sword could slice through a shield and helmet with just one blow. There was something else about it that interested Harvath, though. Stuck to the bag was a piece of masking tape with a string of numbers. Holding it up so Marie could see them, he asked, "Do you know what these are?"

"I have no idea," said Marie, shaking her head sadly. "I took several of those pieces of tape to a friend of Bernard's who is also a mountain guide. I hoped he would be able to decipher it. I thought it might be GPS or something like that. I thought maybe it would help us find Bernard and Maurice, but they seem to be just a bunch of numbers that do not make any sense."

"Actually," replied Jillian as she read the numbers along her bag, "they do make sense. They're grid coordinates."

"Like on a map?"

"Very similar. Ellyson must have established a grid system over the site where the artifacts were found. The first numbers are a reference point, maybe an outer corner or dead center in the middle of the site. The next set of numbers explains what part of the grid the item was found in."

"What about this last set of numbers, the one with a degree marker after it?" asked Harvath. "That's not a longitudinal or latitudinal designation?"

"No. It's degree of elevation followed by a depth designation. I'd say Ellyson was dealing with a very steep surface and was cataloging not only at what point along the slope he was finding things but also how deeply embedded."

"Embedded?"

"Yes, probably in ice. Call him what you will, but the man was thorough," said Jillian.

"Thorough, but not to the point that these strings of numbers will tell us where the actual discovery was made."

"No. They're all in relation to that first set of numbers. Those are the anchor which all the others work off of. We're missing one key piece of the puzzle—the Rosetta stone, if you will, which explains the overall message."

Harvath turned to Marie and asked, "When Bernard failed to return home, did you call the police?"

"Of course," replied Marie.

"What happened?"

"They came and asked the same questions they always ask when climbers have not returned."

"What did you tell them?" asked Jillian. "Did you mention anything about the Hannibal connection?"

"I told the police basically everything I knew, that my husband was climbing the crevices somewhere near the Col de la Traversette and he had not come home."

Harvath looked at Lavoine and asked, "The local police looked through all of your husband's maps, charts, whatever they could find that might tell them exactly where he was climbing on the day he disappeared?"

"The police *and* his climbing friends. They looked through everything, but they found nothing. Doctor Ellyson was trying to keep his work a secret, so it is no surprise Bernard left no record."

It was obviously painful for Marie to relive the experience. Nothing was said for several moments as Harvath set down the *falcata* and wandered among the rest of the artifacts.

"These are all very interesting from a historical

perspective," said Jillian, "but they don't really shed any more light on Hannibal's mystery weapon itself."

"The *Arthashastra* talked about applying poisons to edged weapons, right?" said Harvath.

"Yes."

"Maybe we should have these analyzed then."

Jillian noticed Marie tense and discreetly motioned for her not to worry. "If Hannibal was going to eliminate every Roman man, woman, child, and even their animals, he wasn't going to do it one sword stroke at a time. He had a bigger delivery vehicle in mind. We need to find Ellyson's dig."

Harvath shook his head. "No. This is a dead end. We need to find Emir Tokay."

"And how are we going to do that? We don't have any leads."

"We've got the e-mail address that Marie used to contact Rayburn, and we know Rayburn was involved with Emir's kidnapping. I'd say that's a pretty good lead."

"Only *if* it leads somewhere. Look," she continued, "if we can find the dig, maybe we can find enough physical evidence to help us piece together what this mystery illness is all about and figure out a cure."

"And Emir?"

Jillian was silent as she considered her response. "We don't even know if he is still alive. It's possible that he's been killed. The answers we're looking for might be closer than we think. We're here now and finding Ellyson's dig is at least a possibility we can't afford to turn our backs on."

Jillian was right, but how the hell were they going to locate the dig? Teams much more experienced and much more familiar with the area had searched for the missing men for weeks and had come up empty. How were he and Jillian supposed to accomplish what they couldn't? They didn't even have any new information. The only thing Harvath could think of doing was to re-cover the ground the police had already been over and hope to find something that they had missed. Without much hope, he turned back to Marie Lavoine and said, "I need to use your telephone, and then I'd like to see Bernard's personal effects for myself."

FORTY

After Harvath called Nick Kampos on Cyprus and gave him the e-mail address Rayburn was using under his Elliot Burnham alias, he and Jillian spent the rest of the evening poring over Bernard's personal things. They studied all of his maps, charts, and atlases without finding anything of use. Their eyes blurry with fatigue, neither of them wanted to believe that they had come all this way only to drive straight down a dead end. It was well past two in the morning when Jillian suggested they finally call it a night.

Harvath was absolutely exhausted, but as he lay in bed, sleep refused to come. His mind was plagued with thoughts he had been able to keep at bay for most of the day but which now returned with a vengeance. He was troubled by what his life might be like if he lost his job and was "outed," for lack of a better word, on international television.

As he lay there, his mind and body numb with

fatigue, there was one simple question he could not answer: *Without my career, who am I?*

He had never considered himself a weak man, but doubt was beginning to peck away at the edges of his psyche. The more he tried to push his problems from his mind, the harder and faster they came rushing back at him. Finally, he gave up hope of getting any sleep at all and walked downstairs.

The chalet was quiet. After starting a fire in the fireplace in the reception area, Harvath walked into the kitchen and found a bottle of Calvados and a clean snifter. Filling the snifter, he took the first glassful in one long swallow. Then he removed *Hannibal Crosses the Alps* from the mantelpiece and poured himself another drink. Snifter in hand, Harvath slumped down into an overstuffed leather chair, opened the book, and tried to escape his own world by losing himself in someone else's for a while.

It was half past seven in the morning when Jillian found him, along with Marie Lavoine, poring over boxes of paperwork on the floor of the hotel's office. "What's going on?" she asked.

"Last night I kept thinking about what you said, that the answers to this mystery illness could very well be waiting for us at Ellyson's site. When I couldn't fall asleep I decided to come downstairs and read awhile. I wanted to see why Ellyson was so interested in that particular book about Hannibal crossing the Alps."

"And?"

Harvath pulled the book off the chair next to him and tossed it to her. "Page one seventy-one."

Alcott flipped to the page and read aloud the passage Harvath had underlined in pencil. "Until the Alps give up the remains of an elephant, or a Carthaginian officer, or an African or Spanish cavalryman, we will never know for certain exactly where Hannibal crossed. The possibility of discovering the archeological evidence, however, is not as remote as one might think. During no other period in history have scholars had the access to the Alps and the technological assistance that they have today. Satellites, helicopters, and airplanes have allowed aerial surveys to be conducted which yield views of the valleys, ridges, and peaks never before available on such an accurate and detailed scale." Jillian balanced the book on her thigh and looked up at Harvath, waiting for some sort of explanation.

"Summers in Europe have been getting progressively warmer, and with that heat, Alpine glaciers have begun to recede. As the book says, today's scholars have tools available to them unlike any time in the past. No archeologist worth his salt would ever think of conducting a search like this without as much technological help as he could muster. The Silenus manuscript may have helped Ellyson narrow down the area where the team carrying Hannibal's secret weapon was killed and swept off the side of the mountain, but there was no way it could provide a pinpoint, X-marks-the-spot location. Ellyson may have known the general vicinity of where his needle was, but he needed to shrink the hell out of the haystack."

Jillian was finally with him. "You think he did it with satellite imagery."

"And Bernard Lavoine paid for it."

"With Rayburn's money, of course."

"Of course, but what I'm hoping is that Bernard did it with his own credit card and then just invoiced the expedition or took the corresponding amount from whatever pile of money Rayburn had left here for exactly such an expense."

It was forty-five minutes later when Marie Lavoine uncovered the first credit card statement that made reference to an international satellite company from Toulouse called Spot Image. Soon thereafter, they uncovered several more statements, all referencing the same company. While Bernard had done a lot of business with Spot Image, it was the last set of imagery he had ordered that Harvath was most interested in.

The most logical step was to have Marie call them up, explain who she was and what she wanted. But when the company informed her that their privacy policy prohibited them from providing anyone but the original customer with copies, Harvath knew he was going to have to come up with a better plan.

He had no desire to drive all the way to Toulouse to try to conduct another black-bag job to steal the information. Besides, being a satellite company, Spot Image would be a business that ran around the clock. It wouldn't be empty in the middle of the night with just a couple of security guards sitting behind a desk the way Sotheby's Paris annex was. There had to be someone Harvath knew outside his established intelligence contacts who could lean on Spot Image hard enough to get him what he needed. Suddenly, he knew just who that person was.

FORTY-ONE

Harvath had met Kevin McCauliff several years back while he was still with the Secret Service. Both he and McCauliff had been members of an informal group of federal employees who trained together every year for the annual Washington, DC, Marine Corps Marathon.

McCauliff worked for the National Geospatial Intelligence Agency. Formerly known as the National Imagery and Mapping Agency, the NGA was a major intelligence and combat support agency of the Department of Defense. Though the NGA was very much a member of the intelligence community, Kevin McCauliff wasn't what Harvath would refer to as an established intelligence contact. For a few weeks out of the year, they ran together. That was pretty much the extent of their relationship. The possibility that anyone would be watching for Harvath to make contact with Kevin McCauliff was beyond infinitesimal. And even better, McCauliff owed Harvath a favor.

The imagery analyst was one of the few senior people at the NGA who actually enjoyed the nightshift because, as he put it, that was when all the action happened. The NGA's operator put Harvath through to McCauliff's desk and the twenty-eight-year-old, two-hour and fifty-five-minute marathoner answered on the first ring. "Kevin, it's Scot Harvath," he said from among the boxes of paperwork scattered across Marie Lavoine's office.

"Harvath?" replied McCauliff's familiar voice from over four thousand miles away at the NGA's headquarters in Bethesda, Maryland. "It's almost three in the morning. The marathon isn't until October. Don't tell me you're losing sleep over strategy already."

"I never lose sleep over strategy, Kevin. It's just a race," he replied.

"I'll make sure I remind you of that at mile twenty-five if we get dusted by another pack of young leathernecks this year."

Harvath laughed. They had posted a very admirable time in last year's marathon, but he was a Navy man, and it was gut-wrenching to get blown away in the final mile by a group of young Marines whom they had had a considerable lead over for the entire race. "Okay, maybe it's more than just a race, but that's not why I called."

"What's up?"

"Remember back when I was working the president's Secret Service detail at the White House and got your family on one of the VIP tours?"

"Of course I do. My mother and sister still talk about it—and *you*, as a matter of fact. You swear to God nothing happened between you and Denise?"

McCauliff was like Sonny Corleone when it came to his kid sister, and no matter what Harvath ever told him, the guy never believed anything he said about the evening they spent together. "You're never going to let it go, are you? We had *one* drink and I dropped her back at her hotel. I've told you that a million times."

"I know, but it's over three years ago, and she still talks about you. What would you think if you were in my position?"

"I'd think I need some therapy."

It was McCauliff who laughed this time. "I'll take it under advisement," replied the NGA operative as he switched the phone to his other ear. "So what can I do for you?"

"Have you ever heard of a satellite imaging company called Spot Image?"

"Sure. We've even done some work with them. Why?"

"Do you have a relationship with anybody there?"

McCauliff thought about it for a second. "I know a couple of people. Their U.S. offices are just over in Chantilly, Virginia. What do you need?"

Having seen the clippings Marie had kept from several French newspapers about Bernard's disappearance and the subsequent search and rescue effort, Harvath said, "I'm working a missing person's case overseas right now. The man's name was Bernard Lavoine, L-A-V-O-I-N-E. He disappeared with two other individuals over a year ago on a climbing expedition in the Alps. He ordered a lot of satellite imagery from Spot, and I'm hoping that it might help shed some light on where he was when he disappeared."

"So why isn't someone from DHS calling them?"

"Because the case is personal, Kevin. I'm not operating in an official capacity."

McCauliff was quiet for several moments on his end of the line. "You swear nothing happened between you and my sister, right?"

"Jesus, Kevin. Yes, I swear."

"Okay," he responded, "give me a way to get in touch with you, and I'll see what I can do."

After giving him the number at the hotel, Harvath thanked McCauliff and hung up the phone. Jillian then looked at him and said, "Now what?"

"Now, we wait."

FORTY-TWO

HAMTRAMCK, MICHIGAN

America had been good to Kaseem Najjar, very good. His string of Muslim grocery stores and his mail-order food business were flourishing, his three children attended some of the United States' most prestigious universities, and the man was seen as a pillar of his largely Muslim community just outside Detroit. In America, anything was possible, and Kaseem had proven it.

A refugee from war-torn Sudan, he had the almost stereotypical rags-to-riches immigrant story. He had come to America with nothing but the clothes on his back, and over the course of twenty-five years he had built a dynasty catering to the tastes of those who longed for the foods of their homeland. When it came to the products Kaseem featured on his store shelves, in his mail-order catalog, or on his new web site, he discriminated against no one. His fortune had been built catering to all Muslims. Chili peppers from Indonesia, pistachios from Iran, dates from Libya, special bread flour from Iraq—Kaseem Najjar did not care how hard they were to import. He was a man who never took no for an answer, and that dogged determination was half of what had made him such a success.

The other half of Kaseem's success came from the balance he struck in his life. Though he had never asked for such status, he was proud to be a role model for the Muslims of his community. On an almost weekly basis, a customer, a colleague, or a member of his mosque would ask him the predominant question that seemed to occupy the mind of every Muslim living in the United States—*Where should my allegiance lie? With Islam or with America? Am I a Muslim first or an American?*

Even though he'd been asked the same question thousands of times, he still treated each inquiry as if it were the first time he'd ever been asked. His response, though, was always the same. Instead of an answer, he would pose his own question. "If you had two children," he would say, "who were both equally gifted, beautiful, and possessed of unlimited promise, to which would you devote all of your love?"

It was, of course, a rhetorical question. In Kaseem Najjar's mind, there was no reason to have to choose. This was America, and he could love both his adopted country and his Islamic faith equally. The two were not mutually exclusive as so many perverters of the Muslim religion would like the faithful to believe. His sage response often brought smiles and simple knowing nods from those who asked the question. It also did much to enhance the reputation of Kaseem Najjar as one of the wisest men in Hamtramck.

That reputation, though, was called into question when, as one of the founders of Hamtramck's Al-Islah Islamic Center, Kaseem suggested the center seek approval from the city council for broadcasting the Muslim call to worship over loudspeakers affixed to the center's exterior. The debate this sparked made international news.

Many of the Muslims in Hamtramck considered Kaseem a fool for asking permission for a right that was already theirs. Under the city's noise ordinances, as well as its charter, which specifically protected such religious freedoms, the center *already* had the right to broadcast the call to worship. The calls lasted only one to two minutes, and in their opinion, they were no different from the ringing of Christian church bells.

Kaseem, on the other hand, had been smart enough to see it as a potentially divisive issue in the multiethnic, multireligious community and had decided to tackle it head-on. By rallying his fellow authorities and approaching the Hamtramck city council to ask that the calls be regulated, before a single objection was ever raised, the center had shown itself to be benevolent, sensitive to the rights of others, and above all else, an exceptionally good neighbor. It was an extremely positive PR move for the Muslim community, not only in Michigan but also in post-9/11 America as a whole.

Occasionally, someone would ask Kaseem if he thought the whole incident had been worth it. In his knowing way, he would always smile and then reach for his worn leather wallet. From it, he would remove an article from the *Detroit News*, which he was sure had done more for their cause than anything else. To most nonbelievers, the call to worship was nothing but noise. The *Detroit News* had changed that perception, and the article was picked up by wire services and reprinted in newspapers around the world. With pride, Kaseem would read the translation of the call, which had been read by millions around the world: "Before any prayer session, a man called the *muezzin* climbs to the top of the mosque's minaret and sings *God is great* four times, followed by *I testify there is no other God but God* twice. Then the muezzin calls *I testify Muhammad is the messenger of God* two times, followed by *Come and pray* sung twice. Both *Come and flourish* and *God is great* are then twice called, followed by the final *There is no God but God*."

Of course, the people with whom Kaseem shared the article did not need a translation of the call to worship. They already understood its meaning, but nevertheless there was no arguing with the pride the man obviously felt in having made the religion and practices of Islam a little more accessible to the rest of the world.

Now Kaseem looked at his watch and saw that it was nearing five o'clock in the morning. He had spent all night in his warehouse unpacking the multitudes of pallets that had arrived the day before. They were the first in an exclusive series of shipments that were the crowning achievement of his career, thanks in no small part to the international notoriety he had received from the call to worship undertaking.

Much as British royalty had done in recognizing specific merchants as official purveyors to the crown, a certain rather radical Saudi prince, named Hamal, from the vast, extended Saudi Royal Family had recognized an outstanding, select few merchants who catered not to the Saudi Royal Family but to the greater worldwide Muslim community as a whole. The first and only merchant in the United States to be awarded the honorable distinction had been Kaseem Najjar.

Along with this recognition, Kaseem was awarded exclusive North American distribution rights to the first product ever officially endorsed by the Saudi Royal Family—bottled water from a secret spring discovered beneath the holy city of Mecca, said to have quenched the thirst of the Prophet Muhammad himself. Proceeds from the sale of the holy water went to Islamic charities around the world. As outlined by Mecca's Muslim hierarchy in a communiqué disseminated to mosques around the globe, it was the holy duty of each Muslim—man, woman, or child—to buy and consume at least one bottle of water from the secret Mecca spring before the upcoming Ramadan holiday that fall.

Kaseem had indeed done well in securing the exclusive contract to distribute the holy water in the U.S. Any of the faithful who wanted to purchase some would have to do so at their local mosque, which in turn had to purchase it from him. The arrangement was going to make him even richer than he already was. What he didn't like about it, though, was the Saudis' insistence that he only sell the water to their list of approved mosques in the United States, all of which catered solely to the majority Sunni faith. No provision had been made to sell the water to any of the Shia mosques.

In addition, his counterparts in Saudi Arabia had also insisted Kaseem's company take delivery of several tons of a spice known as *mahleb*. It was made from the pits of black cherries and was readily available throughout the United States, but apparently his Saudi contacts saw a need for a pure Muslim version. Branding was not a concept solely restricted to American companies. The Muslim world was catching on as well. Today it was spring water and cherry pit spice, tomorrow tennis shoes and watches. If the truth be told, Kaseem was very pleased to see the Muslim world begin to keep pace with modern times. He had no doubt that given the choice, his customers would rather buy a Muslim version of *mahleb* than a non-Muslim one.

Though he would never say so out loud, Kaseem realized that his business could very well end up being as profitable as, if not more so than, Jewish companies that specialized in kosher foods.

Another aspect of the transaction was that none of the *mahleb* had been made available to Kaseem to sell through his vast distribution network. Instead, it was intended for some new Muslim spice conglomerate based in the U.S. The Saudis explained that as the conglomerate's import credentials had not been set up yet, they needed Kaseem's company to take delivery of the spice and then repackage it and send it along to the conglomerate's various offices.

A responsible businessman, Kaseem had done a little checking up on the supposed conglomerate. Its principals were all former immigrants like himself and all from Muslim countries, but that was where the similarities ended. As far as Kaseem could tell, none of the men had any experience in the food industry whatsoever. They owned a variety of businesses across the country, most often the types associated with Middle Eastern immigrants who arrive in America and try to get a foothold on one of the lower rungs of the American dream—payday loan, currency exchange, and check-cashing businesses, as well as 7-Eleven–style convenience stores, gas stations, and taxicab companies. They were in fact successful entrepreneurs, but why they would want to get into such a low-margin endeavor like the spice business was beyond him. Maybe they knew something he didn't. None of it mattered, though, as Kaseem had randomly checked samples of the bitter-tasting *mahleb* himself and was convinced that it was the real deal. The last thing he wanted to do was be an unwitting party to importing any kind of illegal substance. Whether his client was a Saudi royal or not, he still had his family's good name and his country to look out for.

As he packed up the last of the *mahleb* to go out via UPS that afternoon, Kaseem's mind was on getting home and getting a little sleep before the morning prayer service. Tired and distracted, he failed to notice that one of the packages he had randomly tested had been put back in with the rest of the shipment and that its lid had not been fully reattached.

The mystery illness from the Iraqi village of Asalaam, the same one once destined to decimate all of Rome, had just made its debut on American soil.

FORTY-THREE

FRANCE

Harvath was in his room scanning the reference book Vanessa Whitcomb had allowed him to take with him, *Greek Fire, Poison Arrows & Scorpion Bombs—Biological and Chemical Warfare in the Ancient World* by Adrienne Mayor, when Marie Lavoine knocked on his door and told him he had a phone call. It could have only been one of two people, and whoever it was had either come up empty or had information that would throw some light on what direction he should take next.

Harvath took the call in Marie's office. "Harvath," he said as he picked the receiver up off the desk.

"Scot, it's Kevin McCauliff."

"That was fast, Kevin," he replied, looking at his watch. It had only been a couple of hours.

"Well, lucky for you, my guy here in Chantilly is friendly with someone at Spot's headquarters in Toulouse."

"What were you able to find?"

"Just like you said, your guy Bernard Lavoine did order a lot of imagery from Spot. The dates from the credit card transactions helped them locate the stuff a lot faster."

"Good. What did they give you?"

McCauliff toggled through the images on his monitor and said, "All of the imagery your missing person ordered was for an area around Mount Viso and a pass just north of it called the Col de la Traversette. The search was pretty broad in the beginning, but became progressively more focused."

"What was he looking for?"

"That I can't tell you," replied McCauliff, "but I can tell you that money didn't seem to be an object for this guy. He ordered every kind of test you could imagine—surface spectral reflectance data, temperature data, emissivity data—you name it and this guy bought it. I'm sure there's some sales rep at Spot who was sorry to lose him as a customer."

Not as sorry as Marie Lavoine was to lose him as a husband, thought Harvath. "What about the last purchases?"

"All scene-specific."

"Meaning?"

"Meaning your missing person had picked a specific spot and was using satellites to drill down on it as hard as he could. After that, there were no more orders," said McCauliff. "Whatever Bernard

Lavoine was looking for, I think he might have found it."

"I owe you one, Kevin."

"Technically," said the NGA operative, "I owed you one, but there is something you can do for me. My sister is going to be in DC for a conference in April, and I want you to take her to a real nice dinner. It'll be the highlight of her trip. But we're just talking dinner here, that's all."

"You got it. Now, can you get me copies of those last images along with any data that goes with them?"

"Already done. All I need is an e-mail address and I can send them off to you right now."

Harvath gave McCauliff one of the remote e-mail addresses he used while on the road and thanked the man again for his help.

As he hung up the phone, Jillian walked into the office. "Marie said you got a phone call. What's happening?"

"We were able to track down the final satellite imagery Bernard and Ellyson were working off of. It looks like you and I are going climbing."

After using the computer and printer of Marie Lavoine's neighbor to download the satellite information, Harvath spent forty-five minutes in Bernard's equipment room putting together what he thought they would need for their climb. Though most of the hotel's guests normally brought their own gear, the Lavoines had been well prepared for those who hadn't. Harvath was able to find not only boots, but also Helly Hansen jackets and pants made from heavy wind-stopper fabric that fit him and Jillian perfectly.

With the pieces of numbered masking tape stuck to the top of the worn kitchen table, Harvath spread out several of Bernard's maps along with their newly acquired satellite imagery. Suddenly, they had a much clearer picture of where Ellyson had focused his search. Harvath had no idea what he and Jillian would find when they got there, but he couldn't help wondering if the search and rescue teams would have been able to save Bernard and the rest of his party if they had had the information that was now sitting in front of him. For some reason, he doubted it. Something told him, just as it had Marie Lavoine, that the disappearance of Bernard and the rest of his party had not been any accident.

As it was at least a two-hour hike to get up to the Col de la Traversette, Harvath quickly divided up their gear. He gave Jillian the lighter items like the flares, food, and first aid kit for her to carry in a KIVA technical pack, and he took one of Bernard's larger internal-frame backpacks to hold everything else.

Marie tried to convince Harvath to postpone the trip for at least a day or two until some of the other local mountain guides, who had been friends of Bernard, were available to go along with them.

Harvath would have appreciated their participation, but he couldn't afford to wait. Besides, the time he spent attached to the Navy's cold warfare specialists, SEAL Team Two, had made him an experienced enough climber, and he was confident he could teach Jillian anything she needed to know along the way. If they ran across a feature that they couldn't tackle, they would just have to turn around and come back.

On the surface it looked good, made sense, and sounded safe, but in the back of his mind, Harvath knew that a million fatal expeditions had started out with the same false sense of security. There was no room for excessive pride in climbing, because there was no more imposing foe than an unforgiving mountain that didn't care if you lived or died.

FORTY-FOUR

The climb to the Traversette was steep, dangerous, and extremely difficult. Both Harvath and Alcott lost their footing several times. The debris-strewn moraine was covered with sharp rocks and jagged pieces of shale. Off in the distance, they could make out the towering peak of Mount Viso. Its craggy, snow-covered face was made even more menacing by the thickening curtain of heavy clouds gathering around it. Harvath knew that the weather was something they were going to have to contend with. Marie had given them an update on the forecast before they left, and the gods were not smiling on their venture. All they could hope for was to be able to move fast enough to beat the storm.

By the time they made it to the pass, their bodies were wrung out. They were above the snowline now, but neither of them cared as they unslung their packs and looked for a place to lie down. Harvath reached for one of his bottles of water and drained it in three long swallows. Dehydration was one of the most common consequences of altitude. He looked down at his gloves, the palms of which were shredded, as were Jillian's. He removed a roll of duct tape from his pack, repaired his gloves as best he could, and then threw the roll to Alcott.

Once Jillian's gloves were patched, the pair shouldered their packs and continued upward. In retrospect, the jagged rocks and loose pieces of shale were a cakewalk in comparison to what they now faced. As the pass wound its way around the north side of Mount Viso, the winds picked up dramatically and the snow they were walking upon quickly turned to ice. Once again, they stopped, and as Jillian ate some of the food Marie had packed for them, Harvath removed two sets of crampons from his bag. Once he was sure that both his and Alcott's were securely attached to their boots, they started walking again.

Harvath chose his steps very carefully. They were on a narrow precipice with the sheer wall of the mountain rising immediately to their right and a fathomless drop, easily thousands of feet, immediately to their left. Very quickly, Harvath gained a new appreciation for how Hannibal could have lost more men and pack animals on this high Alpine pass than at any other point in his campaign.

They walked for twenty more minutes, stopping more and more often for Harvath to check their location on the spare GPS unit he had found in Bernard's equipment room. When they reached the point indicated by the satellite imagery, Harvath held up his gloved hand, indicating that they had finally made it. The wind was now blowing so hard that both he and Jillian had to shout to be heard above it. Snow began to fall, and the icy crystals, propelled by the wind, tore across their faces like shards of broken glass.

Harvath got as near to the left side of the pass as he dared, dug in his crampons, and tried to peer over the edge, but he couldn't see a thing. After checking both his GPS unit and the satellite imagery one more time, he began unloading his pack. He laid out four fifty-meter coils of rope and then pulled out a pair of lightweight Alpine sit harnesses. As he helped Jillian into hers and began tightening it, he noticed her wince. "Are you sure you want to do this?" he asked.

Though Jillian had never climbed before, she seemed more than physically capable, but that wasn't what Harvath was concerned about. Climbing, while demanding stamina, was an absolute mental game and required one hundred percent concentration. He had given her several chances to back out, and she had passed on every one of them. If there was a find down there of any sort, she wanted to see it for herself.

In answer to Harvath's question, Jillian looked

him right in the eye and said, "Just tell me what to do."

He had to hand it to her. She had guts. There was no question in his mind that she was scared—any sane person would be frightened by the prospect of what they were about to do. Even Harvath's adrenaline was flowing, but the difference between a successful climber and a dead climber was what he did with that fear. Would Jillian allow the fear to eat her up and paralyze her the way he'd seen it do at Sotheby's and the department store in London, or would she turn the fear to her advantage and make it work for her?

In all fairness, what had happened at Sotheby's and Harvey Nichols had involved guns and bullets, not ropes and mountains, but Harvath wasn't taking any chances. The entire time they had been climbing, Harvath had been going through a mental checklist of the ways in which he could safely facilitate Alcott's descent into the chasm. The first and most obvious option was for him to lower her down himself, but now without either a line-of-sight visual or proper communications gear, that option was fraught with too many potential problems and was scratched from the list. The next option was for both of them to rappel on the same line, but it would undoubtedly require Harvath to go first, and if Jillian froze for some reason above him, he'd be lucky as hell to get both of them back up to the pass. The option that made the most sense was for them to rappel side-by-side at the same time.

Harvath examined the rock above the pass and looked for anchor points for his hardware. While he decided on the right items to use, he also kept one eye open for anchor points that Bernard might have previously established. The fact that he didn't spot any told him that either they were totally in the wrong location and Bernard had never climbed here, or someone had done a very careful cleanup job. Though Harvath hated to think about it, he had a bad feeling that the latter was probably true.

After establishing anchor points with a combination of pitons and spring-loaded camming devices, Harvath tied a double rope and threw the excess over the side of the pass and into the chasm. He gave Jillian's harness a final check and then his own. Running one of the ropes through her harness, he drew it tight and had her lean back into it while she stood there on the pass, just getting used to it. "Remember, we're going to do this nice and easy. It isn't like you see in the movies. There's not going to be any of that pushing way out from the wall kind of stuff. You just sit back in your harness and we'll lower ourselves slowly, okay?"

Jillian nodded her head, and as an added safety measure, Harvath connected her harness to his own with a long piece of nylon known as a leash.

With their backs toward the drop-off behind them, Harvath gave everything one last check, swung his pack over his shoulders, and then talked Jillian through what was always the most terrifying part of a descent—stepping out and over the edge.

Her feet may have been hesitant, but to her credit, Jillian did everything she was told to do and never stopped. Like many novice climbers, she was afraid to trust the full weight of her body to her harness and ended up gripping the rope a lot tighter than she needed to. Harvath encouraged her to relax, but it wasn't until her hands and the muscles in her arms started to ache that she allowed herself to sit all the way back in the harness.

With the howling wind buffeting their bodies and threatening to slam them into the sheer cliff face in front of them, it wasn't the optimal condition for a first-time descent, but Jillian was doing surprisingly well. Harvath could tell she was scared, but she was keeping her fear at bay by focusing on everything he had told her to do. She was an exceptional student.

Harvath, on the other hand, had several concerns of his own regarding their descent, not the least of which was that due to the weather conditions, a mountain fog had moved in and was making it impossible to see anything beneath them. There was no telling if they would reach any sort of foothold before they ran out of rope, which was all the more reason to take it easy. The last thing they needed was for one of them to end up breaking a leg, or worse.

Twenty-five meters later, the fog diminished slightly and they could make out a wide, sloping shelf of ice ten meters below. Harvath unleashed himself from Jillian and gently increased his speed. By the time she made it the rest of the way down, Harvath's crampons were already firmly planted on the shelf.

"Did we make some sort of mistake?" said Jillian as she stood up and looked around, disappointed. "There's nothing here."

"Maybe, maybe not," said Harvath as he removed one of the satellite images from inside his parka and studied it. "It's been over a year. When it comes to snow and ice, a lot can happen in that time."

Jillian watched as Harvath withdrew two more coils of rope from his pack and established another set of anchor points by hammering pitons into the rock face behind them. He secured the ropes they had used to climb down from the pass so they wouldn't blow away and then got back to work, readying for the next stage of their descent.

After first securing Jillian's rope and harness, followed by his own, Harvath looked at the shelf they were standing on. It sloped upward, away from the mountain, and the number one question on Harvath's mind was *Where did it lead?* Removing what looked like a collapsible ski pole from his pack, he extended the telescoping avalanche probe to its full length and leaned it against the cliff face.

"What are you doing?" asked Jillian.

"You see how the ice slopes up like that?" he said as he pointed at the shelf in front of them.

"Yes."

"That ramplike or wave formation can happen when there's a lot of freeze-thaw, freeze-thaw kind of weather. It builds up very quickly and can be extremely fragile."

"So what are you going to do, walk out there and test it?"

Harvath nodded his head.

"I was kidding," she said. "What if it gives way?"

Harvath tripled-wrapped his own rope around her waist and tied it with a double knot. Once he had rechecked the security of her anchor points, he said, "Then I'll be glad I've got you hanging on to me."

After showing her how to properly feed out the rope, Harvath picked up his probe and started out away from the cliff face along the top of the shelf.

As he walked, large sheets of crisp, ice-laden snow cracked and broke away beneath his crampons. The *pop*, as every footfall punched its way through the crusty snow, sounded like gunfire and could be heard well above the roar of the wind. Harvath looked back more than once, just to make sure Jillian was keeping a tight grip on his safety line.

Using the avalanche probe to test the stability of the shelf in front of him, he took his steps one painfully slow foot at a time. It was like climbing up the side of a slick, steeply pitched, snow-covered roof. With the sharp teeth of his crampons aiding his climb, Harvath was more concerned about the entire shelf dropping away beneath him than he was about losing his footing. As he continued to move forward, he tried not to think about it.

He developed a steady rhythm as he planted his avalanche pole, then took a step, then planted his avalanche pole and took a step. It was almost hypnotic, and Harvath literally had to shake his head to keep his mind focused on what he was doing. When he finally reached the shelf's peak, he stopped and looked around as best he could through the increasing snow. Mount Viso towered high above while the other side of the shelf appeared to run steeply downhill into a large ice field far below.

Harvath had explained to Jillian that when and if he signaled, it was okay for her to follow him out onto the shelf; she should untie the loops of rope from around her waist and follow *exactly* in his footsteps. Giving her the signal, he watched as she removed the rope and coiled the extra loops on the ground where they wouldn't get tangled with her own. Then, like a tightrope walker, she carefully began placing one foot in front of the other and made her way toward him.

She was doing great and was about halfway across the shelf when Harvath heard a series of rumbling noises that sounded like three mortars being loosed. Jillian heard it too and immediately stopped, frozen in Harvath's tracks. For a moment, he thought it might have been thunder, but he knew it wasn't. Thunder came from over your head, not below your feet. For the moment, there was nothing but silence. Even the wind and snow seemed to have died away.

Harvath stood completely still for several seconds, as his ears strained to pick up any further sound, but there was nothing other than his own shallow breathing. After several seconds more, he signaled for Jillian to start moving forward again, *slowly*.

One step. Two steps. So far so good. But three steps later, the shelf began to tremble and made a terrible groaning noise. Pieces of it splintered as if a giant hand was pushing down on it from above. Harvath yelled for her to lie spread-eagle and distribute her weight evenly across the snow, but Jillian couldn't hear him above the noise. Suddenly, the shelf cracked apart and collapsed inward, completely disappearing from sight and taking Jillian Alcott along with it.

FORTY-FIVE

As the ice shelf caved in, there was nothing Harvath could do to save her. Jillian was too far away. It was like watching someone fall through a frozen lake. As her screams echoed off the side of the mountain, Harvath was tempted to look back, but his instincts had taken over and he was totally focused on saving himself.

Flattening his body against the upper peak of the shelf, Harvath slid his ice axes out from their holsters and swung them, along with his crampons, into the ice as hard as he could. Behind him, he could hear the sickening sound of the shelf as it wrenched the rest of the way away and collapsed into the chasm below. At least twenty feet out from the face of the mountain, Harvath said a silent prayer that the receding hunks of ice and snow wouldn't drag his safety line, and him, down into the frozen void.

He lay there waiting to be yanked off at any moment, but the moment never came. As the thunderous roar of the collapsing shelf subsided, Harvath began to entertain the guilty thought that for the umpteenth time in his life, he had cheated death.

With his hands beginning to ache from the death grip he had on his axes, he knew he needed to come up with some sort of a plan, the crux of which had to be getting to Jillian to see if she was still alive.

Looking down, Harvath saw that only about two and a half feet of shelf still remained below him. From the edge of it to the face of Mount Viso, where they had rappelled down with their first set of ropes, was about eighteen feet. The shelf which Harvath had crossed, and which had swallowed up Jillian, had been nothing more than a fragile bridge of ice and snow that covered over the entrance to a deep cavern of blue-green ice. Even though his anchor was firmly established on the far mountain wall, using his rope to swing out over the open expanse, Tarzan-style, was not the best of ideas. Eighteen feet might not seem like much, but it was plenty of distance in which to pick up a full head of steam and slam into the other side. He immediately struck it from his list of possible options.

Ice chasms in general were like a big V, wide at the top and progressively narrower as you got toward the bottom. If one were to imagine a huge triangle with its point downward, it would form a pretty good picture of what things had looked like before the shelf had collapsed. Harvath now stood at the top of the chasm looking across to where his rope was anchored on the other side. Since swinging across was out of the question, the only way he could go was down. The problem, though, was that if he established another set of anchor points on this side, when he wanted to climb back up he'd still be on the wrong side of the cavern with no way to get across. There was no telling what condition Jillian was in. He needed to figure something out quickly. Finally, Harvath had an idea.

After pulling up the balance of his rope from where it had fallen into the cavern, Harvath set new anchor points in the ice above him. Confident that they were secure, he tied a small loop in a portion of the rope that led back across the chasm toward Mount Viso and lay between his two sets of anchor points. Then, after attaching an extra carabiner to the loop of rope, he unslung his pack and removed only the most essential items. The key was to leave as much weight in the pack as possible. It was essential for his eventual ascent that it weigh more than the remainder of the line. The few items he needed to have with him he stuffed inside his parka and then attached the pack itself to the carabiner.

Having tested the anchor points to make sure they would hold his weight, Harvath holstered his ice axes and began his descent. With every crack and pop of ice, he immediately froze. There was no telling how stable the remaining portion of the shelf above him was. If it collapsed, he'd be crushed beneath it, and if the ice around his pitons gave way, he'd be set loose on an unstoppable trajectory straight at the wall of ice on the other side.

Inch by inch, Harvath played out the rope, trying to judge how much farther he had to go. Crystals of snow hung in the air, obscuring everything from view. Twenty feet, forty feet, fifty—soon Harvath began to lose all concept of how far he had rappelled. His muscles ached more from the careful, measured descent than if he had been tackling it at regular speed, but he knew all too well that regular speed was only advisable under perfect conditions. What he now found himself in were definitely less than perfect conditions.

Harvath needed to take a breather, just for a moment, and as he sat back in his harness, he contemplated calling out for Jillian. The upside of the idea was that if she was alive and could call back to him, he'd be able to get a fix on her location. The downside was that the vibrations from his shout could very well bring the remainder of the shelf crashing down on top of him. Harvath decided it was best to err on the side of caution and held back any yelling for the time being.

Thirty feet later, as his crampons touched the icy floor of the chasm, Harvath saw a pile of what looked like broken snow-white surfboards, and sitting atop it assessing her injuries was Jillian Alcott.

She was alive! Harvath couldn't believe his eyes. After securing the balance of his rope, he carefully picked his way across the ice and climbed up the mound of broken snow. "Are you okay?" he asked as he scanned her head and face for any signs of trauma.

Jillian gave him a pained look and said, "I don't think I like ice climbing very much."

Forgetting that she had medical experience as well, Harvath continued in triage mode. "Anything hurt?"

"My right shoulder," she replied as she tried to roll it forward.

"Your legs and everything else are okay? Nothing's broken as far as you can tell? You can move everything? Fingers? Toes?"

"Just the shoulder," replied Alcott. "I think it's bruised."

It was an absolute miracle. "I can't believe I'm looking at you," he said. "What happened? Judging by how much rope I played out, we've got to be at least eighty feet down."

Jillian used her good arm to brush the snow off her climbing pants as she replied, "I did what you told me. I let the rope out nice and slow."

Harvath was dumbstruck. "How? How is that possible?"

"I've got to admit, it scared the hell out of me. I just grabbed the rope as hard as I could."

"But when it drew tight, it would have pulled you in and smashed you against the wall."

Jillian shrugged her shoulders. "Whatever we

were standing on was made up of a lot of snow, because a huge slab of it wound up between me and the cliff face and broke the impact, but my shoulder still bore some of the brunt of it."

Harvath marveled at her. "And you just lowered yourself the rest of the way down here?"

Jillian looked at him as if he was a moron. "I had about five hundred pounds of snow on top of me. The only way I was going was down."

"I think you're going to find going up a lot less stressful than coming down."

"I'd better."

"In the meantime," said Harvath as he fished through Alcott's pack and came up with a headlamp for her that matched his own, "maybe we ought to see what we came all the way down here for."

Jillian took the lamp from Harvath and placed it over her head. As they turned the lamps on, they saw the only path available to them—a narrow ramp that led deeper into the bowels of the ice cave.

The four-foot-wide passageway sloped downward at such an angle that they had to lean back in their crampons to prevent picking up too much speed and losing control.

The walls of ice were so close on each side that they could reach out and touch them both at the same time. It was like walking through a narrow slot canyon.

After several minutes, the path began to level

out, and Harvath and Alcott no longer needed to lean back in their crampons. As they approached the end of the passageway, they crawled beneath a jagged overhang and entered a wide antechamber. The chamber was honeycombed with low tunnels feeding off in all directions. The most magnificent feature of all, though, was a soaring, translucent wall of ice at the far end of the room. Even from where they stood, there was no mistaking what was frozen behind it. Ignoring everything else in the chamber, they walked over to get as close a look as possible.

The ceiling of the antechamber rose steadily higher, and the light from their headlamps cast an otherworldly glow over the scene. Like some sort of enormous, subzero aquarium, the wall of ice held three perfectly preserved elephants.

There was no question what they were looking at. They had unearthed Dr. Ellyson's discovery, and both Scot and Jillian were speechless.

Finally, Harvath tugged on Jillian's parka, and they spread out to examine other portions of the cavern. Moving deeper into one of the tunnels, they began finding bodies—remnants of Hannibal's elite guard. There had to be over thirty of them, most of which were still encased in ice of varying degrees of thickness. Modern equipment lay scattered across the tunnel floor, and they could see places where the ice had been purposely melted away to remove some of the frozen bodies and strip them of their artifacts and God only knows what else.

The naturally formed tunnels bent and doubled back on each other, and Jillian and Harvath drifted in different directions, allowing their own natural sense of curiosity and wonder to dictate their individual courses. Even when they were in separate tunnels, the echo of crampons scraping along the floor of ice notified each of the other.

The lights from their headlamps were the only accompaniment to their own private thoughts as they stared into the face of history. Here and there, Harvath came across random artifacts, propped up against walls or carefully arranged inside narrow alcoves of ice, waiting to be catalogued and placed in plastic bags to be taken back to the Lavoines' barn. They had stumbled upon an amazing work in progress, and though many of the artifacts had already been removed, the historical significance of what remained was still astounding.

Looking at the breastplated soldiers frozen in the walls of ice with their eyes bulging and mouths agape in silent screams was like passing through some sort of ancient house of horrors. It looked as if they had all been preserved in a state of abject terror. And just like the elephants, they seemed as if they could come back to life at any second and burst through the ice with their swords and war hammers held high, ready to do battle.

Besides Ellyson, Bernard, and their Sherpa,

Maurice, no one had seen any of these soldiers for over two thousand years. Harvath could only imagine how Ellyson must have felt upon discovering them for himself. It must have been an incredible rush, both personally and professionally.

Harvath's reverie was abruptly interrupted by the sound of Jillian frantically shouting his name.

FORTY-SIX

Pinpointing Jillian's exact location was no easy task. The labyrinth of tunnels bounced the sound of her voice in so many directions that it was impossible to tell if she was in front of or behind him.

Eventually, Harvath exited the system of tunnels into another large room and found her along with the reason she had been calling for him. Lying at the mouth of the tunnel were three very contemporary yet very dead bodies that had been frozen into bizarre contortions. With their arms outstretched and fingers curled, they appeared to be both begging for help and trying to reach out and grab anyone unlucky enough to come close. Apparently, Jillian had almost tripped right over them.

Taking a closer look, Harvath could see that two of them had been shot in the back of their heads. With his bushy black beard, Bernard was the easiest of the three to identify. Harvath guessed the other man lying next to him was Maurice, which left only one other person. A little apart from the two men, dressed in expensive North Face climbing clothes, was the body of Dr. Donald Ellyson. His throat had been cut from ear to ear, and his parka, as well as his trousers and the ice all around him, were stained a deep crimson bordering on black. Harvath had seen some grisly crime scenes in his day, but this one was pretty horrific.

Jillian asked, "Who could have done this?"

There were a million possible answers, but only one that made sense. "Rayburn."

"Why him?"

"Why not him? He was in charge of the expedition. He knew they were here. It makes perfect sense."

"Look at all the artifacts lying around here. Why would he leave them behind?"

"Maybe he was in a hurry."

"But Marie told us that Ellyson never shared with Rayburn exactly where the dig was. She didn't trust him, remember?"

Jillian was right. "Maybe Rayburn followed them, or maybe he hired somebody else to do it. Whoever it was didn't want these men talking about what they had found."

"You mean Hannibal's weapon," said Jillian as she watched Harvath bend down toward Bernard's corpse. "What are you doing?"

Gently, he removed a gold chain with a small

medallion from around the man's neck. "Ironic," he said as he held the medallion up for her to see. "Saint Bernard, patron saint of mountain climbers, Alpinists, and skiers."

Jillian sadly shook her head.

"I think Marie would want to have this," said Harvath.

"I think you're right," she replied as she walked away from the bodies. She didn't want to look at them anymore, and there was something half buried in ice on the other side of the small room that had caught her eye.

Harvath placed the chain in his pocket and then went through Bernard's pockets, where he found a pair of ancient wrist cuffs made from gold and set with amethysts and small pieces of creamy white marble. It bore the same wolf's head with intertwined vipers as the breastplates. They were definitely something special, and he could see why Bernard had singled them out to bring back. There was something, though, about the way the snarling wolf looked that bothered him.

"Scot, come over here," said Jillian, interrupting his thoughts. "You need to see this."

Harvath tucked the wrist cuffs into his jacket pocket and joined Jillian on the other side of the room, where she was staring at a large wooden chest, its lower half frozen in a solid block of ice.

"Look at these," she said as she pointed to a series of carved figures along the lid.

"The wolf and intertwined vipers," replied Harvath. "The same as on the breastplates."

"Exactly. And these panels along the side seem to tell some sort of story."

Harvath studied the carvings.

"Somebody melted away this ice on purpose," continued Jillian, "to get into the box."

The carvings reminded Harvath of images he had seen in books of the Ark of the Covenant being carried into battle. "Do you think this was used to transport Hannibal's weapon?"

"There's only one way to find out," she said as she carefully raised the lid.

Together, they both looked inside. The long box was intricately partitioned, but other than that was completely empty.

"Damn it," said Jillian. She spent a few more minutes studying the box and then moved on to investigate something else near the mouth of one of the tunnels.

Harvath stayed with the crate, trying to decipher its story. It was an allegory, but its meaning was difficult to understand. "You know what?" he yelled over his shoulder as he continued to stare at the intricately carved relief. "I'm not so sure that these are actually supposed to be wolves."

"No?" replied Jillian, engrossed in something inside the tunnel. "What are they then?"

"I think they're supposed to be dogs."

"You may have missed your calling in life," came a man's voice from behind.

It was a voice he recognized—a voice he knew almost as well as his own. It belonged to the man he had been chasing for months, the man who had set him up in Baghdad and had tried to kill him in Cairo, London, and Paris—Khalid Sheik Alomari.

Harvath wanted it to be a figment of his imagination, but he knew it wasn't. As he turned and saw the al-Qaeda assassin standing there with a fully automatic machine pistol in his hand, Harvath began to reach for his gun. The problem, though, was that he had left it in his pack to help weigh it down. Defenseless, Harvath did the only other thing he could think of. He yelled for Jillian to run.

FORTY-SEVEN

"Call the woman back in here," commanded Alomari as Jillian disappeared down one of the tunnels. "If I have to go looking for her, I assure you I will make her death as painful as I am going to make yours."

"Kiss my ass."

"Wrong answer," replied the assassin as he stepped forward and struck Harvath across the face with his Steyr tactical machine pistol.

Harvath stumbled backward against the chest. It was all he could do to keep from losing his balance.

"We'll try this again. Call the woman back in here, now."

"Call her yourself, asshole," replied Harvath, who could taste blood in his mouth.

The assassin waved Harvath away from the box with his weapon and said, "Have it your way. She won't get far." As Harvath complied, Alomari continued, "I've enjoyed watching you on television.

It's unfortunate that al-Jazeera was not able to address your good side."

"What's unfortunate," replied Harvath, clenching his hand into a fist, "is that *I* wasn't able to address *your* good side."

"You had your chance, though, didn't you?"

That was a fact Harvath was all too well aware of. "How the hell did you find this place?"

"I've been here before," said Alomari as he raised his TMP and pointed it at Harvath's chest. "I didn't think I'd ever come back, but before our mutual friend at Sotheby's died, she suggested I might want to make a return visit. I would have been here sooner, but it took me a while to find a doctor I could trust to pull your bullet out of my shoulder."

Harvath hated him for his command of English, as well as all the other languages he used to move so effortlessly around the world carrying out the dirtiest of al-Qaeda's dirty work. But in his anger, Harvath found some small measure of satisfaction and couldn't help smiling. One of his bullets in Paris had definitely found its mark.

"You find my injury amusing," replied the assassin. "I guarantee you it isn't half as painful as what I intend to inflict upon you and your colleague. Now, take those ice axes from your belt and slowly drop them on the floor."

Harvath had no intention of doing anything the man asked of him. "If you're going to shoot me, go ahead and pull the trigger."

"That would be too easy. I have something else in mind for you. Now drop those axes. I will not ask you again."

"Fuck you," Harvath responded.

Alomari stepped forward and struck him again with his weapon, this time twice as hard.

Harvath's head spun and he saw stars, but he wasn't going to go down without a fight. Trying to focus on the al-Qaeda operative, he gathered his strength and lunged at the man with all his might.

Despite his shoulder injury, Alomari easily sidestepped the attack and watched as, even with his crampons on, Harvath lost his footing and banged his head against the entrance to one of the tunnels.

Before Harvath could slide to the ground, Alomari was on him. The powerful killer pulled him up by the neck of his parka and then swung his machine pistol around hard into Harvath's solar plexus, knocking the wind from him. As Harvath doubled over in pain, Alomari came up from below with a searing punch that connected with Harvath's jaw and snapped his head straight back.

Harvath flailed his arms, trying to grab onto anything to break his fall, but got nothing but air. What finally broke his fall was the icy ground, and when it did, Harvath's head hit it with such a loud smack it echoed throughout the cavern and into the tunnels. Once again, he saw stars, but this time there was something more, an overwhelming blackness that threatened to completely overcome him. Harvath fought it off. The only hope he had of staying alive was staying conscious. Alomari was playing with him, but the minute Harvath passed out, the assassin would finish him off. He knew it as sure as he knew he never should have left his gun in his backpack.

Rolling over onto his stomach, Harvath struggled to get up onto his knees. When he did, Alomari kicked him hard, right in the ribs and right in the same place he'd been kicked by the security guard at Sotheby's two days before.

The extra gear he had stowed in his parka did little to soften the blow. The precious bit of air Harvath had managed to get back into his lungs was forced back out, and his chest started heaving. Somewhere in the back of his mind, a faint voice told him to consider giving up. He was no match for Alomari. The man was much too strong for him. The voice was a sign of weakness, and Harvath despised weakness. Now, he not only slammed the iron door of his mind tight against it, he willed himself to suck in large gulps of air. He had to pull himself together. He had to rally his strength and his wits or he was going to die here, just like Ellyson, Bernard, and their Sherpa, Maurice.

As his lungs heaved for air, Harvath looked around him for anything that could be used as a weapon. He tried to remember what he had stuffed in his parka and whether any of those items could be used to his advantage. He rapidly sorted through the possibilities, but none of them seemed as if they would do the trick. Then it hit him, literally.

There was a jangle of metal on metal as Alomari delivered another searing kick to his ribs. If Harvath could only unbuckle the nylon webbing strung with pitons, carabiners, and other climbing accessories around his waist, he just might be able to use it as a weapon.

Harvath sucked up the pain and fumbled for his buckle. He suffered two more blows before it came free, but he put those blows on account, along with all the rest, determined to make Alomari pay in full. This time he had the right guy, and even if there had been cameras present, he was still going to beat him to within an eighth of an inch of his life. He wouldn't stop until Alomari begged to die. Then he'd drag him back and turn him over to the United States to be interrogated and spend the rest of his life rotting in a jail somewhere while Harvath roasted a pig in his honor each weekend under his prison window.

As Alomari drew his foot back for yet another kick, the belt came free, and Harvath rolled away from his attacker, swinging it in a wide arc. He wanted to fell the man by nailing him right in the back of the legs, but first Harvath had to rid him of his weapon.

With a sharp crack, Harvath brought the equipment-laden piece of webbing around and hit Alomari's hand so hard that his Steyr TMP was torn out of it and sent clattering across the floor. With the weapon out of the way, Harvath could go to work, and go to work he did. Springing to his feet, he swung the belt in a large figure eight above his head and then struck Alomari across the back. The metal pitons tore huge pieces of fabric away from the assassin's parka. Harvath could only fantasize what they would do when he finally connected with flesh.

Whipping the belt around harder this time, he tore straight through Alomari's parka. The man screamed as the last piece of metal hanging from the webbing split open a deep gash in his neck. Alomari could do nothing but recoil as Harvath kept coming at him. Blow after blow, Harvath swung the belt harder and harder. Backing the man up against one of the many tunnel entrances, Harvath beat the assassin mercilessly. Alomari's screams filled the entire cavern as Harvath made good on his promise that the assassin would pay for every innocent life he had ever taken.

The killer's parka hung from his body in bloody shreds as Harvath pulled the belt back for another devastating blow. But just as he was about to whip the belt forward, it went completely slack. It made no sense until he started hearing pitons, carabiners, and other pieces of climbing metal hitting the ceiling and raining down on the floor. *The belt had broken.*

It made no difference to Harvath. He was more

than happy to turn his bare hands on the remorseless assassin, but before he could land the first punch, Alomari turned the tables on him. Harvath took two steps backward when he saw what the man had in his hands. In his absolute rage, Harvath had once again underestimated his opponent, and this time he knew he was going to pay the ultimate price.

"Now I am going to kill you," spat Alomari. He had a double-action, hammerless .357 Ruger KSP revolver pointed right at Harvath's chest.

Harvath dropped the broken belt to the ground, looked Khalid Alomari right in the eye, and said, "You just don't get the point, do you?"

"What point?" he sneered as he steadied his hand and began applying pressure to the trigger.

"This one," said a voice from behind as a twenty-four-hundred-year-old Celtic *falcata* was thrust through the assassin's back.

The powerful sword erupted through his chest in an incredible spray of blood. With its curved blade, it kept climbing upward. Still alive, Alomari was able to see it come back at him and feel the tip of the blade thrust up from underneath his chin and impale his entire face.

As Alomari's dying body fell twitching to the ground, Jillian released the *falcata*'s handle and stared at what she had done.

FORTY-EIGHT

Jillian was unable to stop shaking. "He would have killed us both," said Harvath as he tried to break the spell that had come over her.

"I know," said Jillian quietly. "I know."

As if her handling of the shelf collapse wasn't enough, in killing Alomari, Jillian Alcott had proven that when she really needed to, she could make her fear work for her and not vice versa.

"Here," said Harvath, handing her the Ruger. "This is yours. You earned it."

"I don't want a souvenir."

"It's not a souvenir. It might save your life. Do you know how to handle one of these?"

"I grew up on a farm. I've done my fair share of shooting."

"Killing people is a lot different than killing rabbits," said Harvath, who immediately regretted his words. It was definitely the wrong thing to say, and as if he needed any further convincing, Jillian turned away from him and vomited. He felt so stupid. The woman had just killed a man. Sometimes Harvath simply forgot the code civilians lived by. As they should, people who had never killed before found it reprehensible, even those who did so in defense of themselves or the people they cared about. What Jillian Alcott had just been through would probably haunt her for the rest of her life. Offering to let her keep the pistol was definitely a bad idea, no matter how well intentioned.

Harvath left Jillian alone while he combed through Alomari's pockets. What he found he took—a car key, a high-end Benchmade tactical folding knife, and some spare ammunition. Al-Qaeda had trained him well. There was nothing on his person that could lead anyone anywhere. The U.S. intelligence community was going to be awfully upset at having lost a chance to interrogate him, but as far as Harvath was concerned, he and Jillian had been faced with no other choice.

They spent the next hour combing the tunnels for any clues they could find about Hannibal's mystery weapon. The quiet searching seemed to allow Jillian time to make a tentative peace with what she had been forced to do.

Jillian spent some time studying the intricately carved box they had examined earlier, trying to divine the meaning of its engraving. Finally, she spoke, and when she did, she was all business. She agreed with Harvath that the scenes were allegories but their exact message wasn't clear. There was a depiction of some sort of magical book, which she thought might represent the *Arthashastra*, but paleopathology, not iconography, was her specialty.

Jillian did, though, concur with his assessment that what they had originally believed were wolves on the breastplates were actually dogs. The reason was that on the box, more than just snarling heads were depicted. These animals also had curved tails—a definite *Canis familiaris* trait and not something normally associated with *Canis lupus*.

While Harvath was glad to have her agree with his opinion, it still didn't explain why Hannibal had wanted to use the image of dogs to scare his enemies.

"Did Hannibal use dogs in battle?" he asked as they continued to explore the box together.

"A lot of ancient armies did, but I can't say one way or another if Hannibal used them. If he did, it would not have been unusual."

"And not particularly scary."

"Nope. Besides, if these troops were using dogs, where are they? I don't see any evidence of them down here. Not one leash, not one muzzle, nothing."

Harvath nodded his head in agreement. "So what's the connection?"

"I have no idea," said Jillian as she turned away from the box and ran her hand through her hair. "There are too many pieces missing. It could take months, if not years, of excavating down here with a full team before we could uncover the answers we're looking for."

"We don't have that kind of time."

"What are we going to do then?"

Harvath looked at his watch. Without blankets and a way to make a fire, there was no way they could survive through the night. "We have to go back."

"I wish I had brought a camera," said Jillian.

"Maybe in one of the expedition cases," began Harvath, who stopped when he saw her shaking her head.

"I already checked all of those. There's nothing. Even if we found one, the batteries would long be dead."

She was right. Harvath hadn't thought of that.

"There's one other thing we can do," said Jillian. "Give me your ax."

Harvath handed her the one he'd been using to chop chunks of ice out of the wall to hold against his face. "What are you going to do?"

"Collect samples."

"Samples of what?"

As she headed off toward one of the tunnels, Alcott looked over her shoulder and replied, "Human tissue."

FORTY-NINE

They picked five soldiers at random. The ones buried behind the thickest pieces of ice were Harvath's responsibility, as was the most gruesome task of all—lopping off the top of each skull so that Jillian could collect samples of brain matter. As the mystery illness involved such a serious encephalitis component, she had insisted that in addition to the other tissue samples they were collecting, samples of brain tissue were absolutely imperative. Though Harvath and Alcott were each armed with only an ice ax, they went at their task as if chipping away at a priceless diamond while wielding the most precision cutting instruments in the world.

Jillian's care came out of respect for ancient history. In Harvath's case it was out of his respect for fellow soldiers. Though outside daylight was fading, neither hacked away at their subjects. They carved carefully into the ice until they were able to access the frozen flesh. While Alcott wasn't sure if

Alan Whitcomb would be able to learn anything from the samples, she certainly wanted to give him a chance. Lying within these frozen bodies could be the key they were looking for. Hannibal never would have sent his men into battle without protecting them against their own weapons. Maybe these soldiers, the members of his elite guard, had been inoculated, and maybe their DNA could tell the modern world something about the great weapon they were carrying.

Once the samples had been collected, they hurried back to their climbing equipment; Harvath unfastened his rope and watched as the weight of his pack up above pulled it through his secondary set of anchors. The rope zipped across the empty space above them and landed with a soft *thwack* on the correct side of the cavern, right next to Jillian's.

Attaching their ascenders, Harvath demonstrated how the devices were used to climb back up the rope. He worked with Jillian until she got the hang of it, and then, after he connected the leash between them once more, they began their ascent. Twenty feet from the top, Harvath detached his pack from the line and managed to get it over both his shoulders. After changing ropes at the remnant of the ice shelf, they made it back up onto the narrow Col de la Traversette, packed up their gear, and began the difficult hike back to the Queyr' de l'Ours with only their headlamps to light their way through the dark.

A thick curtain of heavily falling snow was well under way by the time they arrived at the rear of the hotel's property. During their trek, not much in the way of conversation passed between them. Jillian was wrestling with the psychological and emotional trauma of having killed Khalid Alomari while Harvath was trying to figure out how the assassin was tied to Timothy Rayburn in the first place. Rayburn had organized the expedition to recover Hannibal's mystery weapon, and Alomari seemed to be killing anyone who had any knowledge of it whatsoever. Yet there was one person Alomari hadn't been able to kill, and that was Emir Tokay, but only because Rayburn had gotten to him first and kidnapped him. It didn't make any sense. Rayburn and Alomari seemed to be working the same project but from two different angles. Rayburn helped put it together while Alomari worked on taking it apart.

Killing the scientists once their work was complete, as well as silencing anyone with any knowledge of it, made sense, but what didn't make sense was kidnapping Tokay. Why wasn't he killed as well? Why kidnap him?

As they approached the hotel, Harvath tried to quiet his thoughts. At this point, he no longer wanted to struggle for answers. All he wanted was a long hot shower, followed by several Advils and a good night's sleep. The minute they stepped through the hotel's back door and into the kitchen, though, he realized that wasn't going to happen.

"Putain, bougez pas! Bougez pas!" yelled one of two provincial police officers startled by Harvath and Alcott's entrance. Based on their uniforms, they looked to be motorcycle cops, but that still didn't explain what they were doing in Marie Lavoine's kitchen.

Before Harvath could react, the men had drawn their sidearms and had both him and Jillian covered. The last thing he wanted to do was provoke a shootout with police officers, so he just raised his hands above his head and left all of the guns he was carrying where they were for the time being.

Seeing Harvath with his hands above his head, Jillian did the same and asked, "What's going on?"

"Ta gueule!" barked one of the motorcycle cops, while his partner turned and yelled into the other room for their captain. Moments later, a heavyset man in his mid-fifties with thinning hair and bags under his eyes entered the kitchen. At first he couldn't believe what he was seeing, but he quickly recovered and began giving orders to his men.

As they bounced Harvath up against the wall and searched him, they found not only Alomari's tactical machine pistol and .357 revolver, but also the folding knife, Harvath's Sam Guerin identification, and the stacks of U.S. dollars, British pounds, and EU euros that Harvath had been given by his boss, Gary Lawlor, to help finance his assignment. After patting down Jillian, they searched both the packs and found Jillian's tissue samples and yet another weapon, Harvath's .40-caliber H&K USP Compact.

"At least they are all of different calibers," said the captain, in English, as he examined the guns. "That should help speed up the ballistics process."

"What ballistics process?" replied Harvath. "What is this all about?"

"Monsieur Guerin, Madame Alcott, my name is Captain Marcel Broussard of the provincial *gendarmerie*, and it is my duty to inform you that you are under arrest, pending an investigation of your involvement in the murders of London police officer Donald Mills and two civilians at the Harvey Nichols department store, as well as Dr. Molly Davidson, who had been working for Sotheby's Paris office, and tonight's murder of Marie Lavoine."

Harvath was about to protest their innocence and ask what evidence the authorities had against them, when he realized the French police and Interpol would already have more than enough. Security camera footage from Harvey Nichols, though it wouldn't have revealed much of Harvath's identity, would have perfectly captured Jillian Alcott's. Then he and Alcott had been asked to show IDs and have their pictures taken for security badges at Sotheby's. Having been thrown out for an altercation with Davidson the same day she was killed, he and Jillian were the perfect suspects. Now, they had been caught returning to the scene of yet another murder. While not conclusive, there was more than enough circumstantial evidence to hold them indefinitely. He couldn't blame the French police; they were one hundred percent correct in what they were doing, but he also couldn't let them hold him.

As one of the two motorcycle cops stepped up from behind to handcuff him, Harvath swung his head back as hard as he could, shattering the officer's nose. He followed it up with a right-handed chop to the side of Broussard's neck, which dropped him like a trash bag full of mud right onto the linoleum floor. As the other motorcycle cop wrapped his arms around Harvath's waist and tried to tackle him, Harvath laced his fingers together and brought both of his hands down in a lightning-fast snap at the base of the man's skull. Subduing all three gendarmes had taken only a matter of seconds.

Harvath looked at Jillian, who was completely amazed by the speed at which he had moved. Sliding the Ruger into the pocket of his climbing pants, he started giving orders. "Guns, cash, passports, all of it. Gather it up and put it in the small backpack."

Jillian nodded her head as Harvath grabbed the car keys, then bent down and cleaned out the pockets of the unconscious French police officers. Relieving them of their handcuffs, he shackled them in a convoluted wrist-to-ankle, ankle-to-wrist Twister pose that would make it impossible for them to move once they came to. After that, he dumped the chambered rounds and magazines from all of their weapons into the garbage, placed their pistols in the oven, and set it to *bake*.

When Jillian held up Harvath's KIVA pack, indicating that everything was ready to go, he held his finger to his lips and signaled for her to follow.

If there had been other policemen in the small hotel, they would have come running at the first sounds of a struggle in the kitchen. As none had, Harvath felt it was a safe bet they were all alone. That didn't mean, though, that more weren't on the way. Small towns like Ristolas didn't usually get much action, so a murder was likely to attract a lot of attention. The minute Marie Lavoine's body had been discovered, word would have gone out far and wide.

The first thing Harvath noticed as they approached the reception area was the blood. It covered half the hardwood floor. Before he even saw the body, he noticed that most of the pictures had been knocked from the wall and their frames lay shattered in pieces. Harvath wanted to believe that the end had come quickly for Marie, but obviously it hadn't. There had been a struggle, and knowing Alomari, Harvath figured he had taken pleasure in making the poor woman suffer.

When they finally came upon her body behind the small reception desk, Jillian gasped in horror. Marie's throat had been cut, much in the same way as Ellyson's, and her face was bruised and horribly swollen. Alomari had beaten her before he killed her, most likely in the process of trying to extract information. Everyone caves under torture eventually, and if Marie had told Alomari where he and Jillian had gone, Harvath couldn't blame her.

Harvath and Alcott needed to get as far away from the gendarmes and Ristolas as possible. Leaning down, he removed the gold chain with the medallion of Saint Bernard from his pocket and placed it in Marie Lavoine's hand. *At least now she and Bernard were together,* he thought as he straightened himself up and stepped from behind the reception desk.

Walking to the windows near the front door, he peered out from behind the curtains and was not happy with what he saw. The tiny driveway in front of the Queyr' de l'Ours was crammed with provincial police cars. Apparently, Broussard had entered the hotel with the first officers on the scene, the motorcycle cops, and had told the rest of the police to remain outside. From an investigative standpoint it was a smart move. The fewer people tramping through the hotel, the less chance of evidence being damaged. But from an escapee's standpoint, Harvath and Jillian were screwed—doubly so, as he noticed teams of officers moving around to secure the back of the property.

"Shit," said Harvath as he pulled his head back in from the window.

"What's going on?" asked Jillian.

"It's crawling with police outside."

Jillian came up and looked out the window for herself. "What are we going to do?"

"As far as the authorities are concerned, you and I have been on a three-day killing spree. They're not about to let us just walk out of here, and I'm not about to draw them into any sort of fight."

"So what do you suggest?"

After thinking for several moments, Harvath looked out the window again and focused on something at the end of the driveway. "Do you know how to ride a motorcycle?"

"No, why?"

"Because I only have one idea on how to get us out of here, and we've probably only got a million-to-one shot at making it work."

Five minutes later, wearing the visored helmets and uniforms of the two unconscious motorcycle cops from the kitchen, Harvath and Jillian exited the hotel and began quickly walking past the officers waiting outside.

When the gendarmes began asking what had happened inside, Harvath held up a plastic evidence bag containing Khalid Alomari's tactical machine pistol and continued walking. The officers seemed to understand. They knew a murder had been committed, and the presence of such an exotic weapon confirmed what they all secretly believed—that the scene inside was particularly gruesome. Obviously, the captain had dispatched the two motorcycle officers on some important assignment involving the weapon, and they had no time to talk. That was fine with most of them. Hopefully, they would soon be allowed inside and would be able to see the crime scene for themselves. There wasn't a man among them who had ever had the opportunity to see a murder scene before.

They went back to talking among themselves, but when Jillian climbed onto one of the motorcycles at the bottom of the driveway behind Harvath, and with a backpack no less, several of the gendarmes began to suspect something might be going on.

Please let it start on the first try, thought Harvath. It did, and they were half a block away before the first of the cops had run inside the hotel, discovered his colleagues in the kitchen, and come back outside to send the other officers to apprehend the wayward police motorcycle and its two fugitive riders.

Instantly, Klaxons started echoing off the stone structures of the small village. As Harvath drove the high-powered motorbike up both streets and sidewalks, he was thankful it was evening and most people were inside.

While he drove, Alcott stuck to her part of the plan. With their rented Mercedes surrounded by police cars in the Queyr' de l'Ours's driveway, their only hoping of getting away was in whatever car Khalid Alomari had left behind. All they had to do was find it.

Harvath knew that Alomari was professional enough not to have parked right in front of a murder scene, but needing immediate access to the only route to the Col de la Traversette, he wouldn't have parked too far away either.

As they drove up and down each of the village's narrow streets, Alcott repeatedly pressed the remote panic feature on the car key Harvath had found in Alomari's pocket.

The police were less than two blocks behind when Alcott finally got a hit, and the headlights, taillights, and horn of a black BMW 7-series sedan started going crazy. Immediately, Alcott pushed the panic button again and shut down the alarm.

Having seen the proficient way she drove her MG, Harvath had little doubt Jillian could handle the big BMW. Skidding to a halt beside it, he helped her slide off the motorbike and then told her to meet him on the other side of the bridge outside the village.

Once she was in the car with her head down, Harvath took off, the police just turning the corner behind him.

Having been through most of the streets in Ristolas already, he had a pretty good idea of where and how he could shake the gendarmes from his trail.

Racing into the heart of the village, he did two circles around the communal fountain, giving the police plenty of time to at least gain sight of the taillight on the much faster motorbike he was driving, before shooting down one of Ristolas's most crooked thoroughfares.

Revving the high-performance bike into the red zone, Harvath released the clutch and rocketed ahead, putting as much distance between him and the police as possible.

Approaching the deadly ninety-degree turn Harvath remembered from his first pass, he locked up the brakes and laid a skidding trail right up to a low stone wall overlooking an Alpine meadow far below.

The large bike took forever to stop, and for a split second, Harvath thought he was going to be thrown right over the wall along with it. As the front tire slammed into the stones, narrowly missing the iron bench overlooking the valley, Harvath jumped off, flipped open the gas cap, and muscled the bike the rest of the way over. As it fell to the ground far below and burst into flames, he removed his helmet and tossed it as close as he could to the burning wreckage.

He then took off the provincial police parka, stuffed it in a nearby trash can, and ran to meet Alcott at their agreed-upon rendezvous point.

FIFTY

WASHINGTON PLAZA HOTEL
WASHINGTON, DC

Brian Turner had spent enough time with the CIA to know that continuing to meet Senator Carmichael at his apartment was probably not a very good idea. The smart thing to do was to no longer hold any of their meetings in the same place twice. He also had to make sure he picked a hotel where the senator could come up to his room straight from the parking garage and not be seen in the lobby. The chic yet affordable Washington Plaza was the perfect choice. If Carmichael decided she felt amorous after their meeting, they could spend the evening together and order room service, and she could still sneak out via the garage later on with no one the wiser. If she didn't feel like staying, Turner could still take advantage of the magnificent room he had overlooking one of the best outdoor hotel pools in DC and troll the Plaza's very funky bar, known as one of the hottest young pickup spots in town.

Having arrived well in advance of the senator, Turner decided to kill a little time downstairs in that selfsame bar. Ordering his favorite drink, a double-dirty Absolut martini with extra olives, he settled back and listened as one of his all-time favorite albums, *Mothership Connection* by Parliament, played overhead. God, he hated DC, but moments like this, when he found a slice of culture in the vapid city, almost made it worth living there.

Halfway through his third martini, Turner looked at his watch and realized he'd lost track of time. Throwing a fifty-dollar bill down on the table, he zipped out of the bar and hopped an elevator up to his room.

As the doors opened, he prayed to God he wouldn't see Carmichael in the hallway waiting for him, and thankfully, he didn't. Opening the door to his room, Turner had just enough time to take a leak and rinse his mouth out with one of the complimentary bottles of Listerine before he heard the senator's familiar rap on the door.

"Good evening, Helen," he said with a smile as he showed Carmichael into the room.

"What the fuck's going on, Brian?" she replied as he closed the door. "I thought we were only going to communicate via e-mail from now on."

Feeling no pain, Turner's smile never wavered as he replied, "For normal communications, that would make sense, but tonight I have something special to show you."

Carmichael ignored the seat her young lover offered her and instead chose to remain standing in the center of the room. "So what is it?"

"I don't even get a kiss?" asked Turner as he held out his arms, the liquor getting the better of him. "I'm going to start thinking that you don't care about me anymore."

"Are you drunk?" demanded the senator. "I can't fucking believe this. I came all the way down here and you're shit-faced."

"Helen, please," said Turner, bobbing his head a little too much as he accentuated his words.

"*Please* what?" she asked. "Why am I here, Brian?"

Turner smiled again and did a little dance. "Because I have discovered something that will be the final nail in Scot Harvath's coffin. The *coup de grace*, if you will."

Close to heading for the door, Carmichael decided to slow down and hear the young CIA man out. Sitting on the edge of the room's king-size bed and crossing her legs, she replied, "So what do you have for me?"

Turner held up his finger, as if to say, *I'll be right back*, and disappeared into the suite's dressing area, where the closet and room safe were. A moment later he reappeared waving a thin folder in the air. "I told you the proof was out there somewhere."

"Proof of what?"

"That the president really has been using elements of the intelligence community for his own personal hit squad."

Carmichael couldn't believe her ears. "What did you find?"

"After-action reports," he said proudly as he handed her the dossier. "After-action reports for off-the-books, black ops assignments that supposedly never existed."

"How'd you get your hands on these?" asked the senator as she flipped through the pages. "Nobody just leaves intelligence like this lying around."

"It was hardly lying around," said Turner, feeling cocky. He was doing exactly what he needed to do to seal a position in her cabinet. He was proving himself indispensable. "Basically, it all comes down to having the right access and the correct knowledge. I've been at the agency long enough to develop both."

The senator tried to mask how excited she was to get her hands on such valuable information. As she continued reading, she asked, "And Scot Harvath played a role in these off-the-books assignments?"

"They allude to someone who I definitely believe is Harvath," replied Turner.

"How about the president? Can we tie him to any of these operations?"

"Not yet," said the CIA man, "but once I can put Harvath in the picture, I think we'll have the president as well."

"How much longer?"

"If things continue to pan out, I think we're only talking a matter of days. Possibly by the end of the week."

The senator thought about the press cycle, her hearings, and the announcement she was going to make that both the president and his chief of staff had been served. This additional information was exactly what she had been counting on. "Whatever it takes," she said, "do it. And do it fast."

FIFTY-ONE

ITALY

With the French police hopefully searching the valley beneath Ristolas for their bodies, Harvath pulled a map from the glove box and plotted the shortest possible route into Italy.

As France and Italy were both EU member countries, the only thing stopped at their respective border these days was the occasional truck. Even so, Harvath still wanted to be careful and chose a narrow, low-profile route that wound its way through the Alps and eventually deposited them in the Piemonte region's Po River Valley—not far from where Hannibal's army engaged the first Roman legions.

Soon, they neared Turin, and though he and Jillian were both tired, they agreed the wisest choice was to push on to Milan and put as much distance between them and the French authorities as possible.

With its street crime, prostitutes, and drug dealers, Milan was second only to Naples as the seediest city in Italy. While Harvath had always given the fashion industry's tacky capital the widest berth possible, he was happy to find a mid-grade, chain business hotel near the city center. The desk clerk, who suspected Harvath was on a jaunt with his attractive mistress, was more than happy to ignore protocol and accept two nights' lodging in cash along with a hefty tip, in lieu of the presentation of any formal identification.

As he soaked under a steaming hot shower, Jillian went across the street to an all-night café for sandwiches and coffee. When she returned, she found Harvath on the edge of the bed, going through the bag Khalid Alomari had left in the trunk of his car. "Anything interesting?" she asked as she handed Harvath a sandwich.

"You'll love this," he replied. "Along with a prayer mat and a copy of the Koran, he had extra ammo, several very nasty-looking knives, and a garrote wire."

Jillian shuddered. "Death and religion, what a juxtaposition."

"That's the way these people operate. Not all Muslims are terrorists, but without fail all terrorists are Muslims. There's a war raging within their religion. The moderate Muslim faith is under siege by the Wahhabi extremists of Saudi Arabia. That's what gave birth to bin Laden and al-Qaeda. They want to take over the world and they'll do whatever is necessary to make their goal a reality."

Despite the glass of wine she had downed at the café across the street, Jillian was still numb from killing Khalid Alomari. But the more she heard about what a monster he and his kind were, the better she began to feel about what she had done.

"We need to establish our priorities," said Harvath as he reached for one of the coffees.

"That's easy," replied Jillian. "The tissue samples. We've got to get them to the Whitcombs as soon as possible."

"I agree, but I also want the people working on this in my government to get a look at them." Glancing up at Jillian, he added, "Vanessa and Alan are good people, and I don't want to see anything happen to them."

"Neither do I."

"Good. I'd like to arrange for them to get away from Durham for a little bit. Even though we've taken care of Alomari, there's no knowing who he might have talked with and if the Whitcombs are in any danger."

Jillian had not considered that possibility and was obviously concerned. "What do you have in mind?"

"I'd like to have them moved to a special military base where they can continue their work on this case and where they'll be completely safe."

"An American military base?"

"Yes. Fort Detrick, Maryland."

"USAMRIID. The U.S. Army Medical Research Institute of Infectious Diseases," said Jillian.

"You're familiar with it?"

"Of course."

Harvath hesitated a moment and then said, "I'd like you to go with them."

"Me? Why me?"

"Because you've been through enough already. This is only going to get more dangerous, and I don't think it's right to ask you to stay with me."

"First of all," said Jillian as she glared at Harvath, "I'll be the judge of what's right for me, and secondly, you *need* me."

Harvath knew he could move a lot faster without her, but felt he owed it to her to hear her out. "How do you figure?"

"We don't know what the tissue samples we gathered will yield. They might yield nothing at all. Either way, you're not going to sit around here waiting to find out. You're going after Rayburn. You need to find Emir Tokay. At this point, he's the only one who can shed any light on all of this. If, as we said before, he's even still alive."

She had him pegged. That was exactly what Harvath had planned, but he still saw no reason to save the seat next to him for the trip. "I still don't understand why I need you for any of that."

"Emir contacted me because he had pieces of a puzzle he couldn't put together. If he's still alive, he might still need my expertise to sort this all out."

"And if he's not?"

"If he's not and you manage to locate Rayburn, I'm guessing Rayburn will be sitting on all of Dr. Ellyson's papers. That includes the Silenus manuscript and heaven knows what else. You're going to need somebody who can sort through all of that and decipher the most relevant documents as quickly as possible. You can't do this without me, Scot, and you know it."

Not only did Harvath know it, but he hated it. Though she had proven herself quite capable, she wasn't an operator, and the assignment was about to get a lot more dangerous. It was shades of Meg Cassidy all over again, except this time the civilian that fate was forcing him to bring with him into battle didn't have the luxury of several weeks' training with the best the intelligence community had to offer. All Jillian Alcott had was him.

"If I can arrange for Vanessa and Alan to be taken to USAMRIID," said Harvath, "will you back me up on it and encourage them to go?"

Jillian thought about it a moment and replied, "If that's the only way they can be completely secure, then yes, I'll back you up on it."

Harvath glanced at his Kobold Phantom Chronograph and calculated the time difference between Italy and Washington, DC. "I'll need to make a couple of calls to get the ball rolling."

"Does this mean we're sticking together?"

"How can I say no? After all, I owe you my life."

Jillian smiled. “I want to call Vanessa and Alan and talk to them before you do anything.”

“Okay,” replied Harvath as he lifted the phone off the nightstand and handed it to her. “The sooner we get this moving, the better off we’re all going to be.”

FIFTY-TWO

"Yes, he's right here," said Jillian as she motioned for Harvath to pick up the telephone over on the desk. "I'll have him pick up the other extension."

Once Harvath was on, Alan Whitcomb asked, "How much danger are we really in?"

"Enough that I think it wouldn't hurt to take a vacation for a little while," replied Harvath in all sincerity. "As soon as we hang up, I'm going to get everything moving to get you two out of there."

"Jillian said you're going to have us taken to USAMRIID?"

"I think it makes the most sense. They're the lead agency investigating the illness. We'll ship the tissue samples directly there so you can start work as soon as you arrive."

"A little more excitement than we had originally bargained for, but I think Mrs. Whitcomb and I are up to the challenge."

"Good," said Harvath. "Then I'll let you go so I can get things started."

"Before you ring off, I dug up something I think you should hear."

"What is it?"

"A few days ago, when you said that everyone who comes in contact with this mystery illness ends up acting like vampires, it got me thinking. The Iraqis in that village, the foreign aid workers who were trying to help them—that's exactly how they were acting."

"Come on, Alan," said Harvath, "are you going to tell me that what we're dealing with is an outbreak of vampirism?"

"Close," said Whitcomb. "I think what we're really dealing with here is an outbreak of rabies."

Images of the breastplates and the scenes carved along the wooden box they had found in the ice cave rushed to the forefront of Harvath's mind. *Not wolves, dogs.* "Why rabies?" asked Harvath as he tried to piece it all together.

"Like I said, it was your Count Dracula reference that got me thinking. None of us had looked at it that way. It took some doing, but I was able to track down a journal article I had read several years ago. A doctor by the name of Juan Gomez-Alonso from the Xeral Hospital in Vigo, Spain, had published an article in the journal *Neurology* where he explored the similarities between the mythical vampire and the symptoms of human beings infected with the rabies virus.

"Those similarities are astounding. Not only do vampires bite people, but so do human beings affected with the rabies virus. Vampires are said to seduce women; rabies sufferers are known to be hypersexual. Vampires attack people; rabies sufferers often show a dramatic increase in aggressive behavior. Vampires roam the earth at night; rabies patients suffer severe insomnia due to interrupted sleep cycles. Vampires are erratic and suck blood; rabies patients often experience convulsions and bloody frothing at the mouth. Vampires hate garlic; rabies patients are often hypersensitive to strong odors, especially garlic. Vampires avoid mirrors as they do not cast a reflection; rabies sufferers cannot bear the sight of their own reflection and avoid any object that might cast a reflection. Vampires are afraid of sunlight; rabies patients often develop acute photosensitivity. Finally, vampires are afraid of holy water, and rabies patients often develop hydrophobia."

Harvath was astounded. "The symptoms are a perfect match."

"Not only are they a perfect match," replied Whitcomb, "but they explain the other symptoms we couldn't directly attribute to *Azemiops feae* venom."

"So that's it then. The Carthaginians combined the venom with rabies. Now I understand how the dogs fit in."

"Dogs?" replied Whitcomb. "What dogs?"

"The crate I told you about that we think was used to transport Hannibal's mystery weapon," said Jillian on the other phone, "it had a series of scenes depicted in relief along the side. In addition to a magical book, which I believe was a reference to the *Arthashastra*, there were the wolves we had seen on the breastplates, except they weren't actually wolves. After studying them, Scot figured out that they were dogs, and I guess we should now say *rabid* dogs."

"It makes sense," said Alan after thinking about it for a moment. "Rabies is one of the oldest infectious diseases known to mankind. Accounts of it date all the way back to Asia in 2000 B.C. but the best detailed medical accounts date from around 300 B.C."

"Less than sixty years before the birth of Hannibal," said Harvath. "But if rabies is the other component here, something doesn't make sense. I've always understood that once you have rabies, it's fatal."

"You're correct. Once clinical symptoms develop, there is no known treatment for preventing death from rabies. But, if caught early enough in cases of severe exposure, such as bites to the head or neck, anti-rabies serum can be administered; in cases of milder exposures, such as bites to the arms or legs, patients can normally be treated satisfactorily with vaccination."

"But we're not dealing with biting here as a

means of transmission. Nobody bit the people who fell ill."

"Contrary to popular belief, rabies is not solely transmitted by the bite of an infected host. There have been three *modern* confirmed cases of transmission without biting. The first involved a person inhaling virus particles in a bat cave; the second involved laboratory workers who, while using a power saw to cut the tops of skulls off rabies-infected corpses, created an aerosol and inhaled rabies particles; and the third involved a cornea transplant from an infected donor."

"So in other words," said Harvath, "there are multiple routes by which this illness might infect people."

"Unfortunately," responded Whitcomb, "that's true. The *Arthashastra* was quite ingenious in its suggestions for weaponizing and delivering different pathogens. We don't know what strain of rabies Hannibal was using and what resulted when it was combined with the *Azemiops feae* venom. Remember the duplexing examples Jillian cited? The resultant monster illnesses that come from combining two lesser illnesses can be radically different than anyone could ever imagine."

Harvath had no doubt the man was correct, but he still had other questions. "What about Muslim immunity to whatever this illness is?"

"I think we agree that this illness has a cure or at the very least a vaccine of some sort. Regardless of what we know about the illness's major ingredients, the focus must be on finding its cure, whether in the laboratory or via the people who deployed this themselves."

Whitcomb was right. As far as any scientific progress that might be made, the best Harvath could do was to facilitate Vanessa and Alan's transfer to Fort Detrick. And to do that, he was going to have to figure out a way to disregard his orders and communicate directly with one of his best-established intelligence community contacts, without getting caught.

Listening to Jillian say her good-byes, Harvath began to form a plan in his mind.

FIFTY-THREE

RIYADH, SAUDI ARABIA

Ex–CIA operative Chip Reynolds hauled his bulky, fifty-eight-year-old, six-foot-two frame into the shower and let the hot water pound against his head and shoulders. Though he would have preferred to stay under it all day, that wasn't what the Arabian American Oil Company, or Aramco for short, was paying him for.

After toweling off, Reynolds opened the door of his villa and found his breakfast and newspapers waiting. He carried the tray inside to his desk and poured a cup of coffee while he waited for his laptop to boot up. Knowing what a tight grip the Saudi monarchy kept on the media, he only glanced at the local papers. The valuable information came from his network of contacts scattered throughout the country. Though the deputy minister for state intelligence, Faruq al-Hafez, copied him on the daily threat assessment (the creation of which had been Reynolds's idea in the first place), Chip knew that what he was getting was nothing more than a watered-down version. Faruq had never liked him, and Chip knew why.

While still in the employ of the Central Intelligence Agency, Reynolds had uncovered a plot by a Lithuanian mobster to bump off one of the lesser princes of the Saudi Royal Family. The spoiled, drug-crazed brat had run afoul of the Mafioso while vacationing in the Baltic, where his sadistic antics had resulted in the death of two young girls—one of whom was a relative of the aforementioned organized crime figure. The assassination plot was actually quite ingenious, but flawed in that it relied on local talent within the Saudi Kingdom to pull it off.

Reynolds's superiors at Langley had instructed him to coordinate with Saudi intelligence, in particular its deputy minister. Despite Reynolds's extensive background and expertise in the Middle East, including his fluency in Arabic, Faruq refused to work with him, insisting his people could handle the situation. The man had been wrong, almost dead wrong, and had it not been for Reynolds's refusal to be sidelined, the prince surely would have been killed.

When Reynolds's wife died seven years ago of cancer, he decided it was time to retire from the agency. He had given his country a good chunk of his life and wanted what was left of it back. He had watched for years while former colleagues jumped ship for the private sector and cashed in, and he wanted a piece of that action for himself. Saving the young prince's life, no matter how much Reynolds privately believed that he and most of his debauched ilk within the Royal Family ought to take a dirt nap, had secured him a special preferred status within the house of Saud. The fact that he was ex-CIA, could speak their language, and knew his way around the block better than anybody they had seen in a long time didn't hurt his standing either.

But while the al-Sauds might have liked what Reynolds brought to their side of the table, their deputy minister for state intelligence had been shown up by the American and never intended to let it happen again. Ergo, no real substantial intel ever flowed in Reynolds's direction.

Reynolds had diplomatically discussed Faruq's lack of cooperation with the Saudi Royal Family, and things had gotten better for a while, but they always seemed to recede to their current, frosty state of affairs. That said, Reynolds hadn't become one of the CIA's top operatives and wasn't being paid such a big consulting fee for being lazy or stupid, and so he used his skills to bore as far as he could into all of his host country's intelligence agencies. Within forty-five minutes every morning, he had a better handle on what was going on both inside and outside of their borders than they did. Truth be told, his picture was probably more accurate than if the Saudi intelligence agencies had been one hundred percent cooperative with him. Reynolds had always joked that he liked his intelligence like he liked his oysters—raw, with nothing added to enhance the flavor. The last thing he wanted was other people clouding his view of the landscape by trying to impress him with their take on things.

Contrary to the picture of peace, prosperity, and stability most of the outside world saw, the house of Saud was circling the drain. A host of socioeconomic problems that ran the gamut from record deficits, high unemployment, and ultra religious conservatism to resentment of the kingdom's rapid westernization, passionate hate for American troops on Saudi Arabian soil, and the decline in oil revenues as the United States began to open up Iraq's oil fields all came together to create one of the most dangerous political climates ever in the history of the al-Saud monarchy.

Evident to anyone who cared to take a close enough look was the fact that the Saudi monarchy's grip on power over the last two decades had been in precipitous decline. The foolish family policy of ignoring domestic problems in the hopes that they would simply go away had been shown time and again to be an ineffective and potentially suicidal approach to governance.

When challenged, though, the house of Saud did what most petty despots did—they struck back, and struck back hard. Under the pretense of national security and Islamic law, severe crackdowns would be initiated whereby dissidents, leaders of opposition groups, and anyone appearing even remotely threatening to the monarchy were imprisoned, tortured, and in many cases put to death.

It was little wonder then that the rulers of Saudi Arabia found it difficult to accurately gauge public opinion. No half-intelligent subject of the kingdom would ever dare answer a scientific survey or telephone poll honestly, so the house of Saud was forced to rely on a loose network of informants throughout all strata of Saudi society. The problem with the kingdom's informants, though, was that often they reported back only what they thought their handlers wanted to hear. This made for intelligence of varying degrees of quality and reliability, but when analyzed alongside the work product of the only somewhat efficient Saudi intelligence officers, most of whom, including their deputy minister, had their heads so far up their asses you couldn't even see their shoulders, it was barely enough to keep the monarchy's finger on the pulse of the kingdom and stay in control of the country.

As an American, Reynolds had little respect for the brutal way in which the Saudis ran their kingdom, but it was *their* country. The thing he despised about them the most was that they were the region's most earnest spin doctors. For example, in an effort to appear more Muslim, King Fahd had given up his royal title of *His Majesty for Custodian of the Two Holy*

Mosques of Mecca and Medina, the two holiest places in the Islamic world. One member of the Royal Family had even come up with some cockamamie scheme to bottle and sell water from a recently discovered spring beneath the holy city of Mecca, which supposedly once slaked the thirst of the prophet Muhammad himself. Reynolds didn't buy any of it. Though there were some fairly religious members of the Royal Family, they were definitely in the minority. The family's attempt to appear faithful was an absolute sham. Anyone who had heard stories or had seen firsthand the debaucheries of Saudi princes who partied like there was no tomorrow, with absolutely no respect for the tenets of Islam, knew where the ruling family really stood.

To some extent, it was hard to blame them when even their ailing king didn't set much of an example. On his annual vacation to his coastal estate in Spain, Fahd's entourage included 350 attendants, fifty black Mercedes, and a 234-foot yacht, in addition to which he had $2,000 in flowers and fifty cakes delivered daily. With every move it made, the monarchy was shooting itself in both feet, but Reynolds couldn't have cared less. It wasn't his country. As long as the hefty deposits kept being made to his bank account, he'd keep doing his job. His primary concern, the one he was being paid so many petrodollars to see to, was that Aramco's oil continued to flow unimpeded—thereby replenishing the coffers of the house of Saud.

Unscrewing the bottom of the souvenir .50-caliber sniper round sitting on his desk, Reynolds removed a forty-gig, portable USB flash memory drive from its hiding place and attached it to the back of his computer. Not only was the portable drive extremely fast when it came to transferring data, it also had the added benefit of leaving no trace on its host. With this special toy (a gift from one of his friends at Langley) he was able to safely encrypt and store any information he didn't want lying around on his laptop's hard drive. One could never be too careful in the kingdom.

For their part, the Saudis were notorious for filtering Internet content. Their Internet Services Unit (ISU) operated all the high-speed data links that connected the country to the international Internet, and all web traffic in Saudi Arabia was forwarded through a central array of proxy servers at the ISU, which decided what users could and could not have access to. Citing the Koran, the Saudis claimed to be preserving their Islamic values by blocking access to any materials that contradicted their beliefs or might influence their culture. All this while they smoked, drank, did drugs, and whored around in foreign countries. The hypocrisy of it all would have been amusing if the net effect wasn't so lamentable for the average Saudi citizen.

Even though the Saudis had the technology to block access to certain Web sites, Reynolds knew they didn't have what it took to crack encrypted e-mails. Despite all the billions in sophisticated military hardware Uncle Sam had sold his Bedouin buddies over the years, encryption was the one area, *thank God,* the U.S. had refused to do business with the Saudis in. In fact, America hadn't been too keen on Internet filtering, and along with the help of the NSA, the CIA had created a back door for its operatives in Saudi Arabia who needed a secure way to access the Net. They had placed a digital trapdoor in the last place the Saudis would ever look for it. As Reynolds logged onto the ISU's homepage, he smiled at the irony of choosing the eunuchs' locker room as the perfect place to hide the spermicide.

He surfed through the proxy servers over to his Saudi-sanctioned e-mail account and read a string of briefings from his roving security teams who checked in on Aramco's wells, refineries, pumping stations, and various other operations throughout the kingdom. Satisfied that his own house was in order, he decided to see how the house of Saud was faring and opened the e-mail containing the watered-down daily threat assessment. As usual, it was only mildly interesting and not very informative. Reynolds poured himself another cup of coffee and began to whistle *We're off to see the wizard*, as he carefully wove his way through the firewalls and layers of security that protected the Saudi Intelligence Services' data. It was time to peek behind the palm frond curtain.

One of the Saudi ruling family's biggest fears,

and the reason Reynolds held the position he did, was that its state oil company, Aramco, was incredibly vulnerable to attack. With so much infrastructure above ground and unprotected, American forecasters had prognosticated that it would only take a small, well-organized band of saboteurs to completely decimate Saudi Arabia's oil production capabilities, push the al-Sauds from power, and create a worldwide domino effect that could send oil prices soaring over $100, or maybe even $150 a barrel. Geopolitical, social, and economic upheaval would immediately follow. Stock markets would collapse, and civilization would be thrust into a modern version of the dark ages from which it might not ever recover.

It was no wonder Reynolds had nightmares. Saudi Arabia had over eighty active oil and gas fields and more than a thousand wells. There was no way he and his men could be everywhere at once. There had been small, amateur efforts at sabotage in the past, more nuisances than anything else, but it was the "what if" big one that everyone was worried about.

The only way to prevent a major attack was to keep an eye on those most likely to commit one, and that's exactly what the Saudi Intelligence Services' agents were supposed to be doing. The problem, in Reynolds's opinion, was that most of them, including Faruq, weren't even worthy of the envelopes used to mail their paychecks.

Reynolds downloaded the real daily threat assessment and then cherry-picked e-mails and memos that had flowed between the kingdom's various intelligence branches over the last twenty-four hours. As he read, something unusual caught his eye.

Over the last two years, Reynolds had compiled his own terrorist watch list. Almost all of the list's distinguished honorees were radical Muslim fundamentalists from the militant Wahhabi sect, and all were young men the Saudi Intelligence Services currently had under surveillance. The report he was seeing now, though, gave him a strange sense of déjà vu. He had read this same report somewhere before. But how was that possible? He had to be imagining it. Tailing subjects and writing up daily reports were two of the few things the Saudis actually did correctly.

Accessing his removable drive, Reynolds opened the folder he had created for the surveillance subject in question—a young Saudi militant named Khalid Sheik Alomari—and pulled up his previous surveillance reports. It took the security consultant over twenty minutes, but he eventually found what he was looking for. Six months ago, the Saudi agent tailing Alomari had filed the exact same report, verbatim.

It had to be some kind of mistake. Reynolds decided to check the most recent reports on some of the other young Saudis who were known to be close associates of Alomari's and who attended the same militant mosque on the outskirts of Riyadh. Anything having to do with Khalid Alomari gave Reynolds a bad feeling in the pit of his stomach, and it wasn't without cause. The fact that Alomari had been suspected, but never convicted, of several ingenious terrorist attacks within the kingdom, as well as hailing from Abha, the same remote mountain city in the southern province of Asir as four of the fifteen 9/11 hijackers, had cemented his position at the top of Reynolds's list of Wahhabi wiseguys worth watching.

Four more cups of coffee and two and a half hours later, Reynolds had pieced together a very puzzling picture. Saudi intelligence agents had been substituting old surveillance reports not only for Khalid Alomari, but also for four of his associates. Reynolds didn't like it.

For the past two months he and his team had quietly been on heightened alert. From the various streams of intelligence he was tapped into, something big was in the works, but nobody had any idea what it was. If it was an attack on Aramco, it could be anywhere. Reynolds and his people had added extra security in spots where they felt the company was most vulnerable, but other than that, there wasn't much else the company itself could do. There was, though, something that Reynolds could do.

Picking up his cell phone, he dialed his secretary

and left her a message that he was going to be spending the next few days in the field. He shut down his computer, stowed his portable flash memory drive, and grabbed his Les Baer 1911 .45-caliber pistol. Until he knew what the Saudi Intelligence Services were up to, there was no way he could speak with any of his contacts there, especially Faruq. For the time being, he'd have to figure this out on his own.

FIFTY-FOUR

WASHINGTON, DC

It took the man sitting in the car outside the Washington Plaza Hotel three rings before he found his ear bud, plugged it in, and answered his cellular phone. Very few people had this number. When he heard a woman's voice say that she was calling from "The Flower Patch," he knew right away who was behind the call.

"We have your order ready," said Jillian, "but our driver is out sick, so we were wondering if you could arrange to pick up the roses yourself."

Lawlor was all too familiar with the code. Harvath had a person, or persons, who needed to be brought in to protective custody right away. "Can you remind me again what color I ordered?" he asked. "Pink or red?"—meaning were the person or persons foreign or domestic.

"Pink."

Foreign.

"It might take me a while to get there," replied Lawlor.

"Well, we're going to be closing early, so you'll have to hurry."

"Understood. I'm sorry to be so forgetful, but has the bill already been posted to my account?"

"Not yet," said Jillian.

Lawlor knew that meant that Harvath had not yet posted the details for him on their clandestine electronic bulletin board. "I'll keep my eyes peeled for it."

"Good. We'll get it to you as soon as we can."

"In the meantime," said Lawlor as he tried to figure out how to phrase the next piece of information in such a way that it would make sense to Harvath, but not to anyone else who might be listening in on their call, "the special blue roses I asked you to look for overseas are rumored to be available domestically now."

Jillian looked at Harvath, who suddenly had a very concerned look on his face. *Blue roses* was how they referred to their current assignments. Lawlor was talking about the illness. Somehow, it had made its way to the United States.

"The roses haven't been put on sale yet," Gary continued, "but I'd sure like as much information as you can provide me. Rumor has it that they'll be on the market in just a few days."

"We'll get right on it," Jillian said. "Anything else?"

"Yeah, one last thing. I've gotten several calls that Wal-Mart has gotten into the blue roses business as well. You might want to check into it and see what they know."

With that, Lawlor punched the *end* button on his cell phone, set aside the pad of paper he had been taking notes on, and looked up just in time to see Helen Remington Carmichael's car emerge from the hotel's underground parking structure.

FIFTY-FIVE

ITALY

What did he mean by the blue roses are about to go on sale domestically?" asked Jillian.

Harvath looked at her and said, "It means they have intelligence that al-Qaeda has managed to smuggle the illness into the United States."

"How?"

"Who knows? There's got to be a million ways they could have done it. All that matters is that it sounds like they have succeeded in getting it in."

"They haven't released it, though, right?"

"No, but apparently they're planning on doing it within the next several days."

"What are we going to do?" she asked.

"First, we're going to check in with my Wal-Mart connection. It sounds like we may have just caught a break."

Jillian didn't bother asking him to explain.

Harvath depressed the hook switch on his phone and dialed Nick Kampos's cell phone on Cyprus.

When the man answered, it was obvious that Harvath had awakened him from a sound sleep. "Nick, it's Scot. I got a message you were trying to reach me."

"Jesus, Harvath. What time is it?" asked the groggy DEA agent.

"Almost five A.M. your time. What do you have for me?"

"I posted a message on that web site bulletin board thing like you asked, but I didn't hear back from you. Don't you ever check your messages?"

"In all fairness, Nick, I've been kind of busy."

"Well, so have I," said Kampos. "I think I may have a lead for you on Rayburn."

Harvath gripped the phone tighter. "What is it?"

"Hold on a second," he grumbled as he covered the mouthpiece of his phone and coughed several times, trying to get his lungs started before he returned and said, "I contacted a guy we use occasionally and gave him that e-mail address you called me with."

"And?"

"Apparently, your guy Rayburn wanted to look as authentic as possible with his bogus archeology foundation, so using a hotmail-style e-mail account on his business cards, which would have been nearly impossible to trace, was out of the question. He had to purchase the domain name he wanted, and then he set up his e-mail account through some cheapo filipo ISP. And he did all of that with a Visa debit card."

"That's great. Were you able to get any information on the account holder? A mailing address or something?"

"Nope. The information trail on the account holder ends at a bank in Malta. Without a warrant, I couldn't get any further than that."

Harvath was disappointed, but said, "Thanks, Nick. I appreciate you trying."

"What the hell's the matter with you? Do you think I would have left all those cryptic messages with your boss—knowing full well you were in the doghouse—if I didn't have something more for you than that? I said the account holder's *information* trail ended at the bank in Malta, but the financial trail keeps going."

"How far?"

"According to my source, whoever has that credit card has recently been using it in a town in the Rhône Valley of Switzerland, about an hour and a half outside Geneva, called Le Râleur."

"How recently?"

"As recently as last night."

Harvath tore the sheet off the top of his notepad and asked, "Can you fax me the list of exact places in Le Râleur?"

"Why not?" he grunted. "I'm up anyway."

"Thanks, Nick. I owe you another dinner."

"You owe me a hell of a lot more than dinner, but that'll be a start."

Harvath thanked his friend again, then hung up

the phone and turned to Jillian. "We've got a lead on Rayburn."

"Where is he?" she replied.

"In some town in Switzerland called Le Râleur. Ring any bells?"

"I've never heard of it."

"Neither have I," said Harvath.

"So what's our plan?"

"First we need to find a courier service to get those tissue samples back to the States. Then we'll need an Internet café where I can post an update for Gary."

"And then?" she asked.

"Then we need to figure out how we're going to get into Switzerland."

"I take it we're not going to be driving."

"Not with an Interpol Red Notice out on us. It's one thing driving over the border between EU countries, but going into Switzerland is completely different. They check everybody."

"Trains and planes will be out as well then. What does that leave us?"

"Not *what*," said Harvath, as reluctant as he was to go back to Kalachka for more help, "but *who*."

FIFTY-SIX

It was just before noon when Harvath and Alcott, dressed in the new clothes they had purchased before leaving Milan, drove into the lakeside town of Como and abandoned Khalild Alomari's black BMW on a quiet side street. From here on out, Ozan Kalachka would be handling their transportation.

Harvath had been to Como only once before. He and Meg had stayed at the famous Villa d'Este for an entire week. It had been one of the most extravagant vacations he had ever taken. As he and Jillian now killed time strolling the lakeshore, admiring the lavish villas and lush bougainvillea, he couldn't help but remember the time he had spent there with Meg.

Shortly before their appointed rendezvous with Kalachka's man, Harvath entered the tiny café overlooking the water and conducted a quick security sweep. He didn't like to walk into any place he didn't know how to walk out of. Once he was convinced everything was okay, he signaled Jillian and she came inside and joined him at a table. Fifteen minutes later, a middle-aged Italian with a pencil-thin mustache and a copy of the *International Herald Tribune* tucked under his right arm entered the café and looked around.

Kalachka's description of Harvath must have been very good, as the Italian zeroed right in on him. So much for Harvath's copy of the *International Herald Tribune* which he had folded open at the sports section and left in a predetermined corner of the table. Judging from the man's white linen blazer and pastel-colored silk trousers, subtlety was not one of his strong suits. At least the man stuck to the script Harvath had established with Kalachka when he approached their table and said in slightly accented English, "I'm sorry to disturb you, but didn't we meet last summer in Tremezzo? You and your wife were staying at the Grand Hotel, no?"

"Actually, we were at the San Giorgio."

"Ah *sì,* it was the San Giorgio," said the man as he motioned to one of the empty chairs and Harvath invited him to sit down. Once the waiter had taken his order and disappeared, the Italian introduced himself. "My name is Marco," he said as he extended his hand and shook both Harvath's and Alcott's. "I am at your disposal."

Harvath got right to the point. "Our mutual friend explained what we need?"

"Of course, and it's no problem," replied Marco, waving his hand dismissively.

The man was a little too relaxed for Harvath's taste. Leaning across the table and fixing him with his eyes, he said, "This is serious. I expect it to go off without a hitch. No problems at all. Do you understand?"

"*Sì, sì.* This is why I said no problem. Getting out of Italy is much easier than getting in. If your trip was reversed, *then* I would be concerned."

Somehow, Harvath had trouble believing that. "Why is that?"

"Because you are crossing over into the Swiss province of Ticino, and Ticino has legalized marijuana. It's the new Amsterdam. Many Americans haven't heard of it, but it is well known by the Italians. Not only is cannabis legal in Ticino, but it is also much higher quality than what can be found throughout this country. Call it reefer madness, but everyone who smokes wants their marijuana from Ticino. The Italian border guards have their hands full trying to search as many cars and motor scooters as possible coming back into Italy via our local border crossing with Switzerland."

"What about Swiss border guards and going in?"

Again, the Italian waved his hand in the air. "We never see them, except at the crossing itself. There's about fifteen kilometers of chain-link fence defining the border between Italy and Switzerland with holes cut through it all along. I could drop you at the edge of the forest and you would actually be able to find arrows spray-painted on the trees to lead you in the right direction."

"So the drug trade in this part of Europe must be very lucrative then."

"It is what I hear, but I'm not in the drug business. I am an importer of strictly legal goods."

"Really?" said Harvath, skeptical. "Such as?"

"Gold, furs, jewelry, watches, cigarettes—you name it," said Marco. "As long as the taxes on these items are lower in Switzerland, there will be importers, like me, bringing them into Italy."

The man was a criminal, there was no doubt, but Harvath had to admire his entrepreneurial spirit. "How do you plan on getting us across? Through the fence?"

Stirring his Campari and soda, the Italian reflected for a moment and then said, "We are flying you over the border in a kite, my friend."

Ten minutes later, as Harvath paid the check and he and Jillian followed the man out of the café, Harvath wondered what the hell they were getting themselves into.

FIFTY-SEVEN

Marco was the conscientious type of driver who used both hands behind the wheel—one to control the car and the other to make obscene gestures at everyone else on the road. He followed the signs for Menaggio, and when they arrived at the tiny village of Orimento, he parked the car and said, "We go the rest of the way on foot."

The rest of the way on foot turned out to be an hour-long hike past waterfalls and mountain pastures to the top of nearby Monte Generoso.

When they reached the 1700-meter peak straddling the border between Italy and Switzerland, Harvath could finally see what Marco had in mind. In a broad meadow fifty meters downhill, four young men lay next to a pair of oversized canvas bags, enjoying the afternoon sun. It was the bags that gave Marco's plan away. Each was emblazoned with the logo of the local Swiss paragliding club—Volo Libero Ticino.

After taking a moment to catch his breath and drain the last of the water from his bottle, Marco walked Harvath and Alcott down to meet the men, one of whom was his cousin, Enzo—president of Volo Libero Ticino.

The introductions out of the way, two of the club's members began unpacking their gear, while Enzo gave Harvath and Alcott a thorough preflight briefing, explaining how tandem paragliding worked and what would be required of them as passengers. Though Harvath had extensive parachute experience, he understood the key to safe paragliding was in knowing your terrain. As he listened to Enzo go over what to expect during launch, flight, and landing, it was obvious the man was intimately familiar not only with the sport of paragliding, but with Monte Generoso and its surroundings as well. Marco had chosen very well. They would be in good hands.

Harvath and Jillian next climbed into special nylon flight suits, slipped on gloves to help guard against the cold, and then were each outfitted with a helmet and a harness. Once Harvath's technical pack was securely attached to his chest, Enzo clipped into him from behind and a man named Paolo did the same with Jillian.

With one last look to check the brightly colored canopy laid out on the grass behind them, Enzo gave the command, and he and Harvath began running full-steam down the sloping meadow toward the edge of the mountain. After about twenty steps, Harvath began to feel his feet coming off the ground, but just as Enzo had instructed, he didn't stop running until he was told. When the paraglider finally took flight, Enzo let Harvath know that he could sit back into his harness, relax, and enjoy the view. And what a view it was.

With the Swiss city of Lugano and its sparkling lake far below them, Harvath realized this was probably one of the most enjoyable, stress-free insertions he had ever conducted. He looked back to make sure Jillian had gotten off the mountain okay and saw Paolo's canopy floating not too far behind them.

Enzo had explained that depending on the winds, it would take them only about fifteen minutes to reach their landing site, which was a soccer field in the lakeside village of Capolago. Privately, Harvath wished they could stay aloft as long as possible. Up here, gliding through the brisk mountain air, there was no sound but the wind as it rushed past his ears. It was easy to forget, if only for a moment, all of the troubles he was facing back on *terra firma*. It was as if in soaring weightless, a figurative weight had been lifted from his shoulders. He would have given a year's salary to keep floating and never have to touch the ground again.

Because of his parachuting experience, Enzo soon offered to let Harvath take control of the paraglider, but Harvath politely declined. He wanted to enjoy his respite from responsibility until the very last possible moment.

Ten minutes later, the red-tiled rooftops and soccer field of Capolago materialized beneath them and Enzo brought them in for a landing. They had already unclipped from their harnesses and were folding up the canopy when Paolo and Jillian touched down mid-field.

Jillian and Scot stripped out of their flight suits and then helped the men pack up the rest of the gear. By the time they were finished, they were met by a small van sporting the Volo Libero Ticino logo, which drove them the fourteen kilometers into the city of Lugano. Per Marco's instructions, Harvath and Alcott were dropped at a parking structure on the Via Pretorio, near the Piazzetta della Posta.

The silver Mercedes coupe had been left exactly where it was supposed to be, along with its key, a detailed map of Switzerland, and a full tank of gas. Taking the A2, they headed north until they ran out of highway and then turned west toward the Swiss Canton of Valais, Timothy Rayburn, and hopefully a very much alive Emir Tokay.

FIFTY-EIGHT

ALBAN TOWERS APARTMENTS
GEORGETOWN

It had been a long time since Gary Lawlor had conducted a black-bag job. With FBI surveillance teams keeping an eye on Brian Turner, he knew he'd have plenty of time to get out of the man's apartment if need be.

Entering the extravagant Gothic Revival lobby and passing the grand piano on the way to the elevators, Lawlor remarked that either Brian Turner had a hidden trust fund no one knew about, or the young CIA employee was living way above his pay grade.

On the third floor, Lawlor exited the elevator and turned right, down the long carpeted hallway. At Apartment 324, he set down his briefcase and removed a lockpick gun from his suit pocket. Seconds later, he was inside. The former deputy director of the FBI had not lost his touch.

A by-the-book guy, Lawlor had gone over the warrant one final time before getting out of his car.

He knew exactly what he was allowed to look for and what he wasn't—which didn't amount to much, considering the Department of Homeland Security had secured the warrant under the Patriot Act and had, with Neal Monroe's reluctant testimony, been able to make a very compelling case that national security interests were at stake.

Setting his briefcase on the kitchen counter, Lawlor popped it open and marveled at how technology had changed over the years. A product of the Cold War, he was amazed at how much smaller everything was. Gone were the days of complicated installations that all but the most inexperienced observer could detect with enough effort. These days, covert listening and viewing devices were near impossible to spot. Not only that, but the DHS was working with the world's most cutting-edge technology. Even the CIA, and that meant people like Brian Turner, hadn't seen this type of gear.

Once everything was in place, Lawlor used a handheld short-distance radar emission unit to scan the apartment for any place Turner could have secreted documents clandestinely removed from CIA headquarters. The search came up empty, and after verifying all of his covert video and audio feeds, Lawlor backed out of the apartment, making sure he left no trace of his visit.

FIFTY-NINE

SWITZERLAND

It was well past midnight when Jillian and Harvath arrived in the quiet town of Sion, capital of the Swiss canton of Valais, and found rooms for the night.

The next morning, after breakfast and a quick chat with the front desk clerk, they drove through town to an electronics shop called François JOST, where Harvath purchased a high-resolution digital camera, a small digital camcorder, and a top-of-the-line printer. In addition to extremely powerful, high-definition telephoto lenses for each camera, he also purchased a type of lens that had once only been available to people within the intelligence and law enforcement communities. Manufactured by a company called Squintar, the lens had a built-in mirror that allowed a photographer to take pictures at a 90-degree angle. In total, its housing could be rotated almost a full 360 degrees, all while the camera was pointing straight ahead. A popular surveillance tool for years, the Squintar allowed its user to take pictures of subjects without the subjects ever knowing they were being photographed.

Once the salesperson had explained how the cameras worked and had talked Harvath into upgrading to higher memory cards and purchasing extra batteries, videotape, and a dual car adaptor, the pair left the store and headed for the village of Le Râleur.

As they drove, Jillian charged the camera batteries, while Harvath explained their cover and how he wanted to handle things. The element of surprise was the only thing they had going for them. If Rayburn discovered that they were on to him, they would not only lose their advantage, but if he did still have Emir Tokay alive, he might get spooked and kill him, which was the absolute last thing they wanted.

Perched on the banks of a small, glacial lake surrounded by the sheer, rocky cliffs of the Bernese Alps on all sides, Le Râleur was one of the most beautiful villages Harvath or Jillian had ever seen. It looked like it should be gracing posters promoting tourism to Switzerland, as flowers spilled from boxes hung from the windows of intricately crafted wooden chalets, and the whitewashed village church, with its weatherworn copper-covered steeple, gave scale to the towering grandeur of Le Râleur's surroundings.

The first stop they made was at the village tourist information office, which was nothing more than a small glass booth with an ATM and a couple of racks filled with brochures. After selecting what they wanted, Harvath and Jillian got their cameras out and strolled into the heart of the town.

Interspersed with the high-end clothing boutiques, which had obviously been established with the wealthy tourist crowd in mind, were the small shops and businesses that were the true lifeblood of Le Râleur. Harvath and Jillian passed a *fromagerie*, a *patisserie*, a *boucherie*, and a *boulangerie*—all testaments to the French-speaking heritage of the region, *but what could have drawn Rayburn to this place?* Harvath wondered.

His first clue came when they reached the village square and spotted two manned police cars parked alongside each other in front of an old funicular railway. The scene reminded Harvath of something, but he couldn't quite place it. Looking up, he could see that the railway line went all the way up to the top of one of the mountains. Even with his telephoto lens, all he could see from this distance was what looked to be the upper housing for the funicular.

A heavy metal chain blocked the stone steps leading to the railway car, and in case that and the policemen were not enough to dissuade any curious passersby, a large metal placard with *Do Not En-*

ter written in several languages had been hung from the chain itself.

Positioning Jillian at a ninety-degree angle from the funicular, Harvath took advantage of the Squintar lens affixed to his camera and clicked away. Once he had taken enough pictures, he called Jillian back over and suggested they get a coffee.

They took a table on the terrace of a small café facing the square called La Bergère. It was one of the establishments Rayburn had used his credit card in, and from where Harvath was sitting, he could also see the bank where two days ago Rayburn had conducted a cash advance.

Pegging them as tourists, the waitress brought out two menus written in English, Italian, French, and German. Harvath ignored the one that was laid in front of him and instead scrolled through the pictures on his digital camera. Jillian, though, was in the mood for more than just coffee and actually took a look at her menu. "This is interesting," she said after several moments.

"What is?" replied Harvath, not bothering to look up from his camera.

"The funicular railway."

"What about it?"

"There's a story on the back of the menu about the village and its history. Apparently, there used to be a monastery on the top of that mountain, but in the early 1900s the monks couldn't afford to maintain it and ended up selling it to a group of backers who turned it into a sanitarium."

"Like a health resort?" said Harvath, still engrossed in his images.

"Exactly. It attracted wealthy clients from all over Europe, but especially Geneva because of its close proximity. It went out of business, though, in the sixties and fell into a state of disrepair, but was then purchased in the late eighties, rehabbed, and turned into a private residence."

"Whose private residence?"

"It doesn't say. The only additional info is that the peak upon which it is built is at a height of 6,500 feet, and as it is surrounded by mountains and steep, sloping cliffs on all sides, the only way to get up or down is via the funicular."

"Which, for some reason, those heavily armed police officers are now guarding," said Harvath as he looked up from his camera and across the square.

"Have you decided?" asked the waitress as she appeared beside the table with a pad and pencil in hand.

"I'll have a cappuccino and a chocolate croissant," said Jillian, setting down the menu and looking at Harvath.

"An espresso, please."

"I have a question," said Jillian. "I was reading in your menu about the history of Le Râleur and am fascinated by the monastery that used to be at the top of the funicular railway."

Harvath tensed, worried that she might blow

their cover, but then relaxed as he realized that everyone who came to the café probably asked the same question.

"Back then, Madame, there was no funicular. It came much later, with the sanitarium."

"I see," said Jillian. "It must be very romantic living in an old monastery on top of a mountain. I read that it's a private residence these days?"

"Correct."

Jillian leaned in toward the waitress and asked, "Who lives there now, some big movie star trying to get away from it all? I heard a rumor that Michael Caine owns a villa near here."

The waitress looked around to make sure no one else was listening and then said, "It belongs to the Aga Khan of Bombay."

"The Aga Khan?" repeated Harvath.

"*Oui*, Monsieur."

"The Shia Muslim spiritual leader?"

"*Oui*, Monsieur," the waitress said again. "He is very, very rich, this man. Did you know that every year on his birthday, his people give him his weight in emeralds, diamonds, and rubies?"

"I have heard that," replied Harvath, knowing full well the practice had ended a long time ago and even then the man had only been given his weight in gold or diamonds. Still, it was nothing to sneeze at and was obviously the kind of romantic mystique that would cling forever. "That must be why the police guard the funicular."

"Yes, but it's not just the police. He has his own bodyguards too. Sometimes in the evening, if they are not working, they come down here to the village. The police only guard the funicular when the Aga Khan is staying at Château Aiglemont."

"Aiglemont?" asked Jillian. "Is that the name of the monastery?"

"Yes, it means mountain of the eagles."

"Well, I hope the coffee here is as good as the view," said Harvath with a smile. The sooner they got their order, the sooner they could drink up and get out of there. Somehow the Aga Khan was now involved in all of this, and he needed to find out why. He knew enough about the man to know that two police cars at the bottom of a funicular was only the tip of the security iceberg. The Aga Khan would have the absolute best, and the more Harvath thought about it, the more his gut told him he had just discovered where Timothy Rayburn had been able to secure gainful employment.

SIXTY

Why would a major, internationally recognized Muslim spiritual figure be involved in a kidnapping?" asked Jillian once they were in the car and on their way back to Sion.

"I have no idea, but it's important to note that Shia Muslims are the second-largest branch of Islam. It's the Sunnis who make up the world's majority of Muslims."

"So?"

"So you don't often see the two groups working together."

Jillian turned in her seat and looked at him. "Who says they're working together?"

"We came here looking for Rayburn. He's the one who put together the hunt for Hannibal's mysterious weapon. Once the weapon was found and made ready for modern use, everyone associated with it was killed, by an al-Qaeda assassin."

"Or kidnapped. Emir might still be alive," said Jillian.

"Fine," replied Harvath, "but it's no coincidence that both the Aga Khan and Rayburn are known to be in this village. The Aga Khan is the Shia connection, and Khalid Alomari is the Sunni. All of the al-Qaeda are Sunni."

"What's the difference, though? They're all Muslims."

"That's not the way the Sunnis see it. To a good number of them, the Shia are even worse than Western infidel Christians. Hard to believe, isn't it?" said Harvath. "Even holier-than-thou Muslim terrorists are prejudiced against other followers of Islam, but at this point nothing surprises me anymore when it comes to these people. As far as I'm concerned, there are only two kinds of Muslims in the world—good ones and bad ones. Other than that, I really don't care. That's not my department."

"I still don't understand why the distinction is important."

"Most of the terrorism," he tried to explain, "all that militant, radical fundamentalist Wahhabi crap out of Saudi Arabia, is Sunni. The only major Shia problem out there is the Iranians."

"But if they all follow Islam, where does the acrimony come from?"

"Simple," said Harvath. "Thirteen hundred years ago, the Prophet Muhammad died without leaving a will."

"I don't get it."

Harvath turned up the air conditioning and said, "During his time, the Prophet Muhammad had created his own earthly kingdom or caliphate. After his death, his successors were known as caliphs, and it was their job to lead the worldwide Muslim community, or *ummah*. But after the fourth caliph, Ali, was assassinated in 661, a schism erupted between the Sunni and the Shia. The Sunnis believe that Muhammad had intended for the Muslim community to choose a successor, or caliph, by consensus to lead the caliphate, while the Shia believe that Muhammad had chosen his son-in-law, Ali, as his successor and that only the descendants of Ali and his wife, Fatima, were entitled to rule."

"But what does any of this have to do with the Aga Khan?"

"Now we start drifting into the realm of the very interesting," said Harvath as he signaled to change lanes. "The Aga Khan, as I've said, is Shia, and the Shia have a very esoteric interpretation of the Koran. They believe that beneath the explicit and literal levels is another level entirely, and it is on that level that all of the secrets of the universe are contained."

"Including scientific secrets?" asked Jillian, anticipating where he was going.

"Yes, including scientific secrets."

"What's the likelihood that he was involved with the organization Emir was working for?"

"The Islamic Institute for Science and Technology?" replied Harvath. "Anything is possible. It takes a lot of money to fund the expeditions they were engaged in, and the Aga Khan has lots and lots of money. Not only that, but the specific type of expeditions they were conducting would fit very nicely with the Shia interpretation of the Koran."

"Actually, any follower of Islamic science, Shia or Sunni, believes that the Koran contains the keys to the mysteries of the universe."

"True," stated Harvath, "but it's the fact that the Sunni and Shia seem to be working together at such a high level on this that is so interesting. Maybe using Islamic science to rid the world of nonbelievers is the first thing both camps have ever been able to come together and agree on."

"That could be," said Jillian, "but then how does al-Qaeda fit into all this? I see what you mean, at least with the Aga Khan being involved, there is cooperation from at least one camp at a very high level, but who are the high-level operators on the Sunni side? Al-Qaeda? They've always struck me as nothing more than narrow-minded thugs. They're just terrorists."

Jillian was right, but there was a piece of the puzzle that she didn't have. "There is a theory in Western intelligence circles," said Harvath, "and it has been regularly dismissed as being too far-fetched, but the theory is that there is somebody very far removed from the al-Qaeda organization who pulls their strings. I'm starting to think that theory might hold some water."

"Someone above bin Laden?"

"Above bin Laden and beyond Ayman al-Zawahiri, bin Laden's second in command, whom many believe is a lot smarter than bin Laden and could even be the real head of al-Qaeda."

"But that's not what you're talking about, is it?"

"No. You see, during the Afghan war, there was a Soviet KGB agent obsessed with bin Laden. He studied everything he could about him and the burgeoning al-Qaeda organization. Right before the collapse of the Soviet Union, he defected to Great Britain. As these people do, he tried to make himself look as valuable as possible to his new host country. Contained within the intelligence he brought with him were his views and hypotheses about bin Laden and al-Qaeda. At the time, a good portion of that intelligence was seen as pretty fantastic. I mean, bin Laden had been nothing more than a really nasty thorn in the side of the Soviets. The West was on bin Laden's side back then. We wanted them to cream the Red Army and we helped train and equip them to do so. In hindsight, we probably trained them too well.

"Fast forward seven years, and you have the bombings of the U.S. embassies in Kenya and Tanzania, followed by the USS *Cole* bombing in Yemen two years later. Then of course there's September eleventh, and all of a sudden, al-Qaeda cells are popping up all over Britain. Now, the Brits were looking for anything and everything they could get their hands on about bin Laden and al-Qaeda. So, what would you imagine floats back up to the surface?"

"All of the files from the KGB defector," replied Jillian.

"Exactly. This is in part where it starts really coming together. The ex–KGB person, we'll call him Yuri, hasn't given up his passion for bin Laden just because he's the newest citizen of merry old England. On the contrary, he really sees a growing threat in al-Qaeda and predicted long before anyone else that bin Laden was going to go global in a very big, very bad way.

"Yuri took classes at Oxford about all things Islamic and wrote lengthy letters to his case officer at MI6 about why England needed to take the bin Laden threat seriously. Of course, at that time, nobody saw any need to listen to Yuri, and so his letters were buried along with the rest of his intel. Then Yuri made a big mistake."

"Which was?"

"He had unapproved contact with someone active in the espionage community. That's one thing a host country absolutely will not tolerate. They put a roof over your head, and in exchange you give them your old team's playbook and you hang up your spikes. You do not put your spikes back on unless your hosts tell you to."

"So who was he talking to?" asked Jillian.

"The man was a floater. He worked for several different governments, none of whom the British were too fond of. Yuri claimed the man was just an old friend whom he was talking to for a book he wanted to write about bin Laden, but the powers that be at MI6 didn't give a damn. He broke the rules, and he got the boot for it. It was Sweden who finally took him in," said Harvath.

"Interesting," replied Jillian, "but what does that have to do with the idea that someone is pulling al-Qaeda's strings?"

"Yuri believed that al-Qaeda was a front."

Jillian looked at him. "*A front*? A front for what?"

"What do you know about the beginnings of al-Qaeda?" he asked.

"Not much. I know that bin Laden fought in Afghanistan against the Soviets and that when he returned home to Saudi Arabia he was extremely unhappy with the Saudi Royal Family. Somehow al-Qaeda came from all of that."

"Their roots go a lot deeper and cover a piece of terrorism history most people are unfamiliar with. You see, when the Soviet Union invaded predominantly Muslim Afghanistan in 1979, bin Laden was one of the thousands of devout Muslims who heeded the call to help repel the invasion. As the son of one of the wealthiest men in Saudi Arabia, bin Laden brought with him quite a sizable bank account, and it's here that we get to the part that a lot of people don't know about.

"Along with a man by the name of Sheik Abdullah Azzam, bin Laden founded the Maktab al-Khidamat, or Offices of Services, in 1984. It served as a recruiting and command center for the international Muslim brigade that fought throughout Afghanistan.

"It's rumored that the MAK trained, equipped, and financed anywhere between ten thousand and fifty thousand mujahideen, or holy warriors, from more than fifty countries. The MAK had offices around the globe, including Europe and even in the United States. Bin Laden's fame grew like wildfire throughout the Islamic world, and soon all sorts of interesting people were coming to see him. One of these visitors, according to Yuri, began to mold bin Laden's vision of what he could do on a worldwide basis."

"You're saying he was manipulated?" asked Alcott.

"That's too crass a word. It was much more elegant than that. His fervor was already there. It was just a matter of directing it. What's important, though, is that toward the end of the decade-long Soviet-Afghan conflict, a rift started to develop between bin Laden and Azzam. Azzam wanted the MAK to focus its efforts solely on Afghanistan, but bin Laden increasingly wanted to focus on this new idea of 'global' jihad. He had come to believe that not only was jihad a personal responsibility, but all Muslims were honor bound to establish true Islamic rule in their own countries by any means necessary, even violence. Concepts like democracy and the separation between church and state were anathema to him."

"Which immediately made the United States and the rest of the West enemies of Islam," said Jillian.

Harvath nodded his head in agreement. "With the help of the aforementioned outside influence, bin Laden began sketching out rough plans for his global al-Qaeda organization in 1987, but he couldn't bring himself to split with Azzam and the MAK, no matter how divergent their ideas. Over the next several months, bin Laden held many meetings with a certain shadowy international figure who, according to Yuri, urged him to go his own way, but bin Laden either couldn't or wouldn't listen. It wasn't until the next year, when Azzam was assassinated under very mysterious circumstances, that al-Qaeda broke off from the MAK and threw down the gauntlet to the rest of the world."

"You said that al-Qaeda was being used as a front. For what?"

"To ignite global jihad," replied Harvath, "and overthrow any apostate regimes in Arab or Muslim countries they see as corrupt or anti-Islamic."

"And what would they replace those regimes with?" asked Alcott.

"From what I understand, a single Muslim government strictly ruled by sharia—the religious and moral principles of Islam—the law of the Muslim land so to speak. Essentially what they want to see created is another Muslim caliphate. One nation, under Allah, headed by a caliph who would be the recognized leader of the entire Islamic world."

"So bin Laden wants to rule the world. Big surprise."

Harvath shook his head. "Bin Laden's not smart enough to be caliph. He might be the movement's emir-general, providing operational and tactical management, but for all intents and purposes he's nothing more than a Koran thumper, a zealot. He has some useful skills, but not what it would take to run an empire. He's too wrapped up in the fundamentalism. He's nothing more than an extremely clever bully. Once all of the crusader infidels have been driven from the Muslim holy lands and all of the apostate regimes have been disposed of, who would run this new, unified Muslim dynasty he has helped bring to life? Who would be caliph?"

Jillian had never thought about that before. In fact, she had never thought that bin Laden and his organization were anything more than that—bin Laden and his organization, much less that they would ever succeed in achieving their goals. In her mind, al-Qaeda was enough of a terrifying handful without exploring the possibility that they could unite the Muslim faithful and overthrow the rest of the world. "I don't know," she responded. "Bin Laden's a Sunni, so based on their way of doing things, I guess the Muslim faithful would vote for who would be caliph."

"Unless somehow an effort was going to be made to include the Shia in this new Muslim dynasty," replied Harvath.

"But you said the Sunnis saw the Shia as worse than Christians."

"Many do, but Yuri suggested that the person behind al-Qaeda was going to be able to deliver a leader acceptable to both camps."

Jillian thought about that a second and then replied, "Which would mean the person would have to be a descendant of the Prophet Muhammad and acceptable to a majority of the Sunni population. How do you do that?"

"I have no idea," said Harvath as he pulled up in front of their hotel, "but I think I know where some of our answers might be found."

"Don't say Château Aiglemont."

Harvath didn't say it, but the look on his face was enough to tell her that's exactly where he wanted to go.

SIXTY-ONE

RIYADH
SAUDI ARABIA

Chip Reynolds loved the hypocrisy of it all. After spending hours in their mosque listening to a radical imam spew anti-American hate speech, the first thing the three young fundamentalists did was head to a downtown Starbucks for iced Frappuccinos. America might be the great Satan, but their coffee concoctions were nothing short of a divine paradise right here on earth. You can keep your seventy-two dark-eyed virgins, Allah, just make sure the house blend keeps flowing.

Reynolds would have laughed if it wasn't so despicably sad. Radical Islam blamed America and the West for everything that was wrong with their fucked-up countries. He had had his fill of all of it. He couldn't wait to get out. He hadn't been back to his cabin in Montana since his wife had died and didn't think he'd ever return, but he knew at some point he was going to have to try to put his life back together. One more year and he'd have enough to retire *very* comfortably, and no matter what his situation, he'd made a promise to himself that he would try. And once he left, he never wanted to set foot in the Mideast or deal with security or intelligence work ever again.

For the time being, though, he had a job to do. He'd been tailing the three young radicals for the past two days, but in that time there'd been no sign of their buddy, Khalid Alomari. This despite the fact that someone in Saudi intelligence was still filing nostalgic remembrances of surveillance days past, claiming that the four youths had been together almost every day over the last three. Something was definitely up, and the sooner Chip Reynolds got to the bottom of it, the better he'd be able to sleep at night.

After finishing their coffees, the young men were preparing to leave when one of them received a phone call. It was times like these when Reynolds wished he still had access to the CIA's incredible trove of listening devices. Sitting in his Toyota Land Cruiser across the street from the Starbucks with a parabolic microphone balanced on the windowsill, he wasn't getting anything. What's more, even with the air conditioning going full blast, the summer heat pouring through the open window was roasting him alive. It was all putting him in a very bad mood.

Whatever the phone call had been, it must have been important, because Mo(hammad), Larry, and

Curly had an intense, albeit brief conversation, and then immediately hurried outside to their car.

The late afternoon Riyadh traffic made it difficult to keep up with the three men. In fact, on two separate occasions, Reynolds thought he had lost them, only to recover their car a couple of blocks later. They certainly were being cautious, but none of them had the experience to outmaneuver a seasoned espionage veteran like Reynolds.

An hour later, the men turned onto a dusty access road leading to a seldom-used military airfield south of the city. *What the hell were they up to?* he wondered.

As the road twisted and turned, Reynolds often lost sight of his quarry for thirty or forty seconds at a time. He had to be very careful not only not to lose them for good but also to make sure that he wasn't following so closely that they knew someone was behind them. Blending in was one thing in downtown Riyadh or along one of the country's busy motorways. It was another thing entirely out here in the middle of nowhere.

Coming around yet another curve, Reynolds had just enough time to slam on the brakes and skid to a stop. He managed to back his car up out of sight while he watched the young fundamentalists pick up speed as they hit the final straightaway. Five hundred yards away was the airfield's not so deserted and very much armed checkpoint. *Was that what this was all about? A suicide bombing?* It didn't make any sense. Why waste three men on a job one could have done alone? And why hit such a low-value target? Something like this wouldn't even make the news, much less the watered-down intelligence briefing Reynolds skimmed each morning.

Reynolds prepared himself for the worst. As the car closed on the checkpoint, he thought he saw their brake lights, but quickly realized it wasn't brake lights he saw flashing, it was something else. *These guys were signaling the soldiers with their headlights!* Even odder, the soldiers seemed to be responding.

He watched as two men in uniform rushed down from the guard tower and hurriedly opened the gates. Five seconds later, the car with his three suspects sped through and the gates were closed behind them. They never even slowed down. There was no ID check, nothing. Obviously, they had been expected. Reynolds couldn't make heads or tails of it. The phrase "Keep your friends close and your enemies closer" came to mind, but this was like the Southern Black Baptist Conference inviting the KKK in for punch and cookies.

As much as he didn't want to, Reynolds knew he was going to have to get a closer look. He watched as the car headed toward a pair of dilapidated hangars on the far side of the airfield. He pulled off the access road and headed his SUV into the desert. He would have to cut a pretty wide arc to come up on the rear of the airfield without being seen, but it was his only choice.

He drove as close as he dared with the Land Cruiser and then hiked the rest of the way in on foot. Seventy-five yards later, Reynolds spotted the militants' car and took cover behind a narrow berm. The car was parked in front of an open hangar. A Saudi Arabian National Guard UH60 Blackhawk helicopter sat idling on the tarmac nearby. Things were getting very interesting.

Reynolds removed a pair of Steiner binoculars and peered into the open hangar. Seated on top of cushions scattered across the floor, Bedouin style, were the three young militants along with several men in Royal Saudi Land Forces as well as Saudi Arabian National Guard uniforms. The Saudi Royal Land Forces were charged with external security, while the Saudi National Guard were charged with protecting the Royal Family from internal rebellion and from any possible coup attempts by the Royal Land Forces. *What the hell were these guys all doing here together?*

Reynolds had brought his somewhat out-of-date parabolic mike along, but he knew that the engine noise from the UH60 would make it impossible to hear anything. Something big was happening, and he needed to know what was going on. Not having brought the proper equipment to circumvent the electric fence surrounding the base, there was no way he could get in closer. Besides, his running and gunning days were over. If these guys really were up to something that they shouldn't be, there was no question in Reynolds's mind that they would kill him if they discovered him lurking around the hangar. As much as he didn't want to, he knew there was only one person he could call for help. Faruq al-Hafez might not be his biggest fan, but he was completely devoted to the Saudi Royal Family, and a meeting of this magnitude was something he'd want to know and hopefully do something about.

Without taking his eyes from the scene inside the hangar, Reynolds fished his cell phone from his pocket, raised it to his mouth, and said, "Call deputy intel minister, cell." The voice-activated feature began to dial the preprogrammed number, but just as it was starting to ring, Reynolds saw something that made him immediately disconnect the call. Walking out of the adjacent hangar with two large aluminum briefcases in his hands was Faruq al-Hafez himself.

He placed the briefcases on a folding table set up near the mouth of the hangar, popped the lids, and began setting up three stacks of bills. Reynolds watched as a representative from each group came up and collected their money. One of the militants lifted a stack of American currency and fanned through it with his thumb and then shoved the rest of his pile into a dusty, desert-camouflaged knapsack.

The National Guard and Royal Land Force soldiers were far less dramatic than the Wahhabi radical. After a cursory glance, they each piled their money into one of the aluminum cases and shook hands with Faruq. Whatever was going on, everyone seemed to be satisfied.

The National Guard members headed for their UH60 Blackhawk as the representatives from the Saudi army climbed into a Hummer parked on the far side of the hangar. While the militants headed toward their car, the deputy intelligence minister raised a walkie-talkie to his mouth and gave some sort of command. A fraction of a second later, the doors of hangar number two rolled open revealing a sleek Dessault Falcon 50EX business jet. *What the hell is he up to?* wondered Reynolds. The only time Faruq used one of the Intelligence Ministry jets was when he traveled out of the country. There was only one way to find out.

Reynolds removed his cell phone and voice-dialed the man again.

"Hello?" Faruq responded in Arabic.

Reynolds could hear the whine of the Falcon's engines in the background. "It's Chip Reynolds, Your Excellency."

"Yes, Mr. Reynolds. What is it? I'm quite busy."

Reynolds watched as al-Hafez entered the hangar. "I have a security matter I'd like to discuss with you. I'm concerned with some activity we've seen around one of the northern pumping stations. I'm going to be near your office later today and was hoping we could meet."

"That won't be possible," replied the deputy minister. "I'm on my way out of the country and will be gone for several days."

"Vacation?" asked Reynolds.

"Business," said Faruq as he climbed the Falcon's retractable stairs and paused before entering the cabin. "Whatever this is, I'm sure it's nothing. If there's still a problem when I get back, we can discuss it then." With that, the deputy intelligence minister punched the end button on his cell and climbed into the plane.

Hiking back to his Land Cruiser, Reynolds downed a liter of water from the cooler on his back seat and then reached for his body armor. He had one last lead to pursue, and something told him that with that much money lying around, Mo(hammad), Larry, and Curly were going to be in a shoot first, ask questions later kind of mood.

SIXTY-TWO

There was only one road back to Riyadh, and Reynolds got on it as fast as he could. He pushed his Land Cruiser as hard as it would go and beat the militants to the outskirts of the city by a good twenty minutes. By the time they passed him, Reynolds was secreted on a small side street, and they never noticed as he pulled back onto the road and began to follow them.

He had expected the men to return to the small apartment they shared near their mosque, but instead they led him to a large warehouse in one of the poorest neighborhoods in Riyadh. *So much for the Saudi government's campaign to eradicate poverty,* thought Reynolds as he passed dwelling after dwelling where the inhabitants were so poor they couldn't even afford electricity. People could say what they wanted about America, but he had never seen such an enormous or hopeless chasm between the haves and the have-nots than he did in Saudi Arabia.

Risking only one casual drive-by, Reynolds noticed that the building apparently belonged to yet another good-for-nothing member of the Saudi Royal Family—a young prince named Hamal. Reynolds didn't know which type of Saudi royal he hated more—the heavy-drinking, whoring, spend-like-there's-no-tomorrow kind, or the ultra-religious, hypocritical, spit-in-the-face-of-the-world, bite-the-hand-that-feeds-you kind. As far as he was concerned, Prince Hamal fell into the latter category. With an Oxford education and a bottomless bank account, Hamal didn't want for a single thing in his life, yet as a convert to extremist Wahhabism, he never missed an opportunity to strike out at the Saudi monarchy for being bloated, lazy, and corrupt.

Recently, Hamal had taken a page from the British monarchy and had begun issuing royal titles to merchants who were furthering the greater good of Islam and the Islamic world. Much as pastry shops and shirt makers were being recognized as official purveyors to the crown in England, Hamal was recognizing businesses that made life better for Muslims around the globe. While quietly the higher-ups in the Saudi Royal Family were more than a little upset at not having been consulted before the young man embarked on his endeavor, they liked the idea of the Saudi name supporting people who bettered the lives of the followers of Islam. What's more, Hamal was the brains behind the bottled water that supposedly came from a secret spring beneath Mecca. Reynolds thought it was all a crock, right down to how Hamal claimed he was donating all the proceeds to worthy Muslim charities.

That move was surely a winner with the Royal Family. Ever since 9/11, the Saudis had been forced to discontinue their highly successful charity drives on television, which had brought in hundreds of millions of dollars for various Islamic groups worldwide. The U.S. had seen it as blatant fundraising for terrorists, and though the Saudi monarchy didn't necessarily agree, they had buckled under the pressure from their staunchest Western ally.

The money Prince Hamal's venture stood to raise and the positive spin it placed upon the Royal Family meant that the powers that be were willing to look the other way and forget that he had never even attempted to go through the proper channels before setting up shop. At the end of the day, the Saudi monarchy had seen his effort at worst as worthwhile and at best as a way to keep the radical young prince out of their hair and maybe a means by which he could grow to be less of a pain in their collective ass.

After parking his car and surveying the building from the rooftop of an abandoned building down the street, Reynolds knew he wasn't going to be able to leave until he got a look at what was going on inside. Finding a small slice of shade, he waited until most of the neighborhood's residents had left for afternoon prayers before making his way down to the pavement. He had hoped that Mo, Larry, and Curly would leave the warehouse to attend prayers as well, but today just wasn't turning out to be his day.

Stopping at his Land Cruiser, Reynolds pulled a twelve-gauge Remington 870 tactical shotgun from inside the cargo area and wrapped it inside a cheap prayer rug he had bought at one of Riyadh's many souks.

He did one complete turn around the outside of the warehouse by foot, trying to find the best entry point. He stopped outside the blacked-out, bar-covered windows of what appeared to be the warehouse's office, but was unable to hear anything above the steady roar of the industrial-strength air conditioners. With his sweaty right hand shoved inside the wool rug and wrapped around the Remington's pistol grip, the whir of the machines only served to remind him of how goddamn hot he was. Jesus, was he sick and tired of Saudi Arabia.

Continuing on to the loading dock area, Reynolds kept looking for a way in, but the building was more secure than a bank vault. With steel-reinforced doors and bars covering what other few windows there were, the three Wahhabi stooges were obviously a lot more capable of keeping people out of their warehouse than they were of keeping people off their tail while driving. Reynolds realized that the only way he was going to get a look inside was if someone invited him.

By the time he came back around near the office, he had come to the conclusion that the best way to gain an invitation was to first smoke somebody out from inside. Setting his shotgun cum prayer rug against the side of the building, he removed his Benchmade tactical folding knife from his back pocket, popped open the circuit breaker covers for the air-conditioning units, and started knocking them offline one by one.

With one hundred plus degree temperatures raging outside, he figured it wouldn't take too long for the people inside the building to start feeling the heat. The other thing Reynolds hoped he was right about was that with only one car parked in the warehouse's parking lot, there was no one other than Mo, Larry, and Curly inside. Any more than that, and he could end up with a serious problem on his hands.

Picking his prayer rug back up, he leaned behind the office door and waited. Ten minutes later, he heard the sound of someone unlocking the door from the inside. Quietly, he unwrapped the shotgun and threw the rug off to the side.

There was the sound of voices from inside as the man's colleagues urged him to hurry up and figure out what had gone wrong with the air conditioners. Reynolds waited until the man had stepped all the way outside and the door had closed behind him before pursing his lips and making the sound of two quick kisses.

The man spun around, only to be knocked unconscious by the butt of Reynolds's shotgun. The only thing he would remember, if anything at all, was that his assailant wasn't an Arab. That was probably one of the biggest advantages Reynolds had going for him. Saudi Arabia was awash with foreign contractors and consultants, and outside the people he worked with, nobody knew who the hell he was.

There was no knob or handle on the outside of the door. It could only be opened with a key. Fishing a set of keys from the militant's pocket, Reynolds found the correct one, slid it into the lock, and slowly opened the door. It swung silently back on its hinges, and Reynolds stepped out of the heat and into the hallway of the considerably cooler offices.

Less than five feet away, he could hear two men talking. Not knowing how long their colleague outside would be napping, Reynolds decided not to waste any time.

Sweeping through the main office door, he brought the Remington up to the firing position and yelled at both of the men in Arabic to get intimate with the carpeting.

For a moment, neither of them moved. Then, as if they were telepathically connected, they both acted at the same time. One of them snatched up an

AK-47 while the other made a beeline out a side door and into the warehouse.

Before the man with the AK could get his finger anywhere near the trigger, Reynolds hit him with three rounds from the Remington that nearly tore him in half and sent his bloody body flying across the room. *Two stooges down, one to go.*

It had been a while since Reynolds had seen this kind of action, and his heart was pumping a mile a minute as he crept into the packed warehouse. Pallets of bottled water as well as what appeared to be various spices were stacked floor to ceiling.

Reynolds tried to concentrate on finding the last remaining Wahhabi wiseguy. Once he was neutralized, Reynolds could drag their unconscious colleague in from outside and start tearing the place apart.

He heard a noise from the other end of the building that sounded like metal scraping on metal. Peeking out from behind the pallet of water bottles he was using for cover, Reynolds took aim with the shotgun and pulled the trigger two more times, but it was no use. The remaining militant had opened one of the doors near the loading bay and had taken off.

There was no telling what contacts the man might have in the neighborhood, so Reynolds had to act fast.

After a quick sweep of the warehouse that turned up nothing of real value, he ran back to the office and tore the entire place apart as he searched for anything that would explain what the hell these people were up to and what the meeting he had witnessed earlier in the day had all been about.

He was extremely thorough, but the office was shaping up to be another dead end. Ready to give up, Reynolds swept the assorted office supplies off one of the desks in frustration and in doing so sent the desk blotter sailing. As it hit the floor, he noticed several pages sticking out from underneath it.

Picking the pages up, Reynolds began reading. They didn't make any sense. There were lists of currency exchanges, payday loan operations, check-cashing businesses, convenience stores, taxicab companies, and gas stations across the United States. It was all very strange.

Reynolds had no idea what he might have uncovered. It might have been nothing, but taking into consideration everything else he had already seen, he was suspicious enough to want somebody else back in the States to take a look at it.

There was just one problem. Reynolds needed to get the information to someone who'd take it seriously enough not to hand it off and let it get buried. It would also have to be someone who wouldn't ask a lot of questions about how he got it. With a dead militant and the Saudi Royal Family involved, whoever he reached out to not only would have to have a good amount of power, but also be someone he could trust to do the right thing.

Going to the top at the CIA was definitely out of the question. Reynolds had been gone just long enough to lose what halfway reliable contacts he had in the director's office. As he shoved the documents into his pocket, he realized there was only one person who could help him. After wiping down the office for prints, he snuck through the warehouse and used the set of keys he had taken from the first militant to let himself out one of the side doors. When he reached his truck, he waited until he was well away from the neighborhood and wasn't being followed before he picked up his cell phone and dialed the number of his old friend and colleague back in DC.

As the phone began to ring, he hoped like hell Gary Lawlor was at his desk.

SIXTY-THREE

SWITZERLAND

"Where are we going?" asked Jillian when Harvath got back in the car and pulled away from the curb in front of the hotel.

"Here," he replied, and handed her the glossy brochure for Sion International Airport he had picked up in the lobby. "This caught my eye when we were on our way out this morning."

As Jillian looked at it, Harvath added, "It's a pretty impressive operation. Along with being a military airbase, they've poured a lot of money into it in the hopes that this region is going to be the next big thing. Besides having a runway long enough to accommodate the most sophisticated business jets, the airport has just about every service simple tourists like us could ask for."

"I can see that," replied Jillian. "Anything and everything when it comes to charters. Helicopters, gliders, hang gliders, parachute flights, sightseeing flights over the Alps. They don't seem to have missed anything."

"Nope. They even do glacier aviation, the desk clerk told me. It's their specialty. If the glacier is big enough, they can actually land a plane on it."

"So what's the plan then?" asked Jillian as she set the brochure in the door pocket next to her.

"You and I are going to charter a plane and do a reconnaissance flight," said Harvath. "We've already got pictures of what security is like at the base of the Aga Khan's funicular. I want to see what things look like up top."

"Then what?"

"Then we'll try to figure out what to do next."

Staring out the windshield at the mountains rising up on both sides of them, Jillian said, "A line like that doesn't inspire a lot of confidence."

Harvath forced a smile and replied, "I'll try to come up with something a little bit better once I've gotten a look at Aiglemont. Right now, though, let's focus on what we need to get done."

Harvath and Alcott arrived at the Aéroport de Sion posing as climbers looking to charter a plane in order to conduct aerial surveys for a series of upcoming expeditions in the Bernese Alps. Even without reservations, they had no problem finding a willing charter company. Cold hard cash was an amazing problem solver. Not only did they luck out in finding a plane without a reservation, they also managed to land an extremely chatty pilot with an excellent command of English. The first thing he pointed out as they taxied out onto the runway was where the Aga Khan's Cessna Citation X jet was parked. Had the police at the bottom of the funicular not been enough to confirm his presence, now they knew for sure that he was in residence. Hopefully, that meant Rayburn and Emir Tokay were at Aiglemont as well.

The pilot went on to explain that whenever the Aga Khan had one of his aid meetings or get-togethers with his bankers in Geneva, he had his own helicopter pick him up at Aiglemont and bring him back. He never drove.

With his detailed atlas of Switzerland on his lap, Harvath was able to guide the pilot over and around the peaks the would-be climbers were interested in tackling. Each pass was designed to bring them as close as possible to the Aga Khan's mountaintop retreat, which their pilot was pleased to point out and discuss.

When Jillian told the pilot she hadn't been able to capture the structure as well as she would have liked with her video camera, the pilot was more than happy to oblige with another, lower pass. Not only did they get an even better view, but they also got the additional bonus of seeing how the Aga Khan's security team reacted to low-flying aircraft. It was exactly as Harvath had feared. The heavily armed men poured out of the building like angry bees from a hive. Though he couldn't be one hundred percent sure, he even thought he saw one of the men armed with a shoulder-fired missile. The Aga Khan's security team didn't leave anything to chance.

After the pair had gathered all the pictures and videos they needed, Harvath had the pilot do a pass over Le Râleur and return to the Aéroport de Sion. The extent of what they had collected wouldn't be evident until they were able to review it back in the hotel, but from what Harvath had seen already, he had a feeling it wasn't going to be good. The Aga Khan's retreat was impregnable.

SIXTY-FOUR

Back at the hotel, Harvath began printing out all of the digital stills from both their surveillance on the ground in Le Râleur and their reconnaissance flight over Château Aiglemont. As he did, he was still haunted by the feeling that there was something familiar about it, but he couldn't put his finger on what it was.

After removing the art from one of the walls, they pinned up the pictures with thumbtacks. In addition to what looked like the original monastery buildings, Aiglemont had a glass solarium, which probably covered a pool of some sort, a structure housing the mechanical system for the funicular, a narrow concrete or stone patio in front, and a sickly piece of green which turned out to be a small, oblong patch of Alpine meadow that ran along the side of the main buildings and ended in an abrupt drop-off to the valley floor thousands of feet below.

"What do you think?" said Jillian as she stood back and admired their handiwork.

The first thing that came to Harvath's mind was, *I think we're screwed*, but he kept that thought to himself for the time being. "Let's watch the video," he replied.

They attached the camcorder to the TV and played the footage several times over, with Harvath stopping it in different places so he could note the reaction of the Aga Khan's security forces. When he had seen enough, he said, "Those are definitely Rayburn's men."

"How can you tell?"

"Because they are doing exactly what the Secret Service would do in that kind of situation, right down to that man with the shoulder-fired missile. Château Aiglemont might as well be the White House as far as we're concerned. In fact, it's better than the White House because it's protected by mountains on three sides and the only approach is via that funicular."

"So are you saying it can't be done?" asked Jillian as she watched Harvath walk over to the minibar and remove a beer.

Harvath looked at the freeze frame on the television and then up at the pictures tacked to the wall. "I don't know," he replied as he pried off the cap and took a long swallow. "I don't know."

Jillian didn't like what she was hearing. "There's got to be some way. What if we could get inside the funicular car in the village? That would work, wouldn't it? It's a two-car system. They're counterbalanced. For the one at the top to come down, the one at the bottom has to go up, right?"

"True," responded Harvath, "but how would we get them to send the other car down?"

"I would imagine that they would need to resupply at some point, wouldn't they?"

"At some point, yes, but who knows how well provisioned they already are up there?"

"The waitress at the café today said that sometimes when the security personnel are not working, they come down to the village. What if we did it then?"

Harvath took another sip of his beer and thought about it. "We'd still have to get around the police guarding the car at the bottom."

"We could come up with some sort of diversion," replied Jillian. "One of us could distract them."

"And if we got halfway up and they discovered we had managed to sneak onto the funicular, what do you think would happen then?"

"There would be quite a welcoming party when we got to the top."

"Exactly," said Harvath, taking another long swallow. "We'd be sitting ducks. Besides, if I know Rayburn, those funicular cars are wired with cameras, as well as intrusion monitors. Even if we got past the Swiss police, the security personnel at

Aiglemont would know the minute we opened the door on that car, or the rooftop hatch," he added, seeing the look on Jillian's face. "I told you, Rayburn was one of the best the Secret Service ever had. I know better than to underestimate a man like that. We need to come up with something a lot better."

"Supposing he is actually there, could we somehow lure him into the village and then force him to take us back up to the top with him?"

A quiet ping echoed in Harvath's mind as if his mental radar had bounced back off something he had been searching for. "I like the idea of using him to get us inside," he said, "but it's still too dangerous. With a man like the Aga Khan, money is no object, especially when it comes to security. His people will be the absolute best. They know that the funicular is the only way to get to Aiglemont, and they will have anticipated every possible covert and forced use of it to gain access to the Château. For all we know there's even two sets of passwords to get the operator up top to start it moving—one for everything's okay and another for start her up, but I'm bringing company so have the men ready and waiting when we get there. We'd never know. If we do this, it can't involve the funicular."

Jillian was growing frustrated. Harvath was the professional, and he wasn't offering any suggestions of his own. All he was doing was sitting there, drinking his beer, and shooting down every plan she came up with. Jillian decided to give it one final try. "What about a glacier plane? That meadow looked long enough to land one on. Or what about a helicopter?"

"Too noisy," said Harvath, without even considering it.

"You know what then?" replied Jillian, tired of trying to help when all of her ideas were being shot right down. "You figure it out. I'm not going to sit here and be made to feel like an idiot for my suggestions."

"The only reason you haven't heard me suggest anything," he replied, "is because I don't always spit out the first thing that comes to my mind."

"At least we're clear on how much you value my input," said Jillian, her annoyance building to serious anger. "You know what, Scot? I have no idea how you handle problem solving in your line of work. I'm not an intelligence operative. I don't know anything about the military. I'm a scientist. All I know is that as a scientist, I try to rule out the simplest possible answers first and then proceed to the more difficult ones from there. And when working with colleagues on problems, we scientists do spit out what first comes to mind. It's a rather radical process called brainstorming."

Whether it was the insult that shook it loose or not, once again Harvath felt that ping in the back of his mind. It was that feeling of familiarity about

Aiglemont. *"The simplest possible answer,"* he repeated to her. "You're right."

Suddenly, Harvath had his answer. He knew why Aiglemont and its security felt so familiar to him, and he also knew how he was going to get inside. But all of it was going to ride on cashing in on one very big favor.

SIXTY-FIVE

DEPARTMENT OF HOMELAND SECURITY
OFFICE OF INTERNATIONAL INVESTIGATIVE ASSISTANCE
WASHINGTON, DC

Brian Turner. You're absolutely sure?" asked CIA director James Vaile as he sat in Gary Lawlor's office, admiring an oil painting of George Patton.

"I know what I saw," replied the head of the OIIA. "He and Senator Carmichael were both in that hotel together."

Vaile took another sip of his coffee before responding. "This is pretty serious stuff—for everyone involved."

"That's why I wanted to talk to you about it here, away from Langley."

"You know, we normally like to handle our own problems in-house," said Vaile.

"Except your problem has become the president's problem."

That was true, and it was also something the CIA director didn't have an immediate answer for. "What do you suggest we do?"

"As far as the CIA as a whole?" responded Lawlor. "Nothing. But I do want you to make it harder for him to get hold of his information. Let's see how good he really is."

"It could compromise us in a lot of ongoing operations."

"No, it won't. At this point they're baiting for only one type of fish. I don't want there to be any indication that we're on to them. In the meantime"—he paused as he reached into his desk and withdrew a small envelope containing a CD-ROM—"I'd like you to plant this information for me."

"What is it?"

"Open it up when you get back to your office and you'll see. Let's just say that I think it will prove irresistible. Make sure you bury it deep enough that it appears authentic, but not so deep that he'll never find it."

"Consider it done," said Vaile as Lawlor's assistant walked into the room and handed him a message.

Right away, the CIA director could tell something was seriously wrong. "What is it?"

Lawlor looked at his watch and replied, "In three hours, the president is going to convene a National Security Council meeting in the situation room. We just got word that our mystery illness has officially made its debut in the United States."

"Jesus," said Vaile as he set down his cup. "Where and how many infected?"

"The trail starts with a Muslim food importer by the name of Kaseem Najjar in Hamtramck, Michigan, and extends to several UPS workers throughout their processing and delivery system beginning in Michigan and ending in Manhattan. The FBI, as well as teams from the CDC and USAMRIID, are already en route."

"Do we know if it was intentionally released? Are there any more victims?"

"Apparently, that's all they know. Hopefully, we'll have more information by the briefing this afternoon."

"We'd better have more than just information. You saw how fast that thing moved through that village in Iraq," replied Vaile, already racing through worst-case scenarios in his mind. "If we don't get a handle on this, the death count is going to be astronomical. It'll make the plague look like an outbreak of strep throat—" Vaile was interrupted by a text message that came over his secure pager.

This time it was Lawlor's turn to read his friend's visage and inquire as to what was going on.

Looking up from his pager, the director of the CIA said, "The president's chief of staff is looking for me."

"Chuck Anderson? Why?"

"They're concerned that a major offensive with the illness could already be under way and that it's only a matter of hours before they start seeing casualties inside the Beltway. He wants to talk about moving the president out of DC."

"If a major offensive is under way, this thing could turn up anywhere. Where do they want to move him?"

Vaile set down his pager. "They want to greenlight the doomsday scenario."

"Operation Ark?"

The DCI nodded his head. "Anderson is going to recommend that the president, the cabinet, Congress, and everyone else on the continuity of government shortlist be evacuated to the underground facility at Mount Weather."

Lawlor was quite familiar with the emergency command and control continuity of government center built more than a mile beneath the surface of an antenna-studded mountain in northwest Virginia near the West Virginia border. It was a top-secret, self-sufficient subterranean city designed during the Cold War to withstand multiple direct hits from the biggest and baddest nuclear weapons America's most serious enemy, the Soviet Union, might ever unleash. Whenever the media reported the president or members of the government being evacuated in times of crisis to a "secure and undisclosed" location, nine out of ten times it was Mount Weather. "That's what Anderson's paid for," replied Lawlor, "to plan for the worst."

"Oh, yeah," said Vaile. "He's planning for the worst, all right. The president has already initiated the Campfire Protocol. We've got bombers and fighter jets being outfitted with nukes as we speak." Pausing for a moment to consider what America was on the verge of becoming, he slowly added, "I pity any location in this country that shows signs of this illness taking hold."

SIXTY-SIX

SWITZERLAND

It was nearly nightfall when the Crossair Saab 340 HK-ABN aircraft touched down on the tarmac at Sion International and taxied toward the military section of the airfield. It was amazing what a difference a few seconds of video on al-Jazeera could make. Harvath should have been leading an assault force of American Special Operations soldiers up to Château Aiglemont, but instead he was standing in the dim overhead lighting of a small hangar, watching the plane arrive, and reflecting on the enormity of the favor he had cashed in only hours before.

When Claudia Mueller had assisted him a couple of years earlier in rescuing the president from a team of Swiss mercenaries known as the Lions of Lucerne, she was merely an investigator with the Swiss Federal Attorney's Office. Now, though, she was a full-fledged prosecutor with considerably more power and considerably more responsibility. She had reacted to his call just as he had expected she would. At first, she was surprised to hear from him. Their relationship had ended a long while ago and he had never seen the point of keeping in touch. He wasn't what she wanted and she had made it clear that she was moving on. He couldn't blame her. Just like he couldn't blame Meg Cassidy for moving on, but his personal problems aside, he knew Claudia Mueller was the only one who could help him.

Of course, Claudia was skeptical at first, and in all fairness, he would have been too. That was why he had had Ozan Kalachka e-mail her the kidnapping footage showing Timothy Rayburn and then had Kalachka follow it up with a call to one of his contacts within the Swiss government. For his part, Harvath assembled a memo about Rayburn, his aliases, and the credit card information placing him in Le Râlcur and sent it to her hoping that it would be enough.

As a prosecutor, Claudia had become even more demanding about evidence, and when she waxed noncommittal, Harvath hit her with the only card he had left to play. When the two of them had gone to rescue the president from Mount Pilatus, they had been operating on a lot less. That fact brought back a lot of memories for Mueller. Harvath was right, they had been operating on a lot less at the time, but they were not trespassing on private property and he wasn't asking her to commit the lives of other people in the process. Even so, in her short time with him she had learned that Scot Harvath had incredible instincts, and so she decided to trust him.

When the dual-prop Saab 340 HK-ABN pulled up in front of the hangar and dropped its stairs, Harvath felt as if someone had punched him in the stomach. Claudia Mueller was the first one out, and she was twice as beautiful as he remembered. Her long brown hair had been streaked blond by the summer sun, and her skin was a deep bronze. She might have been very busy at work, but Harvath could see she hadn't given up her love of climbing. It was obvious she was still spending a good amount of time outdoors. For a moment, Harvath questioned how he could have ever let her go. Then, just as quickly, he was reminded of the fact that he hadn't let her go, it had been the other way around. Claudia had seen that he was too wrapped up in his career to ever stick out a real relationship.

Nevertheless, she was here now, and Harvath allowed himself, at least for a moment, to believe that she wouldn't have come unless she still cared for him. The thought warmed him until she reached the bottom of the stairs and her left hand trailed down the handrail. On it was something he hadn't expected to see—*an engagement ring.*

Though he had no right to feel betrayed, to Harvath it was as if someone was slicing through his heart with a pair of pruning shears. As he looked at her, he suddenly saw everything that they might have had together, but which she would now have with another man. Maybe he had given up on things between them too easily. Maybe there were things more important than his career.

Harvath tried to shift his mind to something else and focused on the twenty men who followed Claudia off the plane.

Unlike most of the other nations in the world, Switzerland was unique in that, despite its ability to do so, it didn't field a national counterterrorism unit. Instead, the police force of each canton had its own special tactical unit, similar to SWAT teams in the United States. Out of all the canton tactical units, the Stern unit from Bern was the absolute best. Not only did Harvath want to use the absolute best, he also wanted out-of-towners, as there was no telling how loyal the local police were to the Aga Khan. It wouldn't have surprised Harvath in the least to discover that they were on the man's payroll.

Harvath knew that the Stern unit had seen the most action in Switzerland, having deployed on two serious operations, which involved rescuing fourteen hostages from the Polish embassy in Bern, as well as sixty-two hostages from a hijacked Air France 737. If there was going to be trouble, these were the guys he wanted to have on his team.

Harvath met Claudia halfway to the hangar, and she kissed him on both cheeks. Even though it was meant as a friendly, nonsexual gesture, he still felt a charge shoot through his body.

"When I told you to call me if you ever needed anything, this wasn't exactly what I had in mind," she said as the Stern commandos unloaded their gear and carried it into the hangar.

"You know me," replied Harvath, "I never bother keeping in touch unless I've got something exciting going on. Speaking of which, you're engaged?"

Claudia looked down at her ring then back at Harvath and smiled, almost self-consciously. "Yes, we're getting married at Christmas."

"Congratulations. Where's the wedding going to be?"

"My family's farm in Grindlewald. Scot, I'm sorry. I should have told you."

"Why?" asked Harvath. "It's not like you and I are dating anymore. You don't owe me anything."

"Even so, I feel uncomfortable that you didn't know."

"Well I do now, so you can relax. Who's the lucky guy? Someone from the federal attorney's office?"

"Not exactly," said Claudia as one of the commandos came up next to her and set down his bag. "I'd like you to meet my fiancé. Horst Schroeder, this is Scot Harvath, the man I was telling you about on the plane."

Schroeder had to be at least six-foot-three and two hundred fifty pounds of pure muscle. Though he was no judge of man flesh, Harvath couldn't help but notice how handsome the guy was. With his strong, square jaw, solid nose, and broad forehead, the man's face looked as if it had been chiseled from a solid block of granite. "So, you're Harvath," said the man as he stuck out his enormous hand.

"That's right," replied Scot as he returned Horst's grip.

"You've got all the information we need to plan the assault?"

Schroeder was typical Swiss—no bullshit and straight to the point. Either that, or he was a little too up-to-speed on Harvath's past relationship with his fiancée and had taken a disliking to him before their plane had even touched down. "Are you the team leader?" asked Harvath, who had no desire to get into a pissing match with some jealous husband-to-be.

Schroeder nodded his large head.

It pays to know people, thought Harvath as he realized now how Claudia had been able to put a team together so fast. "I've got the pictures and video in the hangar."

"Claudia says you're thinking about conducting a re-creation of Operation Oak," said Horst. "Very clever."

"We'll see," replied Harvath. "The pilots are already inside. They're going to be the ones we need to convince."

"Then let's get started," said the big man as he

clapped Harvath on the back and walked him into the hangar.

Harvath introduced Claudia Mueller to Jillian Alcott and half hoped to see a glint of jealousy in her eye, but there was none. Whether Claudia felt anything or not, she was being a complete and thorough professional. After everyone in the hangar was seated, Harvath began his presentation.

With the help of an AV tech from the military base, he had uploaded all of his pictures, videos, and drawings into a PowerPoint presentation, which he now went through for the benefit of Claudia, the Stern team, and the special pilots he had asked her to arrange. "This is the base of the funicular in Le Râleur," he narrated along with the corresponding pictures. "Two police officers in each car. As far as we were able to tell, they have .40-caliber sidearms and tactical shotguns, but nothing heavier than that."

"How long are the shifts?" asked a man from the Stern team.

"They appear to change about every four hours."

"What about the actual compound?" said Schroeder.

"We did a couple of passes by plane," continued Harvath, "and the reaction of the security team was exactly what I would expect."

"Not very friendly?"

"I'll let the video speak for itself," said Harvath

as he scrolled to that part of his presentation. "These are the main buildings here. Not much action until we go to this next clip and come in for a second, considerably lower pass."

One of the men let out a whistle. "The way those security people run out of that building, they look like rats jumping off a sinking ship."

"Hold it a second," interjected Schroeder. "Can we back it up and enhance that? What is the man at the far edge of the patio doing?"

"Good eye," replied Harvath. Regardless of what he thought of Claudia marrying the guy, the operative was definitely good at his job. "I noticed that too." Turning to the AV tech helping with the presentation, he asked, "Can you sharpen that up a little bit?"

"Not by much, but let me see," replied the young man, who tightened in on the figure in question.

Though most of the resolution was gone, there was enough left for everyone to know what they were looking at. "That man has a Stinger on his shoulder," said Schroeder.

"I guess I can put my doubts about probable cause to rest now," replied Claudia, who had sat down next to Jillian Alcott and was watching the presentation with rapt attention. "We definitely don't allow private citizens to possess missiles in Switzerland."

Harvath had known she would take him at his

word, but he was glad to see her more convinced about the operation as he progressed through his briefing. "You may have heard that this operation is being based on Operation Oak, and some of you now probably understand why. For those of you who do not, let me clarify it for you.

"In July of 1943, Benito Mussolini was placed under house arrest by the Italian government in a hotel on top of Gran Sasso Mountain in central Italy. Adolf Hitler knew that without Mussolini in power, Italy would change sides and align itself with the Allies. In order to prevent that from happening, Hitler selected one of his top commandos, Captain Otto Skorzeny, to launch one of the most daring raids in modern military history. When it was over, Skorzeny had earned the Knights Cross to the Iron Cross and title of the most dangerous man in Europe.

"Much like Château Aiglemont, the hotel where Mussolini was kept was accessible only via a funicular railway, the base of which was heavily guarded by Italian *carabinieri*. Because of the height of the mountaintop, the stability of the air, and the limited open space available for use as a drop zone, a parachute insertion was ruled unfeasible and landing helicopters or airplanes would have been too noisy. So, the teams inserted via glider."

"And that's how we're going in?" asked one of the commandos.

"Pretty much. Skorzeny evacuated Il Duce with

a short takeoff and landing aircraft known as a *Stork*. The initial assault force in our operation will go in via self-launching gliders from this airport. Part of that initial assault force will secure the upper portion of the funicular so the rest of the team can be brought up that way from the village. Once we have Tokay under our control, we'll hopefully be able to evacuate him down the funicular, but if we can't, we'll have to use one of the self-launching gliders."

"They might not hear us coming," said another commando, "but at some point they are definitely going to see us. What then?"

"First," replied Harvath, "we'll be coming in out of the east with first light, so they aren't going to see us until we're almost right on top of them. And secondly, we'll be landing in a meadow at the side of the main building that I don't expect them to be watching too closely."

"That's a lot to suppose," said the commando.

"I'm counting on a glider landing to be something that will arouse curiosity but not alarm."

"And if it does?"

"Then we improvise," said Schroeder, cutting his man off and turning to Harvath. "I see where you're going with this, but Skorzeny also had one other item at his disposal that we don't—Ferdinando Soleti, a high-ranking general in the *carabinieri*."

"Whose men were deployed at the hotel and

tasked with guarding Mussolini. I know," replied Harvath. "Skorzeny faced many of the same obstacles that we do. First, his commandos had to overwhelm the Italian forces quickly enough to prevent Mussolini from being executed. Secondly, the commandos were greatly outnumbered by the Italian troops. And finally, those Italian troops had the benefit of being dug into a serious defensive position.

"The best thing I can offer you are the words of Skorzeny himself, 'The safer the enemy feel, the better our chances of catching them unaware.'" Harvath paused for effect and then continued. "Skorzeny realized his men needed to get out of their gliders and gain control of Mussolini within three minutes if their plan was to be successful. It is no different for us. This operation will require the same three characteristics brought to bear on any successful tactical undertaking—speed, surprise, and overwhelming force of action."

Schroeder nodded his head. "Agreed, but the brilliance of Skorzeny's operation was in having Soleti in the very first glider. Soleti was a *carabinieri* commanding officer. When he climbed out of that glider, the Italian troops were so confused that they had no idea what to do. That hesitation was what Skorzeny needed to gain the upper hand and the successful outcome of his mission. They were able to pull it off without a single shot being fired."

Harvath fingered the Carthaginian wrist cuffs

resting in his coat pocket, the same ones he had been carrying since their near-fatal climb in France, and said, "I think we can get our hands on a Ferdinando Soleti of our own, but I want to talk to you about that in private."

As Harvath wrapped up his presentation, he hoped like hell that Timothy Rayburn was still all about the money.

SIXTY-SEVEN

As they drove toward Le Râleur, Harvath and Alcott filled Claudia and Schroeder in on everything that had happened to them. The tale took almost the entire drive, and had Claudia not known Harvath and been through as much with him as she had, she would have been hard-pressed to believe him. It wasn't until they were less than two kilometers away from the village that Harvath began to outline his immediate plan. In the end, there was no telling if Rayburn would take the bait, but if nothing else, at least Schroeder would get a good look at the security that was in place at the base of the funicular.

They all agreed that Claudia should be the one to make the drop. She was a native French speaker, and though Rayburn would be extremely apprehensive about what she was going to ask him to do, she was the most believable person they could send.

Parking the car on the outskirts of the village,

Harvath pulled one of the wrist cuffs from his jacket pocket and handed it to her. Claudia stared at it, awed by the history and the terror that it represented. As if the golden cuff might somehow have the power to harm her, she affixed it to her wrist with great care.

"You know what to do when you get to the base of the funicular, right?" asked Harvath.

Claudia nodded her head. "I give the police the message, then remove the cuff, put it in the bag along with the note, and hand it to them."

"And if anything goes wrong? How do you let us know you're in trouble?"

"I switch my purse from my left shoulder to my right."

"Good," said Harvath. "Where is everyone going to be positioned?"

"Jillian and Horst will be on the terrace of the La Bergère café directly opposite. And you." She paused. "I actually don't know where you'll be."

"I'll be close, very close. Don't worry."

With both Harvath and Horst to watch out for her, Claudia wasn't worried at all, at least not for her own safety. What she was worried about was whether or not the plan was possible to pull off. Harvath had been right to invoke the memory of Otto Skorzeny, because in every one of his greatest missions his superiors had seriously doubted the man had even the slightest chance for success.

★ ★ ★

Claudia studied her watch, and after the final few minutes had ticked away, she emerged from between two buildings at the far end of the square and headed straight toward the funicular. She took her time, strolling casually, letting the four policemen who were leaning against their squad cars get a good long look at her as she approached.

Harvath watched from beneath the overhang of a nearby building and couldn't help but notice how the men had stopping talking among themselves and how their eyes were glued to Claudia. She really was incredible. Not only was she extremely gorgeous, she was smart and could hold her own without help from anybody else. Harvath was about to berate himself again for having lost her when he saw her flip her hair over her shoulder, turn on her megawattage smile, and cover the last several yards to where the police were standing. It was show time.

Though Jillian easily could have delivered the bracelet, Claudia understood why Harvath had wanted her to do it. Alcott wasn't an operator, and though according to Harvath's account of their time together she had more than proven herself, they needed to be as cautious as possible baiting their trap. Rayburn was already going to be extremely apprehensive, but if he smelled anything, especially Harvath coming, he'd bolt and they'd lose their chance.

Claudia kept the smile coming as she approached

the officers at the base of the funicular. After she flirted with them for several moments, Harvath watched her finger the bracelet and then remove from her purse the note he had dictated in the car. She then slid the bracelet off, placed it in a small bag along with the note, and handed it to one of the policemen. After a little more flirting, she turned, walked back across the square, and disappeared.

Fifteen minutes later, they all met back at the car and headed back to Sion.

"How did it go?" asked Jillian.

"Perfectly," replied Claudia. "They reacted just the way Scot said they would."

Harvath adjusted the rearview mirror so he could see her better as he drove. "Tell me everything that happened."

"When they saw me coming, I think they thought I was a tourist interested in the Aga Khan. I had the feeling they get that a lot. But when I mentioned Tim Rayburn, everything changed."

"How so?"

"They knew exactly who I was talking about. That was for sure. But when I asked them if they could give something to him, they told me they weren't allowed to receive packages for the Aga Khan or anyone on his staff. That's when I pulled the note and the paper sack from my purse. One of the policemen made a joke about why a nice girl like me would want anything to do with a man like Tim Rayburn. That was the man I focused in on.

"Knowing that the Aga Khan spends a lot of time in Geneva, I told him that I had met Rayburn there and that he had told me if I was ever in Le Râleur, that I should look him up. I slid off the bracelet, dropped it in the bag, and told the officer that if my note didn't jog his memory the bracelet surely would."

"And were they convinced?"

"They seemed to be," Claudia replied. "I wouldn't be surprised if the minute I left, they were ringing him up at Aiglemont."

"She's good, eh, Horst?" said Harvath.

Schroeder didn't seem very happy with his fiancée playing the role of the sexy single woman back for a little more action with Tim Rayburn, even if it was for the good of the mission. In response, the commando simply nodded his head and looked out the window into the night sky.

"So we've got about three hours until the rendezvous," continued Harvath, "but I can guarantee you that Rayburn and some of his men will arrive early to try and position themselves with the advantage."

"In the note you told him to come alone," said Claudia. "How can you be so sure he'll bring reinforcements?"

"Because it's exactly what I would do."

SIXTY-EIGHT

Though it cost Harvath several hundred dollars to convince the manager of Sion's hottest nightspot, the Baroque Café at 24 avenue de France, to go along with his request, it was money well spent. The only thing the manager was going to remember from this night was an American with the largest bankroll he had ever seen in his life. The careers of Claudia, Horst Schroeder, and his commandos would remain totally unaffected. At a few hundred bucks, Harvath figured he was getting off cheap. Though the club claimed to have been created in the grand tradition of hot French brasseries such as la Coupole, les Grandes Capucines, le Chien Qui Fume, le Train Bleu, and Chez Flo, its manager had a lot to learn about holding out for more money.

Forty-five minutes before the scheduled rendezvous time, the first of Rayburn's men walked into the bar area of the Baroque Café and took one of the high cocktail tables. The man couldn't have been more obvious, and Schroeder's men, who were posing as bouncers, had no trouble spotting him. The next of Rayburn's men to arrive was much harder to ID. He fit in almost perfectly. If it hadn't been for the fact that one of Schroeder's bouncers had seen him hanging around outside, waiting for a group he could befriend and blend in with, they would have easily missed him.

When the disgraced Secret Service agent did finally show up, he was accompanied by two more men who weren't trying to hide why they were there or whom they were with. With a quick glance over the café, Rayburn found what he was looking for and ignored the hostess as she asked him if he had a reservation. He had plenty of reservations, but spotting the gorgeous woman with the unopened bottle of Dom Perignon on her table and the golden cuff on her wrist—a perfect twin for the one locked in his safe back at Château Aiglemont—was at least for now enough to convince him to go forward.

"Had that been a bottle of Cristal on the table," said Rayburn as he walked up to Mueller, "I would have turned and walked out of here. It's a pleasure to encounter a woman with such class."

Claudia smiled and motioned for Rayburn to sit in the empty chair in front of her. "I'm sorry we don't have more room, but as you know, I requested that you come alone."

Taking another look at Claudia, Rayburn waved

his security detail away and replied, "You seem like a smart woman to me. Surely, you didn't expect me to come to a meeting like this without bringing some colleagues."

"To tell you the truth, Mr. Rayburn, I don't know what I expected. I haven't exactly done this kind of thing before."

"Really?" he replied as he pulled the bottle of Dom from the ice bucket and began peeling the foil away from the cage. "You certainly had me fooled."

"I did what I thought was necessary to get you to a meeting," said Claudia.

Harvath, who had made sure that there would be no available tables anywhere near where Claudia was sitting, now watched as Rayburn's men joined their colleagues at the only spot where they could keep an eye on their boss—the bar at the very front of the café. Convinced that the woman wasn't a real threat, they ordered a round of drinks and were soon paying more attention to the fashionable crowd of diners that packed the trendy café. What did it matter anyway? He hadn't told them why he wanted them to come out with him, only that he needed them to watch his back—that was it. No further explanation. As far as they were now concerned, the only problem their boss was going to have tonight was how to get the stunning woman sitting across from him into bed.

"And how exactly did you know where to find me?" he continued.

Harvath had anticipated this question and had prepped the Swiss prosecutor with the best response possible—the truth. "The e-mail you gave to Marie Lavoine. I used it to track you down."

"That's impossible." Rayburn smiled. "None of my personal information is connected to that account."

"No, but you do use a Visa debit card to pay for it, and that card draws funds from a bank on Malta."

Rayburn was no longer smiling. "That still doesn't explain how you ended up leaving a CARE package for me at the base of that funicular."

"You cover your tracks very well," she said, flattering him. "You only made one mistake."

"Which was?"

"You used the credit card in Le Râleur. Once I knew that, I hired a detective in Geneva and he did the rest."

Rayburn was not crazy that the woman had gotten a detective involved, but he could easily take care of him later if he needed to. For the moment, though, he was impressed. "It sounds like you spent some money to find me. I hope I'm worth it."

"We'll see about that," responded Claudia.

"So why don't you tell me how you came upon those lovely bracelets."

"My father was part of Donald Ellyson's team."

"Bernard Lavoine? He was your father?"

"No, Maurice Vevé. Bernard's assistant."

"The Sherpa," said Rayburn. "Of course. But what does any of this have to do with me?"

"As I said in my note, Marie Lavoine was holding out on you. What was sent to Sotheby's was only a fraction of what she had in her possession."

Rayburn turned his attention away from the champagne bottle for a moment and said, "I knew she couldn't be trusted."

"I couldn't agree with you more, Mr. Rayburn. My father worked just as hard as Monsieur Lavoine and yet Marie never sought to include me in any of your dealings."

"You have to understand, my relationship with Marie Lavoine is very—"

"Was," said Claudia, cutting the man off midsentence. "Your relationship was."

"What are you talking about?"

"Marie Lavoine was murdered, Mr. Rayburn. Just as I am sure my father, Monsieur Lavoine, and Dr. Ellyson were also murdered."

"Why are you looking at me like that?" asked Rayburn. "I didn't have anything to do with their deaths."

"Oh, no?" replied Claudia.

"No."

Mueller held his gaze for several moments and then said, "Whatever the case, it really doesn't matter much now. I came here to do business, not to make any new friends."

"That's a shame," said Rayburn as he finished

removing the wire cage and gently twisted the base of the deep green champagne bottle until the cork came away with a soft *pop*. "I have a feeling you and I might have been exceptional friends."

"I doubt that."

Rayburn poured champagne into their glasses and replaced the bottle in the ice bucket. "Well, then, maybe we should skip the niceties and move straight to business."

"I couldn't agree more," said Claudia as she accepted a glass.

Skipping the toast, Rayburn took a sip of the champagne, smacked his lips contentedly, and then said, "You mentioned Marie Lavoine was holding out on me. How would you be in a position to know such a thing?"

Mueller set her glass down on the table and replied, "All of the artifacts that came out of that chasm were carried out by my father and Bernard Lavoine—*equally*."

"Therefore, you feel you are entitled to an equal share. Am I correct?"

"Exactly."

"Except now we have a problem. According to you, Marie Lavoine is no longer with us."

"Actually, it's according to the police."

Rayburn took another sip of champagne and asked, "What exactly was Marie Lavoine's cause of death?"

"Gunshot wound to the head," said Harvath,

who, disguised as a waiter with darker hair, glasses, and a goatee, had strode up right behind him. He placed the silenced pistol he had wrapped in a large linen napkin and hidden beneath his tray against the base of the man's skull and added, "It was fired from a weapon very similar to the one you're feeling against the back of your neck right now."

Seeing that Harvath had made contact with Rayburn, Schroeder removed his cell phone from his pocket and sent a broadcast text message to his team. Forty-five seconds later, a pair of flashbang grenades detonated in front of the café. Everyone inside, including Rayburn's men, strained to look out the window to see what had happened. As they did, three more flashbangs were pitched into the bar area along with several smoke canisters.

SIXTY-NINE

In the ensuing pandemonium at the front of the café, Harvath and Claudia hustled Rayburn through an emergency exit near the kitchen. Outside, two of Schroeder's men were waiting, and Rayburn was quickly flexicuffed, blindfolded, and stuffed into the back of a waiting car.

They drove him to Sion International and the small hangar on the far side of the military base that they were using as their command center. An office in the back of the structure had been set up as a holding cell and makeshift interrogation room. The first person Rayburn saw as they removed his blindfold and his vision came back into focus was the last person he had ever expected to see again.

"Scot Harvath," said Rayburn as he looked around the room and tried to get his bearings. "What the hell are you doing here?"

Harvath didn't even bother with a response. Instead, he cocked his fist and punched Rayburn right in the mouth.

It was a good punch, and the older man saw stars for several moments. After spitting the blood from his mouth onto the concrete floor, he looked up at Harvath and said, "I guess I deserved that."

"You deserve a hell of a lot more," replied Scot. "That was just for starters."

"Hardly a fair fight," stated Rayburn as he struggled against the flexicuffs binding him to the chair.

"Since when were you ever interested in a fair fight? Besides, this isn't a fight, it's a beating and one for which you are long overdue," said Harvath as he drew back his fist and hit the man again, this time in the stomach.

Outside the room, Jillian, Claudia, and Horst Schroeder listened as Harvath worked over his prisoner. He had to administer his blows very carefully. The first punch to the mouth was the only one he could allow himself to the man's face. He'd been dreaming about that shot for years, but going forward he would have to keep himself under control. If he marked Rayburn up too much, the man would be of no use to them.

Spitting another mouthful of blood onto the floor, Rayburn looked up at Harvath and said, "If you're going to kill me, why not just get it over with?"

"Always looking for the easy way out, aren't

you?" replied Scot as he hit the man again, this time in the solar plexus, knocking the wind from him.

As Rayburn struggled to regain his breath, Harvath began asking questions. "Where's Emir Tokay?"

"I don't know what you're talking about," said Rayburn, doubled over and gasping for air.

Harvath waited until the man's breath had returned and then grabbed his chin with his hand and jerked his head upward so he could look into his face and ask the question again. "Where's Emir Tokay?"

"I don't know what you're talking about," repeated Rayburn.

The man was lying, and Harvath knew it. It was written all over his face, which Scot now let go of and then slowly walked to the other side of the room. "I know you're lying to me, Tim. I can see it in your face."

"What do you see? A facial expression that lasted for only a fraction of a second and gave away my guilt? That's a bunch of Secret Service bullshit."

"Bullshit or not, I've also seen footage of Tokay's kidnapping in Bangladesh. You should have been wearing a mask, or at the very least have chosen a better spot to pick him up."

"What are you talking about?"

"There was a new security camera on the bank across the street. When your goons opened the back door of the car to stuff Tokay inside, the camera captured a perfect picture of you sitting on the back seat."

Rayburn was silent.

"No snappy comeback?" asked Harvath.

"That was never my area of expertise," he said finally. "You were always the wiseass."

"It's a little late to be flattering me, don't you think?"

"See, you can't help yourself, you never could. That's your problem. You say whatever pops into your head and you allow yourself to blindly follow the flag. I've never seen anybody gobble up the duty, honor, and country bullshit the way you do."

"That goes to show that I found something in the job other than just a paycheck. If you're trying to insult me, you'll have to try a lot harder than that. I'm proud of my service to my country."

Rayburn spat out another gob of blood and started to laugh.

"What's so funny?" said Harvath.

"You. You're a fucking recruiter's wet dream. Truth, justice, and the American way. You've been fed it so long, you don't know what anything else tastes like. Step away from the red, white, and blue party line and you've got no idea who the fuck you are."

"And you do?"

"You're goddamn right I do. You and I are exactly alike."

Harvath crossed back over to Rayburn's chair

and was about to crack him right in the jaw, but held himself back. "You and I are nothing alike."

"The hell we aren't," the man responded. "You've spent your entire career in both the SEALs and the Secret Service on the razor's edge of being discharged. You're a smart guy, but nobody ever seems to appreciate how smart, especially when you decide to six-gun things on your own."

"You don't know what you're talking about."

"You forget I was one of your instructors. I read your Navy jacket from cover to cover, and I watched the way you operated right up until I left the Secret Service. You may be skilled, but you never belonged with either organization. You're too smart for them and it drives you crazy being told to sit on your ass when you know how things should be done. Welcome to life working for the government. Your superiors may have called you reckless, but that isn't it. There's a borderline brilliance to the way you operate, but none of them will ever see it. It's only a matter of time before you do something that leaves them with absolutely no choice but to turn you loose—the same way they turned me loose—and then you'll see that you and I are exactly the same. We're defined by what we do. And trust me, once you make peace with that, you'll be a much happier person."

"What are you, a fucking psychologist now? You got drummed out of the Secret Service for helping assassinate a foreign dignitary."

"Really?" replied Rayburn. "Then how come I'm not locked up in some prison somewhere?"

"You really believe your own bullshit, don't you? The reason you're not locked up in some prison somewhere is because you hid the evidence so deep, nobody was able to ever find it."

"I'm surprised at you, Scot. Of all people, I would have thought that you would have been willing to give me the benefit of the doubt."

"Why? Because we had a few beers together back in Beltsville? Because we had been partners once? Fuck you. I'm tired of listening to your bullshit," said Harvath as he wrapped his hand around Rayburn's throat. "I'm going to ask you one more time, and I warn you, the more you lie to me, the harder I'm going to squeeze. Where's Emir Tokay?"

SEVENTY

SWITZERLAND

Rayburn might have been a tough nut to crack, but there was something about Harvath choking off the oxygen to his brain that caused him to be extremely forthcoming. He admitted that not only was he in the employ of the Aga Khan, but in fact he was the man's head of security. When it came to Emir Tokay's kidnapping, Rayburn also came clean. He confessed that he had been involved and that he had orchestrated the kidnapping under direct orders from the Aga Khan himself. Emir Tokay was still alive, and Rayburn drew a detailed schematic of where in Château Aiglemont he was being held.

Other than that, Harvath didn't get much more out of him. Either Timothy Rayburn was the world's greatest liar, or he really was limited in his knowledge of the Aga Khan's involvement with the Islamic Institute for Science and Technology and Hannibal's mystery weapon. Rayburn acknowledged that, per his boss's orders, he had organized Donald Ellyson's archeological expedition in the Alps and was its paymaster, but had no idea what the man was looking for. He claimed that until Marie Lavoine had contacted him over a year later, he had no idea that her husband, along with Maurice and Dr. Ellyson, had disappeared.

No matter how many times Harvath tried to trip him up, he couldn't. There wasn't a single crack in any of Rayburn's stories. Yes, he had kidnapped Tokay, but he had no idea what the Aga Khan wanted with him. Yes, he knew the Aga Khan was involved with the Islamic Institute for Science and Technology, but he had no idea to what extent. As Rayburn so eloquently put it, all of those raghead groups were the same as far as he was concerned. His employer seemed to enjoy having an ex–Secret Service officer as his head of security. It made him feel safer. That said, Rayburn claimed the Aga Khan didn't completely trust anyone, even his head of security. Half the time, Rayburn said his boss seemed to take a perverse pleasure in treating him like a mushroom, i.e., keeping him in the dark and feeding him shit.

Two hours later, it was Harvath who finally cracked. He was exhausted and it was obvious that they weren't going to get anything further out of Rayburn. What they needed to focus on now was recovering Emir Tokay and, if possible, getting their hands on the Aga Khan and doing whatever was necessary to make him talk.

Though Rayburn requested some water and an opportunity to use the facilities, Harvath turned out the lights and left him tied to his chair while he went in search of someplace to get a little rest. In just under five hours, the team would have their final briefing before lifting off for Château Aiglemont.

An hour before takeoff, Harvath and Schroeder went through the assault plan for the final time. There was no telling how reliable Rayburn's information was and so they tried to rely on it as little as possible. With their very own Ferdinando Soleti in hand, Schroeder was convinced that their odds were better than fifty-fifty. Harvath wished he shared the man's confidence.

The biggest tactical decision facing Harvath soon became whether to bring Jillian along with them. When confronted with the decision head-on, she offered the same rationale for coming that she had in Milan—if there were documents at Aiglemont pertaining to the illness, she was the only one who was qualified to ascertain which ones were the most important. If the team encountered a time crunch and was only capable of grabbing a portion of papers, without her there to help, it would be like playing pin the tail on the donkey. In short, they couldn't go without her.

Jillian was right, but Harvath still gave her one last chance to back out. Even though they were hoping to get in and out without a shot being fired, people might still very easily get killed on this assignment. And one of those people could be Jillian Alcott herself. Apprised of all the risks, her decision didn't waver. She was in.

Harvath didn't trust Rayburn any farther than he could punt him and at the very last minute developed a crude piece of insurance to guarantee he wouldn't give them any trouble. Using his knowledge of improvised explosive devices, Harvath cobbled together a little something special with the Stern team's demolition expert for Rayburn to wear underneath his boxer shorts.

Duct tape was used to hold the bomb in place, and seeing how uncomfortable Rayburn was, Harvath said, "It's kind of like a cheap hotel, isn't it? No ball room." Then, holding up the remote detonator so Rayburn could see it, he added, "I'm going to be three steps behind you at all times, and if I even so much as think you're tipping our hand to your men, I'm going to turn that strip of Alpine meadow up there into a real *ballpark*, if you know what I mean."

Rayburn didn't say a word; he just glared at Harvath.

Twenty minutes later, dressed in black Nomex fatigues identical to the ones being worn by Aiglemont's security team, Harvath gave the Stern commandos and glider pilots a final briefing before they all walked out onto the tarmac.

The new Aerotechnik Super Vivat Icarus motorgliders had an enormous wingspan and looked like a typical side-by-side pilot/passenger configuration sailplane that had been crossed with a small Cessna single-prop aircraft. Designed to carry a pilot and three passengers, their maximum crew weight was listed by the manufacturer at 721 pounds. They needed to carry more. Stripping the motorgliders down to the bare essentials, the team was able to get four people plus a pilot in each one.

Harvath and Schroeder would take Rayburn and an additional commando in the first Super Vivat Icarus, followed by Claudia, Jillian, and two more commandos in the second, and the final two motorgliders would contain four commandos each. With such a short landing strip, it was important that each glider land, unload its passengers, and take off again in time for the next glider behind it to come in and touch down. It was going to be a delicate dance and one that they all wished they could have had time to rehearse.

The aircraft were given the call signs Silo One, Two, Three, and Four based on the order in which they would be landing at Aiglemont. While Silos One through Three would be immediately taking off after dropping their passengers, Silo Four would be required to stay on the ground in case the team needed to evacuate Emir Tokay in a hurry. Like the other pilots, Silo Four's captain was a Swiss fighter pilot and had readily accepted his assignment, knowing that if things got bad, he would essentially be a sitting duck. Harvath, though, did his best to assure the man that he was going to see to it that things didn't get too ugly too early.

The eight remaining commandos on the Stern team would be responsible for subduing the police at the base of the funicular in Le Râleur and joining the party once their colleagues had secured the railway's upper housing.

After moving the Super Vivat Icarus craft out onto the runway, their pilots conducted the final preflight checks. Inside the hangar, the commandos did a final check of their own, going over their weapons and communications equipment and stuffing their pockets and pouches with as much extra ammunition as they could carry. When all of the motorgliders had been loaded and the first one was cleared for takeoff, the remaining commandos climbed into their two rental cars and headed out for Le Râleur.

SEVENTY-ONE

LANGLEY, VIRGINIA

Brian Turner looked over both shoulders to make sure he was alone and then sat down at the terminal and logged in. He'd always marveled at how the CIA was more concerned with a hack from the outside than they were with an interior breach of security.

Turner had been fascinated with encryption technology since he was seven years old. While the NSA had heavily recruited him years ago during his senior year at Cal Poly, it was the snap and panache of the CIA that had ultimately won him over. But life at Langley, especially post-9/11, had failed to live up to his expectations. It was nothing like he had seen in the movies, and with all the bullshit rules he and his colleagues were expected to play by, he considered it only a matter of time until America was struck again by another devastating terrorist attack.

That was probably what had attracted him most

to Helen Carmichael. That and the fact that after the Senate Intelligence Committee had toured the new counterterrorism center, or CTC as it was more affectionately known at the CIA, one of her aides had contacted him asking if he would be interested in participating in an above-top-secret focus group. Turner had jumped at the chance and was invited to dinner with the Pennsylvania senator.

It was soon obvious that Helen Carmichael had no intention of conducting any hush-hush focus group, but rather wanted to develop her own personal relationship with him. The first night Turner ever met with her one on one, she took him to one of the biggest power restaurants in DC, Smith & Wollensky, where they dined on thick steaks and discovered their mutual love of dirty martinis. Later, in the back of the limo the senator had rented for the evening, he discovered that she gave the world's best blowjob.

The blowjob was followed by a night of incredible sex at his apartment—sex he never would have thought the senator from Pennsylvania capable of. Helen Remington Carmichael was a hot ticket, and as far as Brian Turner was concerned, her husband was missing out on a first-class freak. The things she did and said when they were together would succeed in getting even the most straight-laced accountant fired from a one-man office.

He was sick of life at the CIA and saw the senator as his ticket out. As the senator's national security advisor, he would hold enormous responsibility when she came into the vice presidency and then, with enough patience, would hold the utmost power when she eventually became president. The petty thefts and incursions he performed on her behalf now were nothing. In fact, Turner saw them as serving the CIA its own just deserts for not better protecting itself from hackers based inside CIA headquarters.

Snarfing a handful of French fries he had purchased at the CIA's all-night cafeteria, he launched his newest, untraceable, personal-best blind mouse program and awaited its results.

Twelve minutes later, Turner practically choked on his Mrs. Fields cookie when his flat-screen burst to life with a file containing the names, dates, payments, and details concerning United States president Jack Rutledge and his own personal covert action team.

SEVENTY-TWO

SWITZERLAND

It took over half an hour of climbing for the Super Vivats to reach their specified altitude. Once there, Silo One's pilot checked his position and then began the process of reconfiguring his craft as a glider. After cooling the engine at reduced power, he brought it to a complete stop, centered the prop, and then retracted it all the way into the nose of the aircraft. He then flipped the fuel shutoff and turned off the engine master switch. Immediately, the craft was enveloped in complete and total silence. Schroeder had never flown in a glider before, but he could now understand why Harvath, and Otto Skorzeny before him, had chosen it as a perfect means for their covert insertion.

Harvath, on the other hand, was already focused on what would happen during the first three minutes after they touched down. With only Schroeder and one other team member to exit the plane with him, they would be naked until reinforcements started landing. Even then, they would total only fourteen shooters against a security force three times that size. On top of that, he'd have to keep one eye on Rayburn, who would remain flexicuffed until just before they touched down, while Claudia kept Jillian safe from any hostile fire. Regardless of Schroeder's opinion, the odds were definitely not in their favor. The only thing they had going for them was the element of surprise, and Harvath prayed it would be enough.

As they neared their objective, the pilot gave the three-minute warning. Harvath ran through the objective once more in his mind as he checked his weapons and then took a moment to try and steady his breathing and slow his heart rate. The adrenaline had already started pumping through his bloodstream and along with it came the same feeling that always visited him before he went into harm's way—fear. He had learned early on that anyone who said that he wasn't scared before such an undertaking was either a liar or a fool. Absence of fear didn't make you brave; it was what you did in spite of being afraid.

Having conducted all of his final checks, Silo One's pilot entered the airspace above the small mountain plateau from downwind, lowered the craft's landing gear, and began his descent. Harvath retrieved the Benchmade knife from his pocket and cut Rayburn's flexicuffs loose.

The approach was perfect. It wasn't until they

were about ten feet off the ground that they all noticed something that hadn't shown up in any of Harvath's reconnaissance photographs. Their landing area was cratered with potholes and littered with rocks the size of basketballs.

Silo One's pilot tried to pull up, but it was too late. He was already committed to the landing, and there wasn't enough lift. Like it or not, their aircraft was going in.

SEVENTY-THREE

The first thing to go was the forward left landing gear, which caused the wing to tip all the way over to the left and gouge into the ground. With the left wingtip acting as fulcrum, Harvath expected the entire craft to spin in a violent circle, but instead, the left portion of the wing sheared completely off, and the plane kept racing forward.

Immediately, Silo One's pilot tried to create a ground loop—a whipping corkscrew maneuver—in the hopes of halting the aircraft. He rapidly rotated the wheel to the right, right up to the stops, while mashing the right rudder with the force of a bat slamming into a baseball. As that was happening, Rayburn took advantage of the chaos and lunged for Harvath's silenced H&K MP7. Instantly, the cockpit was filled with the weapon's distinct *pop, pop, pop* as a three-round burst was discharged in the mêlée. Two of the rounds shattered the Plexiglas canopy above them, while the third creased the back of the pilot's head.

The pilot stayed at the controls for only a second or two more before collapsing over the aircraft's yoke. With help from Schroeder, Harvath wrestled the weapon away from Rayburn and with no choice delivered a sharp, open palm strike to the man's nose. A torrent of blood poured out, and the ex–Secret Service agent roared in pain. His weapon back, Harvath simply ignored him.

One look out the shattered canopy confirmed what he already suspected—the Icarus was picking up speed and they were quickly running out of meadow. Rushing forward to meet them was the edge of the cliff and its drop-off thousands of feet into the valley below. This was a contingency they hadn't planned on.

Based on the reconnaissance photos, they had all known that the landing would be extremely treacherous. The only way it would work was if each pilot began putting a lot of pressure on the brakes the moment they touched down. With all the extra weight they were carrying it would be dicey, and even then, their best projections were that they would stop with just feet to spare.

With a landing strip that only allowed for one aircraft at a time, the idea had been for the team members to unload while each pilot opened the nose of his aircraft and extended the prop back outside so he could taxi back up the meadow, turn around, and come rushing back toward the edge of the cliff for takeoff.

Harvath leaned forward over the seat in front of him and tried to aid Schroeder's commando, Gösser, in peeling the pilot off the aircraft's yoke. It was too late for the brakes. Their only hope was to steer the glider away from the cliff, which they were racing closer and closer toward.

Getting his hands underneath the pilot's arms, Harvath wrenched backward with all his might. As the pilot came free, Gösser grabbed hold of the yoke and yanked hard to the right toward the balance of the meadow and the château.

The remaining tires groaned against the ground in protest as they bounced over several large rocks. The cliff face was less than twenty meters away. Harvath thought about opening what remained of the shattered canopy and bailing out, but he knew that at their rate of speed, all it would take was for his head to hit one rock and he'd be killed instantly. Even if he was able to avoid the rocks, he'd hit the ground so fast, he wouldn't stop rolling until after he had gone over the edge. There was only one way out—they had to turn that aircraft, and that meant not only using the yoke, but the rudders as well.

"To the left!" yelled Harvath as he unbuckled the pilot and struggled to pull him over the seatback and into the second row, where he was sitting. "Turn the yoke the other way as hard as you can and pin the left pedal to the floor!"

"But we'll crash into the side of the mountain!" screamed Gösser.

"Do it!" shouted Schroeder, who understood what Harvath was trying to accomplish. In its current condition, there was no way the Icarus was going to give one inch in turning to the right toward the little expanse of meadow alongside the château. Their only hope was in steering into the damage. Better to hit the side of the mountain than to go over the cliff.

Gösser strained with his whole body and pulled the yoke to the left as hard as he could, but the aircraft refused to respond. Harvath glanced forward, calculated the distance until the drop-off, and prepared for the worst. They were going over the edge.

Then slowly, ever so slowly, the clipped glider started to nose in the direction they wanted it to go. It was almost imperceptible at first, but then the craft made a marked shift to the left. Harvath was about to breathe a sigh of relief when he saw a pile of granite rubble directly in the center of their path.

With no other choice, he braced for impact, using the pilot's body as a makeshift airbag.

The jagged pile of rocks met the plane and acted like a ramp, tearing away half the glider's nose as it was catapulted right at the face of the mountain. Harvath's stomach caught in his throat, and he knew that they were airborne. The mountain stood poised to meet the tiny aircraft head-on, but just as they were closing in on impact, something happened.

They had cut almost a ninety-degree turn. Everything they had going for them was on the right-hand side of the aircraft, which included the remaining wing and the thermals rising up from the floor of the valley. It was one of those thermals that caught beneath the wing and pitched the glider into a barrel roll.

After one complete revolution, the remaining portion of wingspan dug into the rocky ground and completely snapped off, sending the fuselage rolling back up the meadow until it finally came to rest on its side. The smell of cordite in the cockpit from the discharge of Harvath's MP7 was quickly replaced by another, much more terrifying scent—jet fuel.

Harvath lowered the pilot to the leeward portion of the Icarus, then planted his feet on the seat supports and unbuckled his seat belt. "Let's get the hell out of here. Can everybody move?" he asked as he unlocked the canopy.

Schroeder responded first, followed by a grunt from Rayburn. Even Gösser, who hadn't had time to fully buckle in, was alive and literally kicking. The canopy was pinched shut by a large rock, but after several thrusts from the man's heavy boots, it sprang open, and they were able to flee the aircraft and get the pilot to safety before the relatively small fuel tank of the Icarus exploded in a significant fireball.

Safely away from the wreckage, Harvath asked if

everyone was okay. There was a chorus of *yeses*, capped off with the motorglider's groggy pilot coming to and saying, "So much for all-terrain tires."

Rayburn's security men were already swarming out of the château, as Harvath hastily wrapped a makeshift bandage around the pilot's head.

"You don't need to do that," the man said as he tried to get up. "I just want to know which one of you assholes shot me."

"That would be this asshole," said Schroeder, wrapping his beefy hand around Rayburn's arm and jerking him upward.

"Okay," interrupted Harvath, handing him the radio, "you've just been promoted to combat controller. I don't care how you do it, but you've got to find a way for those other gliders to land."

"What are you talking about?" said Schroeder. "There are too many rocks. Those planes will crack up just like we did, or worse."

"Maybe not," said the pilot. "A couple meters more to the right, and we might have had a smoother area to land."

"I don't care what you do," said Harvath as he removed the remote detonator from his pocket. "Just figure it out." Then, arming the remote, he looked at Rayburn and said, "You're on, sunshine. Do everything you're supposed to and you could live to see a ripe old age. Fuck around and they'll be playing 'Great Balls of Fire' at your funeral, if you know what I mean."

Subconsciously, Rayburn's hand moved toward his groin and the explosive device Harvath had forced him to duct-tape beneath his shorts.

"I wouldn't do that if I were you," said Harvath, and Rayburn quickly removed his hand. "I'd try also not to think about Elle Macpherson either," he added as he shoved Rayburn toward Château Aiglemont and its advancing troops.

Convinced that even under duress Rayburn could talk them into the château, Harvath had provided him with a script, any deviation from which he had guaranteed would result in the worst case of jock itch Rayburn had ever had.

SEVENTY-FOUR

"Call everyone into the dining hall," commanded Rayburn. "Someone is preparing to move against the Aga Khan. They tried to take me out while I was in Sion last night. I have more reinforcements coming in via air. Make sure they get to the dining hall ASAP. Let's move. The briefing is in five minutes. Go!"

Rayburn then rushed Harvath, Schroeder, and the other Stern commando past several of the security personnel and up the front steps of the former monastery. Though many of the security personnel looked as if they had questions about what the hell was going on, they obviously knew better than to question a direct order from their boss and immediately went into action.

Inside, Château Aiglemont looked more like an English manor house than a former monastery turned health spa. Medieval tapestries, antique furniture, and even suits of armor accented every inch of the heavy stone walls. "Which way to Tokay?" asked Harvath as he withdrew the map Rayburn had drawn for him.

"At the end of this hallway you make a right, and you'll find a stairway that leads to the subbasement."

"How many guards?"

Rayburn looked at his watch. "Only two, but they will have heard about the meeting in the dining hall by now, and one of them will stay while the other comes up."

"What about the Aga Khan?" replied Harvath. "Where do I find him?"

Rayburn hesitated a moment and then pointed the opposite way and said, "To the right of the stained glass window is a staircase that leads up into the bell tower. Halfway up is a statue of Saint Nicholas von Flüe."

"The patron saint of Switzerland," said Harvath. "How appropriate. What about it?"

"He holds a rosary in his hand. Gently pull down on it, and a door will open. That doorway leads to the monastery's second floor. The Aga Khan's rooms are at the very end."

"Is there any other way to get up there?"

"Not unless you've got a very tall ladder."

Harvath had no intention of climbing a ladder to get to the Aga Khan. Looking at the timer on his Kobold Chronograph, he tossed Schroeder the detonator and said, "We've got less than two minutes.

You and Gösser take Rayburn with you and find Tokay. If he doesn't cooperate, blow his balls off."

"Wait a second," said Schroeder. "I thought we were here to rescue your hostage. Where are you going?"

As important as Emir was, Harvath couldn't pass up the opportunity to get his hands on the Aga Khan himself. "I want the guy behind all of this."

"You can't go by yourself. Let's get the hostage first. After that, we'll be able to watch your back," said Schroeder.

Harvath shook his head. "We don't have time to discuss this. Get Emir, and I'll meet you outside."

Schroeder could tell he wasn't going to get anywhere by arguing with Harvath and so he nodded his head and took off.

Harvath found the doorway at the end of the hall and beyond it the smooth stone steps, which led up to the second level. At the statue of Saint Nicholas, he pulled on the rosary beads, and the statue moved back to reveal a narrow entryway onto the second floor.

Posted outside the Aga Khan's rooms at the end of the frescoed hallway were two husky, ex-military types who reminded Harvath very much of the security guards he'd encountered at Sotheby's in Paris. "Who the fuck are you?" barked one of the men, obviously American by his accent, as he snapped his weapon to attention and pointed it in Harvath's direction.

"FNG," replied Harvath, using the military acronym for *fucking new guy*. "Rayburn wants both of you in the dining hall for a meeting. I was sent to relieve you."

"I'm not going anywhere until Rayburn gives me the order himself."

"What are you, the only guy without a fucking radio in this place?" said Harvath. "Do you know what just happened outside? Didn't you hear that a meeting has been called?"

"Sure but—"

"*Sure, but* nothing, asshole. I was on that plane outside, which is now in flaming pieces, so you'll forgive me if I don't feel like debating this with you."

"Maybe we should go to the dining hall," replied the man's partner.

"Fuck that. Until I hear from Rayburn, I'm not going anywhere."

"Suit yourself," said Harvath as he turned and began walking down the hallway. *So much for taking the compound without a shot being fired*, he thought as he readied his MP7 and prepared to turn and fire.

"Hold it a second," said the sentry just as Harvath was about to spin around and pull the trigger. "I'm already on Rayburn's shit list. I don't need any more trouble. Besides, I could use a cup of coffee."

Harvath eased his finger off the trigger and gently lowered his weapon. So far, so good.

SEVENTY-FIVE

Once the guards had left the hallway and disappeared behind the statue of Saint Nicholas, Harvath prepared to kick in the door of the Aga Khan's chambers. At the last minute, though, he stopped himself and decided to try the handle—it was unlocked. Bringing his MP7 up to the firing position, Harvath pushed open the door with the toe of his boot and carefully stepped inside.

Just like the rest of the monastery, the Aga Khan's rooms were sumptuously appointed. Thick velvet draperies were drawn tight against the windows while ornate chandeliers and Tiffany-style table lamps cast the room in a dim orange glow. Logs stacked upright, A-frame style, blazed in the fireplace. There was a moldy, bookish smell to the place.

At the far end of the main sitting room, which looked more like a study or a library, Harvath found the Aga Khan at a large wooden desk covered with scrolls and old pieces of papyrus. The flat-screen TV behind him was tuned to one of the twenty-four-hour cable news networks.

Dressed in a plaid button-down shirt and khaki trousers, the Aga Khan looked nothing like a stereotypical Muslim spiritual leader. He sported neither flowing robes nor a long unkempt beard. Balding and slightly overweight, his appearance was deceptively placid, more like a grandfather than a fabulously wealthy international power broker. His true character, though, came through when he lifted his head and spoke. Born in exile, the man was completely westernized, and his sharp words were pronounced with a crisp British accent. "Who are you?" he demanded. "What are you doing in here?"

Harvath knew the Aga Khan was dangerous and wasted no time taking control of the situation. Pointing the MP7 at him, he said, "I'm here to ask you a few questions. Now stand up and put your hands where I can see them."

The Aga Khan refused to move. "Do you know who I am?" he stated.

Harvath didn't care. All he was thinking about at this moment was the possibility of mass American casualties from the bioweapon that had been tested in the village of Asalaam and that the man sitting in front of him somehow was the key to all of it. Flicking the fire selector of his MP7 to single shot, Harvath put a silenced round through the top of the man's leather desk chair, inches from his head. "Apparently, you're someone who doesn't listen very well."

With his gold Rolex and matching cufflinks glinting in the light from his desk lamp, the Aga Khan placed his palms on the desk and pushed himself up to standing. "You're going to pay for this," he said as he held his hands up in the air. "I swear to you, you are going to pay."

"Zip it," said Harvath, motioning with his weapon for the man to take a seat in one of the leather club chairs near the fireplace. "I don't want to hear anything out of you unless it's in answer to one of my questions. Do you understand me?"

The Aga Khan sat down in one of the chairs, but refused to acknowledge him. Harvath fired another round, this one right between the man's legs, which sent a clump of batting sailing through the air. Reluctantly, the Aga Khan nodded his head and murmured, "I understand."

"Good," said Harvath as he sat down across from him, turned on the MP7's laser sight, and painted the man's knee with the small red dot. "Just so we further understand each other, this is exactly where my next shot is headed."

The Aga Khan nodded his head.

Harvath balanced the weapon on his lap and kept the laser trained on the Aga Khan's knee as he continued. "Question number one. Why did you kidnap Emir Tokay?"

The man took a deep breath, and as he did, Harvath noticed the dark circles beneath his eyes. He looked terrible, as if he hadn't slept in days. When he spoke, the clipped, powerful speech of a moment before was replaced with a tone of fatigue and resignation. "Why torment me? You know the reason."

"I have my theories," replied Harvath, "but I want to hear it from you."

The Aga Khan looked at Harvath, too tired for games, but with no choice but to play along. "We needed him alive for the same reasons you wanted him dead, but of course you know this."

"I can guarantee you I didn't come all this way to kill Emir Tokay."

The Aga Khan was confused. "You didn't? Why not? You had all of the other scientists killed to ensure their silence."

It was obvious the man thought Harvath was working for someone else. "I'm here because I want to make sure what happened in Asalaam never happens anywhere else."

"Then you don't work for him?"

"Who is *him*?"

"Akrep," spat the Aga Khan, as if the name burned in his mouth. "The Scorpion."

It was a name Harvath had never heard before. "Look, I work for the United States government. Just tell me about Tokay and what happened in Asalaam."

The Aga Khan looked into the fireplace for a moment before responding, "I needed Tokay in order to defend my people from Akrep."

"How? What threat does this man pose to someone like you?"

"It's not just me. Akrep poses a threat to all Shia Muslims. I was foolish enough to believe that he had found a way to unite all Muslims, to bring them back together once again. But I should have known better. He was only using us."

"Using you for what?"

"Money. Money for his expeditions, his grand search for the ultimate weapon that would allow the Muslim people to be on an equal, if not superior, footing in relation to the rest of the world."

"The Muslim Institute for Science and Technology," said Harvath.

"Exactly. The creation of which decades ago had been his idea."

"Who is he? What is Akrep's real name?"

"Who knows? What does it matter anyway? What I should have paid attention to was the one thing he couldn't lie about—his history, the people from which he came. But because I didn't, my people will truly suffer—all people will suffer. Only the Sunni will survive, and that is what he had planned all along."

"You say he couldn't lie about his people. Who are they?"

"They were once the greatest empire in the

world. Hitler was fascinated with them and longed to achieve just a fraction of their power. Even your country has been drawn into their web without knowing it—Libya, Lebanon, Syria, Iran, Iraq, the Balkans—they all have something very special in common."

They were all Muslim countries, but that seemed too obvious to Harvath. He reflected on the fact that all of those countries were home to very serious fundamentalist Muslim terrorist groups, almost all of which had some sort of ties to bin Laden. "Is there an al-Qaeda connection?"

The Aga Khan brushed the suggestion aside. "This goes much deeper than al-Qaeda. Akrep created al-Qaeda and could get rid of them just as easily."

Harvath found it hard to believe that anyone could get rid of al-Qaeda, much less easily, and was about to ask how anyone could believe such a thing was possible, when suddenly his mind flashed back to the conversation he had had with Jillian Alcott just the day before. *What did al-Qaeda want more than anything else? The establishment of a new Muslim caliphate. One nation, under Allah, headed by a caliph who would be the recognized leader of the entire Islamic world.* "Akrep represents the hope of a new Muslim caliphate, doesn't he?"

The Aga Khan nodded his head. "One in which, as he put it to me in the beginning, Sunni and Shia would be represented equally."

"So what's the web the U.S. has been drawn into? Libya, Lebanon, Syria, Iran, Iraq, the Balkans—what's the connection?"

The Aga Khan leaned forward in his chair and said, "All of these places were once part of the greatest Muslim caliphate. A holy kingdom on earth that was unequaled in history and one which Akrep single-handedly intends to resurrect—the great Ottoman Empire."

SEVENTY-SIX

THE PRESIDENT'S PRIVATE STUDY
THE WHITE HOUSE
WASHINGTON, DC

Damn it, Chuck," said Jack Rutledge, who hadn't slept in two days. He punched the remote and turned off his television. "We've got a major terrorist crisis on our hands. I don't have time for this Mickey Mouse stuff. I thought we agreed you were going to take care of this."

"We've been trying, Mr. President."

"So why the hell do I keep seeing Helen Carmichael in front of TV cameras?"

"She's a senator. They constantly court the media. That's what they do."

"Don't give me that crap, Chuck. I thought you were going to talk to her."

"I did," said Anderson. "And the DNC chairman."

"And?"

"Carmichael fought it tooth and nail. Just like we expected her to do and—"

"The DNC chairman promised he'd get to the bottom of it and clean it all up, right?"

"Right," replied the chief of staff, "but—"

"Russ Mercer doesn't take orders from our side of the aisle."

"No, sir, he doesn't."

"What about Carmichael's source within the CIA? Are we any closer to figuring out who the hell it is?"

"A federal judge approved a warrant and we have the man we believe to be the leak under surveillance. Gary Lawlor is coordinating the investigation with the FBI and hopes to have something for us very soon."

"He'd better," said Rutledge. "From what I hear, Carmichael is ready to go public with Harvath's name and service photo any day now. What about the subpoenas she served us?"

"Nothing to worry about. I've met with the White House counsel, and we're going to ignore them."

"We are?" said Rutledge. "What kind of liability does that open us up to?"

"It's just an opening salvo. She knows she can't compel us to appear. But word is Carmichael has had the Capitol police warm up a couple of the jail cells they have up on the Hill."

The president didn't look pleased.

"Don't worry," said Anderson. "It's a media stunt. It makes for good television, but that's all."

"I beg to differ with you," said the president. "It makes for terrible television."

"As far as this administration is concerned, you're right, but she's grandstanding. She knows that no sitting president would respond to her subpoena. It's all smoke. The only way she'll be able to move this forward is to get enough consensus to appoint a special prosecutor."

Rutledge pushed his chair away from his desk and looked back out the window. "Do you want to remind me again why I agreed to run for a second term?"

"Because the people want you," said Anderson, "and because Carmichael couldn't stick anything to you even if she had a roll of duct tape."

"I wish I could be as confident about this as you are."

"Trust me. We're going to come out on top of this."

"Any word from USAMRIID?" asked Rutledge, changing the subject back to the one that he had been obsessing over ever since it broke.

"No. Nothing new. The civilians who were exposed to the illness are still in quarantine and the CDC is working with the people at Fort Detrick, trying to come up with some answers."

"What's your gut tell you, Chuck? Are we going to come out on top of this one as well?"

"I don't know, Mr. President."

"I don't know either," replied Rutledge, "and it scares the hell out of me. We don't have much time left."

SEVENTY-SEVEN

SWITZERLAND

Harvath struggled to piece together everything he was hearing—not only from the Aga Khan, but also from outside the curtained windows where he could make out the sound of an approaching helicopter. Claudia and the rest of the team would not have had enough time to return to Sion and exchange their gliders for something better suited to land on the inhospitable property. All he could think of was that it must have been the Aga Khan's helicopter coming to ferry him to a meeting in Geneva.

The man studied the look on Harvath's face and said, "I urge you to take what I'm telling you very seriously. The Ottoman Empire was the only power to ever fully unite the Muslim countries of the Mediterranean and the Middle East, and keep them united for over six centuries."

"But it eventually fell," replied Harvath.

"Only eighty-plus years ago, which in terms

of history, especially Muslim history, isn't even the blink of an eye. With the rapid advancement of science and Western technology, they were no longer strong enough to keep up a conventional fight. So, instead, they decided on a different course. They stepped back, allowed their dynasty to transform into what is present-day Turkey, and waited for the moment when they could return to reestablish their empire. Millions of Turkish people still greatly identify with their Ottoman heritage. The question *'Kimsiniz Bey Efendi'* is still asked today as it was over seven hundred years ago during the caliphate. *Who are you and what have you contributed toward the greater glory of our people?*

"A core Ottoman leadership still exists, though they don't publicly use the term *Ottoman* to describe themselves. That being said, there aren't many Turks who wouldn't leap at the opportunity for their country to again be seen as one of the most dynamic social, cultural, and religious forces in the world."

Harvath had trouble believing what he was hearing.

"The Ottoman sultans ruled through succession, through one family," said the Aga Khan. "That family didn't just disappear when the empire came to an end. A direct heir to the sultanate still exists. Someone who can trace his lineage back to the very first caliph and a history of Muslim strength and unity that will appeal to all Muslims throughout the Islamic world."

"And Hannibal's weapon? The illness?" asked Harvath, less concerned with the history lesson than with getting the answers he had come for.

"It's all part of their plan to re-create the great Muslim caliphate."

Putting the pieces together in his mind was like trying to stack cinder blocks on top of wine glasses. He needed to bring things back around to the beginning. "How'd you go from being partners with Akrep to kidnapping Tokay as an act of self-defense?"

"The expeditions carried out by the Islamic Institute were extremely expensive," said the Aga Khan. "Hundreds of millions of dollars were being spent. The institute was always running low on money. That's why Akrep came to me. He presented his grand plan for uniting all Muslims and asked if the Shia would help with the financing. We never intended for anyone to die."

"But the bioweapon was to be used as a means of ridding the world of all non-Muslims," said Harvath, skeptical of the man's professed naïveté.

"The idea was to only use the *threat* of the weapon to scare the Western powers and their troops out of Muslim countries."

"And you believed that?" pressed Harvath. "Without some show that the weapon really worked, how could you expect anyone to take you seriously?"

"You're right," replied the Aga Khan. "I soon realized that without proof, there was no way the weapon would be taken seriously. Because it possessed the abhorrent characteristic of needing to be reconstituted in human hosts before it could be used, Akrep suggested we conduct a trial somewhere which would eventually be discovered by the Americans."

"Iraq," responded Harvath. "Asalaam."

"Correct. Not only would we be able to reconstitute the illness and bring it out of hibernation, but the aftermath would send a clear signal to the United States and its allies that they had a very serious new force to contend with. But I allowed myself to forget my history," he replied. "Many Sunnis hate the Shia, but the Ottomans were the ones who gave birth to the idea that we Shia are worse than Christians."

"Yet you went along with them anyway," said Harvath.

"A chance to unite the fractures in our faith was something I could not so easily pass by. Besides, what Akrep was extending was no mere invitation to tea. The subtext was very clear: either we were with him and the Sunnis or we were against them. Based on the information that archeologist Ellyson brought to the institute about what Hannibal was carrying over the Alps, and how it could be used today, we had no choice."

"And you just sat back while innocents were

killed in Asalaam. But, as long as they were Christians, what did you care?"

"But there weren't only Christians who were killed in Asalaam."

"What are you talking about?" said Harvath.

"There were also Shias."

"*Shias?* I was told only non-Muslims perished."

"Then you were told wrong," replied the Aga Khan. "Sunnis made up the majority of that village and they were the ones who survived."

"But how?"

"Because the Sunnis believed the Shia were unclean and inferior in the eyes of God, they used separate wells from which to draw their water."

"So the illness was in the water?" asked Harvath.

"The wells were only part of the process. Akrep never had any intention of bringing the Shia into a united Islam. He double-crossed me and imposed a death sentence on my people. That is why I had Emir Tokay brought here. We needed to know how to immunize our people. I would have arranged to bring more scientists here, but by the time we were able to identify who they all were, Akrep was already having them killed. Tokay was our last chance."

"And has he been able to help you?"

"Insomuch as he had been able to piece together the pathology of the illness, yes. The Sunnis of Asalaam had in fact been inoculated before the illness was released into the village. A substance had been added to the water in their communal well. Absent exposure to that substance, the rest of the village, the non-Sunni population who used their own wells, eventually succumbed to the illness and died."

"So he put something in the Sunnis' water. That's one well in one village. In the rest of the world, most Sunni, Shia, and other religions share the same water source. I don't understand how he plans on inoculating only the Sunni on a global basis."

"That's simple. Akrep discovered a source of water available only to Sunni Muslims. From what Emir Tokay learned, Akrep claimed to have discovered a special spring somewhere in Saudi Arabia. To that water he would add the inoculation and make it available to only Sunnis."

"So he was probably going to bottle the water somehow. Do you know where this spring is or where he planned to do his bottling?"

"No, I don't."

"How was he planning on getting it to the Sunnis?"

"That I also don't know. I was never supposed to know. As I said, Akrep never intended to share the inoculation with the Shia. His goal is to rid the Muslim holy lands of all of the Western infidel crusaders, the Shia, and any other groups the Sunnis see as unfit to walk the sacred soil before setting their sights on the rest of the world. It's no wonder Hitler thought so highly of them. The Ottomans are an amazingly cunning people."

The Aga Khan knew almost as little as Harvath did about the illness, so he decided to change subjects. "You said there's an heir to the sultanate. Who is it? Akrep?"

"No, in the Ottoman tradition, the heir has been sent away for safekeeping and will not be called until the caliphate is ready. For lack of a better term, Akrep is the power behind the throne."

"What power could he possibly have? He doesn't even have an army."

"He may not personally, but Turkey does. And after the United States, it is the largest army in NATO."

"Are you saying the Ottomans can actually call upon the Turkish Army?"

"Eventually they will be able to, but right now it doesn't matter. They have something much more powerful at their disposal."

"Which is?"

"Fundamentalist Islam. Wahhabism, to be exact. The radical Muslim movement from which all modern Islamic terrorism has sprung."

Harvath was all too familiar with the cult of Wahhabism and the sheer devastation it had wrought around the world. "So what are you saying? The Wahhabis are going to do the Ottomans' work for them?"

"In a manner of speaking, yes. The Wahhabis would love nothing more than to see the Islamic world united as a single body, not just religiously, but politically as well. Even before Osama bin Laden became their most recognized adherent, the Wahhabis were calling for the reestablishment of the Muslim caliphate. The attacks of September 11 were a wake-up call to Muslims to rise up and seize power from the corrupt and apostate regimes that govern them."

Once again, Harvath was transported back to his conversation with Jillian. "I don't understand. How are the Ottomans going to use the Wahhabis? And what does it have to do with this illness?"

The Aga Khan looked at him and said, "Revolution."

"*Revolution?* Where? Across the Muslim world?"

"Eventually, but first they must set an example—an example that will empower Muslims everywhere to rise up. It will happen in the holiest of countries most dear to all Muslims and a symbol of corruption and Western influence—Saudi Arabia."

Harvath was stunned. "How can they hope to pull it off? The Saudis rule that country with an iron fist."

"They have been very patient. With the help of al-Qaeda, the Wahhabis have been able to slowly infiltrate the ranks of the Saudi military and security forces. While there are many soldiers and policemen who are not loyal to bin Laden or the Wahhabi faith, there may not be enough of them to make a difference. Time and again in small skirmishes created by the Wahhabis to test the resolve of the military and police, it has been shown that Saudi troops and policemen will not fire on their own people."

Harvath felt the blood go cold in his body. "And if American troops in the region try to help put down a revolt—"

"Hannibal's weapon will be released on them, as well as in the United States. All the Wahhabis will need is twelve hours, twenty-four on the outside, to wrest power from the Saudi Royal Family and take full and unassailable control of the country. Saudi Arabia is the key to the illness, the revolution, everything. And as goes Saudi Arabia, to amend a quote from history, so goes the rest of the Islamic world."

Harvath knew he was right. Considering the Wahhabis' deep hate for America and the vast amount of military hardware the Saudi Monarchy had purchased and stockpiled from the U.S. over the years, the new Saudi Arabia, or whatever the extremists would end up calling it, would immediately join the league of rogue nations.

But that wasn't all. With the Wahhabis' well-defined social and religious agenda, their breed of radical, fundamentalist Islam would begin to spread to the neighboring states and sheikdoms. Much as the Soviet Union gobbled up its neighbors, the exact same thing would happen in the Middle East, with Saudi Arabia playing the role of mother Russia and places like Oman, Qatar, and UAE becoming the next Poland, East Germany, and Czechoslovakia.

As the movement pushed eastward, Pakistan would quickly collapse and along with it any hopes of keeping nuclear weapons out of the hands of the Wahhabis. As Indonesia, the most populous Muslim nation, joined and became the new China, the Western world would be plunged into a clash more devastating than anything it had ever known.

One thing was for sure, while the extremists might claim to be using the illness solely as a bargaining chip now, there was no question that when they were ready, they would set it loose on the rest of the world.

"How did the Ottomans ever get the Wahhabis to agree to all of this?" asked Harvath.

"The Ottomans recognized the power of the Wahhabis and aligned themselves with them early on. That was how they were able to gain access to bin Laden and create al-Qaeda. It is a relationship of religion and politics—a match made in Paradise. The Wahhabis provided the spiritual justification for revolution and the establishment of a single Islamic state while the Ottomans provided the know-how and ability to run it efficiently. The one thing the Wahhabis recognize is that while they may have had a similar social agenda, the Taliban were defeated because they had no idea how to maintain the sovereignty of their country. That is something the Ottomans have more than proven they are capable of."

Harvath's head was reeling. "Without knowing

how they are inoculating the Sunni, how the hell can we stop them?"

"You can't," said a voice from the other end of the room.

The Aga Khan recognized the voice immediately. "Akrep," he said as the color drained from his face.

SEVENTY-EIGHT

Watching the man as he crossed the room, Harvath now realized that the helicopter he had heard belonged neither to Claudia Mueller nor to the Aga Khan but to someone else who apparently had business at Château Aiglemont.

"I was right," said Harvath as one of Ozan Kalachka's two bodyguards stripped him of his weapons. "Everything does have its price with you, even friendship."

"This isn't about friendship," replied Kalachka.

"I'm also willing to bet that this isn't about your nephew either."

Kalachka smiled. "Nephew? I don't have any nephew."

Harvath had underestimated the man yet again.

"I needed to find Tokay, and I knew you would lead me right to him," said Kalachka.

"Why me? Why not Alomari?"

"Assassins have their place in this world, but he

lacked your investigative skills. He also lacked the proper motivation. Not only is your entire country at risk, but someone you bore a serious grudge against was involved as well."

"Rayburn."

"Exactly. It all came together to form the perfect combination. I knew no matter what, you would find Emir Tokay for me."

"But then why did you send Alomari to kill me?"

"I didn't. In fact, when Alomari missed getting to Tokay before his kidnapping, I terminated his employment. Had he done his job, I never would have needed your services."

"He found us in London, though."

"He found you because he tortured the information about Dr. Alcott out of my colleague, Gökhan Celik. By going after Ms. Alcott and Emir Tokay, Alomari was trying to get himself back into my good graces."

"Well, now that you've found Tokay, what do you intend to do with him?"

Kalachka looked at Harvath and smiled. "I've already done it. He's dead."

Without his radio, there was no way Harvath could contact Schroeder and verify whether or not he'd found Tokay, much less if he'd found the man alive. Glancing at his Kobold, Harvath realized that if Schroeder's part of the operation had gone according to plan, he and Gösser would have already gotten to Tokay and moved him outside.

"So now that the last scientist has been silenced, you can set your sights on starting your own personal revolution, is that it?"

"It has already started," he said, pointing to the television set behind the Aga Khan's desk.

Harvath turned and saw scenes of small groups of young men throwing stones and bottles at Saudi police. It looked like a scene from Gaza or the West Bank. "That? That's your revolution? Those are just kids."

"And they're just the beginning. They think the U.S. has convinced the Saudi monarchy to round up all their spiritual leaders and put them on trial. Those kids, as you put it, are going to cause so much trouble on the streets of Riyadh that the Saudi Monarchy will have no choice but to come to the table and meet with the Wahhabi leadership. They will beg the Wahhabis to put an end to the rioting. That's when the real revolution will be ignited."

Harvath looked at him. "Then what, you'll have your Wahhabis bump off the leading members of the Royal Family? Is that how you're going to start it?"

"Quite the opposite, actually. Killing the most prominent members of the Saudi Royal Family wouldn't cause outrage in the streets; in fact, people would be dancing for joy. Instead, the Royal Family is going to kill the top members of the Wahhabi leadership. I think that will prove much more effective."

Saudi Arabia was a religious powder keg, and Kalachka was playing with a terrifying book of matches.

Killing the Wahhabi leadership would send much of the country into a furor. Even a hint that the Royal Family had something to do with the killings would guarantee rioting the likes of which the Middle East and the world had never seen. "That's it then," said Harvath. "You've wrapped up all your loose ends."

"Not exactly," said Kalachka as he withdrew a pistol. "There's one last thing I have to do." Pointing it at the Aga Khan, he pulled the trigger.

The powerful bullet entered squarely between the man's eyes and knocked him over backward in his chair. Bloody pink pieces of brain and scalp spattered onto the ceiling and covered one of the walls.

As Kalachka turned to look at him, Harvath prepared for the worst.

"Despite what you might think, I still do value our friendship," said the man. "And to that end, I will offer you a final chance to live. Come with me. Work for me. I'll make you wealthier and more powerful than you could ever imagine. Of course, you'll have to convert to Islam, but believe me, it's a small price to pay for the riches that await you."

Harvath looked at the man as if he was insane. "Are you kidding?"

"I couldn't be more serious. My plane is waiting right now. Come with me and watch history being made."

"Thanks, but no thanks," replied Harvath. "I'm not interested."

Not a man who agonized over decisions, Ozan Kalachka raised his pistol and said, "Suit yourself."

Though Kalachka had an advantage because he was holding the pistol, Harvath had something he didn't—a clear view of the front of the room.

Immediately, Scot dove for the ground as Horst Schroeder stumbled through the doorway, bleeding from several gunshot wounds, and began firing at Kalachka and his two bodyguards.

Soon rounds were flying everywhere, and Harvath clasped his hands above his head to protect against the hunks of plaster and stone that were being blown away from the mantelpiece above him. He quickly realized that not only were Kalachka and his men trying to take out Schroeder, they were shooting at him as well. Without any sort of weapon, Harvath was absolutely defenseless.

Hiding behind the upended club chair the Aga Khan had been sitting in, Harvath heard another series of rounds make contact with the wall and fireplace behind him and then felt a searing pain in his calf. At first he thought he'd been hit by a ricochet, but as his hand raced to his leg, he realized it wasn't a bullet at all. Several of the fireplace logs had rolled out into the room.

When Harvath kicked the flaming pieces of wood away, one of the logs rolled up against a curtain and set the heavy velvet drapery ablaze. With the bullets still flying, there was nothing he could do to stop it. From the curtains it was only a short jump to the Aga Khan's stacks of books, and within the blink of an eye, almost half the room was on fire. Harvath knew he couldn't stay where he was.

Just as he was about to sneak from behind the cover of the overturned leather club chair, he saw a pair of heavy black boots stumbling in his direction. They were followed by the silenced muzzle of an automatic weapon, and before Harvath could react, its owner was right on top of him.

Horst Schroeder literally collapsed at Harvath's feet, his chest heaving for air. The man was suffering not only from multiple gunshot wounds, but the early stages of smoke inhalation as well. Taking his weapon, Harvath strained to look through the smoke to see if anyone else was advancing in their direction.

"Dead," said Schroeder, his voice hoarse. "All except for one."

"Which one?" asked Harvath as he looked around again and tried to get a fix on whoever was left.

"The fat one. He's gone."

The flames were getting hotter. They had to get out of there. "Can you walk?"

Schroeder weakly shook his head no.

Slinging the weapon over his shoulder, Harvath reached his arms around the Stern commando's chest and dragged him toward the hallway. Once outside, he could hear men shouting and running up the stairs at the other end. *Rayburn's men.* Were they coming because of the fire? Or had they been unleashed to kill? "Horst," said Harvath as he tried to get the commando's attention. The man was having trouble breathing. "What happened downstairs?"

"We found Tokay, but he's dead now. We were waiting for you when the helicopter landed. The fat man said you called him."

It was true, Harvath had called him, but he had never expected Kalachka to show up. He really had underestimated him.

"He knew Tokay by name and asked if he was all right," continued Schroeder, coughing from the smoke and the blood that had pooled in his lungs. "He offered to load him into the helicopter, so we could go help you. We should have been more careful."

No, Harvath thought to himself, *I should have been there with you.*

"The moment we got within range of the helicopter, his men began shooting at us," continued Schroeder. "Tokay was killed instantly. He never had a chance. Gösser's dead as well."

Harvath felt sick and beyond angry with himself as the news sliced right through him. The whole reason they were here was to rescue Tokay, and they had failed. *He* had failed. He had allowed himself to get distracted from their primary objective, and because of it, two men had died and their mission was a failure. "You're going to be okay," he said as he pulled down a tapestry, folded it, and pressed it against Schroeder's chest as a compression bandage. If Schroeder died, not only would Claudia never forgive him, but he'd never forgive himself. This hadn't been Schroeder's fight. He had come to help, and already one of his men was killed. Harvath owed it to him to make sure he and the rest of his team got out of there alive.

"What about Rayburn?" Harvath asked as he laid Schroeder's arm over the tapestry. "What happened to him?"

"Gone. The minute the shooting started, he disappeared."

"What about the remote? Did you try to detonate the device he was wearing?"

Schroeder shook his head. "By the time I knew what was happening, he was out of range." Sliding the remote from his pocket, he handed it to Harvath and said, "Here. He's all yours."

As much as Harvath wanted to chase after Rayburn and Kalachka to make them pay for what they had done, he needed to get the parchments and folios scattered across the Aga Khan's desk. There was no telling what they might be able to learn from them.

The first of Rayburn's security forces were pouring through the door behind the Saint Nicholas statue at the end of the hallway when Harvath placed Schroeder's hands over the tapestry and said, "You're going to be okay," before dashing back inside the Aga Khan's chambers.

SEVENTY-NINE

Harvath could feel the heat tightening the skin on his face as he ran into the room. It was impossible to see, and he had to make his way completely from memory.

Once he made it to the Aga Khan's enormous wooden desk, he bent down beneath the level of the smoke, where he could see pieces of parchment and the pages from ancient manuscripts already starting to curl because of the heat. Opening the top three buttons of his Nomex shirt, he began stuffing it with whatever he could get his hands on.

As he shoved the remaining pages inside his shirt, the sides of the desk glowed a fluorescent orange and then burst into flames. Harvath leapt back as the wood from the burning desk began to snap and pop from the intense heat. At least, that's what Harvath initially thought was happening.

When a bullet narrowly missed his shoulder and sent him stumbling backward, he suddenly realized it wasn't the fire he'd been hearing. Raising the MP7 he had taken from Schroeder, he raked the entire room with gunfire and then dropped to the floor. As he ejected the spent magazine and inserted a fresh one, Harvath greedily took in enormous gasps of air.

"Sloppy work, asshole," yelled Rayburn's choked voice from somewhere within the wall of smoke and flames consuming the room.

Harvath was tempted to empty another magazine and spray the room with lead, but he restrained himself. He needed to stay in control. Fishing the remote detonation device from his pocket, Harvath powered it up and depressed the *transmit* switch again, but nothing happened. Rayburn had somehow deactivated it.

The heat in the room had Harvath close to passing out. He forced himself to think. If he were Rayburn, where would he be? He'd either be standing in the doorway where he could at least have some sort of reasonable air supply from the hall, or he'd be hugging the floor. If Rayburn was in the doorway, he'd make a decent target, but if he was hugging the floor, there could be any number of pieces of furniture standing between the two of them.

"Show yourself, motherfucker," yelled the ex–Secret Service man, "and I promise I'll kill you quick."

Hearing the voice, Harvath ascertained that the man wasn't standing in the doorway after all. He was crawling along the floor, and he was closing in.

Harvath had to bite his tongue to keep from responding. There were only about a million things he wanted to say, several of them quite clever, but if all they wound up doing was help Rayburn zero in on his position, he knew he was better off keeping his mouth shut.

It was a smoke-shrouded Mexican standoff. Neither knew exactly where the other was, but both had a somewhat vague idea. They could have played at it all day if the fire wasn't sucking the last vestiges of air from the room and the flames weren't on the verge of consuming them both. The heat had become so intense he needed to raise his arm to shield his face.

As he did, he heard a scuffing noise intermingled with the roar and crackle of the flames. Rayburn was sliding one of the leather chairs along the floor, using it for cover as he tried to get closer. That was all the information Harvath needed. Creeping as near as he could to the burning desk, he aimed his weapon toward the fireplace and began to spray rounds back and forth two feet off the ground in front of him.

When he connected with Rayburn, he heard the man cry out in pain. Rayburn's weapon clattered to the floor, and then there was silence. Harvath inserted another clip and emptied it in Rayburn's direction. The handle of his gun had grown so hot from the fire he could barely hold it anymore.

Ejecting the spent magazine, he decided he could use it as a diversion by throwing it against the far wall as he ran for the doorway. Counting to three, he pitched the magazine toward the front of the room, and as he awaited a reaction, he heard a groan of wood and plaster from above. A fraction of a second later the ceiling came crashing down.

Harvath dove as far away as he could and ended up tangled in a set of flaming draperies. Had he been wearing anything other than Nomex, he would have instantly gone up in flames.

His exit from the Aga Khan's chambers blocked by the collapsed ceiling, he used a nearby chair to bat the blazing curtains away from the window. Once he had them clear, he pulled his hand up into his shirtsleeve and used it to unlock the hinged windows and push them open.

The burst of fresh air only doubled the fire's intensity, and the raging inferno clawed for any hold it could get on his body as Harvath rolled out the window.

Once on the slippery Spanish tile roof, he moved as far away from the source of the fire as he could. Looking up, he not only saw the rest of the motorgliders circling overhead, most likely awaiting instructions on where they could safely land, but he also saw Ozan Kalachka's helicopter as it steadily rose in the mountain air. Unfortunately, the MP7 slung across his back was made for close-quarters battle. There was no way he could hit the helicopter from this distance.

Down on the patio beneath him, Harvath saw a large plastic case, which most likely contained the shoulder-fired missile spotted during his surveillance flight, but it was also useless. Even if he could get to it in time and pull it out, the sky above was filled with friendly aircraft. Any miscue, and the missile could lock onto a latent heat signature from one of the motorgliders and more innocent people would die. That was something Harvath couldn't live with.

The only thought he could find to console himself with as he climbed down from the roof was that he had a pretty good idea of where Kalachka was headed, and if he moved fast enough, he just might be able to catch him.

EIGHTY

When Harvath finally made it to the ground floor, he discovered that whatever Rayburn had done between escaping from Horst Schroeder and confronting him in the Aga Khan's chambers, he hadn't told his men they were under attack.

Still believing that Harvath and his team were on their side, the Aga Khan's security personnel had carried Schroeder outside, and one of the men who'd had previous training as a military medic was busy tending to his wounds. The rest of the men were busy trying to put out the fire that was quickly sweeping through the complex.

Picking up Schroeder's radio from where the medic had neatly stacked the wounded man's gear, Harvath walked away from the security people and was able to contact the rest of the team. He ordered the men in the village to subdue the canton police and proceed on up via the funicular. He then ordered the motorgliders back to Sion International and told Claudia to get a medical chopper up to Aiglemont to evacuate Schroeder ASAP.

Hearing the chatter across the radio, Silo One's pilot walked across the narrow meadow and joined Harvath, quietly accepting Schroeder's .40 Sig Sauer pistol, just in case the Aga Khan's men figured out they'd been duped and things got unfriendly. With Rayburn crushed beneath the burning ceiling on the monastery's second floor, Harvath had few concerns about that coming to pass.

The first of the Stern commandos were climbing off the funicular twenty minutes later when the medical chopper arrived. After helping Harvath and Silo One's pilot load Schroeder, along with the bodies of Gösser and Emir Tokay, into the helicopter, the commandos casually strolled past all the men fighting the blazing inferno and rode the funicular back down to the village.

On board the chopper, the medics stabilized Schroeder, treated the burns Harvath had suffered, then helped clean and re-dress the head wound of Silo One's pilot. Harvath learned the man's name was Wilhelm, and that in addition to motorgliders, when he wasn't flying as a Swiss Air Force reservist, his area of expertise was private, long-haul business jets.

When asked if he was rated on the Cessna Citation X, Wilhelm smiled and nodded his head. Somehow, he knew exactly what Harvath was thinking. "They'll want us to file a flight plan, you know."

Harvath didn't care. With all the turmoil caused by the fire at Château Aiglemont, it would be days before the Aga Khan's pilots knew that their boss's plane had been stolen.

As the Cessna Citation X raced toward Saudi Arabia at Mach .92, nearly the speed of sound, Harvath wondered how many sand dunes he was going to have to look behind before he finally found Ozan Kalachka. He knew the man had to be somewhere inside the desert kingdom. The only questions were where and would Harvath be able to get to him in time.

For her part, Jillian seemed more concerned with Scot's condition than the condition of the ancient documents, which he repeatedly apologized for letting get damaged in the fire.

With no time for anything but the preflight check before they left, Jillian scrounged what she could from the galley—some crackers, a wheel of Brie, two jars of Caspian caviar, and a bottle of San Pellegrino mineral water—and brought it to him.

Harvath ate what little there was and then tried to concentrate on how the hell he was going to get the aircraft cleared to land in Saudi Arabia and avoid customs. He didn't know anyone with any pull in the kingdom. Regardless of any potential fallout, it was time for him to contact Gary Lawlor directly.

While Jillian studied the pages retrieved from Château Aiglemont, Harvath used the jet's onboard telephone to contact DC. He caught Lawlor on his encrypted cell phone and launched into everything that had happened.

"Claudia Mueller is going to be in some hot water with her superiors," Lawlor remarked.

"I don't think so," replied Harvath. "Kalachka's the one who pulled strings with his contacts in the Swiss government to get the rescue operation approved."

"Either way, they still lost an operator and Tokay."

Harvath squeezed the bridge of his nose with his thumb and forefinger. "I know." He didn't want to think about what happened at Aiglemont, and how he had been conned by Ozan Kalachka. "What about the Whitcombs? Have they had any luck with the tissue samples we sent back?"

"DNA takes a long time to analyze, and ancient DNA even longer. But we've got an even bigger problem on our hands."

"What's happening now?"

"The virus, the illness—whatever you want to call it—has turned up here."

"In the United States," said Harvath. "How?"

"We're still investigating. It seems to have originated with a grocer in Michigan who imports Muslim foods for his mail-order business."

"How many people are infected?"

"Only a handful that we know of, and they're quarantined, of course. But this thing is about to explode," replied Lawlor. "Listen, Scot. The president has initiated the Campfire Protocol—we're running out of time."

Harvath didn't want to believe what he had just heard, but he had worked in the White House long enough to know that the president probably had no choice. The illness had to be contained, and if they discovered nuking entire cities was the only way to do it, Rutledge would be left with no other choice. "Do they already have strike aircraft aloft?"

"They do. If this thing starts gaining ground and the USAMRIID and CDC teams can't pen it in, then they're going to go for ultimate containment."

"How much time do we have?"

"There's no way of knowing."

"Well, if I can track down Kalachka, maybe we can head this thing off. Ultimately, he's the only person left with the answers," said Harvath.

"I agree, but you have no idea where he is."

"We're going to need help. We'll have to reach out to somebody inside the kingdom—somebody we can trust. Somebody who can get us in with no customs and no questions and then help us get the information we need."

Lawlor thought about it for a moment and then responded, "I think I might know the right person. Give me about twenty minutes and I'll call you back."

Harvath hung up the phone and poured another glass of mineral water. The smoke and heat from the fire had made him thirsty as hell. Turning to Jillian, who was still examining the documents that had been taken from Tokay when the Aga Khan had him kidnapped, he asked, "Have you been able to find anything helpful in there?"

"Maybe," she said as she reread a passage from one of the folios. "Apparently, whatever the vaccine is, it works even after the onset of symptoms. Other than that, the rest of it just confirms what we already knew or suspected. Hannibal did in fact manage to secure a copy of the *Arthashastra*. He was fascinated with the *Azemiops feae* viper and the potency of its venom. The Carthaginians conducted countless experiments, combining derivatives of the venom with other chemical and biological components until they finally settled on rabies as the most deadly complement."

"That makes sense, but how were they able to come up with a vaccine for it?"

"Probably by knowing the weapon's key components."

"*Azemiops feae* venom and rabies. Big deal," responded Harvath. "We know that too, yet we're no closer to uncovering a vaccine than we were when this whole thing started."

"What the Carthaginians knew was the actual type of each component. They would have known how the venom was extracted and if anything else along the way was done to refine it. They also would have been dealing with a form of rabies that was current during their day."

"But even knowing the key components, how did they make the leap to an actual vaccine?"

Alcott set down the parchment she was studying and said, "Man has always been fascinated not only with what kills, but also with what cures. Pliny the Elder, a Roman who was one of the foremost authorities on science in the ancient world, claimed that resin from giant fennel and a type of laurel known as purple spurge were effective at curing wounds caused by envenomed arrows."

Harvath remembered reading something to that effect in Vanessa Whitcomb's office. Nodding his head, he listened as Jillian continued.

"In the ancient world, it was common knowledge that people who lived in areas plagued with venomous creatures such as snakes and scorpions often developed some degree of immunity due to their constant exposure. Some believed that the breath or saliva of these people could cure venomous bites in anyone. In fact, there was a tribe in North Africa known as the Psylli who were so immune to snake bites and scorpion stings that their saliva was considered the wonder drug of its day. It was, in essence, one of the first forms of antivenin."

"Do you actually think human saliva was part of Hannibal's vaccine?"

"It's possible, but not very likely if it had to be mass-produced to protect his entire army. More than likely, the antivenin portion of the cure was created in nature somehow."

"Created how?"

"I wouldn't be surprised if the Carthaginians had discovered a way to expose livestock to a form of the venom and extract antivenin—much the same way we do today with sheep and horses."

"And the rabies component of the cure?"

"We used to grow inactive rabies virus in duck eggs. These days we grow it in human cells in a laboratory, but considering what fifth-century B.C. Scythians knew about separating human blood plasma for use in their toxins, who's to say the Carthaginians didn't discover a similar method? The bottom line is that they were masterful at manipulating their environment and the world around them. We can't underestimate any discoveries they might have made."

It wasn't that Harvath didn't agree with her, he did, but that didn't change the fact that they were no closer to discovering a way to head this thing off. If they didn't catch some sort of break and catch it very soon, a lot of people were going to start dying.

Ten minutes later, the onboard telephone rang and Harvath picked it up. Gary Lawlor's voice was on the other end. "I got hold of somebody who is going to get your plane cleared to land."

"Good."

"He's also got something I want you to check out. We may have a break in the case."

EIGHTY-ONE

WESTIN EMBASSY ROW HOTEL
WASHINGTON, DC

If the tone of his message didn't alert Senator Carmichael that he had news worth celebrating, then Brian Turner's choice of a four-star hotel for their next meeting definitely should have. As an added extravagance, he had booked them into the eighth-floor suite that former Vice President Al Gore grew up in when his father was in the Senate and a cousin of theirs owned the hotel. He hoped the significance of their surroundings wouldn't be lost on her.

After arriving early to check in and make sure the room was in order, Turner headed downstairs to the hotel's Fairfax Lounge for a cocktail. Though he could have gone for a third martini, he made good on his promise to only have two. The senator had not been happy with the condition she had found him in the last time they met, although she did warm up considerably when he presented the information he had obtained for her. He knew today would be no different, especially with the bombshell he was about to drop, but he wanted to have a reasonably clear head when he did. Knowing Helen, she was going to be in the mood for champagne and would probably want to spend an hour or two in the sack before running with the dossier he had put together on the president's personal covert action team.

When Carmichael arrived, she was all business. "You must have something pretty big to call me out of my office in the middle of the day," said the senator as she brushed past the young CIA man and entered the luxuriously appointed suite.

"Nice to see you too," he said as he closed the door behind her and crossed over to the minibar. "How about a drink?"

"I've got a floor vote in forty-five minutes, Brian. Why don't we cut to the chase? Tell me what I'm doing here."

She was one hell of a ballbuster, that was for sure, but she was Turner's ticket to the big leagues, and he tried to keep that in mind as he said, "You think you'd show a little more appreciation to the person who was about to hand you the vice presidency of the United States on a silver platter."

"What are you talking about?"

"On the desk," he replied, nodding in the direction of a gift-wrapped package.

Carmichael walked over and picked up the box. Sliding the red satin ribbon off, she lifted the lid and found a plain manila folder inside. "What's this?" she asked.

Turner picked up the room-service menu and flipped to the wine list. "Open it and see," he said over his shoulder.

The senator sat down at the desk and began reading. "How the hell did you get hold of this?"

"I told you before. I'm very good at my job."

"Brian, you're better than good. This is absolutely incredible. This is going to knock Jack Rutledge out of the White House so fast, there'll be skid marks down Pennsylvania Avenue."

"How about champagne? Should I have room service send up a bottle?"

"You have them send up anything you want."

"Cristal it is," said Turner as he reached for the phone to place the order.

Carmichael continued to read. "There's enough here to launch twenty years' worth of hearings." The senator was so excited, she could barely contain herself. "It will take me days just to figure out whether I should drop the whole thing or leak parts of it in dribs and drabs until it reaches such a critical mass that Rutledge and his people will be drawing hot baths and fighting over the razor blades."

Turner had known the minute he uncovered the information that his position in Carmichael's cabinet was all but assured. Now, as she set down the folder and walked over to him, the red satin ribbon dangling seductively from her hand, he knew it was a lock. "When the press asks me where I got my information," she said, unbuckling his belt, "how am I to explain such a fortuitous discovery?"

"You'll tell them it came from a source that was sick of seeing Jack Rutledge mismanage this country's assets and flagrantly flaunting his disregard for the Constitution and the body of laws that make America great."

"That's quite a mouthful," said Carmichael as she dropped to her knees and unzipped his fly.

As she did, the room-service operator came on the line and Turner told her he would have to call back.

In the next room, one of the FBI surveillance agents sitting next to Gary Lawlor removed his headphones, pushed himself away from the video monitor, and said, "Now this scandal has everything. Including its own deep throat."

EIGHTY-TWO

RIYADH, SAUDI ARABIA

Instead of landing at the commercial King Khalid International Airport, Harvath was instructed to head for the Riyadh Air Base, where he wouldn't have to worry about clearing customs.

As the plane made its final approach, Harvath looked out the window next to him. Despite all of the trouble that had come out of Saudi Arabia, he marveled at its capital city. Translated from Arabic, *Riyadh* literally meant "the Gardens," and it was an appropriate name. Situated in the Central Province's Hanifa Valley, Riyadh was not the city of sand which many pictured it to be. Instead it was lush and green, punctuated with an abundance of beautiful parks. Established as an ancient walled city along a historical trade route between Iran and the holy city of Mecca, Riyadh's location, like that of most of the major cities in Saudi Arabia, was selected because of its proximity to a source of fresh water, and Harvath couldn't help but wonder if that water had anything to do with what they were looking for.

After the plane had landed, the pilots taxied to a large parking revetment and shut down the engines. Despite the fact that they were in the shade, when Harvath opened the forward door and lowered the staircase, the heat from outside was like getting hit in the face by a blast furnace. It was easily well over a hundred and ten degrees.

Summer in the sandbox, Harvath thought to himself as he and Alcott made their way down the stairs and over to the Toyota Land Cruiser that was waiting for them. Remembering all the miserable conditions he had to endure as a SEAL, he didn't miss his days of operating in this part of the world at all.

As they approached the car, the first thing Harvath noticed was a cluster of bullet holes along the rear quarter-panel. Running his finger over them, he tried to gauge their caliber.

"I took some AK-47 fire on my way over," said the driver as he came around the side to meet them. He was dressed in the traditional Arab garment that looked like a long nightshirt known as a *dishdasha*. As he unwound the checkered kaffiyeh from his face, they could see he was an American. "Chip Reynolds," he said as he stuck out his hand.

Harvath and Alcott introduced themselves and then watched as he opened the tailgate and retrieved two shopping bags. "I brought you each a change of clothes. The natives are getting a little restless, and the less foreign you look, the better off we'll be."

"What about this?" asked Harvath as he pulled back his jacket to reveal his .40-caliber H&K handgun. Not only wouldn't he be able to hide it beneath a traditional *dishdasha*, but even if he could, he'd have to hike up the entire robe just to get at it. That wasn't going to work.

Reynolds sifted through the gear in the cargo area of his Land Cruiser and pulled out a small briefcase with Arabic writing on it used for carrying sections of the Koran known as a *Juz* that was perfect for holding Harvath's weapon.

He had to hand it to the guy. Reynolds was definitely clever and apparently had thought of everything.

Once Harvath had changed into his *dishdasha* and Jillian into her full-length black *abaya*, complete with a long *niqab* that revealed only her eyes, they were ready to roll.

"Boy, are you a looker," joked Reynolds as Jillian climbed into the backseat. "You're going to break a lot of hearts around here with those eyes."

Harvath wasn't crazy about the man's casual attitude and switched their conversation back to the matter at hand. "How do you know Gary Lawlor?"

Reynolds put the car in gear and headed for the air base's main gate. "Gary and I were in Army Intelligence together. I joined the CIA about the same time he went into the bureau."

"How'd you end up over here?"

"The Middle East was my area of operations. I learned how to speak Arabic and Farsi and actually used to enjoy it over here, Saudi Arabia in particular."

"Gary said you do security work for the Aramco company. A man with your background, I'm sure the CIA was sorry to see you go."

"I'm sure they were, but I'd made a lifetime career out of serving my country. What I'm doing now, I'm doing strictly for the money, and I don't see any shame in it. Why shouldn't I be able to cash in on the few workable years I have left?"

The man had a good point. As they drove out the main gates of Riyadh Air Base, Harvath asked, "I can't blame you, but do you ever miss it?"

"What? Working for the agency?"

Harvath nodded his head.

"In the beginning, yeah, I missed it. I missed it a lot, but I could see the writing on the wall. The company wasn't going to hold on to me forever. What was I going to do, invest in a rocket-propelled wheelchair to chase down bad guys? If there's one lesson I've learned, it's that life is all about change, and stress comes from avoiding change. I think that's the biggest lesson that came from losing my wife. She was extremely supportive of my career, but I knew she wasn't crazy about it. The pay wasn't super and the hours were horrible, but she understood I was in it for something more than that. Do you know what I mean?"

"Yes," replied Harvath. "I know what you mean."

"Are you married?" asked Reynolds.

"No."

"Girlfriend?"

Harvath had to think about his answer a moment. "Not really."

"Well, I'll give you a free piece of advice. It's something I wish somebody had told me a long time ago. The only love I ever had greater than my love for my country was my love for my wife. I wouldn't be half the man I am today if it wasn't for her. I see a lot of people in this game who have chosen their career over having a family, and I think that's a bunch of crap. It's a copout. Even though you're working your ass off protecting life and liberty, it doesn't mean you're not entitled to the pursuit of happiness. The key, though, is in finding the right person."

"There's the understatement of the year," said Harvath as he wondered if Dr. Phil knew somebody in Saudi Arabia was stealing his material.

"How old are you? About thirty-five?"

"About."

"That's when I got married, but I almost didn't do it. It would have been a colossal mistake on my part not to. I guess what I'm saying is, don't let your career stand in the way of what you want out of life."

"I'll keep that in mind," said Harvath, while

what he was thinking was that his career was all he was aware of ever really wanting. He couldn't see past it. He hadn't even tried to until he was faced with what his life might be like without it. Reynolds was an interesting character. Unlike Rayburn, who'd been forced out of government service and into the private sector, Reynolds had chosen to leave and had done so on his own terms after a long and ostensibly satisfying life of service. What's more, Reynolds had somehow been able to have a rich and fulfilling relationship—something Harvath had not yet been able to achieve. As he listened to the man speak, he wondered if maybe it wasn't the women he had dated so much as it was he himself who had been sabotaging his relationships.

After a few more moments of reflection, Harvath realized he had allowed himself to be blown off course and once again tried to bring the conversation back around to the matter at hand. "Why don't we talk about what it is we're driving into."

With time being of the essence, Reynolds avoided any roundabout side road routes, swung onto the main access road into Riyadh, and pinned the accelerator. "As far as what's going on in the city itself?"

"Yeah."

"You saw the ventilation that's been added to the back of my truck?"

"That many holes are hard to miss," answered

Harvath. "You said something about the natives getting restless?"

"The mullahs have whipped a lot of the faithful, particularly the young men, into a frenzy."

"Over what?" asked Jillian from the backseat.

"They claim that the Royal Family has ordered the police to crack down on all militants, even the moderate ones, in response to pressure from America."

"There's definitely some pressure being applied here," said Harvath, "but it's not from America."

"That's just it. The Royal Family seems to be playing right into this guy Kalachka's hands. They're arresting militants left and right."

"Why?"

"They seem to believe that there's a strong possibility a coup might be afoot."

EIGHTY-THREE

As they drove through the tracts of housing complexes outside Riyadh, Reynolds talked about the militants he had been keeping tabs on, why he had decided to follow them, and what he had learned. Then it was Harvath's turn.

Over the next ten minutes, Harvath provided a brief summary of their investigation and everything they had been through. He finished by explaining why Reynolds hadn't been able to find Khalid Alomari and what the man had been doing during his long absences from Saudi Arabia. When Harvath reached the point when the al-Qaeda assassin was killed, he looked in the rearview mirror and saw Jillian avert her eyes out the window.

"You did the right thing," said Reynolds in an attempt to break the silence that had settled over them.

"I know," said Jillian. "I know."

"Let me ask you something else," the man continued, "about this illness. Gary says that it has just shown up in the United States. How'd it get in and where are they seeing it?"

"As far as the FBI, DHS, CDC, and USAMRIID teams can figure out, it started with a Muslim food importer who shipped a package UPS from Hamtramck, Michigan, to Manhattan," said Harvath. "Apparently, anyone who has come in contact with it has become infected, including the importer himself."

Using the rearview mirror to look at Jillian, Reynolds asked, "Do you have any idea how the illness is spread?"

"No, we don't. All we know is that according to the Aga Khan, immunity to the illness is transmitted somehow via water. A holy water of some sort that only Muslims have access to."

"Only Sunni Muslims," added Harvath. "Which is why Gary thought we could help each other out. You said that one of the things you discovered in that warehouse was bottled water, right?"

"Tons of it," replied Reynolds. "The warehouse was enormous, and they had the stuff stacked floor to ceiling. There had to be over a million bottles in there, easy."

"What about the documents you found?"

"That brings us back to my question," he said, looking to Jillian once again. "Could the illness be spread by contact with things that had been purposefully contaminated?"

"Sure," responded Jillian. "The ancients were very fond of lacing fields they knew their enemies were going to pass through with toxic poisons. The enemy would walk through, and the substance would enter their bodies through direct dermal contact or respiratory inhalation. They were even known to contaminate foodstuffs, water supplies, or everyday goods and leave them for the enemy to 'discover,' and that would be that. Why are you asking?"

"From what Gary told me, the contaminated package in the U.S. contained some sort of powdered spice made from ground cherry pits. It was being shipped to an ex–Saudi national who owns a string of very interesting businesses."

"What kind of businesses?"

"Gas stations, convenience stores, currency exchanges, payday loan and check-cashing operations throughout the Northeast."

"So?"

"So what do all those businesses have in common?"

After a moment, Harvath responded, "Cash. They all deal very heavily in cash."

"Bingo," said Reynolds. "And all of those businesses encounter little or no regulation. They're virtual money-laundering machines."

"Or money-dirtying machines."

"According to the list I saw, these guys have operations throughout the United States, even in

Alaska. Short of getting someone inside the Treasury Department, I can't think of a better way to compromise large amounts of American currency. The question is, though, could they use that powdered spice to contaminate paper money?"

"If what I learned in the Secret Service is any indication," replied Harvath, "then definitely."

"How?"

"Our paper is very fibrous, and it doesn't take much for things to get embedded in those fibers. The best example would be cocaine. According to statistics, trace amounts of cocaine are believed to infect four out of every five bills in circulation."

"That's impossible," answered Reynolds. "There aren't that many people doing drugs in America."

"The drug users may be the root source, but they represent an almost negligible minority when it comes to how bills get contaminated. When a powdered substance like cocaine is very finely milled, it passes easily from one surface to another. The biggest contamination culprits are ATMs. Once infected, they were shown to spread trace amounts of cocaine to all the bills they distributed. Counting and sorting machines like those used in banks and casinos are just as bad. Even the machines tested in several Federal Reserve banks were shown to be contaminated.

"Basically, a single bill with trace amounts of a substance like cocaine can infect an entire cash drawer, and when that cash encounters a counting or sorting machine, which fans the bills, the contamination grows exponentially. It makes perfect sense."

Reynolds looked back at Jillian. "You're the scientist. What do you think?"

"From a personal standpoint, I think it's terrifying. But from a strictly scientific point of view, it's absolutely brilliant."

Harvath hadn't liked it when al-Qaeda's strategic genius was praised after the September 11 attacks, and he didn't like hearing this current terrorist strategy described in such a way either, but he understood what she meant. "So is this a viable means of infection?"

"It makes sense," said Jillian. "Contaminated currency would be a perfect, virtually unstoppable way to spread it. It would also have a chilling psychological effect on financial markets worldwide. The American dollar would be quite literally worthless. Not only would al-Qaeda succeed in killing scores of infidels, but they would also decimate the American economy. Quite a one-two punch."

Harvath turned to Reynolds and asked, "How much time before we get to the warehouse?"

"About five more minutes."

"Is your cell phone secure?"

"More secure than most in the kingdom, why?"

"Just in case we don't walk out of that warehouse, Gary needs to know what we've discovered."

As Harvath raised the phone to his ear, he glanced in the Land Cruiser's side-view mirror and watched as a blue Mercedes behind them turned off onto a small side street and another car merged into traffic three lengths back. It was the same car that had been behind them when they turned onto the main road lcaving Riyadh Air Base.

Cupping his hand over the mouthpiece, hc said to Reynolds, "I think we'vc got company."

EIGHTY-FOUR

Reynolds trusted Harvath's instincts. Without even waiting for an explanation, he yelled for everybody to hang on and pulled a hard right turn followed by a quick left.

Pulling a walkie-talkie from beneath his seat, he asked Harvath to describe the car he had seen. Once he knew what they were looking for, he raised the walkie-talkie to his mouth and said, "Bluebird, this is Pelican. Do you copy? Over."

"Who's Bluebird?" asked Harvath as he glanced over his shoulder to see if they were still being followed.

"He's one of my men. His name is Zafir."

"Is he a Saudi?"

"No, Pakistani. He's ex-military and one of the few people I trust with something like this. He's on a rooftop down the street from the warehouse keeping an eye out for us. In about a block he'll have a clear view, and we'll know if anyone is following us."

"Pelican, this is Bluebird. I copy. Over," broke a voice across Reynolds's radio. "What's your status? Over."

"Pelican is inbound with possible company. Please check our tail for a beige, late-model Nissan Sentra. Over."

"Late-model beige Nissan Sentra. Roger that," said Zafir. "Take a right turn at Al Mus'ad and another right turn at Khair al Din. Will let you know. Over."

"Roger that. Pelican out," said Reynolds as he handed the radio to Harvath and prepared to execute the turns.

Three minutes later, Zafir radioed back that they were all clear. Either Harvath had overreacted and they weren't being followed, or they had managed to lose whoever was behind them. Something told Harvath it was the latter. He had a bad feeling that they were about to walk into something they might have a very difficult time walking out of.

Taking the radio back from Harvath, Reynolds did one final check with Zafir, who told him the warehouse had been quiet all day. Even though the parking lot was empty, Reynolds chose to park on the street about a block away. The last thing he wanted to do was draw attention to the fact that someone was visiting.

Fool them once, shame on them. Fool them twice, double shame on them was Reynolds's feeling as he removed the prayer mat, which, just as in his last visit to the warehouse, was wrapped around his Remington twelve-gauge tactical shotgun. The nice thing about this trip, though, was that unless the owners of the structure had changed the locks, Reynolds had his own set of keys.

Working their way around to the office at the rear of the structure, Reynolds tried several of the keys until he found the one that worked. With Harvath helping cover him with his H&K, Reynolds pulled his Remington from the prayer rug, and they quietly crept inside with Jillian right behind them. At the end of the hallway, Reynolds held up his hand and counted to three, at which point he and Harvath both swept into the office and found it totally empty.

Every desk drawer stood open and bare. Harvath checked the file cabinets and found the same thing. The entire place had been cleared out. Somebody had decided they didn't want to wait around to see if the shotgun-toting Westerner was going to make a second appearance.

Motioning toward the opposite doorway, Harvath struck off into the warehouse and signaled for Reynolds to follow. When they entered the cavernous space, they saw that it too had been completely cleared out. All that was left was a battered forklift with two flat tires, a few stacks of discarded pallets, and other assorted pieces of trash. By the looks of it, no one would ever have known the space had been recently occupied. Bending over to get a closer look at one of the pieces of garbage, Harvath heard Jillian say, "Whatever you do, don't touch anything."

Harvath immediately drew his hand back. Wearing a pair of surgical gloves from the plane's first aid kit and using some plastic trash bags she had brought with her from the galley, Jillian began combing the warehouse gathering samples. As she did, Harvath continued his examination of the premises.

In the far corner, he came across a stack of pallets that at some point had been knocked over. Whoever had been clearing the place out must have been in an awfully big hurry, because they failed to recognize that something had been caught underneath. Using the toe of his boot to kick the pallets out of the way, Harvath uncovered a large cardboard box with what appeared to be a military uniform of some sort inside.

Mindful of how the British provided American Indians blankets infected with smallpox, Harvath called Jillian and her latex gloves over to help him check it out.

As she approached, he could see from the bags she carried that she had already collected quite a few samples. "Look at these," she said excitedly as she held up a pair of matching water bottles. "Muslim holy water from a sacred spring near Mecca."

Harvath stared at the Arabic writing on the front of the bottles and asked, "You can read Arabic?"

Jillian shook her head. "It's written in English and about eleven other different languages on the back. Whoever bottled these was planning for some major exporting. We're going to need to get the water tested, but we may have just found how the Ottomans planned on getting the cure to the Sunni faithful."

"Now if we can just find the source," replied Harvath.

Holding up another bag that she dared not open, Jillian added, "I've also collected several packets of what could be our elusive infective agent, but again, until we can test it, I can't be certain."

Harvath complimented her work and then pointed to the box he had uncovered and asked her to pull the uniform out for him.

"What is it?" she asked as she laid it across one of the pallets.

"The top half of a SANG uniform," said Reynolds as he came over to join them.

Jillian looked unfamiliar with the term.

"It's an acronym," explained Harvath. "It stands for Saudi Arabian National Guard. It's made up of tribal elements loyal to the Saudi Royal Family and is in charge of protecting them against the country's regular armed forces or anyone else who might try to push them from power."

"Why would one of those uniforms be here?"

Harvath thought back to what Kalachka had said to him—*Killing the most prominent members of the Saudi Royal Family wouldn't cause outrage in the streets; in fact, people would be dancing for joy. Instead, the Royal Family is going to kill the top members of the Wahhabi leadership*—and Harvath now knew how it was going to happen. "We've got to get out of here."

"I've got all I need," said Jillian as she reattached the *niqab* across her face, gathered up her sample bags, and prepared to head outside.

Reynolds toggled the *transmit* button on his radio and tried to raise Zafir for a situation report on how things looked outside, but there was no response. "Bluebird, this is Pelican. Do you read me? Over," he said for a second time.

The uncomfortable feeling Harvath had had upon arriving at the warehouse returned to the pit of his stomach with a vengeance.

Though he knew better, Reynolds wondered if maybe the radio was having trouble penetrating the warehouse's cinderblock construction and decided to try his cell phone. When the phone showed full signal status, he knew they were in trouble. Zafir was not a man who would abandon his post.

Activating the voice-dial feature of his phone, Reynolds said, "Zafir, cell."

The phone rang several times before dumping Reynolds into the Pakistani's voice mail. Looking up at Harvath and Alcott, Reynolds didn't need to say anything—they all knew they were in trouble.

With all of the windows blacked out, they were

completely blind to what might be going on outside. "Back out the way we came?" asked Harvath. "Or do we try another door?"

For all Reynolds knew, the entire place was surrounded and any of the doors would be suicide. As far as he was concerned, the exit that put them the closest to his Land Cruiser was the one they wanted. That meant either going back through the office or to the door about twenty feet to their right. Either way, the rooftop sniper support he'd hoped to have from Zafir if things went bad was now out of the question. "We'll take this one," he said, selecting the door twenty feet to their right.

As they reached the door, Reynolds saw that it was locked and needed a key to be opened, even from the inside. Keys in hand, he was already searching for the right one when Harvath grabbed his arm. "What are you doing?" he demanded as he tried to twist away.

"Look," replied Harvath, pointing to a pair of barely discernible wires leading from behind the doorframe.

Glancing up, Reynolds now saw them as well. "What the hell?"

Tracing the wires, Harvath discovered that they led to enormous blocks of C4, which were in turn attached to remote detonators. "It looks like somebody was expecting us."

"Not us," said Reynolds as he studied the devices. "Me. I think they knew I'd be back and wanted to teach me a lesson."

"Well, this is one hell of a lesson."

"That's what I get for terminating one of their guys without permission."

"That's what *we* get," corrected Harvath.

Reynolds forced a smile. "Can you defuse it? I don't know shit about explosives."

"I'm not sure," said Harvath as he scrutinized the setup. "This can't be the only door. It's a one-in-six shot they would have been able to get us with this one."

"We need to check the other doors."

Harvath took the doors in the back while Reynolds checked the doors in the front, and Jillian checked all the windows. When they met back up, she said, "All the windows are wired."

Reynolds used the sleeve of his *dishdasha* to mop the sweat from his forehead and added, "Same thing with all the doors up front."

"And in back," replied Harvath, "but with one slight difference."

"What?"

"When we came in through the office door, we must have armed the system. It's now officially active."

"So we're okay then as long as we don't try to go out one of the doors or one of the windows," said Jillian. "Right?"

"That's the way it looks," replied Reynolds. "All

the exits are connected to each other. Open any one of them, and it triggers every charge in the building. There's got to be enough C4 here to take down half the block."

Harvath looked at them and said, "We've got an even bigger problem."

Jillian and Reynolds both looked at him.

"There's a padlocked electrical panel near the office. I was able to pry it open enough to sneak a peek inside."

"And?" said Reynolds.

"I found the system activator."

"Then let's go get it."

"Not so fast," cautioned Harvath. "The panel door is wired. Open it up any further, and all the charges will be set off."

Jillian set her bags down and threw up her hands in defeat. "That's just great. What else could possibly go wrong?"

"Actually, that's only part of our problem. The other part's the timer."

EIGHTY-FIVE

By pressing his face up against the wall as tight as it would go, Harvath had been able to peer inside the electrical panel and read the numbers on the digital timer. They had less than ten minutes left.

With its cinderblock construction, the warehouse was a virtual bunker. Punching through the roof was immediately ruled out, as they had no ladders to get up that high, and even if they did, there was no telling if the roof had been reinforced like the rest of the building. *There had to be another way.*

Scanning the sparse contents of the warehouse, Harvath's eyes fell upon the forklift, and a plan began to form in his mind. With its two flat tires, there was no way they could drive it anywhere, much less straight through one of the walls, but it still might be useful in another fashion—as their very own homemade bomb.

Harvath kept his idea to himself until he got a closer look at the machine. Even from across the room, it was apparent it wasn't an electric model. According to the label on the gas gauge, it was a diesel and more than half full. Locating the vehicle's toolbox, he opened it up but only found a roll of duct tape and a metal claw hammer.

He yelled for Reynolds and Jillian to join him and threw the forklift into neutral as he explained what he needed them to do. With Jillian pushing from the side and using one hand to steer, Harvath and Reynolds threw all of their weight behind it and pushed as hard as they could.

With its heavy forks and two flat tires, it was nearly impossible to get moving, but soon the trio felt the vehicle inching forward. The problem, though, was that they weren't inching fast enough. When they got the machine as close to the center of the wall, and as far away from the nearest doors and windows as possible, Harvath told Reynolds to eject all but one of the shells from his twelve-gauge while he used the claw hammer to tear away the fiberglass housing from around the forklift's gas tank.

The housing shattered and came away with ear-splitting cracks. Once enough of it had been cleared, Harvath pulled off several strips of duct tape and fashioned the shotgun shells in the tightest grouping possible and then taped the entire thing to the exterior of the gas tank. Glancing at his watch, he figured they had less than two minutes. "How good a shot are you?" he asked Reynolds as they ran for cover.

The man replied honestly. "Not good enough."

Harvath was the most accurate with a weapon in close-quarters situations, which meant less than thirty feet. For safety's sake, though, they needed to be back at least two or three times that distance when the forklift's gas tank was detonated.

Hiding behind a stack of pallets, Harvath took the shotgun from Reynolds and said more for Jillian's benefit than anyone else's, "There's going to be a concussion wave, so don't get up right away. Count to three after you hear the explosion and then run like hell for the opening, okay?"

Jillian and Reynolds both nodded their heads.

Leaning out from behind the pallets, Harvath raised the shotgun, took aim, and fired. The bullet hit its mark, detonating the shotgun shells taped to the gas tank and creating an enormous explosion.

The explosion not only tore an incredible hole through the block wall, but also sent the flaming wreckage of the forklift soaring out and into the street.

Without the benefit of sufficient cover, Harvath was knocked backward by the same concussion wave he had warned Jillian about. Before he knew what was happening, Reynolds had lifted him to his feet and was half dragging him toward the opening.

By the time they hit the rubble-strewn pavement outside, Harvath had regained enough of his equilibrium to move under his own power. Without looking back, they ran with all the speed they could muster, knowing the warehouse was about to evaporate in one of the biggest explosions Riyadh had ever seen.

They ran all the way to Reynolds's Land Cruiser, which he had started and was pulling away from the curb before they even had their doors closed.

As the SUV lurched into the street, they felt the ground beneath the tires tremble as the warehouse exploded and sent a billowing fireball into the early evening sky. Hunks of debris rained down on them, denting the hood and cracking the windshield in too many places to count. With one hand on the wheel, Reynolds leaned across Harvath, flipped open the glove box, and revealed a box of twelve-gauge shotgun shells. Taking the Remington from his lap and handing it to Harvath, he said, "Load it up. We need to find Zafir."

Harvath understood.

EIGHTY-SIX

Driving around the block, Reynolds brought the Land Cruiser to a screeching halt in front of the abandoned building Zafir was using as his lookout. Harvath and Reynolds pounded up the stairs and burst out onto the rooftop. Zafir was slumped over his rifle, the walkie-talkie still propped against the wall next to him. Harvath rolled him over and saw that his throat had been cut from ear to ear.

Reynolds lost it. "Those goddamn animals," he cursed.

Crossing to an adjacent roof, Harvath found a plastic tarp and brought it back over to wrap around Zafir's body.

The two men worked in silence, and once they had carried the fallen Pakistani downstairs and loaded him in the back of the Land Cruiser, Reynolds said, "I don't care what it takes. I want the people who are responsible for this."

"We both do," replied Harvath. "Believe me."

The crowd that had gathered to gawk at the smoldering ruins of the warehouse was growing, and given the recent riots that had been springing up all around Riyadh, Harvath suggested they get back in the truck and get moving to someplace safer.

On the way to Reynolds's Aramco offices, they were forced to detour around several small but violent civil insurrections, which Saudi Security Forces nevertheless were having trouble putting down. "They won't shoot their own people. That's their problem," said Reynolds coldly as they passed yet another. "The same thing happened in Mecca in the seventies. They finally had to call in French GIGN units to help them recapture the Grand Mosque."

Yet another reference to Mecca. Everything in Saudi Arabia seemed inexorably linked to the two greatest shrines in Islam, Mecca and Medina. "Do you know about any secret spring there?" asked Harvath.

"I've heard some cock-and-bull story our little exporter Prince Hamal was spreading about one, but who knows? If there's one thing I've learned, it's that Saudi Arabia has more secrets than it does sand. The key is knowing which secrets to leave buried."

"Well, this definitely isn't one of them," said Harvath.

"Do you think that's what's in those bottles?"

"That's what we intend to find out," said Jillian.

"Does Aramco have a lab that she can use?" asked Harvath.

Reynolds looked at his watch. "At this hour it should be completely empty."

"Good. We'll need to get her set up right away. In the meantime, what else can you tell me about the prince who owned that warehouse and the militants he's been working with?"

"Quite a bit," replied Reynolds. "I've got backup copies of my dossiers on all of them back at my office."

"Including photos?"

"Including photos. Why?"

"Because I'm pretty sure I know what their next move is going to be."

After setting Jillian up in Aramco's extensive, state-of-the-art lab with her samples and arranging for one of his men to take care of Zafir's body, Reynolds led Harvath to the elevator and up to where the corporate security offices were located.

His supply of prayer rugs now depleted, Reynolds had forgone the Remington in favor of the Les Baer 1911 pistol he had secreted under the front seat of his Land Cruiser. Upon seeing his office door standing wide open, he pulled the weapon from his ankle holster and motioned for Harvath to be quiet.

Having ditched the Koran briefcase back at the

warehouse, Harvath drew his H&K from the plastic trash bag he was now using and covered their six as he and Reynolds crept down the hallway toward his office. Stepping inside, they saw that it had been completely ransacked.

"Goddamn it," spat Reynolds as he picked up his phone and called the security desk downstairs. After a terse conversation in Arabic, he hung up and said, "I can't believe it. They let the deputy intelligence minister, Faruq al-Hafez, up here."

"The one you saw meeting with the militants and the members of the different military branches?"

"He said it was official business."

"You think he did this?" asked Harvath.

"Oh, yeah. And I'd be willing to bet he was behind what just happened at the warehouse," said Reynolds as he pulled a bottle of Bushmills from his credenza and poured himself a drink. "When I made my first trip there, I butt-stroked a guy with my Remington. He must have seen enough of my face to describe me to Faruq. You want one?" he added, holding up another glass.

"No thanks," replied Harvath. "How can you be so sure he's involved?"

Reynolds took a long swallow of the Irish whiskey and said, "Saudi Arabia has two militaries. One of them is the Saudi Arabian National Guard, which as you so succinctly put it in the warehouse is loyal to the Saudi Royal Family, the al-Sauds.

The other is the Royal Saudi Land Forces, ostensibly established to protect against all external threats to the kingdom, but which in reality was created as a balance against the SANG, should the Royal Family decide to wipe out any of the clans hostile to the al-Sauds."

"Let me guess," said Harvath. "Faruq is from a clan hostile to the Royal Family."

"Bingo."

"How the hell did he get his job then?"

"Just like marrying two children from warring factions, the Saudi Family has put a lot of their lesser enemies in positions of moderate power in hopes of securing their loyalty."

Harvath shook his head. "A lot of good it did them in this case."

"Actually," said Reynolds, "Faruq was extremely loyal for a very long time. He uncovered numerous plots against the Monarchy, even within his own clan, and brought the perpetrators to justice."

"So why the change?"

"He found religion."

"Wahhabism," said Harvath, the disgust evident in his voice.

"Yup, and there's nothing worse than a born-again Muslim."

"But doesn't the Royal Family know he's gone the Wahhabi route?"

"I would hope so. Faruq's boss is one of the Saudi princes—Prince Nawaf bin Abdul Aziz. If

Aziz isn't keeping up on this kind of stuff, he's got no one but himself to blame if things go south. The problem is that the Royal Family operates under a very clouded delusion that it's still in control. Until a man like Faruq fucks up, they think everything is okay."

"In this case, though, once Faruq fucks up, it's going to be too late for the Saudis to do anything."

"Exactly," said Reynolds as he took another sip. "All the rioting we're seeing? Faruq's the perfect person to have sowed the rumors among the Wahhabi leadership. He easily could have fabricated enough evidence to support the claims of a U.S.-influenced crackdown by the monarchy and the police. In fact, he is in a perfect position to actually orchestrate police crackdowns, giving the militants prime examples to rally behind."

"Which brings us to the other reason I'm here. Kalachka said the unrest would escalate to such a point that the Saudi Monarchy would have no choice but to come to the table and meet with the Wahhabi leadership. That's where he plans to have the leadership killed, making it look like the Royal Family was behind it and setting the wheels of a full-on revolution in motion."

"And with the country's fall to the Wahhabis, so begins the resurgence of the Muslim caliphate across the Islamic world. More than one billion strong."

Harvath nodded his head and said, "Listen,

Chip, my first priority is to get to the bottom of whatever this illness is and find a way to stop it. If we can screw Kalachka's plans up in the process, then all the better."

Reynolds set down his drink. "What do you want me to do?"

"I need to find out where and when that meeting between the Saudi Monarchy and the Wahhabi hierarchy is going to take place. That's where Kalachka's people are going to make their move, and if I'm right, Prince Hamal is going to help them do it. He and Kalachka are the only people who can give us the answers we need."

"Wait a second. You think Hamal and those militants are going to pull the trigger? They're all Wahhabis. Why would they be party to killing their own religious leaders?"

"Because," replied Harvath, an adept student of militant Islam, "with Paradise assured for the Wahhabi leadership, if it takes their deaths to bring about a greater good for the rest of the Islamic people, they won't hesitate to take them out."

EIGHTY-SEVEN

WESTERN HEJAZI MOUNTAINS
SAUDI ARABIA

With a few well-placed phone calls, Reynolds discovered that just as Kalachka had predicted, the Wahhabi leadership had managed to force the Saudi Royal Family to the table. But because of the rioting, the Royal Family had been afraid to return to Riyadh for the summit. Instead, they had insisted the Wahhabis come to them at their summer capital just north of At'Taif in the Western Hejazi Mountains.

The Royal Family had been relocating to these lush mountains, known as the garden spot of the Saudi Kingdom, for decades in order to avoid the superheated summer temperatures of Riyadh. As a result, all of the most important members of the Royal Family had palaces built in and around At'Taif.

Less than sixty kilometers from the holy city of Mecca, At'Taif was also home to the King Fahad Air Base, which housed both the Royal Saudi Air

Force's 5th Fighter Squadron and the Royal Saudi Air Force's Western Approach Region Air Defense radar complex, responsible for guarding the kingdom's airspace against hostile penetration.

With opulent summer palaces lying cheek-by-jowl with modern military complexes, all that was missing from the dysfunctional Saudi dream site was religion, and At'Taif had that too. For almost one hundred years, the area surrounding At'Taif had been the principal stronghold of the ultra-conservative Wahhabi faith. In a sense, for the Wahhabi religious leaders traveling in from Riyadh, it was like coming home.

They arrived by a private jet that had been magnanimously chartered for them, only after they had vociferously complained about the Royal Family's unwillingness to meet in Riyadh. Everyone knew the relationship between the Monarchy and the Wahhabis was teetering on the edge of disaster and the credibility of both sides hinged on being able to demonstrate that they acted in good faith in everything they did.

Not above subtle power plays, and in fact quite dependent upon them, the Royal Family chose to hold the summit in the most intimidating palace at their disposal, that of Crown Prince Abdullah bin Abdul Aziz, de facto ruler of the Saudi Kingdom. In addition to Prince Abdullah, other family members in attendance were Saudi defense minister, Prince Sultan bin Abdul Aziz, and Prince Nawaf bin Abdul Aziz, minister of state intelligence. There was a good chance the summit was going to get very heated, and Abdullah wanted as few witnesses to the hostilities as possible. His family had made a big mistake paying what amounted to protection money to build mosques and schools and contributing to the other pet projects of the radical Wahhabis, and he was sick of them running roughshod over his country. They, not the Royal Family, had set loose upon the world the specter of modern Islamist terrorism and as a result had not only blackened both of Saudi Arabia's eyes, but those of the Muslim religion at large. For once and for all, the Wahhabis would listen to him and not vice versa.

With all of the different soldiers standing guard, landing at the King Fahad Air Base reminded Harvath of arriving with the president aboard Air Force One at Andrews Air Force Base in Maryland.

The early morning air was cool and markedly different from Riyadh as they descended the Citation X's stairs. Jillian had worked through the night, analyzing her samples and conferring with the Whitcombs and other USAMRIID personnel back at Fort Detrick. Concurrent with their discussions, teams of FBI and Hazmat agents, warrants in hand, were busy raiding the warehouse of Kaseem Najjar, as well as the cash-heavy businesses owned by every name on the list Chip Reynolds had discovered in Prince Hamal's Riyadh warehouse. Anything and everything that was suspect was placed into airtight containers and transported back to Fort Detrick for further analysis.

Based on the brain tissue samples from Hannibal's elite guard, the Whitcombs had been able to confirm what Alan had suspected—rabies was indeed a prime component of the illness, and the elite guard had been inoculated against it. But inoculation against rabies alone only increased resistance to the illness—it didn't make people one hundred percent immune. This information explained why one of the victims strapped to the ceiling of the Provincial Ministry of Police building in Asalaam—a former veterinarian—was still alive when the Stryker Brigade Combat Team arrived. Another part was still missing from the puzzle.

Hoping to buy time, USAMRIID and the CDC had ordered all first responders to be treated with hyperimmune antirabies serum. The Herculean effort to collect enough doses and have them shipped around the country as quickly as possible was now under way.

In the meantime, Harvath had held a lengthy phone conversation with Gary Lawlor. In the belief that standard rabies vaccine had just bought them more time, Lawlor officially bifurcated Harvath's assignment. Not only was he to do everything he could to uncover both the source and any possible cure for the illness, but he had been additionally instructed to do whatever was necessary to prevent the assassination of the Wahhabi leadership, which all the political minds back in DC agreed would plunge Saudi Arabia into an all-out revolution.

For years, American military and intelligence strategists had been preparing for the possibility of a coup in Saudi Arabia. If the Royal Family was overthrown, a full-blown military operation, code-named Sandstorm, would go into immediate effect. The plan called for mobilizing U.S. armed forces to slice the eastern Saudi province of al-Hasa off from the rest of the country and place it under American control, thereby preventing the Wahhabi extremists from occupying the world's largest proven oil reserves. At this point, though, there was just one problem. The intense summer heat made it nearly impossible to fight in full chem-bio combat gear. Until they were inoculated, neither the U.S. nor any of its allies could fully field enough troops to put Operation Sandstorm into effect.

There was also one other problem. Though it had never been proven and was much debated after the Iraq WMD intelligence fiasco, Washington was well aware that Saudi Arabia had pumped over a billion dollars into Pakistan's nuclear program. Despite repeated denials by the Saudis, there were many who were willing to stake their careers on their belief that in exchange for their generous contributions to Pakistani scientific advancement, the Saudis received one or more nuclear weapons.

Though Gary Lawlor was reluctant to heap

more upon Harvath, he had no choice. Equally as important as getting to the bottom of halting the illness was preventing the Royal House of Saud from losing its grip on power.

Not knowing who might be plotting against the kingdom from the inside, Lawlor was afraid to reach out to anyone in the local diplomatic or intelligence food chain on Harvath's behalf. It was common knowledge that the office of the Saudi Crown Prince leaked worse than a sieve, so a direct call from the president was out of the question. Finding someone they could trust and who would cooperate with them to get Harvath inside would take time, and time was something they were very quickly running out of. Harvath, though, had an idea and knew someone who might be able to make it happen and make it happen fast—Chip Reynolds.

Coached by Harvath on exactly what to say, Reynolds had played the best card at his disposal. Following Harvath's script word-for-word, Reynolds contacted one of the few honest men he knew in the Crown Prince's court—a man he hoped wasn't involved with any attempts at overthrowing the al-Sauds—and told him that he needed an immediate audience. With the seriousness of the summit looming over them, the advisor was reluctant to even broach the subject with the Crown Prince, but with Harvath signaling for him to keep going, Reynolds pressed on.

If there was one thing the Arabs were good

about rewarding, it was loyalty. Reynolds had not only saved the life of a member of the Royal Family, but had also been an excellent head of security for Aramco. If the ex–CIA man really had information about a threat against the Crown Prince's life, then the advisor had no other choice but to make sure he was heard.

Reynolds hated using a lie to gain access to the prince, but he knew it would be the only way they would get a meeting. Eliciting a promise from the advisor not to mention the plot to anyone but the Crown Prince himself, Reynolds hung up the phone and waited with Harvath for what seemed like an eternity for a response from At'Taif. When the call finally came, Reynolds was told that the Crown Prince was willing to see him and the two witnesses he sought to bring along who had "firsthand" knowledge of the plot.

Now, as the trio was bundled into one of Abdullah's heavily armored Suburbans and driven toward his summer palace, Harvath prayed not only that Abdullah would believe them, but that he would agree to turn over one of the most highly visible and highly volatile members of the Royal Family.

EIGHTY-EIGHT

"Shit," mumbled Reynolds as the Crown Prince and several other men entered the reception hall.

Based on the pictures Reynolds had pulled from the hidden flash memory drive back at his house, Harvath had been busy studying the face of every SANG soldier in the room and hadn't paid much attention to the other men on their way in. "What is it?"

"Second guy from the end. That's Prince Aziz, minister of state intelligence."

"Faruq's boss?"

Reynolds nodded his head and was silent until the men approached. "Your Highness," he said, with a slight bow, reaching out to shake Abdullah's hand once it was offered. "Thank you for taking time out of your very important schedule to see us on such short notice."

A courteous smile appeared on the prince's face and he politely tipped his head.

"With your permission, Your Highness," continued Reynolds, "I would like to introduce Mr. Scot Harvath and Dr. Jillian Alcott."

The prince nodded politely at Jillian and then as he extended his hand toward Harvath, said, "You look very familiar to me. Have we met before?"

"Your Highness has a very good memory. I used to be part of President Rutledge's security detail."

Abdullah smiled and grasped Harvath's hand warmly. "I knew it. I never forget a face. Now," he said as he turned toward Reynolds, "what is this all about?"

"Your Highness," interrupted Harvath, "you'll forgive me, but I think we should do this in a private setting with the least amount of people as possible."

"Understood," replied Abdullah, who then issued a string of orders to the men standing behind him.

Accompanied only by his defense minister and the minister of intelligence, the Crown Prince showed his visitors into a wood-paneled study.

In customary desert tradition, he asked them if they cared for any refreshments before getting down to business. All three politely declined. "Okay, then," said Abdullah as he fixed his gaze on Reynolds. "Let's talk about this plot against my life."

Once again, Harvath interrupted. "There is no attempt on your life, Your Highness, at least not directly."

"But Mr. Reynolds said—"

"Exactly what I told him to say."

The defense minister reached for his radio and said in Arabic, "This is preposterous. This meeting is over."

"Not so fast," replied Harvath in perfect Arabic, before switching back to English. "Your Highness, there is a plot to remove you from power, and that is why we're here. Mr. Reynolds cooperated because he believed he was acting in your best interest."

Abdullah raised his hand and motioned for his defense minister to stand down. "I'm listening."

When Harvath had finished explaining, the Crown Prince asked, "Do you have evidence that would support this?"

"Yes we do, Your Highness," said Jillian as she handed Harvath a manila envelope to give to Abdullah. "Tests are ongoing, but this is a summary of what we've been able to gather so far."

"Which is nothing more than sheer conjecture, from what I have heard," replied the minister of state intelligence. "I'll admit, I am not very fond of Faruq, but he has been an unquestionable asset to our organization."

"And the meeting I witnessed with soldiers of the Royal Land Forces, the National Guard, and known militants?" replied Reynolds.

"For all we know," said the defense minister, "they were informants. America isn't the only country that pays for information, you know."

Reynolds conceded the point. "That's true, but what about the faked surveillance reports?"

Now it was the intelligence minister's turn to jump back in. "To tell you the truth, I am more concerned with how *you* were able to get your hands on classified state information."

"If that's what you are more concerned with, then maybe I should be looking for a new minister of intelligence," interjected Abdullah. "Are you or are you not familiar with the militants Mr. Reynolds is referring to?"

"Of course I am, Your Highness."

"And is there any truth to what he's saying about their surveillance reports being falsified?"

"I couldn't say," stammered the minister. "I do not personally review such matters."

"That's not the answer I expected to hear, Nawaf."

"I'm sorry, Your Highness, I—"

Abdullah held up his hand for the man to be silent. "Where is Faruq now?"

"Your Highness, I do not think it is prudent to discuss state intelligence matters in front of—"

"Answer the question," demanded the Crown Prince.

"Sa'dah."

"Yemen? With everything that is going on in our country, all the trouble in Riyadh, what is your deputy minister doing in Sa'dah?"

"The trip was planned some time ago, Your Highness."

"I'm sure it was," said Abdullah, and he looked at his visitors. "Do you have any further questions for either of these men?"

"Just one," replied Harvath as he removed the pictures Reynolds had printed at his house. "We have reason to believe these men are going to try to or may have already infiltrated the ranks of your National Guard here at the palace. Their goal is to kill the Wahhabi leadership and make it look like the Royal Family was responsible. Have any of you seen these men since you've been here?"

Both the defense and intelligence ministers looked at the photos and then shook their heads.

"I would like to circulate these and have every National Guard member at the palace accounted for," said Harvath.

"But the meeting is almost over. If things continue going well, we should have a consensus within a matter of hours and the Wahhabi leadership will be on its way home. Don't you think if these men were going to try something, they would have already done so?" asked the intelligence minister, pressing his luck.

"Do what he asks," commanded Abdullah as he handed the photos to his ministers and then dismissed them from the room.

After taking a minute to collect his thoughts, the Crown Prince turned back to Harvath and said,

"Now that we're alone, we must discuss the involvement in all of this by Prince Hamal."

"We know that will be difficult, Your Highness," said Harvath.

"More difficult than you can imagine," replied Abdullah wearily. "Prince Hamal is my son."

EIGHTY-NINE

Hamal is your *son*?" repeated Harvath.

"The result of an indiscretion in my youth of which I certainly am not proud," said Abdullah, looking away. "While I have been largely successful in keeping his lineage quiet, the boy has been nothing but a source of constant distress for me."

"You'll forgive me for asking, Your Highness, but why have you let him live here? Why not banish him? Send him to Europe or America, anywhere but here where he has been making so much trouble for you?" said Reynolds.

"You don't have children, do you, Mr. Reynolds?" replied the Crown Prince.

Reynolds shook his head.

Abdullah smiled the smile not of an all-powerful ruler but of a father. "If you did, you would understand that I would rather cut off my own arm than to see my son forced from the land of his birth.

That's not to say that I didn't try. I thought that if he had someone to travel with, another worldly young man, a young man of Arab birth, but of a second cultural influence, he might open up and decide life outside this kingdom was more to his liking."

Harvath didn't know why, but suddenly there was that *ping* from a remote corner of his mind as a connection of some sort was made. "Who was this traveling companion you selected for your son, Your Highness?"

"His family was from Abha, a small city in the southern province of Asir. The family's name was—"

"Alomari," said Harvath, putting it all together and finishing Abdullah's sentence for him. "You entrusted your son to the companionship of Khalid Sheik Alomari."

It was the first time Harvath had ever seen a major head of state lose his composure. "I didn't know how evil he was. How could I?"

"You are the ruler of the Saudi Arabian Kingdom," replied Harvath. "You have amazing resources at your disposal. Why didn't you use them?"

"I did!" he asserted. "I was too embarrassed to air my dirty laundry to my minister, so I asked his second in command to do the checking for me."

"You asked Faruq," said Harvath.

Abdullah, his head hung low, responded, "Yes. It was Faruq, and along with the Wahhabis, they succeeded in turning my son against me."

There was still a piece of the puzzle Harvath felt he was missing—a piece that was the key to helping all of the others floating around in his mind to fall into place. "I know this is a delicate question, and please forgive me, Your Highness, but it is something I have to ask."

"What is your question?"

"From you, your son can claim direct descent from the Prophet Muhammad."

"This is correct."

"Hamal's mother. You said she was a foreigner. What country was she from?"

For a moment, the Crown Prince seemed to be at peace, as if he was reliving happier memories from long ago. "We met in Cyprus. A man who had been involved in selling weapons to my brother, King Fahad, for our army introduced me to her. I was a young man filled with the world and forgetful of my responsibilities. She was the most beautiful creature I have ever seen. I was completely captivated by her."

"Her nationality, Your Highness," repeated Harvath. "What was it?"

"Turkish. She was of Ottoman descent."

"And the man who introduced you? The man who had been involved in selling weapons to your brother?"

"Ozan Kalachka."

And with that, Harvath knew who the new caliph was going to be.

NINETY

Crown Prince Abdullah agreed to Harvath's next request on two conditions. The first condition was that he promise not to kill his son. The second was that Harvath, Reynolds, and Alcott convert to Islam before being allowed to enter the holy city of Mecca.

While the second condition came as a surprise to Jillian, Harvath and Reynolds both knew it was not the first time the Royal Family had made such a demand. When the French GIGN team had gone in to help liberate the holy city from radical fundamentalists in the 1970s, they had done so not as French Catholics, but as newly converted followers of Islam.

Once the trio's temporary conversion, which had been conducted on the tarmac of the King Fahad Air Base, was complete, they climbed aboard a Royal Air Force UH60 Blackhawk helicopter with a team of National Guard Special Warfare soldiers.

Dressed in urban camouflage, the Special Warfare team was as serious a group of men as Harvath had ever seen. Outfitted with 5.56mm M4 automatic rifles, 9mm H&K MP5 sub-machine guns, and two M700 sniper rifles, it was obvious the Crown Prince's handpicked team had come to play.

A half mile out, the chopper's pilot radioed to make sure the local security forces were in place and, upon confirmation, swooped in low and fast on their approach.

As they neared the gates of Prince Hamal's sprawling compound in an industrial neighborhood on the dusty outskirts of Mecca, the two AH64 Apache attack helicopters escorting them opened up with a barrage of Hydra 70 rockets and an onslaught of heavy lead from their 30mm cannons.

Hamal's security force was taken completely by surprise, but they soon regrouped and mounted their response. Battle-hardened mujahadeen who had fought in Afghanistan against both the Soviets and the Americans, the men responded instantly.

Before anyone in the Blackhawk knew what was happening, the early morning sky was filled with the contrails of rocket-propelled grenades. Though their pilot did his best to avoid being struck, one of the rockets found its mark, shearing off the rear tail rotor. The pilot yelled for everyone to hold on as the helicopter was launched into a violent spin.

The bird whipped around in circles as it lost altitude and the packed earth of Hamal's main courtyard rushed up to meet it. Harvath could hear gunfire, but with the enormous force created by their spin, it was all he could do to hold on to his breakfast, much less figure out where any of the shots were coming from.

The Blackhawk slammed into the ground, its spring-loaded safety seats barely breaking their fall or, in Reynolds's case, not breaking his fall at all as his leg snapped on impact.

To the Special Warfare unit's credit, they were out the door, weapons hot, before Harvath even had his seatbelt unfastened. Rushing over to Reynolds, he tried to assess the man's injuries, but Reynolds waved him away.

With Jillian's help, he pulled Reynolds as gently as possible from the wreckage of the helicopter and propped him against the mud wall of a large cistern.

Jacking a round into Reynolds's twelve-gauge, Harvath handed it to her and told Jillian to keep her head down as he took off after the Special Warfare team.

Ten feet away he heard the roar of Reynolds's Remington and turned in time to see one of Hamal's security people fall facedown into the dirt. Behind a cloud of blue gunsmoke, Alcott flashed Harvath the thumbs-up. Obviously she had learned something from shooting rabbits in Cornwall. That was the second time she had saved his life.

Getting his head back in the game, Harvath

raised the MP5 provided to him by the Special Warfare unit and slipped into the main building. By the time he reached the team members inside, he had three tangos to his credit, and with every man he dropped, he quickly searched each face for any resemblance to the two militants they were still looking for.

Inside, Harvath followed the unit as they plowed through wave after wave of gun-toting jihadis intent on defending whatever or whoever lay at the center of the compound.

By the time they reached the center, the team was faced with a set of stairs going up to the second story, as well as a door that led somewhere down belowground. Knowing Arab terrorists' penchant for using tunnels, especially when under siege, Harvath chose to accompany the part of the team that was going below grade.

When several rounds into the lock and hinges of the reinforced door failed to open it, the unit's demolition officer placed a shape charge on the door and backed the rest of the men up. Turning away from the blast, he hit a button and blew the door right out of its frame. Another team member then threw two flashbang grenades down the narrow stone staircase.

The flashbangs detonated in quick succession, and the men poured down the narrow opening with the demo officer and Harvath bringing up the rear.

The stairway was incredibly tight, so tight in fact that men had to twist sideways at points just to squeeze through.

Five more feet, and the earsplitting echo of new weapons' fire filled the confined space along with the thick smell of cordite. With no way to see what was happening, Harvath had no choice but to follow the man in front of him.

Suddenly, though, there was a reverse surge as the men turned and tried to run back up the steps. Before Harvath could move, he heard a series of horrible screams as an explosion detonated and a searing orange wave of fire consumed the stairwell.

He dropped to the ground as the flames roared overhead and tried to protect his already burned face.

After the flames dissipated, Harvath checked himself to make sure he hadn't been injured. Deciding everything was okay, he stood and then noticed that the rest of the team hadn't been so lucky. Based on the condition of the demo officer in front of him, he could see that they all had been riddled with shrapnel. Either someone had tossed a grenade into the stairwell or the Special Warfare unit had triggered some sort of antipersonnel device. Either way, somebody was trying very hard not to be followed.

After grabbing the demo officer's bag of charges and flashbangs, Harvath carefully picked his way over the other bodies and down the rest of the stairs.

When he reached the bottom, he found himself in a tight subterranean chamber. Haphazardly placed beams supported the low ceiling and a string of bare lightbulbs lit a long passageway stretching out in front of him. Just as Harvath had suspected, Hamal's complex was indeed attached to a tunnel system.

With the ringing in his ears somewhat subsided, Harvath could make out the sound of one or more people moving somewhere up ahead. His MP5 up and at the ready, he crept cautiously forward, mindful of the potential for further booby traps.

The height of the tunnel rose and fell over a distance of what felt like two or three city blocks. It finally dead-ended at a wooden ladder that stretched upward toward some sort of trapdoor. If someone had been in the tunnel, this was the only way they could have gone. Readying his weapon, Harvath used his free hand to steady himself as he climbed the ladder. He gently applied pressure to the trapdoor, but it wouldn't budge. He tried once again, harder this time, but still it refused to move.

Searching through the demo bag he had taken, he found another shape charge. Affixing it to the bottom of the trapdoor, he attached the necessary amount of det cord, climbed back down into the tunnel, and got as far away as possible. Plugging his ears and opening his mouth to equalize the pressure change that was about to take place, Harvath counted to three and blew an enormous hole right through the middle of the door.

He removed two flashbangs from the bag, scrambled up the ladder, and pitched them up and into the room above him.

Immediately after their detonation, Harvath sprang off the top rung of the ladder and into what could only be described as some sort of bottling plant.

Terrified by the explosions and the heavily armed man who had just crawled out from beneath the floor, workers ran in all directions. They scurried around and beneath rows of automated conveyor belts carrying bottles just like the ones Jillian had recovered from the warehouse in Riyadh.

Heavy stainless steel machines filled the plastic bottles with water and some other compound which Harvath assumed had to be the antidote. They were then sent in orderly rows to be capped, labeled, shrink-wrapped, and stacked on enormous pallets, where they were picked up by a forklift operator and moved to a loading area.

As he was studying the operation, all of a sudden everything around him erupted in a hail of gunfire. Hitting the deck, he saw Ozan Kalachka and the man who would be caliph—Prince Hamal—flanked by two of the meanest-looking, long-bearded, turban-wearing men Harvath had ever seen. With their earth-tone robes and huge machine guns, the bodyguards appeared more suited to the Wild West–style streets of Kabul than a holy city like Mecca.

Harvath rolled beneath one of the conveyor belts and fired his MP5, sending a shower of sparks along the metal platform where the men were standing. Immediately, they returned fire, and Harvath felt water pouring down on him as the bottles up above were sawn in half.

Rolling back out into the open, Harvath applied pressure to the trigger of his MP5 and dropped one of the two Taliban twins bracketing Hamal and Kalachka.

The remaining bodyguard once again returned fire, but this time capped it off with a special twist—a live grenade. As the grenade hit the concrete floor only feet away, Harvath scrambled farther beneath the machinery. He crawled in the other direction as fast as his hands and knees would carry him. And then the unthinkable happened—he got stuck.

NINETY-ONE

It took Harvath only a fraction of a second to realize what had happened—the demo bag he had slung over his shoulder had become hung up on a bolt sticking out from one of the legs supporting the conveyor belt above. As hard as he tried, he couldn't pull it loose, nor could he untangle himself from it. The heavy-duty canvas bag had been meant to take tons of abuse without ever tearing or giving way.

Harvath knew the grenade was only seconds away from going off, and so he did the only thing he could think of. Bracing his back against the underside of the conveyor belt, he planted his legs and gave one big push. He felt the bolts pop away as the conveyor belt tray sprang loose from its supports and flipped over onto the floor, sending a mountain of water bottles along with it. The demo bag was finally free, but all Harvath could do was hit the deck.

As he did, the grenade exploded, the upturned

conveyor belt and pile of water bottles absorbing most of the blast.

Raising his MP5, Harvath shook off the effects of the grenade, leapt off the floor, and ran forward shooting. The remaining Taliban twin tried to return fire, but Harvath caught the man just above his eyebrows, killing him instantly. Reflexively, he then turned his weapon on the remaining two targets and focused on the bigger of them—Ozan Kalachka.

In a move that shouldn't have surprised Harvath, Kalachka grabbed Hamal, swung him around to use as a shield, and put a gun to the prince's head.

"Descendants of the Prophet Muhammad who also have Turkish blood in their veins must be pretty easy to come by," yelled Harvath as he kept his MP5 trained on the man, who, just like Timothy Rayburn, had used and betrayed him. The urge to take the shot regardless of the consequences was overwhelmingly tempting. He could always tell the Crown Prince someone else had shot his son, but that wasn't how Harvath operated. He had given his word. Without a laser sight, Harvath decided against pulling the trigger.

"It would appear we're at a bit of a crossroads," yelled Kalachka from the metal observation platform above the bottling plant floor. "For what it's worth, my offer still stands. What better place for you to convert to Islam than in its holiest of cities?"

"Thanks, but I've already converted. Crown

Prince Abdullah gave me a nice little ceremony, but I don't think it's for me," replied Harvath as he maneuvered for a cleaner shot. "Bad clothes and even worse holidays. My answer is going to have to remain no."

"I'm sorry to hear that," answered Kalachka as he too moved, preventing Harvath from setting up a straight line of fire.

"I'll make you a deal, though," said Harvath. "Give me what I want, and I'll let you live."

Kalachka laughed. "You'll just let me walk right out of here?"

"No, I said I would let you live."

The Scorpion pretended to think about it a moment and then answered, "I think I'm going to walk out of here anyway. Something tells me that even you don't have the balls to risk killing a member of the Saudi Royal Family."

"You think so?" said Harvath as he tightened the stock of the MP5 against his cheek. "Why don't you try me?"

Kalachka took another step to his left and Harvath let loose with a three-round burst that tore chunks out of the wall behind him only inches away from the man's shoulder. There was a look of abject terror on the face of Prince Hamal, and Kalachka shuffled back to his original position. "Maybe we can come to some sort of arrangement," he shouted.

"Like what?" replied Harvath.

"The Wahhabi leaders are as good as dead anyway. Even if I did provide you with what you are looking for, there's not enough time to save the house of Saud. Soon, we'll have three nuclear weapons, and no one will dare move against us."

"How can you be so sure Saudi Arabia even has nuclear weapons?"

"Because I've seen them with my own eyes. It's this country's best-kept secret. Even America isn't sure of their existence. That means, even if you wanted to take them out, you wouldn't know where to find them."

"So what's your deal?" said Harvath, cutting to the chase.

"I'll tell you what you need to know about the illness, but only after you've let me go."

"You need to tell me now. People in America have already begun to come down with it."

"That's ridiculous. This illness has not been sent to the U.S. Not yet, at least. You're stalling," he yelled. "Give me your answer. Do we have a deal or not?"

"Why don't you ask Hamal about America? He's the one with the export business. It seems things may have grown a little bit faster than you had anticipated."

Jamming his pistol into Hamal's ear, Kalachka demanded, "Is this true? Did you ship that poison to America?"

"Yes," Hamal stammered, "but we shipped the water for the Sunni faithful too."

"What do you mean, *we*?"

"Faruq. He coordinated it. He said the only chance we stood against the Americans was to attack them at home so we'd be guaranteed they could never move against us."

"You fool, that was not what we had planned."

"But Faruq said—"

"Faruq is an even bigger idiot than you are."

Harvath had managed to creep several more inches to his right and almost had the perfect line of sight when Kalachka yelled, "That's far enough. No more games."

Harvath stood stock-still.

"Now I know why Faruq was so intent upon cleaning out the warehouse in Riyadh," said Kalachka.

"But it was too late."

"Maybe, but it's not too late for these buildings here. Everything you need is under this roof—the illness, the antidote, everything."

"Give me one good reason why I shouldn't kill you both then and send Prince Abdullah a condolence card?"

Kalachka removed a remote detonator from his pocket and replied, "Because while Faruq might be a mediocre intelligence operative, he is a genius when it comes to explosives. He wired this building the same way he did the warehouse in Riyadh—but with three times as much C4. Either you let us go, or we're all going to Paradise right now, together."

Harvath looked at him and didn't say a word.

"What will it be, Scot? We can end this and both walk away. Don't be stupid. Think about it."

"I think I'll take my chances," replied Harvath as he lowered his weapon two inches and pulled the trigger.

The rounds tore into Prince Hamal's kneecaps and sent the prince crumpling onto the grate beneath his feet. In an instant Harvath had the weapon back up, and as he squeezed the trigger one more time, he said, "If you see him, tell Allah Scot Harvath says hello."

NINETY-TWO

As Kalachka's lifeless body fell forward over the railing, the remote detonator dropped from his hand and clattered onto the platform next to Prince Hamal, who was clutching his legs and writhing in pain. Death was surely better than what awaited him at the hands of his father. He knew the Crown Prince well enough to know that the only reason Harvath hadn't killed him was that his father had wanted to do it himself.

Forcing his hands from his bloody kneecaps, Hamal reached for the detonator, only to have Harvath fire two rounds into the back of his left leg. Running up the staircase to the observation platform, Harvath yelled, "If you move even a millimeter more, the next one goes into your testicles."

Hamal didn't care. His life was over anyway. Stretching his hand out, he reached for the detonator, expecting to feel the fierce pain of the American's bullets piercing his groin, but the shots never came. Instead, he felt a heavy weight land upon his back.

Grabbing Hamal's wrist, Harvath slammed it repeatedly onto the metal grating until he let go of the detonator. Rolling the prince onto his back, Harvath grabbed him by the throat and said, "I promised your father I wouldn't kill you, but other than that, the field is wide open. How do you plan on killing the Wahhabi leadership?"

Hamal forced a laugh and then spat in Harvath's face.

Wiping his cheek on his shoulder, Harvath placed the barrel of the MP5 against Hamal's left index finger and then asked his question again, "How will they die?"

Hamal spat again, and Harvath pulled the trigger, blowing the prince's finger off.

As the man screamed, Harvath moved the gun to the index finger of his right hand and said, "I have more bullets than you have body parts, Hamal. We could be here all day, and believe me, I'll make sure that I keep my word to your father and keep you alive, but you're going to wish you were dead."

Hamal spat at him again, but Harvath held back from firing. Instead, he said, "We know your men are posing as National Guardsmen. It's only a matter of time before we catch them. Everyone at the palace is looking for them. The minute one of them gets anywhere near any of the leadership, it will be all over."

Hamal, his teeth gritted in pain, managed to smile. "You have no idea what we have planned. We have no need to get near any of the leaders."

"What are you talking about?" demanded Harvath. "Tell me, or I'll blow another finger off right now."

"It's too late. It is out of anyone's control."

Harvath was about to pull the trigger when he heard movement on the floor of the bottling plant. The local security forces had discovered the tunnel and were now coming up through the trapdoor. Hamal seemed to know he was saved. He looked at Harvath and through his pain managed another laugh. Harvath raised his MP5 and brought it crashing down into the man's face, knocking out several teeth and rendering him unconscious just as the first of the security forces appeared beneath the platform.

"Prince Hamal is up here," he yelled in Arabic. "He needs medical attention, and then Prince Abdullah wants him detained."

Two security forces operatives ran up the stairs, and Harvath used one of their radios to contact an officer at the compound and have him send Jillian through the tunnel.

When she arrived, she was amazed at the extent of what she found. Tens of millions of dollars had been spent creating a sophisticated, meticulously sealed laboratory complete with full decontamination stations. Whoever had built it obviously knew that they were dealing with something extremely lethal.

After putting one of the lab's full biohazard suits on and clicking her hose into the supply of fresh oxygen, Jillian made her way through the sets of airlocks until she was inside the main lab itself. Harvath waited for her on the other side of the glass, and they communicated via the intercom system rigged to her suit.

It didn't take her long to find what she was looking for. Close to a hundred crudely fashioned black vials sat on the shelves of one of the lab's refrigerators, while nearly ten times that many in purple crowded the shelves of another fridge. They were made from some sort of alloy Jillian had never seen before, and all of them would have fit perfectly in the intricately carved box they had discovered in the depths of the Col de la Traversette.

Upon closer inspection, she saw that the black vials had all been stamped with the same menacing rabid dog's head with entwined vipers, while the purple ones bore the impression of an odd plant or herb, which she assumed must have been part of the inoculation-antidote combination.

Based on the diagrams taped to the lab's rear wall, Jillian was able to figure out that both the illness and the inoculation were extremely potent and required only small amounts to do their work. What's more, the water Hamal was bottling and selling wasn't from any secret spring but rather the Mecca municipal waterworks.

Harvath knew it would take the U.S. at least a day or more before they could get a specialized team on site to help contain the facility, and his thoughts immediately went to Nick Kampos. Kampos could be on site in a matter of hours, and with his experience with the DEA's Clandestine Labs Unit, he could help Jillian secure the antidote until the cavalry arrived. Getting hold of Kampos to help out, though, would have to wait.

Rushing back through the tunnel, Harvath arrived at Hamal's bullet-riddled compound just in time to help Reynolds aboard the CH-47D Chinook helicopter that had been sent to transport the wounded back to the Al Hada hospital adjacent to the King Fahad Air Base.

Once they had lifted off, Harvath used one of the headsets to radio the palace. All of the National Guard troops had been accounted for. There were no signs of the missing militants, and the summit was in the process of wrapping up. Soon it would be all over. Though no attempt had been made on the Wahhabi leadership, Harvath was feeling more nervous about things than he had all day. Removing the headset, he leaned over and shared his concern with Reynolds.

"You think it's safe leaving her back there?" he yelled above the roar of the rotors, referring to Jillian.

"She'll be okay. I'm more concerned at this point with the Wahhabi leadership. We know Kalachka's plan was to kill them during the summit and to have it look like the Royal Family was responsible. But if their men are nowhere near the palace, how the hell do they plan on pulling it off?"

"There's a motorcade," replied Reynolds. "Maybe they're planning on hitting that."

"Two guys plus the deputy intelligence minister? It's possible, but Abdullah's got exceptional security. I think they stole the uniforms so they could get up close to do whatever they're going to do."

"Maybe they've got more than three guys. Who the hell knows? They could have recruited a hundred people and that uniform box we found in the warehouse was only one out of ten others just like it."

There was something about that that made sense. There was also a gnawing at the back of Harvath's mind, as if the answer was already there, just waiting to be teased out. *Why did the militants need the uniforms? If they weren't going to launch their attack from inside the palace, where else would they launch it from? What purpose did the uniforms serve? What would they help them get close to?* The most obvious answer was the Wahhabi leadership, but was there another answer?

Approaching King Fahad Air Base, Harvath saw a long motorcade speeding across the airport from the direction of the Crown Prince's palace.

The meeting had obviously been concluded, and the motorcade was carrying the Wahhabi leadership back to their aircraft. *Soon it would all be over,* thought Harvath. If the militants were going to make their move, it would have to be now, *but how*?

As the motorcade began closing in on a solitary Dessault Falcon 50 Business Jet, Harvath noticed the soldiers scattered across the base, some at attention, some at ease, and he was once again reminded of Andrews Air Force Base and Air Force One. *Why did he keep coming back to Andrews and the president's aircraft?* Then it hit him. Air Force One was at its most vulnerable when it was on the ground.

Suddenly, Harvath knew what the uniforms were for. They weren't for getting close to the Wahhabis—they were for getting close to their airplane. *Faruq was a genius with explosives,* Kalachka had said. The Saudi Royal Family had refused to meet in Riyadh. They had insisted the Wahhabi leaders come to them, and it was the Royal Family who had not only provided the plane, but was responsible for its safety. Now, the picture was clear. Whatever happened, the Wahhabi leadership couldn't be allowed to board or get anywhere near that airplane.

Grabbing the headset, Harvath yelled to the pilot, "We have to stop that motorcade."

"What are you talking about?" the pilot responded.

"The plane they are headed for has a bomb on it."

"But I've got wounded men on board who have to get to the hospital."

"They can wait," commanded Harvath.

"I have my orders."

"Your orders have just changed," said Reynolds as he painfully leaned into the cockpit and pressed his 1911 against the pilot's head. "Do what the man says."

As Harvath relieved both the pilot and copilot of their sidearms, the pilot replied, "Okay, you're in charge. What do you want me to do?"

Harvath knew there wasn't enough time to radio the tower and have them try to make contact with the motorcade, and so he ordered, "Put us down in front of the motorcade, right now."

"Right in front of them? Are you crazy?"

"Do it," commanded Harvath.

Swinging the huge Chinook around, the pilot pushed it full throttle, coming in low and amazingly fast over the top of the speeding motorcade. One hundred yards out, the pilot pulled up and set the Chinook down onto the tarmac, blocking the motorcade's access to the airplane meant to carry the Wahhabi leadership back to Riyadh.

By the lack of reaction on the part of the motorcade, you would have thought they couldn't see the enormous fifty-foot-long helicopter with its twin sixty-foot rotor spans, but Harvath knew what they were doing. Every security person in that motorcade had been warned about the plot to assassinate the Wahhabi leadership. They had no intention of slowing down. In fact, inside those cars they would be readying their weapons, preparing for a showdown.

"Call the tower," Harvath instructed the pilot. "Tell them there's a bomb on that plane and the motorcade needs to turn around and get the hell out of here."

Over his headset, Harvath could hear the pilot radioing his instructions to the control tower. In the meantime, the motorcade was still closing. They were less than fifty yards away. Harvath considered his options and realized he had no choice.

Grabbing the spade grips of the Chinook's door-mounted M60D 7.62mm air-cooled machine gun, he made sure the belt-fed ammo was ready to roll, flicked off the safety, and began firing.

The heavy rounds tore huge pieces of asphalt from the tarmac in front of the motorcade. Though he kept firing, it wasn't until he took out the radiator of the lead Suburban that the armored column came to a halt. The moment it did, doors flew open and security personnel positioned themselves to fire.

At 550 spm, or shots per minute, Harvath's weapon outgunned anything that the security personnel were carrying. Throwing another wall of lead in their direction, yet safely above their heads,

Harvath yelled into his headset, "What's going on with the tower?"

"They're still trying to reach the motorcade," replied the pilot.

"Tell them to hurry up!" he ordered as he raked another series of rounds over the top of the motorcade. "These guys think we're trying to take them out."

Just as Harvath finished his thought, he saw the sunroof of the second Suburban slide back. Seconds later the unmistakable housing of an FIM-92A Stinger Weapons System was slid through the roof, followed by a resolute-looking man who was balancing the entire thing on his shoulder. His eyes pinned on the helicopter, he obviously had no intention of losing anyone on his protective detail, not today.

Harvath had no intention of losing anyone either. "Launch your countermeasures now!" he yelled.

"What?" replied the pilot. "Why?"

"Do it!" screamed the copilot, able to see what his colleague couldn't. "Do it now!"

The pilot launched the countermeasures. Bright flares and flaming pieces of chaff spewed in all directions, showering the motorcade with hot debris and forcing the security personnel not only to shut themselves back inside their vehicles, but also to throw them in reverse and back as far away from the Chinook as possible.

As Harvath prepared himself for a second run, the voice of the pilot came over his headset and said, "The tower has made contact with the motorcade. They are pulling back. I repeat, they are pulling back. Bomb technicians are on their way to examine the aircraft."

Letting go of the grips of the M60, Harvath fell back onto one of the seats and wondered where the hell he could find a beer in this country.

NINETY-THREE

DEMOCRATIC NATIONAL COMMITTEE
HEADQUARTERS
WASHINGTON, DC

Just to prove that she could play ball, Helen Carmichael had abandoned her pantsuit in favor of a gray flannel Armani skirt that came just below mid-thigh, a crisp white blouse with French cuffs, black Jimmy Choo alligator heels, and a matching black alligator belt. Feeling not only on top of the world, but also a bit risqué, she had left the top three buttons of her blouse unbuttoned and had given her navel stud a good polishing before putting it in this morning. Today was going to be one of the most important days of her life.

She had sent Neal Monroe personally to Russ Mercer's office with a peace offering of sorts. Inside the confidential file, which her assistant had been instructed to deliver only to the DNC chairman himself, was but a fraction of the proof she had uncovered, thanks to Brian Turner, that President Jack Rutledge had been running his own private black ops unit. The incendiary file was her ticket to the big leagues. There was no way the party could say no to her being on the ticket, not with what she had been able to uncover.

In addition to tampering with the supposedly "free" and "democratic" elections of several foreign nations, Rutledge had also authorized the assassination of at least half a dozen foreign officials hostile to U.S. policy abroad—and that was only the tip of the iceberg. Rutledge represented all that the world saw was wrong with America, and Helen Carmichael was going to take particular pleasure in watching him burn.

He had also been helping one of his private covert operators, Scot Harvath, avoid service of the subpoena she had prepared demanding he appear before her committee. As if monkeying around with American foreign policy wasn't enough to incense voters, the fact that Rutledge was subverting the Constitution and flagrantly breaking several federal laws was going to send the populace of the United States into an uproar.

Sitting in the back of her town car as it made its way to the Democratic National Committee Headquarters, she had tried to decide where she should start in dismantling the Rutledge administration. Of course, she'd discuss it with Russ Mercer to show she was a team player, but in reality she'd already made up her mind. The world was still enraged about the senseless beating of the Iraqi fruit merchant by a faceless American GI. That was the most logical place to begin. She'd trot Harvath out in front of the cameras and throw the book and anything else she could get at him. It would go a long way in helping to repair America's image abroad, and she would be hailed as the woman who broke the case and made it all happen.

Once she had broken Harvath's back, she could leapfrog right onto Rutledge's and enjoy the ride down as his career and his presidency crashed and burned. Any designs she had had on slowly leaking the information she'd collected were now a thing of the past. It wasn't enough to simply weaken him and cream his ticket in the election. They needed to force Rutledge to resign, or better yet to impeach him before the election, so that the Republicans would be forced to throw another candidate in at the last minute. It didn't matter who they came up with, the American people would be so sick of the Republicans and so distrusting of their party that the Democrats would sail right into the White House. It was so close she could taste it.

As she now sat in Russ Mercer's outer office, Helen Carmichael paid particular attention to how he had furnished the space and what it said about the DNC and its chairman. While her own office in the Hart Senate Office Building had been decorated with mementos from Pennsylvania in an attempt to make her appear fond of the state she represented, once she was in the White House she could finally do what she pleased. In fact, knowing what terrible taste both her future running mate, Governor Farnsworth of Minnesota, and his wife had, she was already looking ahead to what she could do not only in her office at the White House, but with all the other rooms as well.

She was contemplating several pieces of furniture now housed at the Smithsonian that she thought would be perfect in the vice-presidential residence at the Naval Observatory, when Russ Mercer's secretary set down her phone and said, "The chairman will see you now, Senator."

"Here we go," Carmichael said to herself as she stood and smoothed out her skirt. Walking toward the heavy mahogany door, she wondered how Mercer was going to offer her the VP slot. Hopefully, he would have the class to apologize to her first for how unsupportive he'd been. There was also the issue of his meeting with the president's chief of staff, Chuck Anderson, and the things he'd said there, but at this point, she was willing to forgive and forget everything. All she wanted to hear were the words *The party needs you on the ticket.*

As she neared the door, she was suddenly self-conscious and wished she had taken a moment to use the ladies' room to check her hair and makeup one last time. When she had received the message that Mercer wanted to meet with her and that he had a very important item to discuss, she had spent the whole evening prior trying to decide what to wear. She had also had one of her staffers, the pretty, young Asian girl whose name she was always forgetting, come over that morning to help her do her hair and makeup in a way that would make her appear softer and, as the DNC chairman had put it, less of a raging bull dyke. Knocking on the heavy door, she hoped her efforts wouldn't be lost on him.

"Good morning, Helen," said Mercer as Carmichael proudly strode into the room with her head held high and her shoulders back. "Thank you for coming."

She was about to return his greeting when out of the corner of her eye she spied Charles Anderson standing next to the window and stopped dead in her tracks. "What the hell is he doing here?"

"Why don't you take a seat?" replied Mercer.

"Not until you tell me what's going on," she snapped.

"I warned you this whole thing was going to blow up in your face," said the president's chief of staff.

Carmichael ignored him. "Russ, I demand an explanation. What is Chuck Anderson doing in this office?"

"He's here to help prep you for your press conference," replied the DNC chairman.

Part of Carmichael wanted to believe that what she was seeing was the ultimate in strange bedfellows, that Anderson had come to help her craft a statement announcing her run for the White House with Minnesota Governor Bob Farnsworth, but deep down, she knew that wasn't the case. Slowly, it began to dawn on her that Russ Mercer had not asked her here this morning to offer her a chance to be vice president. Though she didn't know exactly what was going on, she could feel herself being backed into a corner, and she didn't like it. Her only choice was to play along until she knew what this was all about. "I don't have any press conference scheduled for this morning."

"You do now," replied Anderson. "In a half hour on the steps of the Senate."

Taking one of the seats in front of Mercer's desk, she responded, "That's very interesting. And what exactly is it that I'll be announcing?"

"Your resignation," answered the DNC chairman.

"My what?"

"You heard me. Your resignation."

"I will do no such thing," said Carmichael.

"You sure as hell will," replied Mercer, "or you'll be going to jail for a very long time."

"*Jail?* This is preposterous. Jail for what?"

Anderson looked at her and said, "Don't play coy, Helen. It doesn't suit you. I warned you that if you didn't back off, this was going to bite you in the ass, and it has."

"What is this? Some kind of intimidation tactic?" demanded Carmichael, who then faced Mercer. "What's your role in all of this, Russ? Are you now a tool of the Republican administration? You ought to be ashamed of yourself. You've really let the party down. You're a disgrace."

Russ Mercer was through being polite. "No, Helen, you're the one who has let the party down, and to tell you the truth, I'm going to be glad to be rid of you."

Carmichael was shocked, but had no intention of giving in. "You're going to have to do a lot better than this if you want to get rid of me."

The DNC chairman simply shook his head, picked up the remote control from the corner of his desk, pointed it at the entertainment center on the far wall, and pressed *play*.

First, Carmichael heard her voice, and then as the TV screen warmed all the way up, she saw herself along with Brian Turner in the eighth-floor suite of the Westin Embassy Row hotel. Immediately, she felt as if she was going to throw up. She sat there frozen, unable to turn away. Thankfully, Mercer turned it off before it got to the most embarrassing part.

"You've been under surveillance for some time," said Anderson.

The senator's mind was racing. There had to be a way out of this. There had to be a way to save her career and still come out on top. "I know how all of this must look," she stammered, "but technically, I did nothing wrong. The man in that video was supplying me with information he felt was his patriotic duty to drag into the light of day."

"Though I'm sure it comes as a total shock, your patriot cum paramour broke a pile of national security laws in obtaining that information."

"That still doesn't change the fact that the president is dirty, and you can't stop me from talking. In fact, this meeting is over. I'm leaving," said Carmichael as she rose from her chair.

"Sit down, Helen," ordered Mercer, "and shut up. You have no idea how easy you are getting off here."

Anderson saw the genuinely confused look on the woman's face and said, "The information Brian Turner provided you with was planted by CIA Director Vaile. They had suspected they had a mole in their ranks and baited a trap for him. As was expected, the bait proved too tempting to pass up."

"I don't believe you," the senator replied. "I don't know how you got Russ involved in all of this, but for some reason he's helping you cover up Rutledge's criminal activities."

"You ought to be a little more forgiving when it comes to Jack Rutledge. I wanted to see you tried and ridden out of town on a rail for what you've done, but the president thought otherwise. He decided to take the high ground and have you resign. As far as he's concerned, there's been enough bitterness between our parties in this country, and though nobody outside this room is ever going to know it, he wanted to try to help mend some of that divide."

Carmichael was silent for several moments before asking, "What's going to happen to Brian Turner?"

"Frankly, I'm surprised you care," said Anderson, "but because you asked, I'll tell you. Him we *are* throwing the book at. Brian Turner is going to prison for a very, very long time. When he gets out, I don't think he'll want anything to do with the worlds of intelligence or politics ever again."

That was it then. Helen Carmichael had tried to play the game by her own set of rules and had lost. There was nothing else she could do for now but concede defeat. "If I agree to do what you're asking, do I have your guarantee that no criminal charges will be brought against me?"

Charles Anderson nodded his head. "You have my personal guarantee, and what's more, you have the president's."

"And the tape?"

"Is part of a federal investigation, but as Brian Turner made a full confession, I don't see why it would need to be entered as evidence at his trial."

"Will it be destroyed then?" she asked.

"No, we're going to hang on to it as part of your personal guarantee."

"Which is?"

"That you'll graciously retire from politics and never mention any of this, including the name of Scot Harvath or what you believe the president may or may not have done."

"That's all?" said Carmichael facetiously.

"Don't be cute, Helen," responded Mercer. "This is a hell of a deal they're offering you."

"You don't have to worry, Russ. Cute is something I have never been accused of being." She then turned to Anderson and said, "So, what will it be? Health problems or the ever-so-popular 'I'm leaving politics so I can spend more time with my family'?"

NINETY-FOUR

CATALINA HOTEL
ZIHUATANEJO, MEXICO
ONE WEEK LATER

After staying in DC long enough to see that the illness hadn't spread, Harvath took off. The president had asked him to come by the White House for a visit so he could personally thank him, but Scot had politely declined. It was going to be a while before he was ready to have anything else to do with that town. In the meantime, he had plenty of vacation days he had never used and figured he was more than entitled to a nice long stretch of time off.

Lying in the hammock on his veranda with the surf pounding against the beach below, Harvath finished reading his day-old copy of the *International Herald Tribune* and set it down next to the ice bucket filled with cold bottles of Negro Modelo beer.

As was often the case with his line of work, the papers had picked up very little of what he had been involved with over the last couple of weeks. There was, though, the story of Senator Helen Carmichael's resignation, which Scot read with particular satisfaction. Having been baited by Carmichael for weeks that something big was coming out of her office, the media immediately fell upon her story.

The fact that she cited wanting more time to spend with a husband who cheated on her, while she cheated on him, as well as a daughter who couldn't stand either of her parents, as her reason for resigning only made the announcement that much more humorous. The bottom line, though, as far as Harvath was concerned, was that when it came to Senator Carmichael, justice had been done.

Before he left for his vacation, Gary Lawlor had filled him in on everything else.

Carmichael's staff was taken by surprise by the news of her resignation and immediately scrambled to find other positions. Based upon a very powerful recommendation from the Oval Office, Neal Monroe was hired on at the DNC as Chairman Russ Mercer's personal assistant.

The "other man" in the senator's life, Brian Turner, tried to cut a deal with the CIA, but the powers that be at Langley had no intention of showing him any leniency whatsoever. He was currently being held in solitary confinement in a federal lockup pending his trial.

Gary detailed how the FBI, CDC, USAMRIID, and DHS had been able to avoid a major outbreak of the illness in the United States by sweeping in early and confiscating the *mahleb* spice deliveries sent by Kaseem Najjar in Hamtramck to all the Muslim-owned cash-heavy businesses on Chip Reynolds's Riyadh warehouse list. With the antidote recovered in the bottling plant in Mecca, all those who had been infected were treated quickly enough to save their lives.

On the jihad front, Lawlor also shared that not only was the Islamic Institute for Science and Technology being dismantled and all of its members interrogated, but Saudi Crown Prince Abdullah had been making significant strides in ferreting out the conspirators involved in the attempted overthrow of his country. As they were discovered, they were tried and sent to Chop-Chop Square, the parking lot of Riyadh's main mosque, where Saudi justice was publicly meted out each Friday. The first to go were the kingdom's deputy intelligence minister and the two Wahhabi militants he had been so actively involved with. There was no word as to the condition or whereabouts of Abdullah's son, Hamal. It was assumed that the Crown Prince had him somewhere under very heavy guard while he tried to figure out what to do with him.

As for Chip Reynolds, he was expected to make a complete and full recovery, at which point he planned on leaving his job with Aramco and relocating back to Montana for a full schedule of hunting, fishing, and deciding what the next phase of his life was going to be. The CIA tried to convince him to come back in-house and help them in their investigations into how Ozan Kalachka had been able to get his hands on classified DOD video, as well as the claim that the Saudis had nuclear weapons, but Reynolds turned them down. He had experienced enough international intrigue to last him two lifetimes.

Both the Whitcombs and Jillian Alcott were given special commendations at a private ceremony at the White House for their assistance in the investigation of the illness. Based on Harvath's report, Jillian was also issued a ten-million-dollar check from the Rewards for Justice program for her role in helping to kill Khalid Sheik Alomari. The last anyone heard, she was planning on using the money to fund a full excavation of Hannibal's elite guard from their icy grave just below the Col de la Traversette.

At last count, Kevin McCauliff had left three messages on Harvath's voice mail wanting to get together to start talking strategy for the DC marathon, while Nick Kampos had faxed several Wal-Mart applications to Harvath's office for him "just in case."

While he knew he was a hell of a long way from being a greeter, Harvath couldn't help but wonder how soon he'd be ready to return to his old way of life. Briefly, the words of Chip Reynolds came back to him, and he knew it wasn't a coincidence that his singleness of purpose had resulted in an actual state of singleness. With thirty-six creeping up on him from around the corner, Harvath was still a young man, but he needed to make some decisions about what he wanted going forward.

Right at this moment, though, all he wanted was to open another beer and start in on the Jay MacLarty novel he had picked up from the lending library in the hotel lobby. After that, he could start thinking about his future. Actually, after that, he was going fishing, but it didn't matter. He had plenty of time and could always think about things tomorrow. For the first time in he couldn't remember how long, Scot Harvath was going to relax.

Opening his book, he was halfway through the first page when one of the desk clerks stepped onto his veranda. "Señor Harvath?"

"Yes?" he replied, laying the book on his chest.

"I'm sorry to disturb you. We have been trying to ring your room, but there has been no answer."

"I know. I disconnected the phone." Why he bothered, he had no idea. Claudia Mueller was the only person who knew where he was, and he'd already called her that morning to get an update on Horst Schroeder's recovery.

"You have an important phone call," said the clerk. "A gentleman has been most insistent. He says he is calling from your office. Would you like me to bring the phone out here to you?"

Harvath began to swing his legs out of the hammock but then thought better of it. "Tell him you couldn't find me."

"Excuse me, Señor?"

"Tell him I'm on the beach or I walked into town. Tell him whatever you want. I don't care."

"Yes, Señor," replied the clerk as he exited the veranda and headed back up to the lobby.

Whatever it is, they'll have to find a way to survive without me, thought Harvath. *At least for the next two weeks.*

AUTHOR'S NOTE

If you are interested in learning more about Hannibal's crossing of the Alps and the use of chemical and biological weapons in the ancient world, I highly recommend *Hannibal Crosses the Alps* by John Prevas and *Greek Fire, Poison Arrows & Scorpion Bombs—Biological and Chemical Warfare in the Ancient World* by Adrienne Mayor.

Both John and Adrienne were extremely helpful in my researching of this novel, and I thank them for their generosity.

ACKNOWLEDGMENTS

My fascination with Hannibal began many years ago when I stumbled across a book about him in the library of my grade school—the Hardey Prep School for Boys in Chicago. I can't remember the title of that book, but I do remember that I couldn't put it down. While the teachers at Hardey always encouraged us to read, doing so while they were trying to teach class was usually frowned upon. I suppose there are worse things to be caught doing than reading, but when I was found out, my argument that Hannibal's journey was much more interesting than what was currently being taught earned me a one-way ticket to the office of Sister Mary McMahon, RSCJ. In the intelligent and compassionate manner that is the hallmark of the nuns of the Sacred Heart, Sister McMahon imparted to me one of the most valuable pieces of wisdom an author could ever hope to acquire—*it's not necessarily what you say, but how you say it.*

In that spirit, I hope my words do justice to the efforts of the people who helped me write this novel. In particular, there were two very important people who worked tirelessly to make this book a reality. The first is my beautiful wife, **Trish.** Not only did she find ways to constantly challenge me to make *Blowback* the best it could be, she gave birth to our second child. Honey, you are beyond incredible. Thank you for your support and for our beautiful baby. I love you more than you will ever know.

The second person is someone who brainstormed with me at all times of the day and night and was always there as my sounding board when inspiration struck. He also came up with a lot of great ideas of his own. With such a wonderfully devious mind, I'm glad my good friend **Scott F. Hill, Ph.D.,** is on our side.

Knowing their nature, the following gentlemen will undoubtedly downplay their contributions to this novel, but I am grateful not only for their assistance, but also the service they have rendered and continue to render our country: the real **"Bullet Bob," Chuck Fretwell, Rudy Guerin** (we're going alphabetically here), **Steve Hoffa,** and **Chad Norberg.**

As always, the Sun Valley crew continues to provide me with the latest and greatest intelligence and intelligence contacts. My deep gratitude goes to **Gary Penrith, Frank Gallagher, Tom Baker,** and **Darrell Mills** (we're going by golf scores here—which direction I won't say).

Tom Whowell gave me my first summer job, and now I have put him to work reading my galleys. Tom, your eye for detail is amazing. Thank you for joining the team as my newest sharpshooter and for such a thorough read.

From the very top on down, the **Drug Enforcement Administration** was a wonderful group of people to work with. My thanks to everyone there, especially the folks out at Quantico and the Firearms Training Unit.

Thanks to my two Washington insiders, **David Vennett** and **Patrick Doak,** who always find a way to make sure my visits to DC are exciting, intriguing, and downright unforgettable.

If it speaks German, eats sushi, or flies, I never write about it without running it by my dear friend **Richard Levy** with American Airlines. Servus to you and Anne.

Thanks to **Bart Berry** of Aquarius Training and Development for the mountaineering assistance. I'll see you when the tuna start running.

Jane Buikstra was kind enough to introduce me to **Dr. Mary Lucas Powell,** who opened the doors of paleopathology to me and gave me a fascinating education.

Captain J. Philip Ludvigson, Captain Armando Riveron, and **Tammy Reed** were very gracious in teaching me the ins and outs of the

U.S. Army's amazing Stryker Brigade Combat Teams.

When you have two people who are so equally important in your career as my terrific agent and my unparalleled editor are, you never know whom to thank first. I took the chicken's way out, and since I thanked my editor first last time, it's now my agent's turn. **Heide Lange,** it's ironic that as an author I cannot find the words to tell you how much you mean to me. Your friendship and guidance make all of the hard work worth it. After marrying Trish, the smartest thing I ever did was asking you to be my agent. Thank you for everything you have done for me.

Now I get to thank **Emily Bestler,** my fantastic editor. You are one of the most talented people I have ever had the good fortune of working with. They broke the mold when they made you. I look forward to many, many more successful years together.

As an author, to have two publishers like **Louise Burke** and **Judith Curr,** whom you like and admire professionally, is a blessing, but to like and admire them even more personally is a gift. Thanks yet again for everything.

There are only about a hundred other people at **Pocket Books** and **Atria Books** I would like to thank—from the sales force to the art, marketing, production, and PR departments, and while I can't thank all of you by name, I want each of you to know how much I appreciate all that you do.

Esther Sung, Sarah Branham, and **Jodi Lipper,** thanks for all of your contributions and for everything you do every single day. None of it goes unnoticed or unappreciated.

Scott Schwimer, my dear friend and colossus of entertainment law, you make Hollywood fun. Thank you for everything, and here's to airbags and crumple zones!

And last but certainly not least, I want to thank you, the readers. You have my deepest gratitude not only for buying my books, but also for telling so many people how much you enjoy them. At the end of the day, it's good word of mouth that really builds an author.

Sincerely,
Brad Thor

Emily Bestler Books

Proudly Presents

ACT OF WAR

BY

BRAD THOR

Read on for a preview of

Act of War. . . .

"Let her sleep. For when the dragon wakes,
she will shake the world."

—Napoleon Bonaparte

PROLOGUE

HONG KONG
ONE WEEK AGO

The air was thick with humidity. *Oppressive.* Typical for this time of year. It was monsoon season and stepping outside was like stepping into a steam room. Within half a block the man was sweating. By the intersection, his clothes were sticking to his body. The Glock tucked behind his right hip was slick with perspiration.

Guns, money, and a bunch of high-tech gear. Just like something out of a movie. Except it wasn't. This was real.

Turning right, he headed into the large open-air market. It looked as if a car bomb packed with neon paint cans had detonated. Everything, even the luminous birds in their impossibly small cages, was aggressively vivid. The smells ran the gamut from ginger and garlic to the putrid "gutter oil" dredged up from restaurant sewers and grease traps by many street cooks.

There were rusted pails of live crabs, buckets of eels, and shallow bowls of water filled with fish. Men and women haggled over oranges and peppers, raw pork and chicken.

Like the first spring snowmelt snaking along a dry, rock-strewn riverbed, Ken Harmon moved through the market. He focused on nothing, but saw everything—every cigarette lit, every newspaper raised, every cell phone dialed. The sounds of the neighborhood poured into his ears as a cacophony and were identified, analyzed, sorted, and stored.

The movements of his body, the functioning of his senses, were all conducted with calm, professional economy. The Central Intelligence Agency hadn't sent him to Hong Kong to panic. In fact, it had sent him to Hong Kong precisely because he didn't panic. There was enough of that back in Washington already; and along with it, the repatriated body of David Cahill.

Cahill had been an Agency NOC based in Shanghai. An Ivy League blueblood type who knew all the right people and went to all the right parties. He saw things in black and white. Gray areas were for professional liars, like diplomats and men who lacked the testicular fortitude to call evil by its name when they saw it. For Cahill, there was a lot of evil in the world, especially in China. That was why he had learned to speak the language and requested his posting there.

As an NOC, or more specifically an agent operating under "nonofficial cover," he wasn't afforded the diplomatic immunity enjoyed by other CIA operatives working out of an embassy or consulate. Cahill had been a spy, a true "secret" agent. And he had been very good at his job. He had built a strong human network in China, with assets in the Chinese Communist Party, the People's Liberation Army, and even the Chinese intelligence services.

Via his contacts, Cahill had been on to something, something with serious national security implications for the United States. Then, one night, while meeting with one of his top assets, he dropped dead of a heart attack right in front of her.

The asset was a DJ out of Shanghai named Mingxia. Her parties were some of the best in China. Celebrities, drugs, beautiful women—they had everything. And it was those parties that had propelled her into the circles of China's rich and powerful.

She was not without her share of troubles, though, and that had made her ripe for recruitment by Cahill. But when he died, Mingxia dropped off the face of the earth. The CIA couldn't find her anywhere. They wanted answers and they had turned over every stone looking for her. Then, two weeks later, she had reappeared.

It was via an emergency communications channel Cahill had established for her—a message board in an obscure forum monitored by Langley. But since her disappearance, speculation at the CIA had gone into overdrive. Did the Chinese have her? Had Cahill been burned? Had the woman been involved in his death? Was this a trap?

She allegedly had information about a crippling attack being planned against the United States, but nobody knew if they could trust her. The Agency was desperate for information. And so it had called Ken Harmon.

Harmon wasn't a polished Ivy Leaguer like Cahill. He was tall, built like a brick shithouse, and he didn't attend fancy parties. He usually drank alone in the decrepit back-alley bars of some of the worst hellholes in the world. He was a rough man with few attachments and only one purpose. When someone somewhere pushed the panic button, Harmon was what showed up.

He had decided to meet the asset in Hong Kong. It made more sense than Shanghai and was much safer than Beijing, especially for a white guy.

Harmon had chosen the coffee shop. A Starbucks knockoff. It was busy, with the right mix of Chinese and Anglos. People chatted on cell phones and pecked away at keyboards. They had buds in their ears and listened to music or watched videos on their devices. *Whatever happened to a cup of coffee and a newspaper? Hell*, he thought, *whatever happened to newspapers?*

There was a front door and a back door, which meant two ways out; *three* if you counted kicking out the window in the women's bathroom leading to a narrow ventilation shaft. The men's bathroom was a death box. There was no escape if you got trapped back there. Harmon didn't plan on getting trapped.

A net of human surveillance had been thrown over the neighborhood. He'd picked out a couple of them. Men who were too fit and too clean-cut. They were Agency muscle, ex–special operations types. They were excellent with a gun and terrific to have on your team if things went sideways, but they were too visible and Harmon had requested no babysitters. His request, though, had been ignored.

He had also asked that they buy the woman a plane ticket so he could conduct the meeting in a nice, anonymous airline lounge at Hong Kong International. It was a controlled environment. Much harder to bring weapons in. Easier to spot trouble before it happened. Tradecraft 101. That request had also been ignored.

Langley felt the airport was *too* controlled and therefore too easy for the Chinese to tilt in their favor. The CIA wanted a public location with multiple evacuation routes. They had cars, safe houses, changes of clothes, medical equipment, fake passports, and even a high-speed boat on standby. They had thought of every contingency and had built plans for each. That was how worried they were.

Stepping inside, Harmon scanned the café. The air-conditioning felt like being hooked up to a bottle of pure, crisp oxygen. He grabbed a paper napkin and starting at the top of his shaved head, wiped all the way down the back of his thick neck. He ordered a Coke in a can, no ice. He had learned the hard way about ice in foreign countries.

Paying in cash, he took his can over to the service station, where he gathered up a few items, and then found a table. It was set back from the window, but not so far back that he couldn't watch the door and what was happening outside on the street.

He carried no electronics. No laptop, no cell phone, no walkie-talkie. He carried no ID. Besides his large-caliber Glock, spare magazines, and a knife, there was nothing on his person that could connect him to anything, anyone, or anywhere. That was how professionals worked.

Removing a small bill from his pocket, he folded it into the shape Mingxia had been told to look for. A heart. He could do swans, too, but everybody did swans. It was the first thing you learned. He normally did hearts when meeting female assets. It was something different. Some of them liked it. Some didn't. He didn't care. A heart was just a heart.

When it was finished, he set it atop a white napkin. It was unique, but low-key, nothing that could be noticed from the street. In fact, you might only notice it as you walked by the table on the way to the ladies' room—and even then, only if you were looking for it.

An hour later, the woman arrived and slowed as she passed the table. It wasn't much, but it was enough to tell him that she had seen it.

While Mingxia was in the bathroom, Harmon scanned the café and the street outside. He sipped his second Coke and flipped through one of the free tourist magazines that littered every café and fast-food restaurant in Hong Kong.

When Mingxia left the bathroom and passed his table again, she found the heart sitting by itself. The napkin had been removed. *All clear*. She hadn't been followed inside. It was safe to sit down. Ordering herself a tea from the counter, she took the table next to his.

She was attractive. Better looking than the photo Cahill had included in her file. He could see why he had recruited her. According to the dossier, she had family somewhere that needed the money. They always did. Harmon didn't want to know about it. He wasn't here to date her, just to debrief her, and if necessary, help smuggle her out of China. He was glad she spoke English.

Reaching into her purse, Mingxia removed the glasses Cahill had given her and placed them on the bench between them.

Harmon had been shown how to use them before leaving the United States. He wasn't a fan, though they were better than the earlier versions Google had developed for the Agency. The Lego-brick-sized projector had been replaced with one about the size of a staple. Even so, the glasses were still too sci-fi for his taste.

It was a better method of sharing information, though, than trading briefcases under the table or being passed an envelope full of reports and surveillance photos. The glasses also had a one-button delete function that scrubbed all the data if it looked like they were about to fall into the wrong hands.

Slipping them on, Harmon turned his attention back to his magazine and pretended to read it.

As the information scrolled across the inside of the lens, his mind began connecting the dots.

"Are you positive about all of this?" he asked.

"Yes," Mingxia replied.

They would, of course, need more than just her word for it. But if this was true, the United States was in trouble. *Big trouble.*

"What's this bit in Chinese that keeps popping up?" he said. "*Xuě Lóng*?"

"It's the codename for the operation."

"What does it mean?"

"Xuě Lóng is a mythical Chinese creature said to bring darkness, cold, and death."

"What's the translation?"

"In English, it would be called a snow dragon."

CHAPTER 1

KARACHI, PAKISTAN

Scot Harvath caught sight of himself as he checked the truck's side mirror. He was wearing the traditional shalwar kameez—baggy, pajamalike trousers with a long cotton tunic. His skin was tan from having spent the summer outside. He had sharp blue eyes, short sandy brown hair, and was in better shape than most men half his age. He needed a shower and shave, but for a former Navy SEAL in his early forties, he looked pretty good.

Sitting next to him, driving their white Toyota SUV, was twenty-eight-year-old Chase Palmer. Eight years ago, he had been the youngest soldier ever admitted to Delta Force, or the "Unit" as members referred to it. His hair was lighter than Harvath's, but their appearances were so similar they could have been taken for brothers.

Cradling an H&K MP7 submachine gun in the backseat beneath her burka was twenty-five-year-old Sloane Ashby. In her short military career, she had racked up more confirmed kills than any other female soldier, and most of the men. With her high cheekbones, smoky gray eyes, and blonde hair she looked more like a college calendar coed than a "kick in the door and shoot bad guys in the face" operator.

Harvath moved his eyes back to the taillights several car lengths ahead. The night was alive, *electric*. Motorbikes buzzed in and out of traffic. Trucks clogged the streets. Between the curtains of diesel exhaust, he could smell the ocean. They were getting close. Activating his radio, he said, "Look sharp, everyone."

With over twenty-three million inhabitants, Karachi was the third-largest city in the world and Pakistan's most heavily populated. It was an easy place to hide. *Staying hidden, though*, thought Harvath, *required discipline*. It meant not going to your favorite restaurant just because it was your last night in town. But that's exactly what Ahmad Yaqub had planned.

There had been debate over where to grab Yaqub. Should they do it in Karachi while he was under the protection of the ISI—Pakistan's Inter-Services Intelligence Agency—or should they wait until he returned to his stronghold in Waziristan?

The Secretary of State wanted to wait. He wanted to pay a rival faction in the lawless border region between Pakistan and Afghanistan to snatch him so there'd be no American fingerprints on the job. Hitting an ISI motorcade in Karachi was asking for trouble. *A lot of it*. The clock, though, was ticking.

Yaqub was an Al Qaeda–linked Saudi who had traveled to Afghanistan for the jihad and had married into a powerful Waziristan clan. From his mountain compound, he helped fund and coordinate terror operations against corrupt Pakistani and Afghan politicians, as well as anyone else seen as enemies of Islam and the Taliban.

His greatest coup had been the assassination of Benazir Bhutto in Rawalpindi. She was the American-backed "puppet" who had been predicted to win the election and become president of Pakistan. She had made no secret of the direction she would take the country and how she intended to crush the Taliban.

Yaqub knew there would be an investigation into her death and had left just enough clues to confuse everyone. Some believed a rival political faction had ordered her death. Some blamed the Taliban. Some swore it had come from deep within the ISI, whose continued hold on power was dependent upon chaos reigning throughout the region. Where these clues didn't lead, though was back to Ahmad Yaqub. Or so he had thought.

But people in Waziristan talked, especially when money was involved. The Taliban often lamented that cash was the greatest weapon the Americans brought to the battlefield. Money frightened them more than the drones that killed without warning. American dollars were like a cold wind in winter. No matter how well constructed your house, the wind could always find a way inside. And a particular gust of American dollars had done just that.

The U.S. had made the apprehension of Ahmad Yaqub a top priority. They had moved heaven and earth to compile as much information on him as quickly as possible. The best intelligence on Yaqub had come from a private intelligence agency run by an ex–CIA spymaster named Reed Carlton.

As part of the Carlton Group's force protection contracts with the Department of Defense, they had developed unparalleled human networks throughout Afghanistan and Pakistan. Nobody collected better intelligence in the region than they did; not even the CIA.

Within twenty-four hours of being tasked, the Carlton Group had reached out to its networks and had assembled an impressive dossier on Yaqub. They knew exactly where he was, how long it would take him to do his banking and assorted business in Karachi, and where he'd be spending his last evening. But the Carlton Group's expertise didn't end there.

In addition to hiring top people from the intelligence world, Carlton also recruited the best talent from the Special Operations community. One of his greatest accomplishments had been landing Scot Harvath.

Harvath had served on SEAL Teams 2 and 6, with the Secret Service's Presidential Protection Division, and under a prior president who had successfully used him to covertly hunt and kill terrorists. Harvath and the President had enjoyed a simple understanding—if the terrorists refused to play by any rules, Harvath wasn't expected to either.

Carlton saw in Harvath a bottomless well of raw talent. When he hired him, he had not only honed Harvath's exceptional counterterrorism skills, he had also taught him everything he knew about tradecraft and the world of espionage.

When he was finished, Harvath had become more than just a talented hunter and killer of men. He had become an apex predator—a creature who sat atop the food chain, feared by all others.

There was one other plus Harvath brought to the current assignment—plausible deniability. The Carlton Group was a private organization. If Operation Blackbird went sideways, there wouldn't be a trail leading back to the White House.

In order to give the United States even greater insulation, Harvath had suggested using Kurdish Peshmergas instead of American operators for the hit. The Peshmergas had trained with U.S. Special Forces, were tough, and could be relied on no matter how bad things got.

The Peshmergas would be augmented by a couple of trustworthy Pakistanis from the Carlton Group's network who had supported delicate, in-country covert operations in the past. Harvath and his people would not get involved unless absolutely necessary. That was the best he could offer. The U.S. had to move on Yaqub. Time was running out. It had to be now and it had to be in Karachi. The Secretary of State had reluctantly agreed.

Once they had the green light, Harvath and Carlton began planning the operation. There was layer upon layer of detail to be covered—weapons, logistics, contingencies, and personnel chief among them. The key was to get Yaqub in transit. That was when he'd be most vulnerable. Harvath knew exactly who he wanted with him on the assignment.

Chase Palmer was smart, aggressive, and very talented. By twenty-eight, he'd seen more action than many Unit operators ever would and was already looking for his next adventure. Having worked with him on a previous assignment, Harvath had been quite impressed and knew he'd be perfect for the Carlton Group. That was all it had taken.

With Chase on board, there was only one other operator he had wanted along.

With the Taliban and Al Qaeda having put a price on her head for all her kills in Afghanistan, the Army had removed Sloane Ashby from combat. They had assigned her to the Unit compound at Fort Bragg, where she had become a trainer for Delta's all-female detachment known as the Athena Project. She was a good instructor, but she was far too young to be mothballed and she missed the action. When Carlton met her and offered her a position, she had jumped at the chance.

Noting the intersection they were approaching, Sloane said, "Khayban-e-Jami coming up."

They had driven the routes between Yaqub's safe house and his favorite restaurant multiple times. The team knew every intersection and had plotted multiple points where they could grab him. When they did, the Peshmergas would have to move fast. The key was incapacitating his bodyguards as quickly as possible.

Yaqub's destination was a popular restaurant called Bar-B-Q Tonight. It was close to the Karachi Yacht Club and just across the street, ironically enough, from Benazir Bhutto Memorial Park. Whether that provided an added sick appeal for Yaqub was anyone's guess.

"Fifteen meters to the intersection," Sloane called out.

"Damn it," Chase swore as the car immediately in front of them began to slow. "We're going to lose them. The light's changing."

Yaqub's two-car motorcade had already entered the intersection, trailed by the Peshmergas.

"Try to stay with them," Harvath replied.

Chase leaned on the horn. "C'mon, Chicken Little. Be a man. Move your ass."

"Easy with the horn."

"This guy's gotta be the only idiot in Karachi who doesn't push through a yellow light."

"We'll be okay," said Harvath. "Let's just not draw attention to ourselves."

Chase tried to steer around him, but there wasn't enough room.

"Not good," Sloane stated from the backseat.

"Everybody, stay calm," Harvath instructed. He didn't like the idea of being separated from the motorcade or the rest of his team either, but there was no use blowing their cover. They'd been very careful and had made sure not to get too close, repeatedly switching positions. The ISI was well trained and would be looking for a tail. There was also no telling how many of the motorbikes or scooters zipping through traffic might have been spotters.

"We know where they're going," Harvath continued, "and we've got eyes on—"

Before he could finish his sentence, a massive truck came barreling through the intersection and slammed right into the car carrying the Peshmerga fighters.